Britain,
AD 43

For the people of Caer Cad, 'skin' is their totem,
their greeting, their identity.

Ailia does not have skin. Abandoned at birth, she is an outsider
in her own village, forbidden from learning and marriage.
Despite this she grows up an intelligent and brave young woman –
one for whom the Mothers, the tribal ancestors, have
chosen a higher destiny.

With a dark threat growing on the horizon – the aggressive expansion
of the Roman Empire – Ailia must embark on an unsanctioned
journey to protect her people, and their pagan way of life, from the
most terrifying threat they have ever faced.

Set in Iron-Age Britain on the cusp of Roman invasion, SKIN
is a mesmerising, full-blooded novel about the collision of
two worlds, and the remarkable young woman on
whom the fate of her tribe rests.

SKIN

Ilka Tampke was awarded a Glenfern Fellowship in 2012. Her short stories and articles have been published in several anthologies. She lives in Woodend, Australia. *Skin* is her first novel.

Visit Ilka's website: ilkatampke.com.au

Follow her on Twitter @IlkaTampke

SKIN

ILKA TAMPKE

HODDER &
STOUGHTON

First published in Australia and New Zealand in 2015
by The Text Publishing Company

First published in Great Britain in 2015 by
Hodder & Stoughton
An Hachette UK company

1

Cover and page design by Imogen Stubbs
Map by Simon Barnard

A CIP catalogue record for this title is available from the British Library

Hardback ISBN 978 1 473 61642 4
eBook ISBN 978 1 473 61640 0

Printed and bound by Clays Ltd, St Ives plc

Hodder & Stoughton policy is to use papers that are natural,
renewable and recyclable products and made from wood grown in
sustainable forests. The logging and manufacturing processes are expected
to conform to the environmental regulations of the country of origin.

Hodder & Stoughton Ltd
Carmelite House
50 Victoria Embankment
London EC4Y 0DZ

www.hodder.co.uk

For Adam, Amaya and Toby

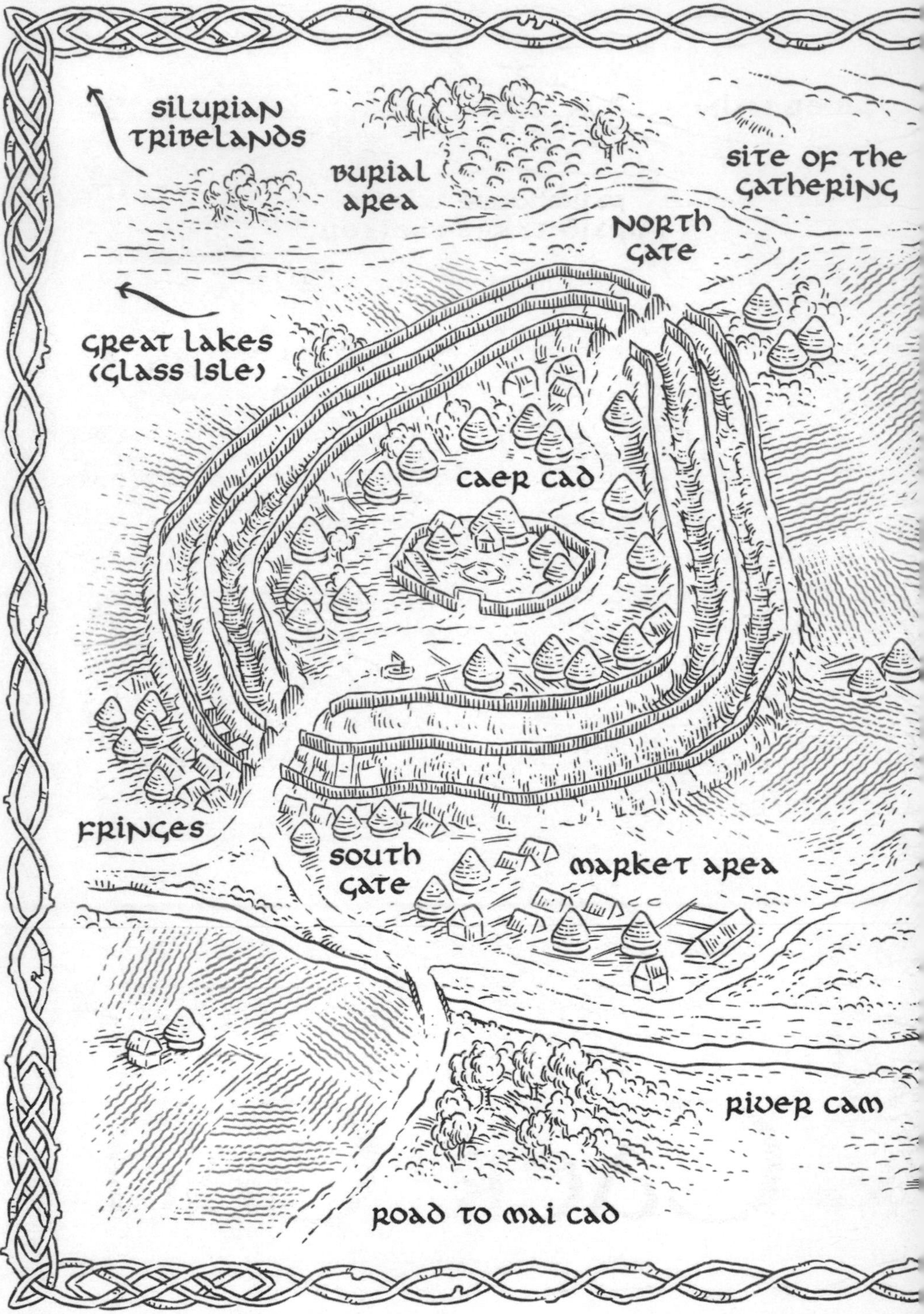

silurian
tribelands

burial
area

site of the
gathering

north
gate

great lakes
(glass isle)

caer cad

fringes

south
gate

market area

river cam

road to mai cad

RIVER NAIN

FARMHOUSE WHERE
FRAID TAKES SHELTER

OLD FOREST

DUN'S FARM

SISTER
HILL

EASTERN
TRIBES

CAER CAD

The Great Deluge

The world was born of a great flood. These waters were Truth
and washed over everything. Some saw the river as it came and
were well minded enough to transform themselves into salmon.
By this means they survived. They were the wise ones.

SOUTHWEST BRITAIN, AD 28

I WAS NOT yet one day old when Cookmother found me on the
doorstep of the Tribequeen's kitchen. She was on her way to our
herb garden after tasting her stewed pork and finding it wanting in
rosemary. I very nearly felt her leather sandal upon me before she
noticed my tiny, swaddled shape.

I knew the story well.

'Mothers of earth!' She carried me inside, laid me on the table and
peeled open my wraps, powdery with frost.

I was a girl. Misshapen, no doubt, for why else would I have been
left for the Tribequeen's servants to care for? Cookmother ran her
callused fingers across my wrinkled back, my flailing limbs and swollen
belly. My cord had been torn, its stump still raw and crusted, and my
eyes were sunken with thirst. But she found nothing else wrong. I was

perfect. A poor mother then, or a mother in shame? But Cookmother could not recall any women from the fringes who'd been due with child.

I squalled at the smell of her. I had not yet known a mother's touch nor the taste of her milk.

Cookmother sat down on a stool and let her leine fall open so I could suckle greedily from her well-veined breasts, still full to bursting for the second warrior's new child.

And when she had to tear my mouth away to tend to the spitting cookpot, she laid me down on a goatskin in front of the fire, where Badger, the old black-and-white bitch, was resting from the mouths of her own hungry pups outside. And when I howled—two hours on a stone step at midwinter had given me a coldness that needed touch and I had not yet drunk my fill—Cookmother placed me beside Badger's flaccid abdomen and my little mouth easily found a nipple. Badger lifted her head and smelled me curiously, too exhausted from seven successive litters to snout me away.

Over the months that followed I fed often in this way. Cookmother said I was half reared on dog's milk. She wondered if this had some part in what became of me.

Perhaps because I was well formed, or because the season's harvest had put all in good temper, I was kept in the kitchen as Cookmother's own. She had treated many lost babes, then given them to the warrior families or, if they were too weak, to the builders, for a child-soul in the foundations would bring great protection to a new house.

But I lay in a tinderbox lined with lambskin while Cookmother ground the grain, dried the meat and ran the Tribequeen's kitchen. She was busied all the sun's hours and my cries were often silenced with a sharp word and a finger dipped in pig fat or salted butter. But at the end of each day I was nuzzled to sleep in her own bedskins and the murmurs of her dreams were my nightsong.

Her temper was hotter than a peppercorn and my cheek often felt the sting of her palm, but when I was two summers old and burned my wrists at the rim of the cookpot, it was she who applied a fresh poultice while I writhed and screamed, and she who held me through the night when the smarting was unbearable. And when the Tribequeen called for girls of able wit to be sent for service to one of the eastern tribekings, it was she who shut me into a wooden chest with a command to be silent, and told the messenger I had taken to wandering the fringes and who knows what infections I was picking up there.

Cookmother was plump and warm, like a fresh-filled sausage, although to look at she was as ugly as a toad, with a toothless laugh and skin as pocked as porridge. Her legs (when I burrowed beneath her skirts, hiding from a loud-voiced farmer or loosed bull) were so gnarled that I wondered, in my earliest innocence, if she was half kin to a tree. This was before I knew the workings of the body and learned these dark, knotted roots to be pathways of blood.

The tribelands in which I grew were those of Durotriga in Southern Britain. Of the many regions within it, ours was called Summer, a wetland country, named for its abundant yield of barley, oats and wheat, where grass grew as lush as a deer pelt, and teemed with rivers.

My township, perched on the plateaued crest of Cad Hill, was Caer Cad, one of the largest hilltowns of Durotriga. The walled banks and deep ditches that encircled it were beginning to crumble, for peace had sat upon this tribe for many seasons. The only strangers breaching our gateways now were traders from the Eastlands, who chuckled at our round earthen houses built all alike, their doorways aligned to the midwinter sunrise. They called them anthills and thought us simple. But our journeymen and -women did not seek to display their knowledge through mighty buildings. Their greatness lived elsewhere.

I was an inquisitive child with a watchful eye. What pleased me most was seeing life at its arrowhead: Badger and the endless stream of pups that spewed from her swinging belly, the ice crystals in the river at wintertime, the spill of young fish that filled it in spring.

What frightened me was being alone.

There were five in our house. Of my three kitchen sisters, Bebin was my favourite, steady and never shooing me away when I followed her to market or to the Tribequeen's sleephouse. I was less fond of Cah, sharp and changeable as the west wind. Ianna was our spinner, without wits for much else.

In the kitchen we slept abreast, close to the crackle of the hearth. Sometimes one of the girls would sleep in the stable if the night was hot or the human smells were too wretched. But I would never sleep alone. I needed the comfort of fire and a body against me.

Despite my affliction, Cookmother's rugged care never wavered. She told me always that fear could be fought with a curious mind. *Hold questions like a torch before you.*

After evening porridge was eaten, my favourite stories were those of the skin totems.

'Speak of the deer!' I would bid her, curling in her broad lap.

'Graceful. Gentle. They are kin to the woodlands and survive best by quietness.'

'And the salmon?' I urged.

'Ah, the queen of all skins,' she proclaimed, for she was salmon-skinned. 'Keepers of wisdom. We hold the past, and the seeking of homelands.'

'And what of mine?' I wound my small arms around her neck.

She would tell me each time that I belonged to no totem. That I belonged to nothing but her.

4

Though she nursed almost every one of the warriors' children, there was no blood youngling who had ever called her Mam. I was the one, she whispered to me each nightfall, who was truly her own.

She called me Ailia, meaning light.

—

I was seven summers old when my life was spared for the second time.

It was midwinter. The Gathering. The people of Durotriga had come together, as they did every seven years, to remake the union of our tribe. For six nights we had woven together our tribelands in song, called forth our animal kin, and eaten and drunk together. Now it was the seventh day, when we would offer the gift that spoke most deeply of our gratitude to this country and to the Mothers who formed it, the gift that would hold our ties strong until we next met.

I hoped to the Mothers it would not be me.

The near-dawn was bitter as we gathered in our hundreds around a large, raised mound, surrounded by fires. Cad Hill was to the south of us. We were on Mothers' land now, the most sacred ground of Summer, deep-sodden by our northern river, the Nain, which kept the Mothers close. Many had journeyed days to come here; we had only to pass through our northern gateway to reach this place. The land had been felled and cleared, but it was not permitted for beast to graze it, or tribesman to walk upon it outside of ritual time.

This was the turning of the winter. The journeymen worked quickly to be ready for the breaking of light over the far grey hills. They called for girl children born in the year of the last Gathering to come forward. Braced by our closest kin, or whoever loved us most, we approached the space before the crowd.

Tethered horses steamed at the nostrils and gave off a strong blood heat from the slabs of muscle on their flanks and necks. I flinched as they stamped and twitched in the cold. They'd been whipped and taunted. They were ready to run.

I stood at the end of the row, gripping Cookmother's hand. When I glanced sideways I saw a line of only ten or twelve wide-eyed faces, fewer than one would expect among so many tribespeople. No doubt some tribeswomen had kept their daughters hidden, had not heeded the Mothers' call, each knowing that their daughters would now never be truly of the tribe because they were not willing to give them to the tribe.

Llwyd, the Journeyman Elder, highest trained of our wisepeople, paced our number and one by one sent girls back into the crowd. They scurried and tripped, collapsing into their families' joyful sobs. One by one we were rejected if our health, our strength, our radiance of spirit were not sufficient for the Mothers.

At last there were two of us. We could hardly have been more different to look at. I was tall and well grown with a vine of light-brown curls escaping my braids, whereas she was small and slight, her dark hair smooth as water.

Llwyd came to me first.

'She is half-born,' said Cookmother. 'A foundling. She has no skin.' Her voice was steady but I could feel her legs trembling through her skirts.

'Unskinned?' said Llwyd. He looked up and down the length of me. 'She is otherwise perfect—perhaps the Mothers want her anyway. After all, they know her skin.'

'Please—' Cookmother's voice cracked. 'I'm training her for plant-craft. Let her serve us in another way.'

Llwyd crouched before me and squeezed my arms and legs. Although I had been told countless times of the honour this gift would bring to my soul, I started to rock with terror.

Llwyd took my hand. 'Will you be our gift?'

6

My legs weakened but I did not fall. 'Yes,' I whispered.

Llwyd stood.

All watched, awaiting his word.

He walked to the other girl. She must have been far-born as I had never seen her at markets or festivals. 'Is there any reason, why I should not choose *this* girl?' he asked.

The girl's companion was no older than fourteen summers. Too young to be the child's mother. 'This is my sister,' she said, 'and last of my kin.'

'She, also, is perfect,' said Llwyd. He looked out to the gathering. 'We will give the child with skin.'

'No!' The sister grabbed the girl, who had begun to wail.

Now my legs buckled and Cookmother lifted me into her arms.

'You will be honoured for your gift,' said Llwyd, reaching for the girl.

It took two journeymen and the Tribequeen's first warrior to wrench the child from her sister. The air was jagged with the older girl's screams.

Cookmother hurried me back to the safety of the crowd and kept me clasped to her chest. Nightshade was thrown onto the fires and my nostrils flooded with its dizzying smoke.

The journeymen and -women started to sing down the songs of our tribe in powerful harmony. I could sense the expectation in the gathering, the pulsing of hearts and the coursing of blood. This ritual was part of our story, part of our truth, but the terribleness of it was never forgotten.

The chosen girl's sister still screamed. The warrior held her, his arms spasming with the force of her struggle.

The girl was led between the fires to the top of the mound. The ovates poured henbane down her throat. Soon she would feel no pain. The singing became louder. Cookmother squeezed me closer.

I wanted to hide my face in her tunic, but I knew all must bear witness to this giving. Especially me.

The ovates took off the girl's under-robe. Unclothed, she was as fragile and veil-skinned as a baby mouse. Water, dark with plant steepings, was poured over her blue-cold skin, the trickle of shit wiped from her thighs, and she was called to be ready.

I was lost in the wondering of how this would be the greatness of her body's growth. That the fresh folds and twig bones of her would never know the height nor flesh nor wisdom of a woman. As I stared, she met my gaze. Though she had nothing of my high forehead or my pointed nose, her wild green eyes were a mirror of mine.

The ovates began to circle her as the first lip of light emerged on the horizon.

Llwyd stood on a platform before us and called the dedication: 'Mothers, receive this lifegift as tribute and request. Let the spread of this new blood soak into your earth, flow into your rivers. Let it nourish your body and ease your hunger. Let what we give you now, torn apart, be returned to us as whole.'

As he spoke, the lesser journeymen were tying the ropes around the child's ankles, wrists and neck. These in turn were fastened to the ropes that trailed behind the horses. There were nine horses for the task. Two for each arm, two for each leg, the largest and strongest for her head.

The journeymen positioned her; she was already halfway to the Otherworld with the herbs. They kissed her and stepped away.

She stood with limbs outstretched and tears on her face. The singing reached a wailing peak. It was time. She was, for a moment, creation, the rising sun itself, before the riders mounted, the journeyman shouted, and the horses surged with unstoppable force, to the north, south, east and west of her.

The Singing

At first there was chaos. A void without form.
Then the Mothers began to sing.

AD 43

I STIRRED WITH the crow's first cry, instantly awake. It was the day before festival; tonight the fires would be lit for Beltane and I had been sleepless half the night in anticipation.

Despite the cold morning, I was damp with sweat in my bed, pressed on one side by Cookmother and the other by Neha, my beautiful grey-and-white bitch. She was the final born from the last of Badger's litters and the most like her in temperament: wary of any who stroked her. But to me she was as devoted a protectoress as could ever be wished for and I would not so much as empty the nightpot without her by my side.

I lifted Cookmother's arm and rolled out from under it, reaching for my grey woollen tunic that hung over a stool by the bed. The other kitchen girls still slept, Bebin and Ianna curled together. Only sour-tempered Cah slept alone. The fire in the hearth was barely smouldering. It was Cah's turn to keep it last night but she had clearly forgotten again. I stoked it quickly. It would bring great shame on Cookmother for our house fire to die.

As I tied my tunic with my leather belt, Neha brought me my sandals. 'Good girl,' I whispered, lacing them firm. I tugged a comb through the tangle of hair that spilled down my shoulders, then I grabbed a basket and we slipped out through the heavy cowskin covering the door.

Outside, the air prickled with spring. Past the Tribequeen's low stone gateway, the path was dotted with festival offerings of cheese, eggs and milk left in small rock hollows or poured straight onto the cobbled ground. Some had left bread or jugs of ale. Each gave back the best they could.

Soon the winding pathways of the warriors' houses gave way to the open streets of the town centre, where our craftspeople worked. Caer Cad was already awake. Smoke poured from the house peaks and the open forges were lit. Many makers were already bundling their metals and pots into baskets for market, restless, like me, with the promise of festival. Most greeted me as I passed, but some looked away.

I turned into a narrow path where the rich smell of roasting wheat told me Mael's bread was ready. Inside his bakehouse, I leaned against the warm oven while he chose his largest loaves.

'Take care when you attend the Tribequeen today,' he warned. Mael had grown heavy on his own graincraft and had a great fondness for the foretelling of ruin. He was mocked for both of these, but I always offered him a ready ear and in return he was free with the news of the township.

'Why so?' I asked.

'There was a rider from the east last night. The Bear is fallen.'

'Slain?' I questioned. There had been no news of war.

'Nay. Died in his bedskins. An old man's death, bless his soul to have reached it.'

The Great Bear, Belinus, king of the Catuvellauni, whose rule spread over most of the eastern tribes of Albion. He was greatly admired, even by those beyond his reign, like us.

'Who will wear his crown?' I asked.

'This is the question.' Mael bent down and swung open the door of the oven. 'Togodumnus has claimed the capital but his brother, Caradog, will want his share of the tribes, and he is a flaming arrow. Whatever smooth waters Belinus has sailed between Britain and Rome, Caradog is sure to whip up.'

I could not help smiling at his prophecy. 'I think we are safe from the Romans here, Mael.'

'Are we?' He dripped with sweat as he pulled out the bread stone. 'The Bear knew how to throw a bone to the Roman dog. He gave them all the skins and the tin they could want and kissed their fingers for the privilege. They had no reason to attack again. With that young cock Caradog crowing about Britain's great freedom, who knows what Rome will do to subdue him?'

I placed the loaves in my basket. Even within my short remembering, the tendrils of Roman ways had touched Caer Cad. Aside from the pretty cups and the dark wines that filled them, there were new arts like coloured glass, oils from fruit, and different coins that served in trade. More and more barrow-loads of our lead and grain were carted out and rolled onto ships bound for the Empire. But the tribes had always been, and remained, the law-keepers of this land.

Rome's army had come one hundred summers before and the eastern kings had defended their freedom with trade and terms. There was always talk that they would come again, that they would not be so easily withheld, but I was not afraid. Cookmother had taught me that the roots of the tribes reached deep and it would take more than Roman swords to dig them out.

I thanked Mael for the bread and he smiled at me through blackened teeth. 'First time through the fires tonight?' he asked.

I nodded.

'Then Mothers bless you.' He chuckled and the knot tightened in my belly.

Outside, Neha sprang to her feet. Sun streamed over Sister Hill to the east. Already there were women busied at its crest, softening the ground for the poles and laying the offerings.

Of the year's four great festivals, Beltane was the most beloved by the tribes. A night of fire, of joy, where the heat of man against woman broke open the winter, called back the sun and readied the ground for a strong, sweet harvest. For girls who had first bled since last Beltane, such as me, tonight would be their first union. I was twice seven summers.

Barking filled the air. Neha had galloped ahead. I ran after her, hoping she hadn't bitten the wheelwright again.

When I rounded the corner I found her snarling at a young tribesman marking his fightcraft in the street. I pushed through the crowd around him and called Neha off. 'I'm sorry,' I panted, grabbing her scruff. 'She's not fond of strangers.'

He laughed. 'She mistakes me then. I am no stranger to Cad.'

I stared at him. He was well cast, of medium height but heavily muscled, his beard lime-bleached in the style of the warrior. Despite the crisp morning, he practised without a shirt, his silver torque glinting on his shaved chest. He was familiar but I could not place him.

'Are you returned from fosterage?' I asked, hooking my unbraided hair behind my shoulders.

'Ay.' He sheathed his sword. 'I am Ruther of Cad.'

Orgilos's son. Often spoken of. Fostered to the east for

fight-training, then to Rome to learn their soldier's craft, he would have been almost twenty summers now.

I nodded. 'Blessings upon your return.' Neha growled under my firm grip. 'Hush!' I hissed. 'Forgive her. She's cursed with a wolf's temper.'

'And her mistress?' He stared at me. 'Is she so cursed?'

I answered with a brief smile, then pulled Neha and turned away.

'Do you not offer your name?'

'Ailia,' I called over my shoulder.

'Skin to Caer Cad?'

I stopped, wordless. It had been many summers since I had met this question.

In the silence, a woman's voice called. 'She's unskinned, daughter only to the doorstep!'

My face burned. There were those who were angered by my place in the Tribequeen's kitchen. Years of taunts had taught me to walk away without looking back, lest their spit wet my face.

'Unskinned?' said Ruther. 'Yet you hold your head like a queen.'

'Because she attends the queen's kitchen,' called another. 'And the Cookwoman pets her like a house dog.'

I kept walking. Ruther was right to be surprised. Not often would one without skin move through the town so freely. A pebble struck my shoulder, hard and sharp. I stopped as the sting gave way to a warm ache and a trickle of blood down my back.

'Cease!' shouted Ruther into the crowd. 'Do you strike a maiden's back? And for nothing but an accident of birth? Do you still live in this darkness since I have been gone?' He turned to me. 'Go home, daughter of the doorstep,' he said. 'Be proud of your boldness.'

Before I turned the corner, I glanced back. Ruther had unsheathed his sword and was swiping and twisting it again to a tide of admiring murmurs. Who is he, I wondered, who cares so little for the laws of skin?

'Handsome, isn't he?' said a townswoman as she passed.

'If your tastes are such,' I answered.

'He thought you sweet enough.'

As I hurried home, I saw the thick smoke of the fringe fires coiling above the town walls.

Just beyond the southern gate, wedged along the lower banks of the ramparts, was a tight-packed warren of stick huts and hide tents, foul with littered bone scraps and poor drainage. These were the fringes. Home to the skinless. Shunned by the tribe.

Summer was strong in deer spirit. Except for those who had travelled or married in—bringing with them skins of the owl, wolf or the river—most born here were skin to the deer.

Born to the skinless, or lost to their families before naming, the unskinned were not claimed by a totem. Their souls were fragmented, unbound to the Singing. If they remained little seen, they were not despised, not usually harmed. The townspeople gave them enough grain, cloaks and work, if they would do it. But they could not live within the town walls because no one could be sure of who they were.

I quickened my pace and Neha trotted beside me.

Skin was gifted from mother to child by a song.

I had no mother. I had no skin.

But I had been spared. Just.

—

'Who cast the stone?' spat Cookmother, dabbing an ointment of comfrey on my back.

In the quiet of the kitchen, I sat between my worksisters on a long log bench draped with pelts. We held bowls of bread soaked in goat's milk and huddled close to the hearthstones as the morning sun had not yet warmed the thick walls of our roundhouse.

'I did not see.' I winced as Cookmother covered my wound.

'I'll strangle them with their own innards if I learn of it.' She lifted my dress back onto my shoulders, and I leaned against her warm bulk. It was by Cookmother's insistence alone that I remained in the Tribequeen's kitchen.

As we ate, I told the girls of the Great Bear's death, and of my meeting with Ruther.

'It is said he can match twenty Romans with his sword,' said Ianna, her wide eyes blinking.

'More likely to share their wine and whores, I've heard,' said Cah.

'Speak not against Orgilos's son in my kitchen, thanks be,' said Cookmother, stirring the fire pot.

Bebin rose and took up a flame to light the torches. 'Was there another returned with him?' she asked.

'Who could you mean?' jibed Cah.

We all knew she spoke of Uaine, also fostered to the east. She had awaited his return for three summers.

'He was alone,' I murmured.

Bebin turned away and my heart fell.

'Uaine will be schooled to a high warrior now,' said Cah. 'He will set his sights beyond a kitchen girl when he returns.'

I could have struck her with a fire iron, but I knew Bebin had more sense than to listen to Cah.

Bebin walked the curved room, igniting the torches, each one revealing more of the swirling red circles that marked our walls. She lit only the kitchen's eastern half—the realm of the living—where the floor and shelves were crammed with baskets, grindstones, grainpots and buckets. The western half, where our beds were laid, was the place of the dead and must remain always in darkness.

'Empty your bowls, Cah, Ianna,' snapped Cookmother. 'It is time for your lessons.'

Cah groaned.

'What was that?' said Cookmother. 'Rather wash out the shit trough, would you?' She reached over and snatched Cah's bowl.

'I had not finished,' said Cah.

'You have now. Get your cloak.'

Bebin smiled as she caught my eye. Four years my elder, she had finished her schooling, but every morning except wane days and feast days, Cah and Ianna, both my age, were still expected to go to the shrine, where learners gathered before dispersing to the rivers or to the craft huts for schooling.

I followed them to the door and watched them walk off, laughing. Learning was wasted on both of them. Ianna had no brains for it and Cah had no gratitude. They had no idea of their privilege. I would have cut off my first finger to be in their place for just one summer. But I was not permitted to go with them or hear any talk of what they learned. It was forbidden for the unskinned to be taught.

Neha nosed my hand. I squatted beside her and buried my fingers in the swathe of white fur around her neck. She was not a large dog—her shoulder only at my knee when I stood—but her carriage was proud. She turned her snout to meet my caress. Her face was unusually marked—half-grey, half-white in perfect division—but it was her eyes that drew the most curiosity: the one belonging to the white side was ice-blue, the other brown. It gave her an eerie, lopsided stare that, combined with her wary temper, many felt marked her as a friend to the dark spirits. But I knew her soul was true and I had taken many years of comfort from her odd-eyed gaze.

'Come, Ailia,' called Cookmother from the hearth. 'Fraid will be ready for her bath and you know she does not like to wait.'

Names

The moon has a name—a Mother's name—
but it is too powerful to say.
We say only brightness or light of the night.
We are too small to say its true name.
A name. A soul. They are the same.

I PUT DOWN the brimming water bucket and struck the bell at the Tribequeen's outer door. Although I had passed this threshold daily since I had turned twelve, it still made my belly flutter. I paused at the inner door and she called me through.

Inside, the air was heavy with birch smoke and the scent of the walnut oil she rubbed in her hair. She sat, straight-backed, on a stool by the fire. Dressed only in her linen night-tunic, without the layers of bracelets and neckrings that marked her as our leader, she looked pale and thin.

I was one of the few permitted to see her un-metalled, but I never forgot that she was Fraid, unchallenged Tribequeen of Northern Durotriga, skin to the deer. She carried the nimble wit of her totem and enough of its caution as well. Few tribeswomen rose to rule but

Fraid had a stomach for it that her brothers did not, and the shelves lining the walls were laden with gifts—carvings and jewels—that bore testament to the bonds she had wrought with our neighbouring tribes.

'Come,' she said.

I could not read her face as I walked toward her. Her high brow was smoother, more innocent, than one would expect of a woman who had borne the weight of a tribe for twenty summers. Yet usually I could detect the twitch of the lip, the lift of the jaw, which told me if matters in the tribe were not well. Today I could not.

I glanced at her bed. No warrior lay within, though she had taken many since her husband had fallen to fever last midwinter. The bed of her brother, Fibor, was also empty and her youngest daughter, Manacca—seven summers old and the only one yet to be fostered away—had torn past as I returned from the well. Fraid was alone.

Yet when I drew closer, I was startled to see Llwyd the Journeyman, sitting motionless on the carved bench to Fraid's right. Her concern must have been great to call her highest advisor before she was properly cloaked.

Clutching the bucket, I bowed deeply.

'Quickly, Ailia,' said Fraid. 'I'm poorly slept and hungry.'

I pulled a bowl from the shelf and ladled it full of the barley porridge bubbling on the hearth. Etaina, Fibor's wife, must have prepared it before she left. 'Might I serve you food also, Journeyman?'

'Nay, I fast for the rites.' Llwyd smiled at me. Rarely did I see him outside of Ceremony or council. He wore the bone-coloured cloth of all journeymen Elders and, where it parted at his shoulder, I saw the mark of the deer scarred and dyed into his upper arm. His beard was the colour of pewter and his brown irises were misty with age, but the creases in his face showed there had been laughter in him. There was laughter still.

The journeypeople were those who had travelled many years in their learning. They were our teachers, our law-keepers, our ears to the Mothers. They knew how to travel the dream states, the trances, from which they saw what was true.

I unhooked the cookpot and placed it on the hearthstones. Then I hung an empty cauldron, filled it with wash-water, and sat down at Fraid's feet.

'This death will hasten an attack, I am sure of it,' Fraid said to Llwyd between mouthfuls. 'Not only because it makes cracks in our leadership, but because Caradog speaks so provocatively against Rome.' She sighed.

'He has always spoken so,' answered Llwyd.

'Yes, but he had his father to blunt his words.'

'True,' Llwyd nodded. 'Belinus was an artful leader, equally skilled with word and sword. But Caradog has his own strengths. He is a tribesman, a lover of our Albion.' His voice had the warmth of a long-burned fire.

Fraid placed her bowl on the bench beside her. 'Do you suggest that we offer an alliance with Caradog? Should I send an envoy to pledge our fighting men and our coinage?'

Llwyd glanced at me and I turned back to the fire, embarrassed that he had caught me listening. 'No,' he said. 'You have worked hard to protect the independence of this tribe.'

'Caradog may seek to bring us into an alliance by force,' said Fraid. 'After all, he already controls the tribes on three sides of Durotriga.'

'Caradog will seek to subdue the tribes whose leaders hold Roman sympathies,' said Llwyd, 'and that, good Tribequeen, is not us.'

I unhooked the simmering pot and poured the steaming water into a clay bowl, sweetening it with a pinch of dog-rose from a pot on Fraid's shelf.

She winced at the heat as her feet slid in. 'Nevertheless it will not hurt to keep the tradelines strong. After Beltane, I will send an envoy with new samples. I will send the knave Ruther.'

I glanced up as I rubbed her feet with a slippery slab of tallow.

'Why him?' asked Llwyd. I could not read the tone that had darkened his voice.

'He's been Roman-taught. He knows their ways. Perhaps he can help smooth what Caradog upsets.'

'Be at peace, Fraid,' said Llwyd, lightening again. 'Caradog is a man of fire, but he is fuelled by love of the Mothers. If he leads us to war with Rome it will be an honourable war.'

'But can we win such a war?'

Llwyd paused. 'We will win it if the Mothers desire it.'

'We will win it if our armies are strong enough,' said Fraid.

I looked to her. It was not her way to speak so irreverently.

Llwyd frowned.

'Forgive me,' Fraid sighed. 'It is only my worry speaking. But I cannot share your good faith, Journeyman. The messengers have long spoken that the fool Emperor Claudius searches for glory. The Romans are awaiting the right moment to strike, and this time they will not allow themselves to fail.'

As I dried Fraid's feet, I could not tell if it was her words or Beltane nerves that made my belly clench. I loosened her night braid, setting her dark hair tumbling down her back. As I retied it, the pulse in her neck throbbed under my fingers.

'You speak freely in front of this girl.' Llwyd stared at me.

'She can be trusted,' Fraid said. 'What do you think, Ailia? How will we fare under another Roman attack?'

My mouth fell open in surprise. I knew nothing of statecraft or the arts of war. I could not read omens in the night sky or the spilled innards of a slain lamb. I shook my head. 'I don't know.'

Fraid laughed. 'Of course you don't. It is festival eve, not the time for such questions.' She turned to Llwyd. 'I will speak on this with the council when the fires have burned down.' She held out her fingers to be cleaned and I gathered my sticks and brushes. It was a mark of shame for nails to be ragged or dirty and I was the only one she permitted to tend them.

Fraid was bold in keeping me as her attendant. She chose me because she liked my touch and she said that, of all the girls, I was the most at ease with a woman of power.

I was fortunate beyond words. Privileged in ways others without skin can only dream of.

Why was it not enough?

—

I walked down to the well near the southern gate, murmuring thanks to the Mothers before I cast my bucket into the long, dark drop.

The passage from womb to world was only half a birth—the body's birth. Our souls were born when we were plunged, as babes, into river water, screaming at the cold shock of it, given our name and called to skin.

Deer. Salmon. Stone. Beetle. The North wind. Skin was our greeting, our mother, our ancestors, our land. Nothing existed outside its reach.

Beyond skin there was only darkness. Only chaos.

Because I was without skin I could not be plunged or named. I was half-born, born in body but not in soul. Born to the world but not to the tribe. I could never marry lest skin taboos were unknowingly betrayed. Deer did not marry well to owl. Owl to oak. At Ceremony I had to be silent, and keep to the edges. For where would I stand? What would I chant?

I lived with these losses, but the one that hollowed my chest was that I was not permitted to learn. All learning began and ended with the songs of skin. I ached to learn. Weaponcraft, oak-lore, the knowledge of the stars. I hungered for the poems that brought shape to this world of earth and water—the hardworld—and mapped the spirit places of the Mothers' realm. Poems that told us what had come before, what made a life right and true.

I pulled up the bucket brimming with water from deep in the mountain.

When Fraid gave me my freedom, I would find my family. I did not know how, but there would be a way. I would find my birthplace, my kin and my skinsong, and then I would be able to learn.

Then I would be born.

Balance and Order

We eat enough, but pay fines if our belts become too large.
We couple freely, but never with force.
We observe the rise and set, the wax and wane,
the winter and summer.
What we take from the forest, we give back.

'SALT FOR THE grain cakes. Mustard.' Cookmother called out the list for market as she fossicked through the pots crammed on the shelves and floor. She was always promising to tidy her stores but never did, and refused to let anyone else. 'Honey, of course. Not the watered-down sap from that cheat with four fingers. Get the elder honey from that nice Dobunnii girl with a bit of a rump.' Cookmother grunted as she got up. 'Don't forget the goat, of course, and Ailia, on the way back, pick some yellow dock and meadowsweet from the marshes.'

I nodded as I sharpened my harvest knife and slipped it into my belt. Cookmother's knees could no longer abide the steep walk, so Bebin and I went to market each moonturn, though Cookmother was always convinced we'd be fiddled.

Following the sound of market drums and bleating livestock, we made our way down to the flatlands from the southern gate. Sellers from all of Summer were gathered below, on the banks of our largest river, the Cam. We quickened our pace. The best pickings went early at market.

Neha tore ahead toward the sprawling pens of lambs and goat kids, where we found her wolfing a fresh-cut calf's tail from our favourite seller. We haggled over the fattest of his young goats and walked on, dragging it on a rope past the ponies and hunt dogs.

Dried salmon and geese hung above tables laden with fresh carcasses. Beyond the flesh stalls were sacks brimming with salt and herbs from the trade routes, and waist-high baskets of grain and fruit. The air teemed with smells of blood, sweetcakes, dung and smoke, and the shouts of sellers calling their wares. Bebin and I wove among them, making our greetings and stopping to gossip. News of the Great Bear's death had spread through the township, but it could not dampen the thrill of the upcoming festival and the whispers of who would be paired at the fires.

Two young men jostled to watch us pass. 'Hold the bulls,' one called, 'we have found our Beltane lovers!'

'Do you hear cocks crowing?' Bebin asked me loudly as she pushed past them.

It was only this spring that the men of market had been noticing me. I had grown taller. Bebin came only to my shoulder, though she was as curved as a goddess, whereas I had the chest of a knave. My bloods had flowed for almost a year, but I would never be one with a wet nurse's chest and I was glad of it. I was fair enough of face, but too strong-nosed and sharp-chinned to be called sweet, unlike Bebin, who was as succulent and wet-eyed as a baby calf. She was dark like our first people, whereas I was of middling colour, with hair the hue of beech wood and eyes as green as moss. Though I loved Bebin dearly, I would not have traded my strong shoulders for her round hips. I could not help thinking there was more use in the first.

We moved swiftly past the jewellers, toolwrights and potters to reach the sellers of cloth. As well as honey, salt and a goat, I needed to buy ribbon for my hair at Beltane. I had always worn blue. Tonight I would wear red.

As I was stuffing the loops of ribbon into my basket, I heard Bebin yelp. I looked up to see her darting around the next corner. The stubborn kid slowed me in following her, but when I had cajoled it past the medicine sellers (and paid for the pots of resin it kicked to the ground), I found her on the far side of the market, standing with Uaine, watching the young men and women practising for the games tomorrow.

I lingered, allowing them their whispers and laughter, as I watched the threshold maidens shooting archery targets. A pang of envy shot through me as a fair-haired girl raised her bow and drew back a sinewy arm. Ribbons of deerskin hung off the belt around her narrow hips. She released the arrow and hit the trunk at its centre, smiling as the crowd applauded. I marvelled at her mastery.

Fraid had come down to observe the play, for the results of this contest would help her choose which of the fresh-bled maidens would run first through the fires tonight.

Neha nosed my palm and I rubbed her cheek. If it were a contest of commanding a wayward dog I would win without rival.

'Do you not join the games, Doorstep?'

I jumped at the voice so close to my ear. Neha growled.

In a tartan tunic pinned by a silver brooch, Ruther held himself as though the gates to the Otherworld would fly open at his command.

'Don't call me that. It is no kindness to be reminded so.'

'Is it not a compliment? Are not the thresholds sacred?'

My gaze snagged on the bow of his lip, before I turned back to the games without answering.

'Why are you not among them?' he asked.

'I am not permitted.'

'Have you not bled?' He was as forthright as a siring bull.

'Ay, I am aged for my first Beltane, but you know as well as I that I cannot contest the Maiden's crown.'

'Because you are without skin?'

I frowned. 'Yes. Because I have not been taught any of the contest skills.'

He snorted. 'Foolish waste.'

I turned to him in surprise. 'It is not for us to judge the laws of the tribe.'

'Why not? Do they stand above questioning?' He leaned closer. 'I am recently returned from travel where I found a world greatly different from this.' He paused, his breath warm on my ear. 'I have seen cities where men claim their place by merit alone. Where they are no more bound by clan than the eagle by ground.'

'If the laws are not held,' I whispered, 'then what protects us?'

His eyebrows shot skyward. 'This is what I seek to learn.'

There was something that angered me in these words and in the smile that accompanied them. 'Is it not tribal law that has placed you as nobleman?'

His smile fell away. 'Have you not seen me fight? I will earn my position by my sword against any warrior of Albion.'

'And a nobleman's schooling has bought you that skill.'

He stared at me and I looked straight back. His eyes were as blue as flame. 'So are you permitted, at least, to attend this night?' His voice was low. 'After all, even cows and pigs run the fires.'

I reddened. 'Of course.'

'And will you dance?'

'Ay.' No one was denied the dance.

'And take a fire lover at your will?'

The hairs on my arm rose to stand. 'Yes.'

'Good then,' he said, suddenly too jovial. 'Perhaps I shall meet you there.' He stepped forward, draping his arm around Uaine's shoulder. 'Good brother!' he exclaimed. 'I did not see you there, and who is this delicious sweetmeat with you?'

I stared as he laughed with Uaine, gathering the ravel of my wits. It did not take one any more learned than myself to see that he was not to be trusted.

—

The afternoon was busy with preparation for tomorrow's feast.

Ianna and Cah helped Cookmother to knead the barley cakes while Bebin and I decanted the barrels of beer and lined the roasting pit with straw.

All had to be completed before our kitchen fire was doused at sunset. Our hearths burned ceaselessly throughout the year, except at Beltane, when they were extinguished, to be re-lit, reborn, by a flaming tallow stick carried back from the fires after the dance.

We were deep in work when the horn call from the shrine announced the late-day hunt.

I ran back to the kitchen and gathered the pots and vials from the medicine table. Cookmother packed her tools and we left for the shrine. She gripped my arm as we wound through the back streets. The shrine lay at the midpoint of Cad's central roadway, but we took a less visible path so that fewer would see it was I who accompanied her. 'My knees cannot bear the distance,' she panted. 'Next time you will have to go alone.'

Although I could not be taught, for years, at Cookmother's skirts I had watched and gathered, unsanctioned, the arts of healing. Because her hands had become gnarled by labour and her back twisted with age, it was I who had ground the heavy medicine stone, wrapped marsh reed tight around a cut, and pressed deep into a swollen belly to discover the lay of a babe. By the time I was nine summers old I had dressed hunt wounds open to the bone and sewn a man's flesh with an iron needle while five men held him down.

There were physicians among the journeymen of Summer, but none as trusted as Cookmother. And none she trusted more than me to assist her, as I had until late last night, distilling the frog poisons and bud essences that would aid the hunt.

We passed the last of the roundhouses and emerged back onto the open street. Turned earth surrounded the entrance to the shrine, where calves and foals, offerings for Beltane, lay in shallow graves, their bones safeguarding the shrine.

A lone journeywoman, barely older than me, left the hall as we entered, the green robe of the novice seer billowing behind her. Cookmother stopped, offering the greeting of the salmon, and the journeywoman murmured the deer skin greeting in response.

I stood, head lowered, saying nothing, but I turned to watch as she walked away. Hers was the path of hard learning: long days in the groves, listening and questioning, twenty summers gleaning the sacred truths and rites of our country. Many sought this path, but only those who showed great fire of mind could begin it. For women of knowledge could travel far further than even their journeybrothers. The journeywomen were those who could cross—mostly by spirit but sometimes by flesh—beyond the hardworld to the spirit realm, the place of the Mothers.

'Is she Isle-trained?' I whispered to Cookmother.

'I have heard she will go this summer.'

I fought a wave of envy. While the men went to the Island of Mona, the most gifted journeywomen from all of Albion trained their craft at the Glass Isle. I knew little else of it. Only that it was water-bound, protected by mists, and closer than anywhere else to the Mothers' realm.

Within the cool darkness of the shrine, the men of the hunt were seated on rows of benches, giving thanks before the altar. Ruther was not among them and I was relieved not to be distracted as I worked the plants.

Fibor, Fraid's brother and first of her warriors, stood waiting to dedicate the hunt, but first Cookmother had to ready their eyes and arrows with juices. She worked quickly, brushing frog poison over their upheld spear tips.

The men began the low chant to ready themselves.

Strong like a bear
Strong like a bear

I followed behind Cookmother, holding the bottles as she tipped droplets of goldenseal into their eyes to bring them clear vision.

See like a bird
See like a bird

She turned to me in annoyance. 'Bah, Ailia, my own eyes are failing me. You finish it,' she said, thrusting the bronze pipette into my hand.

'Are you sure?' I whispered. Only ever within the walls of the kitchen did she charge me with treatment.

'Ay—begin, begin,' she urged. 'The mixture will not hold for long.'

I finished walking the circle of upturned faces, dripping the poison into each pair of eyes. 'It will pass in a moment,' I whispered to one, who winced with the sting.

Eyes streaming, the men stood, making the cries of the animal they would hunt: the short blasting snorts of the doe, the guttural grunts of the tending buck. They mimicked not in disdain but in kinship. The eating of totem meat was forbidden, except at Beltane when it was hunted, just once, and eaten to remake the bonds.

Fibor called the dedication and strode to the doorway. The men gathered their weapons and followed him out to the roadway, headed for the forest's edge where the dimming light would embolden the deer and draw them out from the shelter of trees.

'Return with deer or shame!' Cookmother cried after them. She took my arm. 'Well worked, Ailia,' she said.

'The knave Ruther proclaims himself loudly.' Bebin passed a branch of fresh hawthorn to me as I stood atop an upturned woodbox. We were decorating the Great House and it was tiring work; five men on end would not reach its roof peak and five farm huts would not cover its floor.

'Too loudly,' I agreed, tucking the sprig of white blossoms behind a beam. Delicate petals showered on her head as I wedged it in.

'Still,' she said, 'you seem to have caught his eye at market this morning.'

'As many others catch his eye.' I jumped off the box and dragged it under the next beam.

'Choose carefully if he comes seeking you tonight,' Bebin paused as she followed me, finding her words. 'He is changed from what I remember of him.'

I straightened to face her. 'How so?'

'I'm not sure. There's a newness in him. Something not of the tribes.'

'And Uaine? Is he so changed?'

'Perhaps,' she answered. 'But Ruther is somehow at its source.'

I laughed off her warning. 'He is the son of a high warrior to the deer. He won't come looking for a skinless girl.' I paused. 'No one will.'

'Oh, Ailia.' She took my hand. 'It will be you who'll do the choosing. There are knaves who'd have had you long since.'

'None of honour.' I picked a bud from the branches cradled in her arm. 'And even if there were, I have no clan ties to offer in marriage.'

Bebin threw back her head and laughed in the way that saw her first coupled at every festival. 'Beltane is no time for making marriages. It's the night to throw rings off!' She set down the branches on the box and turned to me. 'This is the marriage of earth and sun! Clan ties mean little tonight.'

I nodded. 'There's a petal on your cheek.'

'Sweet friend,' Bebin said, looping her arm around my waist. 'Do not be nervous. All will be well.'

Not until the sun nudged the western horizon did we hear the shouts and barks of the returning hunt. Bebin and I were in the courtyard, stoking the roasting pit outside the Great House. We rushed to the queen's gate, where a crowd was gathering to meet the hunters.

Fibor came first, then the others strode through the gate, a strung milking doe swinging between them, its pelt matted with blood. The last of the hunters carried its young—a single buck, unharmed, no more than one moon old.

We followed them to the Great House, where the doe was laid on the ground at the door and received by Fraid, before the hunters swiftly gutted and lowered it, without beheading, into the pit. There were cheers and laughter from the crowd and Neha surged forward with the rest of the dogs, snarling and snapping for her share of the innards.

I stood back while the doe was covered with straw, stones and finally earth. As I turned to go back to the kitchen, I noticed the baby buck standing wide-eyed and alone beside me, paralysed by the noise and the dogs. I scooped it up, its spindly mass no heavier than a basket of bread. It struggled feebly then collapsed, trembling, into my arms.

Fraid called to the crowd. 'Look how the sun is nearly set. Go to your homes, put out your hearths and ready yourselves for the fires!'

With shouts of excitement, the crowd dispersed and Bebin came to my side, cooing and fussing over the baby deer.

'Ailia!' Fraid called. 'Go and lay out my metals. I will follow soon to dress.'

'Can you take him back to the kitchen?' I asked, pushing the buck into Bebin's arms.

As I walked to the sleephouse, I saw townspeople tying rowan branches to their doorways. The boughs would protect against the dark spirits who could steal forth when the Beltane fires burned a hole to the Otherworld. The rowan was a reminder to us that when we sought light, there was an equal risk of finding darkness.

—

From the baskets and boxes that rimmed her walls, I pulled out all of Fraid's metals onto a table draped with cloth, wondering what she would choose tonight. Next to the coloured armbands, anklets, neckrings and her silver festival torque was my favourite of her ornaments: a bronze hand mirror with the swirling face of a Mother engraved on its back. I picked up the mirror, savouring the weight and lustre of the metal and the texture of its scored pattern under my fingertips. I loved the spinning patterns that flowed from the hands of our makers. None of the Roman crafts were ever as beautiful.

On a wooden stand beside the table was the Tribequeen's diadem, the tribe's most sacred piece. With its hammered gold and flame-coloured stones, it seemed as if lit from within.

Glancing at the doorway, I set the mirror down. Then with both hands, I lifted the crown—heavier than I expected—and placed it on my head. When I held the mirror to my face, I gasped. Before me was a queen. A Mother.

'Ailia?' Fraid was at the doorway. 'What are you doing?'

I wrenched the crown from my head and pushed it back onto its stand.

'This headpiece marks the first consort to the deer,' she said, striding toward me. 'Do you seek to defile it?'

'No!' I assured her, furious with my stupidity. 'I am sorry, Tribequeen. I...I was beguiled by the metal—'

She stood before me, surprise knotting her brow. 'You might have my favour,' she said, 'but do not forget that I am at the very limits of my grace in keeping you here. Do not give me cause to release you. You are here by a spider's thread.'

'Yes,' I whispered, bowing my head.

'Oh, Ailia,' she sighed as she sat on her stool. 'This is not as I expect of you. Come.' Her voice softened. 'You are unsettled as we all are by the news from the east. Now, we shall forget this and you will help me dress.'

I nodded in gratitude and brought the robes from her cloak stand.

She raised her arms so I could slip the silk under-robe over her bare torso, followed by a dress of clan tartan threaded with silver. She wrapped her chain belt twice around her waist and let the heavy bronze charm rest against her belly. I helped her slide her narrow feet into leather sandals ornamented with twisting metal and coloured stones. Then she sat very still while I blackened her fine eyebrows with berry juice and rubbed roan into her cheeks.

Admiring her own beauty in the bronze mirror, she caught my eye in the reflection. 'You run the fires also tonight, do you not?' she said.

'Yes.'

'Would you like me to colour your lips?'

I nodded and crouched beside her.

Her fingertips were cool as she patted powdery roan across my mouth and cheeks. Then she feathered a small juice-soaked brush over my eyebrows and dabbed rose oil at my temple and throat.

'There,' she said, handing me the mirror. 'Does it please you?'

My eyes widened in the mirror. The colours made them sparkle and had turned my lips to petals. My tinted cheeks tempered my jaw, drawing my face into perfect alignment. I was beautiful.

Fraid, too, seemed astonished. She looked at me as though seeing me for the first time. 'I may have chosen the First Maiden this morning, but it seems the Mothers have chosen you.' She laughed.

She asked for rose oil to be rubbed into her arms and shoulders so they would gleam in the firelight. As I stroked her skin, I marvelled at how it was just like my own: warm, alive, pale from the winter sun. It held her as mine held me, and wept blood when cut, as mine did also. Our skin was the same. Yet hers had a name and mine had none.

After admiring my face, Bebin brushed my unruly hair and wove the crimson ribbon down its full length as I kneeled on the floorskins before her. I could hear the distant shouts of the men dragging the last of the branches up to the bonfires on Sister Hill. Ianna and Cah were already dressed and readied, waiting outside, watching the Beltane moon rise.

Cookmother groaned, struggling to feed the buck by the fire. She grew more and more impatient, guiding its whiskery mouth to her nipple. 'By Mothers, there's scarcely a drop left in these useless sacks,' she muttered, kneading her breast. 'I'm too old for this. Bebin, you need to start breeding so I can be free of this cursed nursing.' She would feed the buck until it was strong enough to be given back to the forest. When the hunt took a feeding mother, this was what we had to do.

Cah's face burst through the doorskins. 'Come!' she called. 'It will be over before we leave.'

Bebin squeezed my shoulders. 'Let's away.'

'I'll catch up,' I said, rising. 'I want to settle the buck first.'

'Butter heart!' She shook her head. 'Be quick at least.'

Milk bubbled from the buck's nostrils when he had drunk his fill and Cookmother put him down on the floor with a thud. 'It'll stink of deer shit in the morning,' she muttered, getting up.

I fashioned the tiny deer a nest of straw in my own bedskins and cradled him into it. He quivered at my touch. 'Hush, youngling,' I cooed. 'You're safe here.'

I stared at his dewy face, the whisper of spots across his back, and wondered at the wash of love that rose in my chest. Was this skin love? Was this my kin? I had grown on deer country. Surely my kin could not be far from here. But no one had claimed me. It was said that those without skin were still seeking their souls. I took a deep breath as I stroked the creature's knobby spine. If I was without a soul, what was it that heaved and thrashed within me?

Neha approached, sniffed the buck, and flopped down beside it.

'That's it, girl. You watch him for me.' I stood to leave.

Cookmother was poking inside the rosewood chest where her most precious oils and powders were kept. She pulled out a tiny leather pouch and brought it to me, pressing it into my hand. 'I meant this for your next birthday,' she said. 'But every maiden needs a threshold gift on her first Beltane, so take it now.'

Inside the pouch was a gold pin in the shape of a fish. I shook it out into my palm, then fastened it to the front of my new yellow dress.

She crushed me with her embrace and I breathed in the warm, sour smell that had swathed me all my childhood. 'Let me take the red ribbon out and thread a blue so you can sleep in peace another summer,' she whispered. 'Men's hunger is like a dog's—always sharp.'

'Leave it so. I am ready.'

5

Sacred Love

Through sacred love the fields are made fertile.
Through sacred love we are freed from famine.
Through sacred love the world is renewed.

I WALKED THE torch-lined path to Sister Hill with Bebin, Ianna and Cah. The moon hung fat and low in the eastern sky, teasing a honey fragrance from the elder blossoms that brushed our shoulders as we passed. We all wore dresses of yellow and orange, and our hair ribbons whipped in the wind. Laughter trailed down the hillside and the air felt ripe with magic.

Cah pulled a flask from her belt pocket and took a long swig.

'Ay, Cah, do you not want steady wits for the rite?' said Bebin.

'Surely it is a night to abandon steady wits?' She offered it around but we refused. 'Mind you are not chosen by Fec, Ailia. He is as ugly as a boar and carries contagion, I am told.'

'Cah!' chided Ianna.

'Well, it's true. I see you smile.'

'You'll not have Fec,' whispered Bebin into my ear. 'It will be a noble match for you this night.'

As we neared the crest, the unlit woodpiles reared like two beasts silhouetted against the western sky. Circled around them were the journeymen and -women, chanting purifications for the flames to come. Tribespeople milled around the poles set for the dance. Men had worked for three days to dig holes deep enough to hold the trunks upright. Eleven had already been positioned. The raising of the twelfth would commence the rite.

At the pole-bearer's cry, we all surged back, making space for the men to bring the trunk. It was a grown oak, freshly felled, its skin smoothed to a silk sheen and wound tight with twelve ribbons along its length. It took ten men to manoeuvre it over the final hole, shuffling forwards then back until they were in place.

'Down!' came the call and the pole rose skyward. Tribeswomen packed the base with dirt so it stood as firm and straight as the others. I craned my neck to see them all: stretching from earth to sky, the ribbons like water, swirling about them.

A drum strike began. It was time to dance. The crowd fanned open to form a circle.

Instinctively, I moved to the back. Already the music was coiling around me and I was swaying and treading with its pulse. There was little my bones loved more than to dance.

'Come!' Bebin tugged my hand. 'It's your threshold year—you must dance at the poles.'

'No,' I said, horrified. 'I am not permitted.'

She grabbed both my shoulders, thrusting her face close to mine. 'Ailia, you are true and whole and you love the Mothers more than any I know. Come and dance. No one will protest it this night. The Mothers know your heart—'

'Wait—' But she was pulling me into the centre.

There were twelve maidens to a pole. We each caught a dangling ribbon and began to walk. The weight of so many eyes upon me was crippling, but I listened to the drumbeat and forced myself forward.

A second, faster rhythm began, counter to the first, and this was our call to start the steps: a fast-moving pattern of footwork, twisting one leg behind the other. I watched Bebin ahead of me, her hips and shoulders rolling smoothly. The ritual was deep in her body and she wove its spell effortlessly.

The tribespeople began to sing and the drums gathered pace. My feet kicked up dirt as I danced. Panting, I kept my eyes fixed on Bebin, her hair sailing behind her. Faces blurred as they flew by. The drums become faster, the chant yet louder. Soon I was sweating, heat pouring through me. My chest cried to stop but I danced faster and harder.

Now I felt the magic we pounded in the dirt. Now I felt the power of the dance to wake the Mothers from their winter sleep. Now it was no longer a dance, no longer twelve maidens. It was a wheel wrought of our bodies and as it turned I was flooded with an intense joy. I ran and ran until I was no longer there. There was earth and sky and the poles that bridged them but I, Ailia, had melted away and there was only the dance. Only the wheel.

A voice was raised in a mighty call and the drumbeat ceased.

We stopped, breath ragged. The fires were to be lit. I hurried back into the crowd, my heart still hammering.

Llwyd stood between the two woodpiles, arms raised. We fell silent to hear him speak. 'Our earthly world—our hardworld—is a place of wildness,' he began. 'The forces of chaos run through its veins. They are our breath and our devastation.'

The crowd gave a rumbling cheer.

'By our knowledge—by skin—we are aligned to these forces. Yet we know in our souls they can never be harnessed. The wildness is stronger than us and we are always subject to its mystery and power.'

Voices began to swell.

'This night, beloved people of Summer, we kindle the fires that will cleanse our cattle, seed the belly of our earth, and bless our souls. Then—' he paused for a moment, '—let the forces of chaos run free!'

The crowd erupted into cheers. Two lesser journeymen approached, bearing burning sticks. Over stamping and shouting, they called the final incantations to the Mothers and the towering woodpiles were ignited.

Fire surged upward into the indigo sky. I watched, motionless, staring at the flames, my cheeks smarting with heat. I had been separated from Bebin and forced back to the edge of the gathering. But as I looked out over the grainfields, pastures and forests that stretched beneath the hill and the magnificent rise of Cad beside it, my heart brimmed again with the gladness I felt in the dance. All my people were here around me, rejoicing in the land that held us. All we could ever want was given to us. For this moment, the ache for skin was gone, healed in the love and warmth of the fire.

There were shouts and we scrabbled to make way as two white bulls were driven toward the flames. They stalled at the mouth of the firepath, bellowing in fear, eyes rolling and muscles twitching.

Llwyd called their blessing, and they were forced, galloping, through, burning sticks at their rumps. The crowd roared.

Now the farmers were herding all of Cad's cattle up the hillside. The air was filled with their screams and the smell of their terror as they, too, were run through the flames and onto the safety of their summer pastures.

When the animals had been purified, Fraid called forth the First Maiden. I pushed my way forward to see her. A deerskin cloaked her naked, painted body, and beneath her antler crown, the mask of the doe covered her face. None could see who had been chosen. She was the earth now, a Mother.

The drums began again and the young men of Summer formed a line before her as she walked the length of them. They stood tall and bare-chested, baring their teeth and making animal cries to attract her attention.

We all swayed and stamped as we waited for the Mother to make her match. From the corner of my eye I noticed Ruther, standing well back from the line, and I wondered why he, of all the young men, would not contest this honour. Finally the Maiden held her hand out to Juc, the newest of the warrior initiates. He dropped to his knees to accept her and then together they ran through the fires to the crowd's screams of excitement.

Now all were free to run the fires. The threshold maidens were brought forward first and Llwyd called blessings on their wombs as they entered the flames. Young men raced to the other side to meet them when they emerged.

Tribespeople were dancing furiously, drunk on the fireheat. Maiden and knave were writhing in pairs, then racing down the hill-side or coupling right there by the fire.

I hovered at the edges and saw Bebin bounding away with Uaine. Ianna and Cah were nowhere to be seen. I turned back to the fires. They were why I had come.

When all the tribespeople had run and only those without skin remained, it was my turn. I walked to the threshold. Once I had run through this passage of fire, I would be something other. Something new.

The heat was scaring. It pushed me back, yet I forced myself forward.

'Run! Run!' chanted the few who awaited their turn.

I ran. Embers blistered my feet and stung my eyes, but I pushed on blindly. The passage went on and on. The heat was too great. I stopped, panicked. Were the fires collapsing? There was no way forward. I cried out, my voice drowned in the roar of the flames. How had others endured this torment? Every part of me commanded me to turn back, but I kept going. There was a final, unbearable surge of heat. My bones softened like iron in a forge, then I burst out the other side into the cool night. I had done it. I was through.

I beat out the sparks smouldering on my dress and looked around, unable to wipe the smile from my face.

'Found you!' Ruther was at my side.

I threw my arms around him, unexpectedly happy to see him, then screamed with laughter as he scooped me up and began to run. With my height, I was no easy load, and he staggered as we careered down the hill. I could not stop laughing with his every clumsy step.

Where the hill met the flatland he set me down and we fell to the grass, panting as our laughter faded. Out of the fire-warmth, it was dark and cold. I could not make out his features as he took my face in his hands.

'Do you accept me?' His voice was hoarse from chanting.

'Ruther, I am unskinned.'

'I follow the laws of my own judgment, Doorstep. Do you?

'Don't call me so!'

He pulled me closer. 'Will you take me?'

His hips were hard against mine. My singed skin howled for his touch. 'I will.'

His mouth descended and I startled at its strange, serpent softness and its taste of ale.

We stood and walked a short way to the shelter of a fennel bank. Then, with the crackle of fire masking my sharp cries of pain and pleasure, and the cool grass beneath my back, the doings of a man and a woman were made known to me.

We slept entwined, part-hidden under the fennel. I awakened with the starlings' cry. In the rosy light I watched Ruther's face: his smooth, broad cheeks and lips half smiling, even in sleep. The thick muscles of his chest and shoulders were slack. There was so much force in him, yet last night he had been gentle.

His eyes flickered open and he seemed to take a moment to remember where he was. 'Tidings,' he croaked.

'And to you.'

'Forgive me,' he said, 'You will not be called Doorstep and I do not remember your true name.'

I could not help but laugh. 'What if I were a nobleman's daughter?'

'But you are not.' He stared at me through bleary eyes. 'You're of the groves, aren't you?'

'No,' I said, frowning at his forgetfulness. 'I am of the Tribequeen's kitchen.'

'A kitchen girl! I *have* chosen highly.'

I lowered my eyes and rubbed off the ash smeared on my legs.

He sat up and pulled the leather tie from his hair, scratching it loose. 'I'd have picked you for an initiate, though. There's a presence about you—' He reached for me, snuffling my neck like a boar. 'You are beguiling.'

I smiled. 'The fires beguiled you.'

'No,' he said, pulling me close, 'it's you.' His kiss tasted bitter and stale, but he was so assured in his want of me, and so splendid behind the creases of sleep, that I had to return it.

'What have you done?' He held my face between his warm hands. 'You're fine-faced—true—but so are many women...' He frowned and drew back his head. 'Have you charmed me this night?'

'No,' I said. 'Why would I have wish or knowledge to charm you?'

He stared hard at me. 'Then, by the Mothers, I am caught,' he declared. 'By a kitchen girl. And without skin!' He laughed in disbelief.

'You're not caught,' I said, annoyed. 'We are fire lovers, nothing more. Have no fear.'

He offered me his water pouch before taking a long draft himself. Around us people were rising and wandering back to the township. Ruther stood and took a long piss against a tree.

'Mule!' I laughed.

When he sat back down he stared at me again. Neither smoke nor little sleep had dimmed the blue of his eyes. 'Woman, I speak in truth.' He lowered his voice. 'I know not what magic was worked last night, but there is a force in you that has disarmed me entirely. I am here for only one more day before I ride the trade routes again. Will you join me at the feast today?'

'I will be serving—'

'Then tonight?' he pressed.

There was something of the child in his demand and it did not kindle my affection. 'If I am free.'

He reached for a last embrace and laid his head upon my chest. My thoughts spun as I looked out over the fields of Cad, Ruther cradled like a babe in my arms. He lifted his head. 'Would you remind me of your cursed name?'

I laughed. 'Seek it for yourself, if you are so persuaded!' I stood up, brushing the twigs from my skirts, and bade him farewell.

Cah spoke of feeling weakened by the doings of a man. But I felt strengthened as I walked back to Cad, as if I had a new part to myself.

—

'At last,' said Cookmother as I walked through the door. She handed me a cup of warm goat's milk. Bebin and Ianna had also returned.

We awaited only Cah before we would go to the river to scrub the ash from our faces and smoke from our hair.

Over porridge and milk we shared our night's stories. Ianna squealed when I told them of Ruther, but Bebin and Cookmother were silent.

'Cah had Fec,' said Bebin.

'Fec?' said Ianna. 'But she said—'

'Hush,' chided Bebin, as the doorskins were pushed open.

Cah walked in without greeting, dark shadows ringing her eyes.

'Come, Cah.' Ianna leaped to her feet. 'We've been waiting. We have to bathe before—'

'Stop clucking,' groaned Cah, but she gathered her soaps and brushes without further complaint.

'Ailia,' Cookmother called as we were walking out the door.

I turned around, though I knew what she would say.

'Be careful, Lamb. Not too far in.'

All along its length, tribespeople were ducking and splashing in the River Cam, taking their year's first bath in its sacred water. Our springs and rivers were the openings to the Mothers' realm. Water was their gift.

We walked upstream where the waters broadened to a deep bathing pool, at least fifteen paces wide and well hidden by trees. Cah disrobed first. I admired the compact strength of her. Her long hair was black as charcoal, but her skin was pale and her eyes were blue. She was handsome when she did not scowl. Ianna was not blessed with beauty. Her hair was the colour of carrots and her face often matched it. Her fleshy belly and thick legs laid bare her weakness for Cookmother's milk pudding and any other sweets besides, but she was as smile-ready as she was slow-witted. Bebin was the queen of us. I could only shake my head at the creation of her.

44

I pulled off my sandals, dress and under-robe, then sat down on the bank, letting my feet trail in the shallows. The cool morning pimpled my skin. As I looked at my thin legs, dotted with bruises, slightly bowed, and my narrow feet with their widespread toes, I wondered what meetings and marriages had crafted this body? What story flowed in its blood? Were these my mother's legs? My father's feet? Was there a sister somewhere with toes like mine?

Ianna shrieked at the water's edge and clutched her arms around her. 'Ooh, the wind is cold enough. How will we manage the water?'

'Just start with your toe,' said Cah. 'Stand on the large rock there and tell us how cool it is—sometimes the brook is warmer than the air.'

'It will freeze our blood, I tell you.' She leaned over the jutting edge of a large river stone. As sure as I knew she would do it, Cah was behind her and, with a solid shove, Ianna was toppled, arms flailing, into the water.

'You're a wretch!' she cried when she surfaced. 'Mothers! I'm chilled to the innards.'

Cah was rolling with laughter and I could not help smiling at the sight of it, but I did not like her way of humour.

I stood up and walked to the rock. 'Don't try it with me, Cah,' I said as I leaned over to help Ianna.

She was still chuckling, but she left me alone.

The river ran with snowmelt and we could not stay long submerged. We sat on the bank, scrubbing each other's backs with handfuls of salt and tallow soap, then plunged back in to rinse the lather, laughing at the spidery whiteness of each other's limbs in the dark of the water. We stayed talking, daring each other to hop back in, over and over. The girls skimmed across the width of the river while I remained only where I could stand. Swimming was taught to all children of the river tribes, and was yet another skill I was unworthy to learn.

'It must be time to go.' Bebin heaved herself onto the bank and the other two scrambled after her.

Although I was the weakest swimmer, I was always the last to leave the water. I was waist-deep in the soft current when something flickered across my thigh. 'A fish!' I called in delight. It glided back past my belly, as long as a hare and bright as the moon. Rarely had I seen salmon in this part of the river. 'Sisters, see this fish!'

They peered over the edge, but the salmon dived into the darkness. As soon as they turned away it appeared again, breaking the surface an arm's length from me, its skin glinting in the sun.

'Look!' I cried.

But again it plunged from view when the girls craned to see it, and they returned to their drying and dressing.

I stared into the muddied water and shivered as a ripple touched my back. Then the fish was in front of me, nibbling fragments of reed caught on my thigh. I wanted to laugh with the tickle of it, but I stayed silent so it would not be frightened away.

Ianna and Cah began to walk back.

'Bebin,' I said softly as she squeezed water from her hair. 'Look at this pretty creature.'

She peered down. 'I see nothing at all.'

'Don't you see it eating, right here beneath the surface?'

'You're still fire-maddened from the rites,' she said, smiling. She wriggled her robe over her arms and picked up her basket. 'Hurry and catch me up, or Cookmother will be in a temper.'

I stared at the fish and reached to touch it. It darted away, but not before I felt the quiver of its muscle, the slick of its skin. 'You are real,' I whispered.

Bebin was right. It was time to return. But I could not tear myself away from this intriguing animal. I plunged under the water to clear my senses. When I broke the surface, the fish was gone.

Freedom

We are born neither good nor evil.
It is our choice that determines which of these we become.
To make this choice we need absolute freedom.
How else may we be judged unless we are free?

I CARRIED THE last platter of loaves into the Great House, weaving between guests to join Cookmother at the hearth. Rich smells of long-cooked meat mingled with those of herbsmoke, blossom and crowded bodies. The fire roared at the room's centre, a whole sow blistering above it. The roasted doe had been broken onto steaming platters by the hearth.

At least a hundred tribespeople were seated on benches in three rings around the fire. Nearest to the fire, on the most finely carved bench, and facing the eastern doorway, sat Fraid. She wore woven wool in the deepest hue of red and her arms were weighted with bracelets of silver and gold that she would hand to the poets as they pleased her. Fibor sat on her left, then Etaina and Manacca, Fraid's daughter.

Before them stood a visiting poet, robed in woad-blue, plucking a harp. The instrument was of an ancient style, strung with human hair and with as many strings as were ribs in a human body.

To Fraid's right sat Llwyd and, beside him, two lesser journeymen of Cad. The other high warriors and their families completed this circle. Among them, facing the Tribequeen, was Ruther. I was suddenly shy as I stood beside Cookmother, and did not return his gaze.

In the second ring were the craftsmen and low warriors, and behind them, the land-owning farmers of Summer.

When all were settled, Llwyd stood and dedicated the meat. As first warrior, Fibor took an iron knife from his belt and speared a thick chunk of doe's shoulder, which he passed to Fraid with a bow. The feast had begun.

Cookmother toiled at the fire, ladling stew into bowls. My task was to fill the tribesmen's outstretched beer horns and I could hardly keep pace with their shouts for more.

When I reached Ruther, he grabbed my free hand and pulled me into his lap. 'Greetings, *Ailia*.'

'I am needed for serving,' I protested, laughing.

'There are others to serve.' He leaned forward to slice a morsel of pork and fed it straight from his knife tip into my mouth.

Juice trickled down my chin as I chewed, and he licked it away.

The room roared with voices. Feasts were the tribe's time to firm friendships, soothe old arguments, bring gifts to Fraid, and, of course, hear news.

'All quiet!' commanded Fraid, raising her arm. 'You will know by now that Belinus, High King of the Catuvellauni has passed to Caer Sidi, the home of the dead. Let us hear from the visiting songman. He came only this day from our neighbour to the east. Tell us, poet, how it stands in the eastern tribes since the death. Are they resolved to settle under Caradog?'

The young poet bowed and lifted his harp. Our songmen spent ceaseless summers learning by heart the poems of our country, but their most admired skill was that of forging verse in the moment it was spoken.

He sang:

> *When the Great Bear dies*
> *Barely are his pyre and carcass ready*
> *When he's swarmed by many well-kinned flies*
> *Though none who'd rule as steady,*
> *None who'd walk the narrow bridge*
> *That spans the Empire and our home,*
> *None who reap the privilege*
> *Of holding hands with Rome.*
> *Caradog has risen,*
> *He rules with Mothers' might,*
> *When Rome chimes at his hut bell,*
> *Will he run? Succumb? No. Fight.*

The guests bellowed their applause.

Fibor had emptied more beer horns than most. 'I am glad to see the Great Bear down,' he proclaimed. 'Perhaps now the Catuvellauni will have a king who will stand firm against Rome.'

I felt Ruther's back stiffen. 'Belinus held the ear of the Emperor himself,' he said. 'We all reap the spoils from the tradelines he opened.'

I glanced at him, amazed he would challenge our first warrior.

Fibor set down his cup. He was well known for his hatred of Rome and less so for the delicacy of his tongue. 'Belinus wiped Rome's arse for the privilege of its pretty things. His son knows the honour of freedom.'

'On matters of trade,' Fraid interjected calmly, 'the Great Bear's achievements are undisputed. But he is gone. Let us speak of the future.' She turned to the poet. 'Are the other petty kings and queens concerned that this death will prompt an arrival on our eastern shores?'

'It is so feared,' said the poet. 'Caradog is beginning to strengthen his support among the tribes.'

'Take them by force, you mean?' Fibor chuckled. 'I wish him courage. The Emperor will think twice before launching an attack on a warrior such as Caradog.'

'Caradog *insults* the Emperor Claudius,' said the one who held me. 'He goads him by claiming we Britons are the uncapturable people.' Ruther looked around the circle. 'Think for yourselves, tribesmen, what this will provoke in Rome.'

I moved to stand but Ruther tightened his grasp around my waist.

'Son of Orgilos, it seems you have become quite a friend to Rome since your travels there,' said Fibor.

Ruther stared back at him. 'Is it not wise to understand the mind of those who would be our captors and our rulers?'

'Understand this,' said Fibor. 'We are the free people. The Romans have captured the world, yet we remain uncaptured.'

Murmurs of agreement rumbled through the gathering.

'I have heard that they see Albion as a place of dark magic! An otherworld!' said Etaina. 'They are too frightened to come. This is why we remain uncaptured.'

'Hah!' sneered Ruther. 'We are uncaptured because Belinus met Rome's hunger for our landwealth. Why would they attack when they already held purchase on all they desired?'

The circle fell silent. I was stunned by the recklessness with which Ruther spoke. Surely Fraid would not permit him such liberty? With his thick forearm gripping my waist, I felt as though I were caught on a wild horse.

'You return to us greatly informed of the opinions of Rome, Ruther,' said Fraid. 'We are privileged to have such knowledge in our midst.'

Fibor grunted but I felt Ruther soften.

'When do you leave for the Empire lands, Ruther?' asks Llwyd. Until now he had said nothing but I watched how closely he listened.

'Tomorrow if the weather holds, and if you will bless it, Journeyman.' Ruther dipped his head to Llwyd and I breathed out with relief that at least he showed respect to our wiseman.

'And what do you carry by way of trade goods?' Llwyd continued.

'Metals.' He took a large bite from his flesh hook, chewing as he spoke. 'And dogs. Our skins are in favour.'

Llwyd nodded. 'Long-traded goods,' he said. 'What do you make of the new trade taking hold at the eastern ports? I hear it is very lucrative and that the Romans exploit it in ever greater quantities.'

Ruther frowned. 'Of what trade do you speak?'

'Do you not know it?' Llwyd paused. 'I speak of the sale of our men and women to Romans as slaves.'

There was a murmur around the circle.

'A foul trade,' said Fibor. 'Roman slaves are whipped like dogs and owned until death. What snake would sell his own tribesman to such a life?'

Ruther snorted. 'Do not our own noblemen—our tribekings and queens—also have servants?'

'Yes,' said Fraid. 'But their labour is owned, not their souls.'

It was true. As a servant to the Tribequeen, I was constrained by the laws of skin but not by my servitude. I finally wriggled free of Ruther's hold and stood, taking up my jug.

'Wherever the Roman slaves may come from,' said Ruther, holding up his horn, 'they are put to good use in the building of fine cities.'

The circle was silent. His light words were poorly judged.

I made my way around the circles, filling horns that had run dry.

'They please you then, these cities of the Empire lands?' asked Llwyd quietly.

'Why, none could be displeased—'

Fibor protested, but Llwyd raised his hand. 'Tell us of them.'

Ruther straightened, pausing to cast his gaze around the room.

I filled Llwyd's cup, then stopped behind him to listen.

'Imagine a city that covers the earth from one horizon to the other—' Ruther's eyes blazed—'where there are columns of stone that would dwarf an elm. Where buildings are not small or round or made of stick and mud, but are square and high and built of cut stone, each with not one, but many rooms. Where underground pipes bring rivers of clear water into every home through bronze fountains that can be levered to run at will. And there are yet other pipes that carry away their shit. Imagine, never having to empty a pot!'

Timid laughter rolled through the audience.

'They adorn their floors with pictures made of a thousand tiny tiles. Their stadiums make ant mounds of our hill towns,' he continued. 'And every corner of the known world can be visited in one stroll of a market square. This is the glory of Rome.'

'Yet who serves this glory?' demanded Fibor. 'Who lays these pipes?'

'Slaves!' challenged Ruther.

'Such a city cannot endure,' said Fibor. 'It is immorally built, and in time it will crumble.'

'And yet it does not,' said Ruther. 'All are enlightened by the brightness of this city. Even the slaves bask in its warmth.'

'And what of the groves and springs for ritual?' asked Llwyd. 'Where are they found in these cities?'

'There are shrines in every street. They do not need forests or springs to worship.'

Standing close, only I heard Llwyd's intake of breath. 'And they are not weakened in denying the springs?' he asked.

There was a trap in these questions and I wondered for what purpose.

'Weakened?' Ruther laughed. 'Journeyman, I am a tribesman first, and I love my own people above all others, but make no mistake, these are among the strongest people under the sun's light.'

There were gasps among the warriors.

'I question the loyalty of this man!' Fibor stood and Ruther immediately followed, putting his palm to his sword handle. Where there were disputes between warriors at feast times, they were often resolved with a test of swordsmanship. But not this day, not at Beltane, a time of coming together.

'Cease, both of you!' commanded Fraid. 'By Mothers, speak more cautiously, Ruther.'

'I am sorry.' Ruther bowed lightly to her. 'It was clumsily uttered. I would no sooner see us subject to Roman rule than anyone here, but there is greatness in the new world that cannot be denied. Greatness of man. Even a fool can see it.'

Fibor's eyes flared. 'Anyone who is true to the tribes—even a fool—sees no such thing.'

'Shall we test it?' said Ruther. 'Give me a fool.'

Fibor's eyes narrowed until his gaze fell on me. 'Ask the beer maiden. She is untaught, unskinned, little more than a fool, albeit a pretty one. How does *she* judge the greatness of man?'

'Yes, ask her.' Ruther smiled broadly.

'Step forward, girl,' commanded Fibor.

'Stop!' said Fraid. 'Ailia, do not answer. The skinless will not speak at festival time. Fibor, cease this game.'

'Wait.' Llwyd held up his hand. 'I wish to hear her answer. Ailia,' he said, turning to me, 'what is your response? How is greatness to be judged?'

All eyes were upon me and suddenly my breath was short. What would I say? I stepped forward, heart pounding. 'I—I have seen nothing of the greatness of which Ruther speaks,' I began. 'But I do know that all wisdom is born in the springs…' With these words, a strange calm descended over me and my voice steadied. 'If a man obscures our sight of these by a thousand tiny tiles, then surely he is the fool.'

'And this from a kitchen girl!' Fibor roared with laughter and the other guests joined in.

Ruther looked away.

Llwyd's gaze was fixed upon me.

The feast rolled into the night. Ruther barely allowed me to leave him, pulling me back to his lap when I tried to get up, slipping his warm hand into the sleeve of my leine to stroke the fall of my breast. When the sow's carcass had been picked clean and the men had fallen to slumber from drunkenness, he led me to the stables to couple again.

Afterwards, he lay panting, his head on my chest. 'Last night was by no means my first time in the fields,' he said when his breath had steadied, 'but I have never known such nearness to the Mothers as by you this Beltane.'

I smiled, confused by his praise. 'Still it does not bother you that I am without skin?'

'No.' He propped on one elbow and stared at my face. 'You know so little of the world. In Durotriga you all live as you have lived for thousands of summers. But the eastern tribes are leaving the hills and are settling in river towns—large towns that are already shaped by the Empire. People of all skins fill these cities. The ties of skin are loosening there. Does that not interest you, Doorstep?'

'By the will of the Mothers, I am blessed with a name. Will you use it?'

He laughed and rolled back, pulling me onto his chest.

What he described did interest me. How could it not? But it frightened me also. The laws of skin had denied me much but I knew in the heart of my bones that they were true. It unsettled me that Ruther did not see it so.

He yawned. 'You should come with me to the Empire lands, Ailia. Journey with me and see for yourself what I have spoken of.'

I chuckled. 'How could I come?'

He wriggled up to sitting, roused by the idea. 'You will come as my servant.'

I sat up, our spell broken, and began to dress. 'It is too soon for me to leave Cookmother. She needs me for her work.'

'The herbs? Any girl can help her with that—you are meant for something greater.'

I flinched. 'You'll not say that when my poultice saves your limb should you come to me with battle wounds.' I strapped my sandals.

'Where are you going?'

'To my bed.'

'Will you not return with me to my house?'

'As your servant?'

He frowned. 'Forgive me, is that not what you are? Have I done wrong to call you so?'

I sighed and softened. 'No, you haven't. But I would rest in my own bed this night.'

He drew a deep breath of my scent. 'You've pierced me, Doorstep. When I was not battle-ready.'

I kissed his mouth then slipped out onto the moonlit courtyard. As I walked to the kitchen, my eyes stung from sleeplessness and my body hummed with a sweet, dull ache. But I was glad to have run the threshold of Beltane, glad to discover what lay beyond.

Water

All wisdom lives in our rivers.
The brink of water is where knowledge is revealed.

THE MORNING'S FIRST light showed Bebin's bed was empty.

As I wandered out to collect fresh water, I met her stealing through the Tribequeen's gate, still in her feasting dress. I led her to the back of the kitchen, where we could stand in the warmth of the rising sun and talk without being heard.

'Where have you been?' I whispered.

'With Uaine,' she murmured, heavy-lidded.

'He is pleased to return then?' I smiled.

'Ay.' She turned to me, her brown eyes brightening. 'I think he will sing me his song.'

I nodded. Wordless. I was not prepared for how deep it cut.

The skinsong. The betrothal. An invitation to join with another as kin. It was how we knew if the Mothers blessed the union. When the skinsong was sung, the one who listened could remain silent, declining the bond. Or they could sing their skinsong in return. It was in the blending of songs that the singers knew if they were favoured to marry. If the harmonies shifted the soul, the bond was true.

Bebin had sung me hers, once, in friendship and, of course, I had heard Cookmother's many times. But I would never hear one from a tribesman in betrothal. Because they would know that I could not return it.

I kissed Bebin's cheek and wished her happiness.

—

Ruther and Uaine returned mid-morning to prepare for their departure. They would take some of Fraid's best horses and many of her dogs and hides.

I found cause to pass Ruther many times in the stables and storehouses until eventually he pulled me into one of the grain huts, pulling the door closed behind us. 'How can a man prepare for travel,' he said, kissing my throat, 'with such a bird flying past?' He loosened his belt. 'Must I show you once more, my feeling for you?'

I took a strange pleasure in luring him from his task, testing this new power I held. My back was pressed hard against the storehouse wall when the door swung open and Bebin stepped in. She stopped when she saw us, then turned and left.

I found her in the Great House, straightening the skins that covered the benches.

'May I speak, Ailia?' she said, as I joined her.

'Of course.'

'Think on your intention with Ruther. The union of man and woman is a life-giving act. It summons magic in one way or another—use it cleverly.'

I fondled the tattered edge of a boar skin, shamed by her wisdom.
'But Ailia—'

I looked up.

'Do not think I am displeased that you are favoured so.' She smiled her quiet smile.

I glanced at her sideways. 'You are still not impressed by him?'

'No, no, he is a fine man indeed,' she protested. 'I hear he even employs a history-keeper to travel with him and sing praise-songs as he walks into new townships, like a king into battle.'

We both spluttered with laughter at the arrogance of it.

Smoothing my fingers over the animal skins, I marvelled, as always, at the variation between them: the soft, patchy pelts of the cattle, the spiked shiny bristles of the boar, and the deep lustrous fur of the reindeer, in which I buried my whole hand. Each held its own beauty and worth.

The sun had just begun its descent when a small group gathered at the southern gateway to farewell Ruther and Uaine.

Ruther's last kiss was sweet but I was relieved as I watched him ride away. I could return to the kitchen's steady rhythm and settle my thoughts.

Cookmother busied all of us with harvesting early berries from the Tribequeen's gardens, but when I could not even sort the green from the rosy without error, she took pity on me and went to fetch a delivery of medicine. 'You are useless to me here, sex-drunk and giddy,' she said, handing me a muslin-wrapped bundle and a small bottle of honey. 'Take these to Dun's farm. Tell the woman there to heat the powders and honey with sheep's milk, drink it, and rub a little on the chest. Throw what remains on the ground to the south of the

58

house. Tell her there's enough within for four days.'

I committed these instructions to memory and called Neha to my heel.

'Keep clear of the Oldforest,' said Cookmother as I packed the bundle into a basket and checked for my knife.

'Yes, Cookmother,' I droned in response to the warning I had heard a thousand times.

To the east of Caer Cad lay a forest that was forbidden by lawsong to all but the journeypeople and their highest initiates to enter. To get to Dun's farm I had to walk the river path until it met the Oldforest, then along the track that skirted its western edge.

Late sun warmed my shoulders as I walked upstream past the last of the farmhouses. Neha bounded beside me, barking at the insects that hummed near the water. The river spirits were restless and the very earth seemed to prickle with life.

The grazing pastures gave way to wild grasslands clumped with meadow flowers, and soon we drew close to the dark edge of the Oldforest. Before the pathway left the river, I crouched down to fill my waterskin.

The Cam flowed right through the heart of the Oldforest. It was said that the water journeyed to the Mothers and back again before it emerged, sweet and cold and full of secrets from its passage.

I looked out over the river as I drank. It was wide here and sharply banked. A thin mist trailed over its surface. Strange, when I left Cad the day had been clear, but now the water was dark under low cloud. I stood, knotting my waterskin back onto my belt, when I heard a long moan.

Neha growled and I heard it again. It came from upstream, near the forest's mouth. Neha darted toward it. I followed her and peered over the bank where she had stopped.

There, crouched in the shallows, not five paces away, and hunched in pain, was a man. He was unclothed to the waist, his dark hair spilling over his bare shoulders, and he was rocking as he moaned.

'Are you...in need?' I called.

He looked up in surprise.

'By the Mothers,' I whispered when I saw his face.

A large iron fishhook was pierced through his lower lip. He stared at me from dark brown eyes, trembling.

'What a wicked wound!' I dropped my basket and splashed into the water. 'Let me help you.'

But he startled, like an injured animal, jerking his face from my touch.

'Hush,' I said, crouching before him. 'I cannot help you if you don't let me look.'

Slowly he turned toward me. He was barely beyond learning age—perhaps three or four summers my elder—but his beard was thick and he was finer than a king, with searching eyes, hollow cheeks and the ripe, brooding lips of a displeased god.

Neha had followed me in. She whimpered, licking the brown skin of his shoulder. Only now did I notice that she had not barked.

My soaked skirts billowed around me. 'Are you a fisherman?' I asked, bewildered. 'Where is your shirt?'

He went to speak but flinched with pain.

'Let me try to free it,' I coaxed. 'I am trained in wound work.'

He paused then shifted toward me.

I eased open his lip and inspected the hook. 'You'll have to come back with me to the township,' I told him. 'It will take a smith's tool to cut it cleanly.'

His eyes flared and he shook his head.

'You will not come?'

He shook again.

I stared at him, wondering at his stubbornness. 'This wound will catch heat if you do not clear the implement,' I explained. 'If you won't come, then I shall have to cut it now.'

He searched my face, making some kind of reckoning of me, then nodded.

'Be steady,' I warned, loosing my knife from my belt. 'There is a ring at one end of the hook and a barb at the other. I will enlarge the piercing and slide it out. Can you hold?'

His eyes widened but he nodded again.

'I have some knowledge of surgery. It will be quick.' I gripped the knife close to the blade. 'Ready now,' I said. 'Hold here about my ankles and squeeze if the pain is too strong. I've helped a few women in birth, so I can take some squeezing.'

A trace of a smile flickered in his face as he braced himself against my legs.

I stretched his cheek flesh taut with one hand and positioned my knife with the other. 'There!'

He gasped as I sliced deftly. Deeply. Through the crimson surge I opened the cut and tugged hard on the hook, taking care that it did not re-lodge in his flesh as it passed. Proudly, I held it up for him to see.

'Mother of earth,' he gasped, blood streaming down his chin, 'you have the touch of a slaughterwoman!'

I stared at him, disbelieving. Where were his thanks? 'Come out of the water,' I called as I climbed onto the bank. 'I need to treat the piercing.'

He did not move. I watched him from the shore. A trickle of blood ran down his chest and stomach. He was lean, but his muscles were long and well worked, the body of a messenger.

'As you wish,' I said.

He waited in silence as I plucked stalks of nettle from the river's edge and squeezed their juice into my palm, mixing it with honey from Dun's bundle. I stepped back into the shallows. 'This will stem the blood,' I said, dabbing it on his swelling lip.

There was vividness around his skin, like spray from a waterfall. Our faces were close. He lifted his eyes. His gaze was a blow to my belly.

'What is your business here?' I whispered.

'As yours. Taking drink.' He winced with the movement of his lip.

'But the hook? The wound?'

'Unfortunate,' he answered.

'But where are you from?' I pressed. He was certainly a stranger to Cad.

'Surely that is my question to ask, Journeywoman.'

'Journeywoman?' I gasped, laughing at his error. 'Not I! Much as I would wish it were so.'

He frowned. 'Then where...?' His question drifted into silence.

As he stood in the knee-deep water, I saw the full height of him. His trousers were rough-made (he was no nobleman) and of a strangely patterned weave. A whistle, carved of bone, was strung on a plait of leather and wound around his narrow hips.

'Might I know your name at least?' I asked, standing beside him.

'Taliesin.'

A bard's name. Or a magician's. But he was too young to be either. Why did he not state his tribe or township?

'Yours?' he asked.

'Ailia of Cad.'

'Ailia,' he repeated. 'Light.'

'Yes,' I said, surprised. Few knew the meaning of my name.

'What is your skin?' he said.

Never had the question laid me so bare. 'I...I am skin to the deer.' It was a lie I had never told. Why could I not bear him to know me unskinned?

'I am skin to the salmon,' he said.

62

Cookmother's skin. I looked away. Something in me had shifted with my lie. 'If you walk with me a short while back to town,' I said, distracting myself, 'I can show this wound to my Cookmother. She will know how further to treat it.'

'I cannot come.'

His firmness stopped me asking his reason. 'Then perhaps we should meet again a day or so hence, that I might check it again,' I said, relieved, at least, that he would not discover my untruth.

He nodded hesitantly. 'Come here again tomorrow and I shall show you my wound.'

'Here?' I said. 'Surely your home—?'

'Is too far,' he said.

I stared at him, then reached for his hand. 'Let me help you out of the water.'

'No!' he said, almost shouting.

Startled, I dropped his hand.

Neha barked. I was suddenly unsure of myself, uneasy with his strangeness. 'Be very careful with your eating and drinking,' I said as I wiped my knife on my skirt and put it back in my belt. 'So you do not tax the wound unduly.'

'Good advice.' He found my eye. 'I won't kiss you for thanks. It might tax the wound unduly.'

My face burned as I stepped back onto the bank to repack my basket. I glanced about for his tunic and sandals, but saw neither. 'In which direction do you walk?' I asked over my shoulder.

He did not answer.

When I turned around, there was only Neha, barking at the river. I looked to the forest and called his name, but he was gone. Disappeared like the mist from the sunshine.

The Salmon of Knowledge

Around the pool of wisdom grew nine hazel trees. Each tree
dropped a nut into the water, and they were eaten by a salmon.
By this act, the salmon gained all the world's knowledge.
Whoever first eats of the salmon's flesh will, in turn,
gain all the world's knowledge.

I HAD SCARCELY walked through the kitchen doorway, when Cookmother thrust two steaming bowls of broth into my hands and bade me take them to the sleephouse.

'Llwyd is with her,' she said. 'And he was here earlier also, asking of you.'

'Of me?'

'Ay.' Cookmother was bent over the cookpot, and I could not see her expression.

'For what purpose?'

'None that he was confessing to me.'

Fraid's daughter was playing outside by the fire pit with a straggle of other children. 'Tidings, Manacca,' I called as I hurried past. 'Do you want some broth?'

'I'm not allowed in,' she cried, turning back to her skittling stones.

There was a scent of disagreement in the room as I shouldered through the inner doorskins of the sleephouse. Fibor and Etaina were not within. Again Fraid sat with Llwyd alone.

'Does he forget the reputation of Britain's knowledge?' said Llwyd. 'We are known the world over for our teaching.'

I passed him a bowl and he took it gratefully.

'Initiates travel from Germania to be taught here, from Gaul,' he continued. 'Albion is at the very centre of learning, Tribequeen.' He sipped his broth.

'But he has seen the new world,' said Fraid. 'He sees freedom in it.'

They were speaking of Ruther. I handed Fraid her soup and slipped to the edge of the room.

'He mistakes wealth for freedom,' said Llwyd, 'and might for wisdom.'

They drank in silence for a few minutes. 'You may leave,' said Fraid, turning to me.

'Shall I not wait for your bowls?' I uttered before I could stop.

'No, Ailia.' She frowned in surprise. 'I asked you to leave.'

I waited as the heavy skins of the inner doorway flapped closed behind me. Fibor or Etaina could return at any moment, but I was hungry to know what was being said inside. I leaned toward the doorskins and could just hear their muffled voices.

'Why do you remove her?' Llwyd asked. 'I thought she held your trust?'

'She lay with him at the fires. I do not want our words recounted at his pillow.'

I heard Llwyd chuckle. 'She certainly commands an allure beyond that of a kitchen girl.'

They both laughed, then quieted.

'Ruther's words have unsettled the journeypeople,' said Llwyd.

'With Belinus's death, we do not need one of our own warriors crying the greatness of Rome.'

'I will summon the council tomorrow to discuss what we shall do.'

Footsteps approached the sleephouse. Manacca squealed outside.

My heart thudding, I continued to listen as the footsteps passed.

'I have looked to the stars and to the birds,' said Llwyd. 'We stand at the dawn of a change. And Ruther's words at the feast have given it shape.'

'Surely his knowledge of Rome can only strengthen us...?'

There was a pause before Llwyd answered. 'What strengthens us is the Mothers. We have to hold them close. We have to protect our bond to them.'

'But is it not already strong? The journeymen are powerful, as you have said—'

'There is one weakness,' said Llwyd.

Fraid sighed and I heard the exasperation in it. 'We have agreed to raise this no further, Journeyman. It is no riddle I can solve. Why speak of it now?'

'Because the Great Bear is dead. And a vulture is circling his carcass. When it lands, make no mistake, we will need the strength of the Kendra. We will need the presence of one who has sung.'

'The bloodline is fallen.' Fraid's voice had a strange edge. 'We cannot conjure her from chalk or iron. With or without a Kendra, we must plan our defence against Rome.'

I stood frozen in the dark corridor between doors, straining to make sense of their words. Who was this woman? This Kendra? Why could she not be discussed?

'No army of the tribes will triumph without her blessing,' said Llwyd. 'She is the voice of the Mothers.'

'Then why has she not spoken?' said Fraid.

'She will speak,' said Llwyd. 'We must make sure we are listening.'

66

'Ailia!' Llwyd's voice rang through the early dusk.

I had fled the sleephouse as I heard him prepare to leave, and now he sighted me hurrying toward the kitchen. I stopped and waited while he caught up.

Despite the stoop of his back, he moved with a journeyman's grace. 'May I walk with you?' he said as he reached my side. If he was suspicious of me he did not show it. His eyes caught the day's dying light. 'I was impressed by your words at the feast yesterday,' he said as we walked.

'I suspect the knave Ruther was less so.'

Llwyd chuckled. 'Though it appears it did not quell his interest.'

Now it was I who laughed. 'No, it did not.'

'Were you always of the kitchen? Raised by the Cookwoman there?'

'Since near birth.'

'And you have learned the plants by her?'

I glanced at him, unsure what to confess. 'I assist her when her bones stiffen, deliveries and the like.'

'Nothing more?'

I faltered. Llwyd was the keeper of all Caer Cad's learning. It was only by his sanction that healers could practise their arts.

'Tell me,' he continued, ignoring my silence, 'has an animal appeared to you since Beltane? An animal of unusual countenance or strangeness?'

We had reached the kitchen. The doorskins were pinned open. I saw the firelight glowing through the doorway and caught a waft of Cookmother's sour milk dumplings on the evening breeze. Suddenly I was very keen to be inside. I thought hard on his question. 'None strange,' I said.

He kissed my cheeks. 'Go well, maiden, enjoy your sweetmeats.'

It was only later, as I lay between Cookmother snoring at my back, the buck curled in my arms, and Neha grunting at my feet, that I remembered the fish I had seen as I bathed in the river.

I rushed through the next morning's tasks, then set about grinding a tincture, making sure I was noticed by Cookmother as I pounded the white meadowsweet petals to a paste.

'What do you make?' she duly asked.

I could not tell her that I was to meet Taliesin, a stranger of tribe unknown, who waited within a breath of the forbidden forest. She would never have permitted it. So I did, for the second time, what I had never done before: I played fool with the truth. 'Dun requested something further to dull the pain,' I announced. 'I promised I would bring it this afternoon.' I stared down at the quern, my cheeks burning with the lies, and with the shame of not yet delivering even the first batch of herbs.

'Good then.' She poked a wooden spoon into the mixture. 'Throw in a little nightshade if he's making such a fuss.'

With my face and neck splashed with rosewater, my braids tied, and Cookmother's fish pin at my breast, I hurried out the south gate and down to the Cam. I soon reached the Oldforest, where only Neha saw me again stop by the river, instead of turning north toward Dun's farm.

He was not there.

'Taliesin?' I called, answered only by a mocking silence. I sat on the bank with the afternoon yawning around me, feeling stupid for thinking he would come. Finally I picked up my basket, whistled Neha to my heel, and began to walk away.

'Ailia!'

He stood dripping on the bank, sunlight splintering off his wet shoulders.

I walked back and stood before him. He was even finer today with his hair in damp tendrils around his face, water beading on the ridges of his cheeks. Again he wore nothing but a pair of rough trousers, roped at the waist, and the carved bone whistle at his hip. 'Would you not have waited?' he asked.

'I have waited long enough,' I said.

'Be gone then, if you wish to stay no longer.'

I snorted. 'I will check your wound at least.'

'At least.' He presented his lip.

'What is this?' I traced my fingers over his mouth. There was nothing left of yesterday's cut. Just a thin silver scar. 'It's perfectly healed,' I said in awe. 'How can it be?'

'You tended it. Did you not think your own herbcraft was potent?'

'Well, yes, but—' I faltered, hoping his swift healing would not bring our meeting to an end.

He flopped onto the grass.

'How did...why were you in the water?' I asked, sitting beside him.

'I had to cross the river.' He stroked Neha's ear; she in turn licked the water from his hand. 'Sweet-tempered dog.'

I laughed. 'Not normally.'

'She senses a truly noble spirit,' he teased. It was the first time I had seen him smile.

A silence fell between us. He picked up a pebble and cast it into the river. The *plop* echoed in the quietness. 'What payment is required for your treatment?'

'I expect no payment.'

'Why not? Is it of no value?'

'Yes, but...' Again, I was tripped by his question.

69

'I accept no service without payment.' He sprang to his feet, strode to the forest and slipped out of sight between the trees. Who was he that his lawsong permitted him to walk in the Oldforest? Moments passed and I feared he might have gone again. But then I heard rustling and he reappeared with a long stick of birch.

'This one is perfect!' He squatted on one knee, drawing a small blade from his belt, and tapered the stick to a point. When he was satisfied it was sharp, he walked to the edge of the water and stepped into the shallows.

He stood motionless, his spear poised. He was delicate, far less of a warrior than Ruther, but there was something older, darker, in his spirit that gave him another strength.

He drew back his arm. 'Hah!' he shouted as the spear shot forward. He splashed, stumbling, then turned to me, grinning as he raised his stick with a fat silver salmon thrashing at its tip. I laughed, delighted at his skill. Pulling the fish from the spear, he stilled it with his blade on the grass. When it had ceased twitching, he carried it to me and laid it at my feet. As he leaned forward, I caught the grain and honey scent of his hair.

'Beautiful,' I said.

He looked up. 'Shall we feast?'

Our gaze held and I could not look away. There was something so knowing and yet needful in his earth-brown eyes, and I was so unexpectedly pierced by him that, for no reason I could fathom, I found I was crying.

'Why do you weep? Would you have preferred a minnow?'

I shook my head, laughing through my tears.

It did not take him long to shape a small fire pit, fill it with branches, and fashion a firedog from three green sticks. With river reed he plaited a rope and tied the fish to the sticks by its mouth. 'Can you make a flame?' he asked.

'Not well,' I admitted. Unskinned, I was not permitted to craft fire. Only to tend it.

He frowned. 'Watch then.' He gathered a handful of tinder and bade me hold it. 'Blow gently,' he said while he sparked it with fire flint from his pouch.

It began to smoke in my palms as I blew.

'Not bad,' he said and I hoarded his compliment like a jewel.

As the fish began to sizzle, a blister bubbled in the skin of its flank.

Taliesin leaned forward and burst it, then held his thumb to my lips. 'You must have the first taste.'

Tentatively, I took his thumb in my mouth, sucking the shreds of fish skin and juice from its tip. We shared the dense red flesh straight from the bone, sweet and smoky, and washed it down with river water that we drank straight from the flow.

It was only when we were sitting on the bank, legs outstretched and bellies full, Neha gnawing the bones beside us, that I realised what he had eaten. 'The salmon! Are you not forbidden to eat it?'

He glanced at me. 'Has plantcraft claimed all your knowledge?'

I looked away, fighting a wave of shame.

'I can eat it beyond my skin home. To strengthen my skin.'

'Perhaps if you told me your skin home—' I stiffened, '—I'd be less ignorant of that at least.'

'Beyond your travels, I am sure.' He shifted as he sat.

'But where?' I pressed. Why had he cause to hide this?

His face clouded with irritation. 'Does my skin home determine your opinion of me?'

'Of course not.'

'Then why do you pursue knowledge of no consequence?'

I was silent, caught again by his prickly logic.

He laughed softly. 'What would you say if I told you that I do nothing but swim up the river and down again, resting a moment here

71

or there. Taking my food where I can find it. Harming no one.'

'I would say that you mock me. And if not that, then you do not earn your place in your tribe. Though there is something sweet in the freedom of it.'

He nodded. 'Well answered.'

And I felt ripe with pride that I had pleased him.

He fondled the bone whistle around his hips, carved with symbols I did not understand. I fought the urge to ask of them, and then it dawned upon me that I was with someone who believed I had skin, someone who did not know that I was forbidden to learn. 'Tell me what the patterns mean.'

'These?' he said, lifting the whistle.

I nodded.

'Close your eyes.' He picked up my hand and rubbed my fingers over the nubs of bone. 'These are the marks of my ancestors.'

My eyes opened. 'What does it feel like,' I asked quietly. 'Your skin?' My heart was thumping.

He frowned. 'As yours—'

'But I mean yours,' I said quickly. 'Tell me how it feels to possess the salmon's skin.'

The afternoon was very still. No breeze or bird cry broke the silence that had fallen around us. When he answered, I knew from the music in his voice that he spoke from his core. 'The salmon is my story.' He gave a light, desolate laugh. 'It is the mirror of what little is perfect in me.'

I yearned to assure him there was much that was perfect in him. But I was beginning to see the bruises beneath the pride he held like a shield before him. 'Tell me more,' I whispered.

'What should I say?' He shrugged. 'We all understand our totem.'

'Is it not something different for each of us?'

His eyebrows lifted. 'Perhaps. For me it is survival. The salmon song will always exist. My body dies, but my skin never will.'

I nodded, choked with the truth of it. I was bound to nothing that would endure.

'Would you like to hear a story?' he asked.

'Yes.'

He gouged ruts in the ground with a twig as he spoke. 'In the time of the Singing there were shapes in the water. No eyes, no fins, no soul. They could not swim. They just drifted in the river. One night a Mother of fire threw a burning log into the water and the sparks ignited the shapes and turned them into red salmon that darted around.

'The Mothers of sky were angry that the Mother of fire had made something so beautiful, and said that they would cast them away to the four corners of the oceans. But before they did this, the fire Mother put a little of the soil from the riverbank into the salmons' noses, so they would never forget the smell of their birth-place. They would swim until they found the smell that matched the one they carried within them. And even if the journey killed them, they would die at home.' Taliesin looked up. 'I should not have told you this.'

'Why did you tell it?'

'Because you asked of my skin. And my stories are my skin. As are yours.' He drew his knees to his chest. 'If I fail this life, my skin stories will take me to another.'

'You will not fail this life—'

'How would you know?'

I reached out to touch his forearm wrapped around his legs. His muscles were as taut as wood, but his skin was softer than a horse's muzzle.

He smiled, before pulling his arm away.

We sat together until evening coloured the western sky. I learned nothing of his tribe or history, only of his favourite season (late summer) and companion dogs (hut-reared wolves), his love of prey birds and dislike of combat arts. But the lightness of his words could not mask the sharpness with which he watched the world and the tenderness with which he met it. He could not be of low birth; he was learned.

I stood, calling Neha to my side, terrified that I would not see him again. He was so tall that I had to tilt my head to find his eyes. 'Thank you,' I said. 'Payment has been well made. Yesterday's dab of honey for today's fish and stories.'

'A fair exchange,' he agreed. 'There is no further business that binds us.'

'No,' I said. 'None at all.'

'I shall meet you here tomorrow then?'

'Yes,' I said with too much relief. 'I will see you then.'

As I walked home through pastures and wheat fields doused in amber light, Taliesin's words swirled around me. I knew what he said was true: for those held in skin, this life—this fleshform—was just a fragment in a river that was ever-flowing. Totems did not die, nor did the souls who had joined with them.

But for those like me, death *was* the end. A casting back to the void. For most of the skinless this was too much to bear, it was why they relinquished their days to the comforts of beer at the fringe fires. A life without ritual. A life unlived.

Now, more than ever, I knew that this would not be my way. I whistled for Neha, who had bounded into a field in pursuit of a hare. I was going to search for my skin until the last breath flowed from my body.

'There you are!' Cookmother said, as I slipped into the kitchen. 'Take these to the council.' She pressed a jug of beer into each of my hands, too distracted by preparing meat for the councillors to question the lateness of my return.

I walked straight back out into the dusk. Tribal council met on the third night of the wane, or whenever Fraid required it. Most often in the Great House, but if the evening was mild, like tonight, they would gather directly under the stars that would guide them.

I wove between them, filling the horns of the twelve tribespeople who formed our council: Fraid at the strong place, Llwyd to her left. Fibor and Etaina, Ruther's father, Orgilos, and seven others.

'Your son has disturbed us, Orgilos.' Fibor's voice still carried some of Beltane's heat.

'He speaks not for me nor I for him,' said Orgilos.

Fibor drank. 'It is said that the apple does not fall wide of the tree.'

'Sometimes pigs eat the apples and shit in the fields,' Orgilos responded.

Etaina threw back her head and laughed. 'My sister's daughter is also newly returned from fosterage,' she said. 'Ruther is but one of many who begin to proclaim the light of Rome. In the eastern tribes, there are many minded as he is minded.'

'And what of their loyalty, wife?' Fibor raised his cup as I refilled it.

'Dissolving in grape wine and olive oil,' said Fraid. 'We are protected by distance. And the strong minds of the western kings.'

'We are protected by skin,' said Llwyd, and the council's silence acknowledged it.

I stood behind Fraid, outside the circle. The eastern horizon was deep-water blue with one lively star rising to its surface.

'You call us to determine if we should prepare for war, sister,' said Fibor to Fraid. 'We are fools if we do not. We know the Romans lust for these tribelands.' He looked around the circle, eyes blazing, 'They will come. If we are not prepared, then they will fuck us like a dog!'

Fraid turned away.

'Perhaps we should strengthen the earthworks around the hill,' agreed Orgilos. 'As a precaution.'

'At the very least!' cried Fibor. 'And replenish our stones and renew the chalk—'

'As you know full well, we rebuild the ramparts according to the rhythm called by the Mothers—at the seventh winter solstice,' said Llwyd.

'Will the legions wait for the Mothers' call?' said Fibor.

'The legions will fall at their call,' Llwyd answered, 'when it is spoken by the woman who carries our song.'

The council murmured.

I stiffened, aware of the discomfort rising among them. Again, this woman. Who was she, who carried such hope? I burned to find out.

'This is the true heart of our argument, council.' Llwyd looked around him. 'We have not known a Kendra for one and twenty summers. Albion hungers for her born Mother. Bleeds for her. Without our Kendra, we start to rot, and the Emperor Claudius can smell it. This is why the Roman beast begins to stir.'

'You believe one journeywoman will keep the Roman legions at bay?' said Fibor.

'She is not one journeywoman,' said Llwyd, unflinching. 'She is the Kendra of Albion.'

'She is not here,' said Etaina softly.

I recognised the yearning in Llwyd's silence.

'It is true that we hunger,' Etaina continued with care. 'But is it not the Mothers themselves who keep the Kendra from us? With deepest respect, Journeyman, perhaps they call us now to act in our own strength.'

Fibor grunted his agreement. 'They ask us to fight for ourselves.'

Llwyd stared at them. 'Have you drifted so far since she has been gone?' he asked. 'Without her, we have lost the very reason that we fight at all. She is our bridge to the Mothers.' His voice trembled.

The sky was now dark. The council was quiet. No one could deny that Llwyd spoke the truth.

'We will start the work to the ramparts at the next wax.' Fraid stood to end the discussion. 'And we call for our Kendra.'

The Hardworld

The Singing is the Mothers' world, the making of things.
Once they are made, the world is hard.

'GRAB IT FIRM, Ailia. Don't be timid or it won't flow.'
I was squatted in the sheepyard with my fingers squeezed around a swollen teat. The Tribequeen's ewes were heavy with milk and we were all needed to empty them. I had paired with Cookmother, who was bent over the animal, holding it still as she barked instructions.

'Tell me of the Kendra,' I asked over the hiss of milk.

She looked at me in surprise. 'What do you know of the Kendra?'

'Little. This is why I ask.'

'Be still, you wretch!' she cried as the ewe bucked its head. 'She is gone. Dead for thrice seven summers, without a daughter to bear her cloak. Albion yields no other Kendra.'

'But will she return? How is she found? How is she known?'

'How will I endure your ceaseless prattle?'

'Please,' I urged. 'You bid me always to be curious—who is she?'

Cookmother sighed. 'Her name means most knowing woman. Her wisdom descends by blood and rises by training. Keep milking, don't slow!'

I tugged on the fingers of skin that hung from the udder. 'Why is she so little spoken of?'

Cookmother leaned closer. 'Fraid has bade that we do not speak of it. Because it is feared that in losing her, we are distanced from the Mothers.'

My eyes widened. 'Does she journey?'

'Of course she journeys. All wisewomen journey,' Cookmother snapped. 'How else are they called journeywomen?'

'But the Kendra?' I pushed.

'Her journeys with the Mothers endure. They are not fleeting.' Cookmother pauses. 'The Kendra learns with them. They are her teachers.'

I took breath at the words.

'Ay, it is an honoured path she walks.' She lowered her voice, glancing sideways to ensure that we were unheard. 'But dangerous also. The Mothers are strong. And they can be cruel. They will take of her what they want.'

My fingers clenched the teat. 'What, Cookmother? What do they take?'

The ewe jerked, kicking the pail, and splashing milk over the ground.

'By the Mothers!' cried Cookmother, setting the pail upright with a thump. 'Concentrate on the task, Ailia, you have no need to know of this.'

'I *want* to know.' I was surprised by the strength in my voice.

'Then listen,' she said, her eyes locked to mine. 'There was a time the Mothers stood much closer. It was easy to see them. Now the new world bleeds into ours and the Mothers are fading. It is harder for the journeywomen to enter their realm. The learning we need is different. We still call upon our Mothers, but perhaps the time to walk with them has passed. Perhaps the need for the Kendra has passed.'

Never before had I known her to question the old ways. 'Journeyman Llwyd would not agree,' I whispered.

'Llwyd has not known what I have known.'

I stared at her, startled. 'What have you known?'

She shook her head in agitation. 'Enough!' she said. 'Ask me of plantcraft. You're well gifted for it and that's what you are born to. No more, no less.'

A flame of protest flared in my chest but I said nothing more.

'Cookmother?' I ventured, when we had milked without words for some moments.

'Ay?' she grunted.

'How did she die?'

'Drowned, I recall. Drowned in a river.'

The late morning brought an unseasonal heat, sedating the township with the scent of warm earth. Work slowed as townspeople paused to give thanks for the Mothers' gift of an early summer.

Bebin and I took hours to boil and strain the sheep's milk, and I had almost given up on seeing Taliesin. But then Cookmother settled for a rest after highsun, and murmured her drowsy approval when I told her I was going harvesting for spring roseroot.

'If you give me half an hour, I'll come with you.' Bebin looked up from the table where she was shaping the sheep's cheese into soft boulders.

'Oh no,' I faltered, 'I want to pick from the north side of the hill and if I wait any longer the buds will close.'

Her smile could not mask her disappointment and I resolved to attend to her soon.

This time it was he who was waiting, sitting on the bank, when I turned the last bend of the river path.

I was damp with sweat as I dropped down beside him. 'How do you fare in this fearsome heat?'

He shrugged, making me feel foolish for my trifling question. 'As I fare at all times.'

Neha clambered joyfully over him.

'And how is that?' I retorted.

He looked at me as if to answer, then shook his head. Something needled him today. 'One such as you would not understand.'

'What do you mean "one such as me"?'

'One who lacks nothing.'

'Lacks nothing?' I laughed at the untruth. 'How little you know.'

He worried a small tear in the seam of his trousers. How had I displeased him?

'You should ask your hutmother to repair that,' I ventured.

'I would if I had a mother to ask. But I do not. Hut or otherwise.' He glanced at me. 'Nor father.'

I stared at his profile, stunned. By the Mothers, he was as I was. Yet he must have known his mother once, for he was skinned. 'I am sorry for it.'

'Why?' He straightened. 'It was not your doing.'

I sighed. His spirit was covered in bruises. A wrong word and he would snarl like an injured dog. Yet when I coaxed him to come closer, it was as though I had captured a piece of the sun in my hand.

I stretched out my legs, sticky with sweat. Heat rose off the earth as if the Mothers themselves were feverish. 'Pity we cannot eat those berries,' I said, looking at a bush laden with black fruit on the far side of the river.

'We can,' he said.

'Oh no—'

'Come,' he insisted, rising. 'Swim with me.'

'I can't,' I confessed. 'I cannot swim.'

'But you are of the river tribes,' he questioned, 'how can you not swim?'

'Why should I?' I snapped. 'Our bodies are not meant for water.'

'Yes, they are,' he said, sitting back down. 'We all began life in water. Was it not where we were safest?'

He picked up my hand, stretching my fingers, and let it fall in my lap. Then he squeezed my thigh through my skirt. 'Large hands. Strong limbs,' he pronounced. 'This body was meant to swim. I will teach you.'

'No!' I laughed. It was forbidden for me to be taught. Besides, I would be so graceless.

'As you wish.' He walked to the bank and launched himself into the rolling water.

I trailed my feet among the reeds in the shallows. The river was wide here, perhaps twenty paces across, swollen with spring melt. Taliesin stood chest-deep in the current, his shoulders gleaming like polished wood. 'It's colder than a widow's bed!' he called.

'What did you expect?' I laughed. 'It's full of mountain snow!'

He swam to the other side of the river and climbed onto the bank.

I watched him as he plucked and savoured the fruit, mocking me with his unhidden pleasure. 'All right,' I shouted. 'Teach me to swim!'

He stuffed his mouth with more berries before crossing back. Standing before me, water running off his skin, he took a berry, warm

82

from his mouth, and slipped it gently into mine. 'Get in,' he said, as the acid sweetness broke on my tongue.

The water swirled cold around my thighs.

'You'll need to take off this.' He gathered my billowing leine and tugged it over my arms.

Facing him in my thin linen under-robe, my resolve started to slip away. 'Taliesin,' I said. 'I spoke in truth—I have never swum.'

'I will not let you drown.' He took my hands. 'Let the water lift you. And kick your legs.' He walked slowly backward, pulling me into the belly of the river, as I gripped his wrists. 'Good,' he nodded, his dark eyes blazing.

Never had my body been so immersed. Never had it felt the icy eddies and nagging currents of deep water. Breathlessly, I let go one hand as he pulled me further. Now the river was too deep even for him to stand and we were both water-bound and jubilant, joined only by our fingers.

The current surged, testing our hold. 'Taliesin!' I gasped.

But instead of tightening his grip, he cast me free.

Water drowned my protests as I slipped under, flailing in panic. The current had dragged me downstream several paces before I felt his hands around my ribs. 'Why did you let me go?' My heart hammered under his palms.

His expression was bemused, unrepentant. 'To see what you could do.'

'I can do nothing!' I clung to him like a frightened child. 'You need not test it a second time.'

'No.' He cradled me.

Our faces were close. I was suddenly conscious of how tightly I pressed against him, but was too nervous to loosen my grip.

He carried me to the shallows of the far bank, but no sooner had I relaxed my hold, than he ducked out of my reach.

Incredulous, I watched him glide back to the other side, where Neha paced the bank. 'Swim back, Ailia!' he called.

Furious, I ignored my fear and plunged forward in a frenzy of kicking to berate him. But when I could find neither the surface above me nor the riverbed below, I panicked again, swallowing water and clawing at the current. I heard Neha barking. My chest burned. Would he not come?

'Kick and lift!' I heard the muffled command through the prism of water.

Desperate, I thrust forward again and kicked with all my strength, gasping for air whenever I broke the surface. I struggled forward until my legs sank in exhaustion, finally finding foothold on the riverbed.

'Do your promises mean nothing?' I panted. 'What teaching is this?'

'That which has seen you cross the river alone,' he said without apology.

I glared at him, then burst into laughter.

Then he showed me, more carefully, the art of travelling through water until finally, with him coaxing beside me, I swam smoothly from one bank to the other and back again.

I had almost forgiven him as we climbed out to dry.

'What is your greatest fear?' he asked.

We lay back on our elbows in the sun. His questions were like cast stones, falling straight to the depths.

'To be alone.' It burst out before I could catch it and I prayed he did not think me too brittle. 'And yours?'

'A witless conversation.'

I stared down at his long fingers splayed in the grass.

'And your greatest pleasure?' he continued.

In an instant of truth, I realised it was him, but I could not confess it. 'Knowledge,' I answered, thinking of when I was happiest.

'Mine also.'

'Hah! What do you love in it?' I had never spoken in such a way with another.

He thought a while. The sun had dried his hair to crisp coils on his shoulders. 'That it saves us.' He glanced at me and saw the question in my face. 'What else is evil but ignorance?' he said.

'A brutal assessment.'

'But true.'

'And for those who are untaught through no choice of their own, what is their salvation?'

He stared at me. 'It is a great waste that you have not been made journeywoman.'

'Why do you say so?'

'Because you would look so fetching in the robes.'

I shoved his arm and he collapsed onto the grass.

'Because you have a mind that asks,' he said, sitting up. 'Like a river that finds new paths. Such minds are rare as jewels. I am surprised it has not been recognised.'

I reddened under his praise. 'My tribespeople need me for other purposes.'

'It is not for the tribespeople to determine. If the Mothers want you, they will call you to journey.'

'But skin is needed to journey—' I flinched, almost confessing myself.

'Of course,' he said, frowning.

I took a deep breath, wondering how long it would be until he discovered how far from a journeywoman I was. Until that moment, I would drink of the cup he offered. 'Taliesin, can you tell me of the Kendra?'

His eyebrows lifted. 'You ask me of your own Kendra?'

'But Albion is without a Kendra.'

He looked at me with an expression I could not read.

'Is it so illicit a truth?' I ventured. 'Might no one speak of it?'

'How is there no Kendra?' he interrupted, his voice sharp. 'What has happened?'

'I don't know—' I faltered. 'The township is forbidden to speak of her. I am told she is lost...drowned. There is no other.' I had gone too far with this question. He would learn too much of my ignorance.

'Drowned,' he repeated to the river. 'Then what holds your people to the Mothers?'

'Why...the same that holds yours...' I floundered. 'The journeypeople?' I thought of Llwyd's distress, of Cookmother's words. 'Perhaps...not enough.'

Taliesin shook his head, his mood suddenly as dark as when I arrived. 'You know that the Kendra is the bridge! If she is lost, there is no hope.'

With every question I risked exposure but I had to know. 'No hope for what?'

He would not meet my eye. Agitation rose off him like heat. 'No hope for me.'

His words made no sense. 'Why?' I urged. 'What does she bridge?'

His expression was incredulous. 'Surely you know? She opens the gates between the hardworld and the realm of the Mothers. She stands with the Mothers as they are singing.'

'And...' I breathed, 'what does she do?'

He stared. 'She sings.'

'How do you know this?' I asked.

'How do you not?'

I hurried home through the warm evening, my head spinning with him. I could not fathom how he did not know of our Kendra's loss or why his own hopes hung upon it.

He was as dazzling and unfathomable as the night sky: in equal measure splendid and despondent, vital and injured, tender and cruel. He had an Elder's wisdom, yet the wariness of a child, and in the force of these splits, the whole earth turned within his sprawling frame.

It was almost dark when I stole though the south gates of Caer Cad, my pockets stuffed with herbs, hastily picked.

Bebin stood as I slipped into the kitchen.

'Tidings, sister,' I greeted her. 'Where is Cookmother?'

'With the queen, thanks be.' She pulled me outside so that Cah and Ianna would not hear us. 'I do not know what you have been doing these past turns of the sun, but I cannot explain your absences to Cookmother much longer,' she whispered.

'Is she angry, Bebin?'

'I will not lie—today she smelled smoke, but if you settle quickly we can assure her that you have been returned an hour or so hence.'

'Thank you,' I breathed in relief.

She paused, glancing around the queen's compound, then lowered her voice. 'Where have you been, Ailia?'

'Only harvesting,' I said. 'The heat—it brings such lushness of growth.' I had to look away from her doubtful eyes. I had never lied to her before. I had never lied before meeting Taliesin. And yet the lies were in service of something pure: my knowledge of a man who was awakening me. Surely no harm could come of it?

It was nearly the hour for sleep. We were seated around the kitchen hearth, nibbling on fresh cherries of sheep's cheese. I fed a morsel to the fawn, lying in my lap, and he nudged my hand for another. He was growing strong and lively on his food. It would be hard to let this one go.

The striking of our doorbell startled us all.

'Who comes now?' grumbled Cookmother. 'I tell you, I am not going to a birthing tonight. You go, Ailia—feign that I am not here.'

Smiling, I set down the fawn and went to the door. Outside stood a strangemaid, who had turned away and was staring out to the night sky. She had some height but carried it weakly and her skirts were torn and filthy. 'Tidings,' I said to her bent back.

When she turned I almost gasped at the sight of her. She was perhaps only five or six summers my elder, but looked much older, as if life-robbed by some means. Her face was little more than skin draped thinly over the skull beneath it: a wide forehead and a wasted chin. But behind the defeated flesh were the bones of a face that might once have been beautiful. Her hair was unbraided and stiff with dirt, her mouth fixed in a grimace. Festival time brought many wanderers from the outlying settlements, searching for food or work. But seldom had I seen such a wretch as this even at the furthermost fringes.

She looked at me from eyes sunk deep in her skull. 'I am looking for the maiden Ailia.'

It was a shock to hear her speak my name. 'I am she. What business do you have with me?'

She took a step toward me, staring. Her stance was unsteady and she seemed to struggle to make clear sight of me. But despite all this, there was a force in her that set my heart pounding. 'You are she,' she muttered. Her gaze steadied on my face. We both stood trapped in this reckoning of one another.

I reached down to restrain Neha, but her ears were folded back and she nosed at the woman's hand. 'What do you seek?' I asked again.

'The townspeople tell me you're a favourite of the Tribequeen.' Her voice was rasping, too loud in the quiet night. 'I need work and a bed to sleep. Will you ask the queen for a place in your kitchen?'

I laughed. 'I'm sorry, strangemaid, but I have no power to refer you. My own place is held by threads!' My words were true, yet even if they weren't, I would never commend this maiden. 'Besides—there is no room.' I lied to soften the refusal.

'There must be room.' Her voice sharpened. 'I can do whatever needs to be done.'

The weave of her tattered shawl was unfamiliar; she had travelled far and I knew, as she would also have known, that there was always need for tenacious workers in the Tribequeen's hutgroup. Perhaps Cookmother would hear my petition if I made it. The scent of stale beer and piss rose from her skirts. 'No,' I said. 'There is no room.' I fought a stab of shame at another lie.

She shrank back. 'Where else might I ask then?'

'Perhaps the warriors,' I stammered. 'Orgilos has not long since lost a daughter to fosterage.' I clucked repeatedly at Neha, who, unfathomably, had settled at the woman's feet and would not come.

'The hound, at least, accepts me.' She stooped to rub Neha's head. 'You know your own skin,' she cooed.

'You are skin to the dog?' I asked. I had not yet met one of this totem.

'Ay.' She straightened.

Where was the dog's strength in this sorry maiden? I bade her farewell but she would not turn away. Her eyes dropped to the golden fish pin at my breast.

'Take it,' I said, tugging it free from my cloak. 'You can trade it for food and shelter for a few days.'

'How kind,' she sneered, closing her fingers around it. Her nails were ragged and rimmed with dirt. As I turned away she grasped my wrist. 'Do you not even ask my name?'

'What is your name?' I whispered.

'I am Heka.' Her nails dug into my skin. 'Of Caer Hod.'

It was an outlying hilltown of Durotriga, known for the purity of its chalk and the strength of its learning. How had she fallen so far through its web?

'Is it true that you are without skin?' Still she gripped my arm.

What did she care of it? 'Let go my arm.'

'Answer me.'

'Yes.'

She nodded slowly, her eyes not leaving mine. 'It is your greatest suffering, is it not?'

Now my heart thumped as though she were an adder before me. There was something in her that reached inside me and grabbed hold of the truth. 'Yes,' I whispered.

The trace of a smile twitched in her mouth. 'Stupid bitch.' She released her grip. 'You will regret not helping me.'

I recoiled in shock. Name-calling was punishable by law of the journeymen. I could have told Cookmother, even Llwyd, and had her brought to justice. I said nothing.

She turned and hobbled into the darkness.

Neha returned to my side.

'What did she want?' Bebin joined me at the doorway.

'To come into the kitchen.'

'Her?' said Bebin. 'Look how she staggers in her step. She's rotten with drink.'

I peered after her. Indeed she was nothing more than a wobbling drunkard and I was right to deny her.

Freedom

Freedom in love precedes all other freedoms.

I SAT ON a stool outside the kitchen in the morning's first light, feeding the fawn milk from a jug. He was surer on his legs each day and starting to gambol around the kitchen garden. When he'd emptied the jug, he bounded away on milk-drunk legs, the early sun making a bright aureole of his downy coat. I laughed at the pride I felt at his growth.

Neha ambled out of the kitchen. 'Greetings doggess.' I fondled the loose skin of her cheek. She sat beside me, echoing my love of the little buck.

A crunch on the ground made us both look up. Next to the stable, across the courtyard, was the strangemaid from last night, Heka, watching me.

Neha's tail thumped on the ground. Why did she not growl?

'Be gone!' I called, rising to stand. 'What business do you have here?'

She held my eye before turning away.

A few moments later, Cah emerged from the same passageway, carrying a bucket.

'Did you speak to the rough girl?' I asked as she passed me.

'Yes,' Cah sneered. 'I gave her some milk.'

—

'What is sweeter than mead?'

My eyes were closed against the brilliance of the day.

We lay on our backs on the grass, weary and river-soaked from my second lesson in the water. As the sun baked us dry, Taliesin tested me with a series of riddles.

'Sweeter than mead?' I mused. 'A kiss?'

'Wrong!' I heard the smile in his voice.

'Then what?'

'Conversation.'

'Ah yes.'

It had been almost impossible to find my escape today. Cook-mother's eyes had narrowed with suspicion at my third day of harvesting. I knew I could not sustain these lies much longer. But Taliesin was worthy of the risk. His temper was buoyant and I left the subject of the Kendra untouched.

'What is swifter than wind?' he asked.

'A warrior?' I ventured.

'Wrong again. The answer is thought.'

I rolled onto my side to face him. 'Ask me another.'

'What is lighter than a spark?'

'Tell me.'

'The mind of a woman between two men.'

'True enough!' I smiled.

'What is blacker than the raven?'

'Is it death?'

'Your first correct answer.' He lay with his forearms crossed over his face, shielding his eyes from the sun. I stared at the swell of his mouth, pressed against his upturned shoulder. Would that I could be that mouth. That shoulder.

'What is whiter than snow?'

'Life…?' I murmured, my thoughts dissolving as I watched his lips form the words.

'Of course not!'

'What then?' I said, surprised at his vehemence. 'What is whiter than snow?'

'Truth.'

'Truth,' I repeated, propping up on my elbows to look over the river.

'There is no greater power,' he said, his eyes still covered.

I agreed with his words, but I was flooded with confusion. For was it not he who had caused me to lie?

'Only one in five correct,' he mocked. 'Do you want one last chance to redeem yourself?'

My gaze caught on the trail of hair that halved his belly. 'Yes.'

'What is sharper than the sword?'

I thought for a moment. 'I don't know.'

He turned to face me. 'Knowledge, Ailia! It was the easiest of them all. Knowledge is sharper than a sword.'

'Taliesin?' I sat up, resolved that there be some truths.

'Ay?'

'Are you a free man?' I asked softly. 'Or journeyman? Or other?'

He was quiet before answering. 'I am free in one place, bound in another.'

'Yet another riddle. I wish for some understanding. I would know *something* of you.'

'But you know many things. I'm a fine fisherman, a clever riddler, handsome as a stallion—'

'With a colt's conceit!' I laughed. 'But this is all dressing I can already see. Give *me* a truth. Tell me something of your history. Have you brothers or sisters? Are your people farmers? Traders?'

Taliesin sat up. With a twig he began scratching small circles in the ground between us.

'If you cannot tell me of yourself,' I said, 'then tell me of your people. Are you under Fraid's queendom?'

He shook his head.

'So you are a traveller here. Were your kinspeople subject to Cunobelinus while he lived?'

He frowned. 'Now it is you who speak in riddles. I do not know these names.'

My thoughts whirled. What class of hidden person was this who did not know the name of Britain's first High King? Was he lawless? A forest dweller? An isolate? I could not have borne for that to be so. 'What is the shape of you?'

He threw the twig into the river. 'You seek to know me by things you cannot see. I could tell you something, but would it be true?' He turned to me. '*This* is my shape, clear before you. If it is not enough—'

'Of course it is enough!'

'Then do not ask for more.' His shoulders slumped as he saw me flinch. 'This is the best of me.'

I silenced the protestations that sprang to my lips, for could I not have said the same of myself? I lowered my head. 'There will be no more questions.'

'Shall we agree on it?'

'We agree.' My eyes remained fixed to my bare feet. I felt chastised, adrift.

After a long pause, he spoke gently. 'There is one question I can answer...We spoke of it yesterday, and I answered glibly.'

I looked up. 'What question?'

'You asked of my greatest fear...'

The air was very still. 'Yes,' I murmured. 'What is it?'

'I will show you.' Springing to his feet, he crouched beside me. 'Hold your dog and make no sound.' He walked to the river and, as he had done before, speared a young salmon, this time with his knife.

'I am not hungry!' I snapped, annoyed by the needless killing.

'It is not for you.' He tucked the carcass into his belt and walked several paces up river where he stopped, raising one arm above his head. Staring skyward, he stood unmoving, then, with his other hand, reached for the whistle at his hips and brought it to his mouth, piercing the sky with its shrill cry.

I startled, perplexed, but soon enough there was a dark shape gliding and circling above us and, with another call from the whistle, a grey and white goshawk, solid as a fattened lamb, swept down to perch on a boulder at the water's edge not five paces from where Taliesin stood.

I was indeed impressed. The art of command of a wild animal was a privileged learning, one not easily bestowed. He had been long and well trained to hold this knowledge.

Neha lurched forward under my grasp but I gripped her scruff, growling at her to keep back.

'Greetings,' called Taliesin, holding the dead salmon out before him.

The bird's brilliant yellow eyes darted from Taliesin to me, cautious, yet drawn.

'Are you hungry?' he cooed. 'Would you like to feast?'

Even I was transfixed by the seduction in his voice.

'Ailia, come,' said Taliesin steadily.

Bidding Neha to be still, I rose and walked to his side. I had never stood so close to a hunting bird. My breath caught at its wild beauty, the ripples of grey on its white breast, its beak, sharp as a blade. 'It's magnificent,' I whispered, flinching as it turned its head.

Taliesin shook the salmon. There was fear in the quiver of his breath and the scent that rose from his skin. 'Come,' he murmured, never tearing his gaze from the bird, 'come close and you will have your prize.'

With a sudden beating of its mighty wings, the goshawk lifted and flew toward us, snatching the fish in its powerful claws, and carrying it into the open sky.

Taliesin watched as it soared from view, then turned back to me, staring long and deeply at my face.

'What is it that you fear?' I asked, self-conscious under his scrutiny.

'Your freedom,' he said.

'Freedom?' I yelped. 'I am bound as tethered cattle. I am beholden to the Tribequeen, to Cookmother—'

'Yet your soul is free. You are as the hawk. You could lift me from the water. I would see what I have never seen. But it would mean my death.'

I stared at him in confusion. 'I could never harm you,' I whispered.

Neha barked beside us. A cool wind set up from the south.

'Do you know goshawks mate for life?' he said softly.

'As do wolves,' I muttered, not breaking his gaze.

He leaned forward, his sun-dried lips catching as they grazed over mine. We were poised, unbreathing, barely touching. And then we broke.

His mouth was deep and sweet as river water. I reached up, burying my fingers in his warm hair, drowning in the turned-earth scent of his skin. My chest and hips collapsed against his and I felt his moan of pleasure, his thundering heart.

We paused for breath and he laughed.

'Why do you laugh?' I asked, frowning.

'Because I am happy.' He paused. 'Aren't you?'

Then I quelled his wondering look with another kiss that rolled my senses so completely I did not know if I was seeing, touching, hearing or tasting him, only that he was everything, and life was all it needed to be if he loved me in return.

I had intended to leave well before sunset, and yet I stayed with him, entwined, until the evening fell on the fields around us.

We had spoken of all but ourselves. Whatever I had asked of the world between our embraces—animal-lore, forest craft—he had answered. It was clear that he had been deeply schooled, yet he wielded his knowledge humbly, less like a warrior and more in the journeyman's way. He did not speak to me as if I were novice, but sought my thoughts, as if I were queen. His kisses eroded the banks of me, his words surging through the new paths and spaces.

As darkness fell we stood, pressing together again, hungrier, and more urgent now that our parting was upon us. From the skin to the core of me, I craved to join with him. So different from Ruther, he did not help himself to my breasts and hips. I reached for his hand and placed it at my chest but he pulled it away.

'Ailia,' he said. 'Do not hope for too much of me.'

What is this? I began to plummet. Was this the love of the bard's poems? This lurch from ecstasy to despair in moments. 'Do you not wish—' my voice was barely a whisper, '—do you not wish to meet me tomorrow?'

'I will meet you tomorrow.'

'When? How?' I asked it of myself as much as of him.

But he was shaking his head, suddenly impatient to leave. 'You will find me.'

'Will you walk with me, just a little way?'

'I cannot. I am sorry.'

'Are you expected elsewhere before nightfall?' I implored. 'Are there those who will worry?'

'No questions,' he said.

When I looked up from tying my sandals, he had gone. I sped home with Neha on my heel, Taliesin burning on my skin.

—

It was well after dusk when I slipped into the Tribequeen's gateway. The compound was silent and cast in grey moonlight. Hastening my step, I conjured the reasons for my lateness: the thick-grown blackberry, the lost paths.

As I approached the kitchen I saw that a bundle had been left on the doorstep. A festival offering for the Tribequeen? It was oddly shaped and there seemed to be a dark liquid around it. Only when I was quite near did the horror of it become clear. It was no bundle. No offering. It was my fawn. Slain at the neck and freshly so. And stuck sharp through the thin skin of its too-large ear, like some mocking adornment, was an object well known to me. My fish pin.

This was Heka's work.

I sank down, resting my palm on his flank. The cool night had already stolen his warmth and he was cold beneath the dewy fur. I gazed at the delicate faggot of legs, at the gentle face, its eyes half-closed. Such evil I had never known.

The moon darkened and a cold rage lifted me to standing. My heart clenched like a warrior's fist and breath hissed through my throat.

Without thought, I pulled off my sandals, the bare soles of my feet pressed on the dirt. I closed my eyes. My urge to harm Heka, as she had harmed, was so powerful I was swaying with it.

And then I felt it. A shivering. Something pushing, as though the earth's spirit was nudging at my feet. With my next breath it was within me, coursing up from deep in the ground. Life laws had been broken by Heka's act and now it was as if the Mothers' own anger rose up through me, stirring and fuelling my own. With deep breaths, I pulled it forth until my belly flooded with the strength of it. With a hard spasm, it rose from my core, erupting in a choking howl. And on this sound was carried all my fury: my desire for Heka to suffer for this fawn.

I fell against the wall of the kitchen, panting heavily. I did not know what I had sent forth, only that it was black with intent. And I was spent like a hunter after a kill.

I eased the jewel from the buck's ear, gathered him into my arms and buried him with my bare hands at the queen's gateway.

When I finally burrowed in beside Cookmother, I was hollow with grief. I squeezed against her broad back, but it was no use. I could not rest. Something had awoken and was stirring within me.

The Geas

A sacred prohibition, a curse, a taboo.
Touch the forbidden object, cross the forbidden
threshold, and suffer dishonour, even death.
A journeyman or woman will place the geas,
but if the need is true, anyone can call it.
A geas called by a woman is the most powerful of all.

'WHAT ROTTEN SOUL yields this sick act?' Cookmother grunted as we scrubbed the blood from the doorstep.

Questions of my lateness had been silenced by the death of the fawn.

'Who would do it, Ailia? Who is so spirit-ill in the township?'

I did not expose Heka's name. To do so would reveal that I had relinquished Cookmother's gift. But this was not all. There was an infection festering between this strangemaid and me, and it filled me with shame.

Cookmother freed me from my tasks. 'Find the wretch who would slay the queen's totem, and call for retribution. Or I'll have Llwyd himself set a geas,' she called.

It was Mael the breadmaker who told me that Heka slept at the fringes. 'She touts a trade that she learned at the Roman ports—' his eyes bulged as he heaved a tray onto the bench, '—where women are bought and sold like loaves.'

A slate-grey sky bore down on Caer Cad. I walked out the gates and into the labyrinth of rough huts and tents that made up the fringes. The stench of human shit rose from the narrow paths, and eyes glinted from the doorways as I passed. 'Get gone!' I yelled as a swarm of screeching children peppered me with pebbles.

Neha's bark led me to Heka. She sat under a makeshift thatch, gnawing on gristle, next to a man withered with age.

'Heka?'

She looked up.

'I would speak with you,' I said.

She came reluctantly to her feet and stood before me. 'Speak then.'

Under the daylight, I saw the dirt that browned her skin and the lice teeming in her hair. For a moment her wretchedness overwhelmed me. Most came to the fringes by skinlessness, others by crime or injury. She was sister to the dog. What held her here? Had all refused her as I refused her? Then I pictured the fawn. 'The animal slain—you have done grave wrong with it. You had business with me, not a babe of the forest.'

'What say you?' She screwed up her face, affecting confusion.

'Don't play the fool, you injure the Tribequeen's own kin in the killing of the Beltane fawn.'

She laughed. 'And how is it my work?'

'This.' I pulled the pin from my pocket and held it before her. 'You left your mark. Were you so dull-witted as to think I would not know you?'

'Ah, the pin. That has been lost to me since yesterday morn—thank you for its safe return.' She reached to take it but I snatched it away.

'Heka,' I stammered, 'do you deny it?'

She took a bored breath. 'If ill was done by the pin, then it was not by my hand.'

She could not weasel from this. It was a lie without shame and I could almost taste the pleasure she took in it. 'Who else would seek to disturb me so?'

'I do not know. But whoever it was, it was not I. Ask your work-sister, Cah. She walked with me yesterday. We drank together, here, at the fringe fires. She will tell you.'

Cah? What was *her* business here? My certainty cracked and doubt drifted in. I began to wonder if indeed the pin had been lost and I had accused her falsely. 'Tell me the truth, woman, or, by the Mothers, you will suffer for your lies. I will ensure it.'

Heka laughed again. 'You set me a geas? Ooh! By which journeyman is it sanctioned? Which skin laws enforce it?' She scratched a lesion at her throat.

'I know it was you,' I said, despairing. 'I know it.' But my voice was thin.

Heka snorted and turned away.

I brimmed with fury as I walked back through the fringe huts, but it was an impotent, crippled anger that found no justice. Never before had I been deemed worthy of such ill. Yet I could not cast off the thought that it was somehow deserved. That her lies were payment for mine. Then I thought of the precious buck and I was stiffened with hate all over again. My geas had no sanction, but it was made with the full weight of my heart.

I stopped before I reached the southern gate. I could not return to my kitchen tasks in such distress. There was only one who could help me make sense of this, and, while I had leave from Cookmother, I would test his promise to me.

With Neha at my side, I stole back along the first rampart, and slipped through the northern entranceway, down the hill. A farmer was driving cattle in the next field and women were washing blankets at the Nain, but none noticed me as I edged south through the crop fields then out along the Cam.

It did not take me long to reach our place. The water mirrored the dark sky, its burbling drone more a warning than a comfort. *Come*, I willed him, wrapping my summer cloak tightly as I waited.

Neha barked at something in the river.

I peered over the bank and my eye caught an arrow of light as a fish shot to the deep. After a moment it surfaced again, the weak sun catching on its flank. It was the fish from the bathing pool. I was sure of it. 'Hush, Neha,' I chided, as she let forth a torrent of barking.

I crouched, watching it ribbon through the water, its belly crimson and silver, black at its spine. Never had I seen anything so beautiful. I laid my hand on the river's surface and the fish glided under my palm. The touch of its skin halted my breath. In a flash, it had darted upstream.

I cried out in dismay and to my delight it returned, then swam away once more. I stared after it, enchanted. Did it want me to follow?

It flipped joyously as I began to walk. I quickened my step until I was not ten paces from the edge of the Oldforest and there I stopped. Cookmother had always warned me to keep a fair distance from the forest's edge, that its spirits had a long reach. But I could not take leave of this animal.

The fish darted back and forth, cajoling me forward, until I stood right at the forest's threshold. I stared into the shadowy corridors that were hardly touched by the day's thin light, my flesh pimpling in the sudden cold.

Neha barked beside me but the sound was distant.

The salmon leaped once more then lunged into the forest. Now I had no doubt: it was asking me to go in. What harm could come when

I had the invitation, the protection, of such a magical creature?

I took a step, then several more, until there were dark, moss-covered trunks, not only before and beside me, but also behind me, and I was fully encased within the forest.

Neha did not follow.

It was an eerie world in which I found myself. Filtered light through the canopy lent a veiled, moonlit quality to the narrow path. The air in my nostrils was cold and scented with rot. Silence surrounded me, save for the faint barks of Neha and my muffled footfall on the forest bed.

I did not tear my eyes from the fish, who led me steadily now, without jumps or turns. My mind knew nothing but its rhythmic undulations, like a trickle of blood through the black water.

When it slowed, I was deep in a grotto: a hidden place as lovely and secret as any I had seen. A small waterfall dropped into a wide pool ringed with mossy boulders and surrounded by hazel trees. Their branches spread over the water like gnarled fingers, laden with fruit as crimson as the fish's skin. Every few moments a nut dropped into the water, where it bubbled and sank, prompting a thin mist to rise off the surface.

I stood at the edge, as the fish circled. Before my eyes, its colour strengthened until it was the hue of a fresh wound. It plunged and surfaced several times. Then there was stillness and it was gone.

In an instant, my dress and sandals were off and I was into the water. My legs blanched with the coldness but I pushed further in. Underfoot were sharp stones, silty mud, wriggling things. But with my next step, I could not find the riverbed. There was no floor. When I inched forward, my toes felt a ledge, and beyond this, only space and water.

Hesitantly, for I had never swum alone before, I glided out over this deep place. I let myself drop until I was fully submerged but still there was nothing beneath me. It was a well of some kind, a spring, within the river. The water at its opening was ice-cold as I flailed above it, eddies pulling me downward. This was where the fish had gone.

With a deep breath, I dropped under once more and peered into the darkness, straining to sight a flash of red.

'Ailia!' Taliesin's voice echoed through the water.

I broke the surface, searching frantically. 'Taliesin!' I called, splashing back to the bank. 'I am here!'

'Ailia—' Again I heard his voice but it was distant, muted, as if through a barrier.

I called to him as I clambered from the pool, but my shouts were met with silence and a heavy mist that had rolled in from the heart of the forest. Pulling on my dress and sandals, I ran among the trees, calling, but the mist denied me sight and he did not speak again.

When I was finally still, shaking with cold, the truth of where I had come struck me like a blow. The fish's hold was broken and suddenly I was terrified. 'Neha!' I screamed, running back to the forest entrance, 'Neha, where are you?'

I ran without rest, stumbling on roots and stones until the trunks started to thin and I sighted my dog waiting patiently.

'Thank the Mothers,' I murmured into her neck when I reached her. As she licked my face, I lay back on the grass, laughing to be out of the forest and free of its seduction. How foolish I had been, how lacking in strength. 'You were cleverer,' I whispered to Neha. 'You knew to resist.'

I promised myself never to be drawn again, but no sooner had I done so than I remembered the voice calling through the mist. Was it some mischief of the forest? No. It was Taliesin, I could have sworn it. He was there.

When I pushed through the doorskins, only Bebin and Ianna were in the kitchen, hemming cheesecloths at the table.

'Where is Cookmother?' I asked.

'Gone with Cah to attend a dirt-dweller near death from skin-sores,' said Bebin.

I stared. 'Which dirt-dweller?'

Bebin shrugged. 'Someone Cah had knowledge of.'

'I will be back soon,' I said, retying my cloak.

'Be sure that you are, sister,' called Bebin after me. 'I will find stories for your absences no longer.'

Even as I hurried down to the fringes, I knew what I would find when I got there. I pushed my way through the knot of people gathered outside the tent I had visited that morning.

Inside the cramped space, Cookmother was bent over a figure lying on linen wraps on the ground. An evil smell poured from her. Though her face was swollen and badly blemished, I saw it was Heka.

Cookmother gasped with relief at my arrival. 'Quickly, Ailia, help me! There is infection in the blisters and my compresses will not clear them.' Bundles of herbs lay strewn around her and she was wringing hot water from bloodied linen strips. 'Nothing relieves her—'

'She is cursed!' cried a voice from the crowd around us. 'Skinsores are the mark of the lie-teller. A blemish for each lie told.'

'Confess your lies, if you've told them, dirt-dweller,' said Cookmother to Heka. 'It may be all that saves you.'

But Heka was beyond hearing or speaking. Her eyelids flickered with a roll of fever.

'May I sit with her alone?' I asked.

'Do what you can.' Cookmother hauled herself to standing. 'My cures are spent.'

Heka's skin was ashen. Her face, throat and arms were covered in rosy eruptions, their white centres weeping with pus. Heat poured from her and she moaned with pain.

Had I done this? These were violent sores and had come quicker than any flesh-law would allow. If this was my curse, it had manifested more swiftly than even a journeyman's geas.

Heka groaned as a boil broke at her temple.

If I had in any way crafted this horror, I could not allow it to continue. I leaned close to her. 'Heka—'

Her eyes sprang open at my voice and filled with a wild hope. 'Lift the geas,' she whispered.

'Who killed the forest's child?' I murmured into her blistered ear.

Her breath laboured through her swollen throat. 'It was I.'

I swallowed. 'For what reason?'

'So you would know what I have known.' Her words were unfathomable.

'What have you known?' I stared at her, but she spoke no more. The fever was robbing her breath. I could not allow her to burn a moment longer or she would surely break her ties with this world. 'It is lifted.'

Straightaway the redness began to pale. I pressed her brow and felt it cool.

'Thank you,' she whimpered.

'Ailia?' called Cookmother from the entrance.

'Come!' I cried. 'Your herbs have prevailed. She becomes well.'

'What? By Mothers, you are right.' Cookmother bustled in and stood beside me, smiling.

We gathered up the bandages and took them to the well. I was silent as we washed them, struggling to fathom the power of my geas. At my wish, Heka had been sickened and healed. The truth of it shocked me, but I could not deny it. Was it something in the forest—the fish, the pool—that had bestowed me this strength? I burned to ask Cookmother, but how could I confess that I had entered the forest? That I had transgressed her gravest foreboding?

The afternoon brought heatwork in the making of cheese. It called for our largest iron cookpot, four women to lift it and hours of patience for stirring the milk.

We worked tirelessly, seasoning the curd with droplets of sweat. Bebin and Ianna chattered without pause and Cah broke in with her usual barbs, but I remained quiet, my thoughts spiralling, until at day's end, in need of giving them voice, I asked Bebin to walk with me.

We stood on an upturned bucket to mount the earthen ledge circling the hilltop behind the first wall. Walking north along the ledge, we reached a place where several spiked beams had rotted and tumbled into the ditch below. Here we sat with our legs dangling, staring out to the eastern horizon, watching the nightfall.

There could surely be no colours like those of a Summer dusk, the bruised pinks, mauves and greys falling like gauze on the vivid green flatlands. A wane moon was ascending and we could hear the distant natter of day's end drifting from the town.

Bebin looked up at the emerging stars. 'The bull's head is almost mid-sky. Tomorrow will favour unions.' Although she had only the first degree of training, she was gifted in star-reading and I loved to hear her speak of it.

'Then it is a shame your traveller is not returned,' I teased.

'Nor yours.' She glanced at me. 'Where are your thoughts, Ailia? Have they followed Ruther to Rome?'

'No,' I laughed. 'I've barely thought of him.'

'So what has quieted you today?'

I scratched a small welt that had risen on my hand, then looked down in alarm as it bled. Did my skin now begin to betray my lies?

It was time to speak before my flesh confessed what I did not. I inhaled and told her that I had stepped into the Oldforest. I told her of the fish, the drop in the water, Heka's mark on the fawn and the command of life I had shown that day. The only thing I did not speak of was Taliesin.

She listened, round-eyed. When I was finished, she was grave. 'You must not go back in. I warn you with all my heart. The Oldforest is dangerous to those without training. I know only little, but I have heard of such drops as the pool you found—' She paused, her face taut with worry.

'What are they?' I urged.

'They are holes in our hardworld.'

'But where do they lead?'

Bebin shook her head. 'That is journeywomen's knowledge. But I do know that they are tears in the truth of things and if you fall through them you are unprotected.'

'Why does it draw me? This fish? This place?'

Again she shrugged. 'Perhaps they sense easy prey. You are untaught and pure-hearted.'

As she spoke I was ashamed of my ignorance, my easy surrender to the enchantment of the fish.

'These are powerful places, only for people with knowledge. Stay clear, I beg you, sister. Cookmother will insist on the same.'

I grabbed her arm. 'Don't tell Cookmother,' I pleaded. 'Promise you will speak nothing of this to her.'

Bebin nodded. 'As you wish,' she agreed. 'But it is not well to hold secrets from those who would protect you.'

'Just this one,' I said. 'There will be no cause for further secrets to be kept.'

'Only if you promise me something also,' she said.

'Ay—what is it?'

'That you won't go in again to the forest—not one time hence.'

'I promise,' I said.

We both looked out over the lowlands. A breeze carried the scent of willow blossom up from the river.

Even as I promised, I knew that I must go in just one last time. Taliesin was caught there, hidden from me. I would find him. I would bring him out of the forest's darkness and into the light.

There was news of a rider as we returned, and all through the township, people spilled from their doorways, bearing torches, gathering to share the news.

The rider had come from the Artrebates, a powerful tribe that shared our northeastern border. King Caradog had overthrown their tribeking and taken control of their tribelands.

Caradog was building an army.

Rome would not like it.

Rome would stop it.

It was right at our doorstep.

The Skinsong

The skinsong is within us.
It is the cord that leads us back to the Mothers.

THE NIGHT SKY was paling to a bloody dawn when I reached the hazel-ringed pool the next morning. I had crept from the kitchen in darkness. Neha had led me, untorched, along the river, but I had walked through the forest alone, with only the faintest first light and the water's soft gurgle to guide me.

A figure stood by the pool's edge, dark against the white mist.

With a surge of relief I ran to him. 'Where were you yesterday?' I murmured into his chest. 'Why did you not come?'

His face was troubled. 'I am not a dog to be summoned at will.'

'Of course, but I...I heard your voice—' I faltered, dismayed at his sharpness. 'We must leave here, Taliesin, both of us. It is dangerous for me to be in this place, and already I am fraught with changes—'

'What changes?' He frowned.

'There is no time to tell you now, will you come?'

'Tell me what is altered in you,' he insisted.

I groaned, and hurriedly told him of Heka, the fawn, the skinsores.

He looked at me. 'You set a geas then called it back. What is the strangeness in it?'

'It is not the art of a kitchen girl!'

He snorted. 'Your gifts are plain enough. Is that the whole of it?'

'No. There is more. I have been too easily enchanted. Never should I enter this forest, but I was led by a river fish against my will.'

'And yet you come again today,' he said.

'Only to find you!' I cried. 'We have always met outside the forest. Never within. We must return to that place, Taliesin, or find a new one, far from the Oldforest.'

'I cannot leave here,' he said.

'But that is madness. Why not?'

He turned away. 'We made an agreement—no questions.'

'No!' My frustration erupted. 'I cannot honour this agreement. I am kept in an unending fog with you. You draw me here, where I am entirely forbidden, and now you say you cannot leave. Look at me!' I commanded.

He turned back, his eyes bright with anger.

'Who are you, Taliesin? What do you want of me?'

'Nothing!' he shouted. 'I ask nothing of you—I never have. Leave, if what I offer is not enough.'

'How dare you make such a challenge to me. Does it mean so little whether I stay or go?'

He strode a few paces upriver and stood with his back to me.

'You retreat to a hole like an animal,' I spat. 'Why will you not stand where you can be seen? Do you so fear the light?'

'It is not that I fear it,' he said, his voice low, 'I know it is not there.'

'Of course it is there,' I scoffed. 'There is always light.' I walked to his side. 'You wrap yourself in a blanket of mystery while I shiver alone outside. It is selfish. Cruel.'

He laughed, coldly.

'By the Mothers, what is funny in it?'

'It is not the first time I have worn those words.'

'So now you claim them?' I cried. 'I seek you against the gravest of warnings, yet you do not choose to return the effort.'

'There is no choice in it.'

'There is always a choice.'

He turned to me, his face twisted. 'Do you not think this is hard for me also, Ailia? It is harder than you could know.'

His words caught in my chest. Suddenly he was softer than a pup and I could not kick him again. 'I am weary of these questions without answer,' I said quietly. 'If you wish to see me you will leave the Oldforest. I cannot come here again.'

His eyes closed then opened slowly. 'As you wish.'

I stared at him in despair. Then, beneath the indifference that masked him, I saw such anguish in his dark eyes that I could do nothing but pull him toward me, cradling his head as it dropped on my shoulder. 'What strange and magical creature are you?' I murmured into his hair. 'I did not mean it. I will not stop coming, I cannot. But there is one thing that you must tell me at the very least. One question that cannot be left unanswered...'

He lifted his head and met my gaze.

'Is it love that we have in the chasm between us?' I whispered. 'Tell me. This alone I need to know.'

He did not speak.

My hands dropped from his shoulders and fell to my sides. I waited but still he did not answer.

He did not love me. This was the truth he had found so hard to share.

We stood like this, each staring at the ground, as I reeled with the pain of it. At least now it was known.

Finally he took my hand and led me through the mist to a boulder by the river's edge, where we sat down. The flow was quiet in the dawn, and shafts of salmon-coloured light spun off the water's surface. A hazel branch dropped one red berry and we watched it drift downward.

In the breaking day, Taliesin began to sing. His voice was piercingly tender. But as soon as I heard it my belly flooded with dread. I braced my palms against the cold rock.

He was singing me his skinsong.

> *Human kin, hear my skinsong,*
> *The song of my mother,*
> *The song that has made me born.*

I heard its first cycle in silence. I was not expected to sing here, only to listen. His song told of a childhood lost to the rivers and forests, a lonely life, a father unknown, and a mother's betrayal. Its sadness shifted the fluids of my heart.

He began the last verse. The music of the skinsong was always gifted by the mother, but this—the summation—was where Taliesin must shape his own words:

> *I was born in the waters of wisdom,*
> *Spawned of knowledge more ancient than creation*
> *But I was wrong-born: half here, half there*
> *Swimming forward and yet backward tears the soul,*
> *Lets memories out and chaos in,*
> *But the smell of my birthplace is in my flesh.*
> *My love, I call to you*

I've swum oceans searching,
Now I catch your scent
I am destined to find you, but it will be a fight,
My flesh will ebb, my bones will crumble,
but I will not sleep until I have reached the pool where you swim.
Your scent is in my flesh
and I will search the world to find it.

When we had finished, we both stared into the water, the silence bleeding between us.

He loved me utterly and I could not return it.

'Why do you not sing?' he whispered.

In his eyes I saw his slow understanding that I would not join with him. And I was horrified that he should think this, because I had never yearned for kinship with anyone so deeply in my life.

For this reason, I could not tell him why I did not sing. I loved him too much to speak the truth: that I was unmarriageable, unloved by the Mothers. That I had no song. It was better he thought I withheld it than know I did not possess it. While he believed I had a song, at least, he might continue to hope for me, continue to love me.

I could not bear the disbelief in his face. I had never felt so treacherous, so ignorant. For the first time it was I who stood and left without farewell.

The rising sun was clearing the mists as I pounded over the forest path. But though I ran swiftly, the edge did not come. I stopped to check I had not led myself awry, but no—the river was still close. As I entered by her, I would exit by her, so I held tight to her banks. Taliesin's song pushed into my thoughts, but I drove it out, running yet faster to be free of this forest and into the open where I could think in the light.

I stopped, motionless, at the smell of woodsmoke. There was a fire nearby, downstream. I crept forward. If there was a camp or worse—a journeymen's grove—I had to pass unseen.

The smoke thickened and I wondered, with a gust of hope, if somehow Taliesin had lit this fire—if I had discovered his home. Then I froze again. Through the dense trunks I glimpsed a hutgroup on the other side of the river.

I stole through the trees until I reached an old willow at the water's edge. Hidden behind its trunk, I peered over at the settlement, amazed that I had run this very path yesterday and seen nothing.

It was a small hut group, the huts built in a circle amid pens of dark sheep. But at the centre of the hutgroup burned the largest fire I had ever seen. It was tended by tribespeople I thought at first to be men. But they worked half-clad in the fireheat, and soon I saw they were women's shoulders that carried fuel to the firepit and women's arms that cast it in.

Propped against the huts were many swords and knives. This was forge fire. But who were these women who worked fire without men? They were young, barely past maidenhood, but steady and formed as grown oak. Even at a distance, their dark eyes burned.

I stood transfixed by their stature, their purpose. I squinted to see the talismans and cloth patterns that would mark their tribe, but the smoke was settling over the river, veiling my sight.

A wren whistled behind me. The forest grew ever lighter. If I did not return home in time with bread, then I would be forced to confess my disgrace to Cookmother and my broken promise to Bebin.

I took a last look at the women, then turned back to my path. When I emerged from the forest, Neha was still standing guard at the entrance. She whimpered as I greeted her, more anxious than usual to rekindle our bond. Something was not right as I cast my eye around the fields. The sky was too bright. With a horrified glance at the sun, I realised that the day had almost reached highsun. It had been dawn only moments hence! Had I watched the women of the fire for so long? I began to run. There would be no explaining this lateness now.

An icy silence greeted me as I entered the kitchen.

Bebin's eyes flickered a warning as she hurried out at Cookmother's command. Ianna and Cah were at lessons.

Cookmother sat at the hearth, facing the door. 'Sit,' she said.

I walked to her and sat on the floor at her feet.

'Bebin went to the bakehouse,' she began, 'as you were not here to make the errand.'

'I am sorry—'

'Silence,' she spat. 'While she was at the bakehouse, Bebin saw Dun's wife, wasted with worry. Dun has worsened, is near gone.'

My stomach curdled as I realised what I had done.

Cookmother sat unmoving. 'She asked Bebin why the herbs never came.' Her mouth was rigid. 'Why did the herbs never come?'

'Is it too late?' I whispered. 'Let me take them to her this moment.'

'Bebin brought her here and I gave her the herbs. Tomorrow will tell us whether they came too late. Now I ask you a second time: why were the herbs not taken?'

In all my days with Cookmother, I had never once failed to do her bidding. Not one life had been lost at my hand. I had served her craft tirelessly and the thought that I had breached it now was too much to bear. The wrongness of this neglect, Taliesin's unanswered song, and all that had befallen me since Beltane surged within me and I could carry it no longer. 'I have been swept up in a tide of change since the fires,' I wept. 'I have been wronged, and oddly powered, and then seduced into the Oldforest—'

She inhaled sharply. 'What is this? You have walked the forest?'

In truth, it was a relief to be caught. 'Yes.'

'That which I have entirely forbidden?'

There was to be no more hiding. 'Ay. It was a fish, a crimson-skinned fish that magicked me in. Then this morning, there were women with a great fire—'

Cookmother flinched as if physically struck. Her voice, when it came, was trembling. 'Tell me what you have seen.'

'Only a hutgroup,' I said. 'And women of such grace working the fire...'

Cookmother's hands flew to her mouth. When she lowered them they were shaking. 'Did you walk among them? Touch them or speak with them?'

'No.' I was becoming frightened. 'They were across the river, hidden by smoke. I just saw the shape of them. I did not call.'

Her shoulders dropped with relief. 'Thanks be,' she breathed.

'Cookmother?' I said, unnerved. 'Who were the women?'

She would not meet my eye. 'They were outcasts, dirt-dwellers not permitted even to fringe the towns,' she said. 'They'll slit your throat for your sandals.' She fingered the carved bone talisman at her belt as she spoke.

I frowned. 'I would swear they were no outcasts.'

'Be assured, that's what they are. And hear this, Ailia—' Now she held my gaze. 'If the threat of the forest alone is not enough to repel you, then let me promise you this: if you go to the forest again, I will cast you from this kitchen.'

My mouth dropped open in shock.

'Unlawful contact with the forest invites darkness and I will not permit it near my kitchen.'

Never had she threatened such a thing and the fear of it conjured a fresh batch of silent tears.

'Ach, come,' she grumbled, pulling my head to her lap. 'This is your path, by me,' she murmured as she stroked my hair. 'You are meant for my learning. Hear me please, Lamb. Never go to the forest again.'

'But what of the fish?' I hiccupped into her skirts.

'Stay clear of the place where you saw it.'

And what of Taliesin? cried my heart, but as when I spoke with Bebin, I could not find the voice to name him to Cookmother. Her comfort was all I had. I could not risk it.

There were footsteps outside, the girls returning.

'Speak not of the forest to anyone,' Cookmother hissed. 'Anyone!' Then she pushed me off her lap and rose to her feet.

Cah burst in, flushed with excitement. Ianna trailed behind.

'There is news in the township,' said Cah, her eyes alight. 'Verica, the Tribeking of the Artrebates has fled to Rome. He protests Caradog's theft of his kingdom and asks for Rome's help to retrieve it. The Emperor Claudius has agreed. War is coming.'

Truth

Truth is life-giving, the sustaining power of creation.
The realm of the Mothers is a place of truth.
By truth the hardworld endures.

FROM THIS MOMENT, there was little else but Rome on the lips of the town.

Messengers arrived every few days telling of Roman forces amassing on the shores of Boulogne. Some said they were ready to sail, hungry to reinstate Verica and the other exiled British kings who would rule by Roman law. Others reported that these soldiers were scared, that the General Plautius could not rally them, that they feared the thick mists of this island and called it a place of dark magic, of hurricanes and creatures half-human, half-beast.

We heard that the brothers Caradog and Togodumnus held an army poised at Cantia to fight back the legions. Then we heard that they had gone home to their wives and children, assured that the Romans were still months from sailing.

The moon fattened and thinned twice. Cookmother permitted me to take no medicine outside the township walls. I could not even fetch the bread alone. Only to serve Fraid did she release me from her sight.

Nightly Fraid argued with Llwyd as to the best way to proceed. Send forces straightaway? Wait to see whether Rome would move into the west after they landed? And always the Kendra. The Kendra who bore the power of the Mothers. Who would weave the spells that would confound and frighten the invaders. Who would guard the precious heart of Britain—its knowledge, its skin.

I knew that Llwyd sat in silence for hours of each day calling for the Kendra to come. Over and over, he opened the bellies of wild hares and studied the entrails that fell steaming onto the crisp dawn ground. He watched the sky: by day reading birdflight, and by night, the stars, looking for omens that would lead him to her. He grew thin and wasted, fasting as offering for her revelation, drinking only the bark teas that I brought him for his vision as he sat in the temple.

The arguments between Fraid and Llwyd were echoed among the townspeople. Some spat on Verica's name, calling him a Roman-loving dog. Others claimed Caradog was too hostile, too greedy in broadening his rule, and needed Rome's firm rebuke. It was the division in the town that most disturbed Fraid as I brushed and shined her hair each night with oil. How could we fight them when we were fighting ourselves?

She ordered the works on the hill's defences to be hastened. The ramparts were fortified and lined with a dazzling new layer of chalk. All was built in precise alignment with the sun's path, ensuring a strength far beyond what a craftsman's hand alone could bestow. When our structures echoed the order of the skies, they harnessed the power of the Mothers themselves.

All this pleased Llwyd but it was not enough. Only the Kendra, he said—often with tears in his eyes as days without food made him weak—would bring us to unity and truth.

And I lived with my own war between the ache to see Taliesin and the forces that held me from him. I was bound every waking hour to Cookmother's tasks, shackled by a gaze that gripped me tighter than a prisoner's neckring. Only by night was I free to be with him in my thoughts, where I relived every memory of his touch, and imagined those that might come. Like Llwyd, I did not eat; my belly battled food and I grew thinner. Like Llwyd, I was yearning for the one who would deliver me from this hunger.

'Get up, Ailia.' Manacca shook me awake.

It was midsummer eve, the night of the southern solstice. I had drifted to sleep on the floor of the Great House, though we were all supposed to keep vigil through this, the shortest night. Now dawn approached and we had to walk to Sister Hill to watch the break of the year's longest day. Despite Rome's encroachment, or perhaps because of it, we clung even more tightly to our rituals.

Bebin and Cah tugged on their cloaks as I helped Manacca tie hers, blinking tiredness from my eyes. 'Do you come, Cookmother?' I asked, prodding the mound snoring beside me.

'Soon, soon,' she murmured, breaking wind as she rolled over.

I smiled at Bebin as we headed through the door and out of the compound to join the river of torches streaming through Cad's southern gateway. I took a deep breath of the warm air and tightened my hold of Manacca's hand. This was the first time I would walk beyond the town walls in more than two moons.

The solstice fire was beginning to die down as we reached the top of Sister Hill. Young knaves took up hoops of branch and reed, doused them in grain spirit, then held them to the embers to ignite. We all chanted for the wheels to be sent forth, cheering and laughing as each flaming circle reeled down the slope, tumbling into the Cam below.

'They're like shooting stars,' I whispered to Bebin.

Manacca squealed as another was launched.

The fire had been lit at dusk and had burned through the night, with Llwyd and the lesser journeymen keeping vigil. Now, as the hour of light drew closer, they allowed it to die down so that the solstice sun would know no contest as it banished the darkness.

Fraid stood flanked by her high warriors at the western point of the fire, wearing her diadem and a thick gold torque. She would be first to hear the visiting seer's predictions, first to be touched by the year's strongest light.

With their shoulders wreathed in summer oak leaves, the journeymen chanted by the dwindling fire. Their low, rumbling drone invoked the fire spirits to yield their truths to the seer who sat in trance beside them. When they had sung, the seer would scry the firebed and read the embers.

The ground under my sandals was sticky from a wild mare's slaughter. Her bones, flesh and white pelt had bubbled through the night in a cauldron on the solstice fire. Llwyd ladled the broth into a bowl and passed it to the Tribequeen. She drank to renew her place as first consort to these tribelands, then passed the bowl to her warriors, and finally to the seer.

When all had drunk, Llwyd brought us to silence with his raised staff. Despite his frailty, he was still majestic in Ceremony. 'The solstice fire has burned tirelessly through this night,' he called. 'This promises an early ripening and a plentiful harvest!'

We cheered. Good news was greatly needed now.

'It is time for the fire to speak,' Llwyd continued. 'But first look to the west.'

Sinking into the horizon was a moon that was one day from fullness.

'Today our mighty solstice sun will set against the full moon's rise,' Llwyd said.

A murmur rippled through the gathering. There had been unease in the township about the sky patterns as we approached midsummer, but only the journeypeople could speak directly of such things.

'Such a constellation occurs only once in many lifeturns,' said Llwyd. 'The two great sky spirits are each at their most powerful. As they oppose one another in the east and west, the skin of our tribelands will be stretched between them. We may be held in perfect balance,' he paused, 'or we may tear.'

A rumble of panic rose in the crowd.

'Be still,' said Llwyd. 'Keep to your houses at sunfall this day, that you will not be caught by the force of the pull. That you will not tear the skin. But now—' he looked to the seer, '—it is the hour for augury. The coming sun, so challenged by the moon, will speak only its truest messages through the fire. Come forth if you would hear the fire speak.'

The tribespeople surged forward, eager to learn what was foretold for them in fortune or marriage. They would need to be swift; there was less than an hour before sunrise. Among the milling bodies, I noticed a familiar hunched form, standing with her back to me. Almost as if she could feel my stare, Heka turned, meeting my eye. Her skin was still pocked with the scars of the blisters.

A large-shouldered tribesman stepped in front of me, obscuring my view, and I pushed her from my thoughts. The seer had begun. He stood at the lip of the firebed, calling the Mothers to speak. He was a slight man; his beard seemed too dark and his brow too firm to have attained the degree of seer, but he had been trained at the Isle of Mona in the northwest, and the words of such a man were highly valued. Using an iron stick to prod wisdom from the long-burnt wood, he spoke to one tribesperson after another, turning the embers, sometimes casting in an acorn to watch how it burned. Fraid and Llwyd stood beside him, whispering as they heard the portents.

Finally it was Bebin before him. The crowd was thinner now, as many had heard their fire words and had dispersed to the hillside for the rise. I stood beside her. The embers were turned for a fresh message.

'A high marriage is shown,' said the seer.

I squeezed Bebin's arm.

'There is the sign of metal and the symmetry of a skin.'

'These are traders' wears,' I whispered, 'they tell of Uaine.'

'Hush.' She smiled.

'It is indeed a man of trade and a favoured match,' said the seer. 'Accept the marriage and its consequences.' He set down his stick. 'That is all. The sun threatens to dawn.'

Bebin pushed me forward. 'Please—scry for my worksister,' she said, as I shook my head. 'Just one more.'

'Not Ailia,' commanded Fraid. 'The fire will not speak to one without skin.'

'With your permission, Tribequeen,' said Llwyd, dipping his head. 'I would like to test it.'

Fraid frowned. 'As you wish, Journeyman. But quickly—' she glanced at the sky, '—the fire must soon be doused.'

The seer looked at me and took up his stick. 'Of what do you wish to learn?'

My heart was racing. I had never heard my own fire portents before. 'Skin,' I said slowly. 'I ask of my skin.'

The seer turned to the fire and I stared at him as the light flickered on his deepening frown. 'There is nothing,' he said, finally. 'There is no story in the wood.'

'Because there is no story in her!' called a man from the crowd. 'The Mothers do not see her.'

'I said it would be so,' said Fraid, turning away.

'Let me help,' said a low voice beside me. I turned to see Heka, poised, readying to throw a handful of acorns.

'Thank you, no help is required—' I stammered, prickling at her nearness.

'But it is,' she said. 'After all, did you not help me as I stood at the gates of the Otherworld?' She glanced at me and I saw that her spite had not lessened in the weeks since I had tended her. 'Perhaps I can help wake the Mothers.' She cast the acorns into the embers. Too many. Their explosions broke open the thickest log, releasing a red trickle of sap. Heka turned to the seer. 'Now what does the fire say?'

The crowd watched. We all knew the method was flawed, but the seer was transfixed by what it had conjured.

'The sap,' he said, 'It foretells the running of blood.'

'Whose blood?' I gasped.

'Yours. Another's. There are many rivulets—perhaps the blood of many.' He looked at me. 'You will find skin—'

My breath caught.

'—but its cost will be blood.'

'What is this rot and nonsense?' Cookmother's voice thundered into the silence, pushing Heka aside as she shouldered to the front. 'Even I know that sap in the fire can mean many things. The coming of rains for one, which is well needed here. Or the waters of babebirth. Don't set to terrifying the stupid girl with these horrors,' she said to the seer as she clutched my arm.

Llwyd leaned forward, looking into the fire. 'No, Cookwoman, I, too, see the message that has been spoken.'

'I think there is little cause for concern,' said Fraid. 'She's my kitchen servant. Unskinned and without influence.'

'The fire says otherwise,' said the seer.

'Yes.' Llwyd turned to Fraid. 'She must be watched.'

My shock was lost in the babble of townspeople hurrying to take their place on the hillside before the rise. I stood between Bebin and Cookmother, the closest I knew to kin. We all fell silent as the sun neared the horizon, painting the sky a brilliant turquoise. A lone drummer struck a steady pulse.

We watched, motionless, as it dawned: the most beautiful and powerful sun of the year. When the crimson orb was fully birthed, Llwyd began the incantations. Many tribespeople took up the chant and some began to dance, but I had no heart for singing or dancing.

I looked out to the far edges of Summer, squinting against the rising sun. Perhaps Cookmother was right and there would be no spilling of blood. Perhaps I could trust in the light.

Heka's grey-shawled figure sat alone on the hillside at the edge of my vision.

—

'Do you see, girl?' said Cookmother, shuffling beside me through the town's winding paths. Bebin had stayed at the hill, but I had left early with Cookmother to prepare the solstice feast. 'Do you see what comes when you play fool with the forest?'

'But you said it would not be as the seer foretold!'

'I said it,' she spluttered, 'but I cannot be sure of it. Heed the seer, if you will not heed me. Settle yourself, as I have done, to your days in Cad.'

'I am told I will find skin!' I wailed.

Cookmother tripped on a loose cobblestone and I grasped her arm to steady her. She stood, catching her breath. 'Have I not given you the comforts of kin?'

My heart folded. 'Yes,' I said. 'But—'

'Then stay within the safety of Cad. Don't stir up what is at rest.'

Then I voiced a question I had not even asked myself. 'What if I am called to more?'

'You are not!' she cried. 'How could you be called? You're not even—' She looked away.

'Not what?' I demanded. 'Not even a tribeswoman? I know that. But you have always said otherwise. You have always told me I am whole to you.'

Her lips pressed firm. 'This is a tiresome business, Ailia. You are needling more than a mouse in a grainsack and I wish you to stop it.'

'And what of my wishes?' I said. 'What of my hopes and questions? Do you not think *I* hunger to know why the forest has spoken to me?'

Cookmother was seldom rich in good temper, but never had I seen her so vexed. Her eyes darkened. 'You are no tribeswoman.' Her voice was low and hard. 'You are not wholly born and you shall not go in again. Do you hear?'

But I would hear no more. Instead, I ran. I ran back through the township, ducking and stumbling through the narrow paths. Ianna greeted me as she returned from the hillside, but I was too wild to answer. All I saw was where I did not belong and where I would never find Taliesin. I flew through the town's entrance and down the hillside, turning west when I reached the Cam.

Eventually I came to an outlying farm where a winter cattle house stood empty while the beasts grazed the summer pastures. Exhausted, I pushed open the heavy door and crept into one of the pens, where I burrowed beneath the straw.

Cookmother's faith had always given me a place. Without it, I had nothing. I cursed the woman who birthed me then condemned me to this tribelessness. The only one I wanted was equally lost and utterly forbidden to me. I curled into a ball and let myself weep.

A rustle behind me made me look up. Neha had found my hiding place. She dropped beside me, whipping the straw with her tail, summoning a spill of fresh tears that she licked from my cheeks.

We lay in the barn for many hours, although there was a feast to serve and the girls would have had to work harder without my help.

It was near day's end when I emerged from my refuge. I took a moment to farewell the solstice sun as it grazed the horizon, then I turned back toward Cad. There, rising between the eastern hills, was a moon as round and red as a bowl of blood. This was the moment of which Llwyd had warned. It was too late to hide. I tried to move but I was caught between them, my fluids suspended by the pull of each orb. For an instant I felt myself stretched taut to breaking across the sky, then the moon wrenched free of the horizon, and I fell to the ground intact, released from their struggle.

Had it held? I worried as I scrabbled to standing. Or had the skin of our tribelands been torn?

=

Cookmother said nothing when I returned to the kitchen, though the clatter of pots spoke loudly enough. She served stew and oat bread to each of the girls, but it seemed I was to fetch my own. At the sleeping hour, she told me I could not lie in her bed. This she had never done.

My heart thudded with outrage as I lay next to Bebin.

'Don't worry,' she whispered, 'she will soften by the morning.'

'Be silent,' hissed Cookmother.

The kitchen slept but I could not settle. Outside the insects droned. The night yawned on, noisy with snores and tossing bodies. I got up. My foot caught on a basket as I passed, spilling barley kernels across the floor, but I could not stop to tidy them now.

Outside the air was warm, the moon still dazzling. Dogs howled through the township and I muzzled Neha with my palm. My senses were wakeful, my mind too alert. I would never sleep this night. I clicked Neha to my side and began to walk.

The rush of the Cam was louder by night, frogs beating at its banks. The moon lit my path. I quickened my pace. I was headed for the forest and I did not question it. Looming like a beast in the darkness, its breath drew me in. But even stronger than this, I knew Taliesin was close. He was what pulled me.

If Cookmother would not recognise me, then I was not bound by her command. If skin would not claim me, then I was outside the laws of skin. I realised now that there was freedom in being cast out: that I was beholden to nothing but my own will, my own desire.

I shivered in readiness for Taliesin's touch. This was the night that earth and sun would join in us. I could not give him my song. But he would have everything else. I crouched down to kiss Neha—who still would not follow—and went in.

The canopy stole much of the moonlight. I crept forward by my ears and fingertips. The forest pulsed with danger but I was not scared.

Soon the trees thinned and there was enough light to see the sparkle of the river and the trunks that lined the path. There was no hutgroup, no fire, no women.

I came to the place where the hazel boughs reached over the pool, the blush of their berries still red, even in moonlight.

He came from the mist.

I greeted him but he did not return it, his bare shoulders rigid under my embrace. He was still angry, I thought as I released him. And yet he had come. Or was he here only to cut himself free of me?

He walked to the edge of the pool and stared into the water. 'Shall we swim, Ailia? I know you have grown fond of it.'

'No,' I said, relieved, at least, to hear him speak. 'Not at night.'

'I have always loved to swim in the dark.' His voice was distant.

'My mother used to call me her night salmon.'

I walked to him. Perhaps, if I was gentle, I could lure him back. 'Tell me something of her,' I ventured. 'Your mother.'

'Short of temper. She had little patience for motherhood.'

'But she must have loved you,' I said.

'Not enough to return for me.' He looked straight ahead.

'Taliesin—' I touched his back, '—I can be no comfort to you unless you speak to me. I don't understand—'

'No.' He turned to me, his expression bitter. 'You do not understand. You will never be a comfort to me. You see only the light.'

'It is not so,' I said, recoiling. 'I have known darkness, but I do not let it rob me of hope.'

'Then you are a fool awaiting the next blow to your back.'

I stared at him. 'Do you know so little of joy?'

'I know pleasures,' he spat. 'A strong ale, a woman's thighs.'

I winced. 'There is more than that.'

'The blind may believe it,' he said. 'I know of the world's truth.'

'But there is truth in the light! Your own riddle said it so—'

He snorted with disdain. 'A riddle to comfort the stupid.' His eyes glittered in the darkness. He was made ugly by this cruelty. I had never thought him so.

'A life in darkness is no life at all,' I said. 'You might as well bid goodbye to this world and go searching in the next.'

'Yes,' he agreed. 'Useful advice.'

'No!' I cried, gripping his arm. 'Don't speak it—' My chest ached with the sting of this soured meeting, the fear of his threat. 'Why do you seek to wound me so?'

'Why did you not return my song?'

I stood poised at the edge of a cliff. I took a breath. 'Because I have no song to return,' I said softly. 'I am a foundling. Half-born. Unskinned. There. Now you have the truth of it.'

There was a pause. 'But you are skin to the deer—'

'No,' I said, faint with shame. 'It was a lie.'

'A lie,' he whispered. 'Why?'

'Because I did not want you to know the truth of me.'

'Unskinned?' He stared at me with an expression I could not fathom. 'You will never journey—'

'Of course not.' I felt my heart beginning to harden like his. 'I am no journeywoman. I am nothing, as you yourself have said so plainly.'

We sat in silence, the truth like a wound between us.

I awaited his goodbye. I prepared mine. But there was something more to be told. 'I have confessed myself to you,' I said. 'Will you now tell me who you are?'

He stared out into the night, his face unmoving. Eventually he spoke. 'I am not of the tribes.' He paused. 'I come from a different place.'

'What place?' I asked.

He turned to me. In the dim light his eyes were shadows. 'It does not matter what place. Without skin, you will never reach it.'

'Are you one of the outcasts I have seen in the forest?'

'No.' He shook his head. 'I am sorry I cannot bring you more truth.'

I laughed in my sadness. 'You are the only thing that is true to me.'

Beneath our feet was a soft, damp blanket of leaves. He sat, pulling me down beside him. 'How are you permitted to be here so late?' he asked.

'I follow my own command now in these matters.'

He laughed heartily until I also was chuckling at my own boldness. The grey light smoothed his skin to a velvet softness. He was the dissolving of me. We both looked to the water as another red nut fell.

'I am so sorry,' I whispered.

He turned to me. 'I love you no less unskinned, Ailia.'

My breath stopped. 'How is it so?'

'How could I not? I love what sits here before me. You are free and alive and brave beyond words. But without skin you will never come to my place and I cannot stay in yours. We can meet only like this, fleetingly and bound to this place. It is no offering for one as beautiful as you—'

'I will have you however I can,' I said.

He leaned forward and kissed my mouth. Never had I known such tenderness.

My senses were needle-sharp. All else beyond him paled. But beyond this moment, there was no ground between us, nothing to stand on. He was the cliff, the danger. I jumped.

We fell back, legs tangling. This time it was he who was hungry, tearing open my dress to savour the rise and taste of my breasts.

I drank the briny scent of his shoulders and neck: sharp and sweet as bitten apple. This was not the frantic clutching I had known with Ruther. This was the earth's renewal brought to flesh.

In seconds we were ready, aching to join, but when I reached down to lift my skirts, he pulled away as if the wanting was too strong.

'Why do you stop?' I leaned up to kiss him, to bring him back, but he pushed me away.

'I cannot—' His face filled with anguish.

I could barely speak for my confusion.

He sat with his back to me, his breath heavy.

Throbbing, swollen with need, I hardly dared ask the question that came to my lips. I did not want to open the chasm between us. But I had to know. 'You asked if I could journey. Is *that* what would bring me to your place?'

A ragged cloud darkened the moon.

'Yes,' he said.

My blood quickened. 'But that means...you are of the Mothers' world.'

Silence.

'*Are* you of the Mothers, Taliesin? Are you of their place?'

'Yes,' he whispered, and then he was gone.

I did not look up. To watch him go now would have broken me apart. My skin burned. I had to cool myself or I would crack.

I loosened my dress and under-robe, letting them slide to the ground as I stood. Naked, I stepped into the pool. The water was cool silk against my skin. I shut my eyes and sank to my neck.

But my eyes sprang open. I was not the only life in this pool. Something quickened at my shoulder and I knew it was there: my fish. This time I knew it was male. Only a male creature could bear the fierce heat of me now.

Through the black water I could not see it, but I felt its sinewy current as it circled me in tightening rings until its rough scales grazed my chest. It turned, darting and nibbling at the points of my breasts, bringing a pleasure so exquisite I cried out aloud.

For a moment it was gone, and then was there again, brushing my thighs as it swam past my legs, then between them. It was such sweet relief to be finally touched, that I could not help but make space for it, as it nosed at the creases and folds of me.

And when it burrowed, snaking into my body's darkness, the force of my yearning for Taliesin broke open and I was lost in a shudder of pleasure so great that my legs buckled and I dropped fully beneath the water, where the fish kept on with his ways until I was thrown into such jolts of release that I felt I would never need air again.

I turned and tumbled. My legs reached for the river floor but could not find it. Still the fish was around me, within me. Which way was above and which was beneath? Pressure mounted in my chest as

I grew desperate for air. Then even the fractured moonlight ebbed away and I was surrounded only by blackness and water. I was weakening. I sensed the fish was still near but I could not feel him now, nor anything else. The darkness closed in and I started to sink.

Ceremony

In Ceremony, we are fully in accord with the Mothers.
In Ceremony, we are kin to the world.

WHEN I OPENED my eyes I was on the riverbank. My body was
bruised and strewn with tendrils of reed. A violent cough
brought silt water erupting from my stomach. Exhausted, I rolled
onto my back and looked up at the sky, pale and pink, through the
canopy of trees. The day was young.

I sat up. I had washed up on the opposite bank from where I had
entered the river, yet my robes were beside me. How had this come to
be? Had I lost my memory? It had to be so, although Taliesin and the
fish hung strikingly clear in my mind. I dressed quickly and walked
downstream, looking for a place to cross back. Cookmother would
have woken and I shuddered at the reprimand that awaited.

The sun broke into the forest, setting every wet leaf ablaze.
Although I was only across-river from a familiar path, there was a

strange otherness in the scene around me. All was as it should have been: wind on my skin, lark-song in my ear and grass at my thighs when I squatted to piss. But the colours were more vivid, the shapes more distinct, as though every tree, blossom and stone were proclaiming itself. I quickened my pace, keen to be free of the forest's magic.

Soon I had walked long enough that I should have been at the forest's edge, but I was still deep amid trunks. The shadows were shortening. Cookmother would be sending Bebin out to search.

At the next step I stopped. Once again, I smelled fire and heard faint voices drifting on the smoke. Was it the women? The outcasts? Perhaps they could guide me. Perhaps they would have some knowledge of Taliesin. I left the path and walked toward the voices. This time there was no river between us, no veil of smoke. This time I was on their ground. Cookmother had said they were women of violence. I had to go carefully.

I stopped just short of their clearing and watched from behind a wide beech trunk. Their fire was yet mightier than when I saw it first. The women walked a circle around its edge. Over the roar of the flames I heard their chant, rising in pitch as they completed three rotations and began in the opposite direction. Others worked bellows at the base of the fire, shouting to align their blows. Their arms were muscled and patterned with ash. They did not look like outcasts. They were as gracious as any women I had seen.

As the sun lifted over the trees their chant became louder. The fire surged and its radiant heat warmed my face as I peered from behind the trunk.

One woman stood on a raised platform, calling the chant. She must have been a journeywoman or some weaver of magic, for although her fleshform was only of moderate height she carried a glamour so tall I had to tilt my head to see her face.

Abruptly her magic receded and I saw her in her earthly scale. Her short hair was dark and woolly, her eyes like blades as they searched the forest. She lifted her hand to silence the women. 'Where are you?' she called into the open space.

My heart thumped as I drew behind the trunk.

'Show yourself.'

She was speaking to me. I stood frozen. I had no choice but to go forward. I emerged from the trees and walked into the clearing, bowing my head.

'Name yourself,' the woman called.

'Ailia,' I said to the ground.

'Address me by name.'

I looked up. Her eyes were upon me. 'Forgive me. I do not know your name.'

'Address me by name!'

I was faint with the fireheat and the fear I would condemn myself by this ignorance. I closed my eyes and drew deep breath. Without warning, there was a name at my lips that had formed itself outside my knowledge. 'Tara,' I murmured. Then louder so she could hear: 'Your name is Tara.'

She laughed a warm, throaty laugh and called me forward.

I approached warily, Cookmother's warning ringing in my ears, but when she thrust out her hand to be kissed, I was soothed by the touch of her. 'It is good to have a visitor,' she said. 'We were not expecting it. Take some milk, then join the work.'

'What work is being done?' I asked.

'We are strengthening the fire,' said Tara. 'Tonight, if the metals are willing, we pour a sword.'

Smithing was men's work in the town, sacred work, and I had heard only snippets of it from the crafthuts. How the favoured days for sword-pouring were few and how on such days the fire must burn long to trap the daylight, so the power of the sun itself would be captured in the sword. It was not craft for the unschooled and I told Tara I had no learning in it.

'Baah.' She waved me off. 'You have come. You will learn.'

One of the women took me to a hut, where she gave me a heavy leather tunic and a long horn of sheep's milk. 'How did you come?' she asked.

I thought of the fish and my thoughts clouded. 'I am not sure.'

Worry passed briefly over her face. 'Come. There will be time after the rite for the figuring of you.' She walked to the door.

'Please,' I said. 'Tell me who you are.'

The woman turned, frowning. 'Are you so unprepared? We are the makers of weapons.'

'Are you...outcasts?'

'No,' she said, bewildered. 'We keep the wisdom of fire.'

They were some class of journeywomen. But of which township? And why had Cookmother told me they were outcasts?

Outside the women had resumed their chant. I stepped into the circle, into the space they made for me. The chant was long and intricate and at first I could not voice even a word of it, but after some hours and many cycles it came as effortlessly as breath.

Thoughts of Cookmother and Cad faded as I circled and sang. These journeywomen admitted me to their ritual without skin. I should have protested it, but I did not.

Daylong we worked the fire. As evening came, I sensed the rising anticipation.

Tara called and two women left the circle, returning with a crucible that they set upon the pulsing embers. They left again and returned with pieces of copper and tin, metals that had not been used for swords in Cad for many summers.

The metals were given to the pot and the singing began in earnest. My voice was hoarse from chanting and my feet ached from the ceaseless walk, but now I saw that the day's work had been only a prelude to the true song. I opened my throat and let the sound flow out of me.

For many hours we walked, sang and waited, through the night, for the metals to shift their form. Each woman worked the bellows, swapping as they tired. I did my turn, resting my legs yet tiring my arms as Tara called us to raise the heat higher and higher.

Finally we saw the first sign of magic: the faintest reddening at the crucible's centre. The metals were changing. All our energies were renewed as the redness lightened to orange. Corners softened, peaks bent and spread in the base of the pot. We hastened our movement, strengthened our song.

'Watch as you walk!' called Tara. 'The colour will tell us when it is ready to take form. It must be pale like the sun.'

I did not know how long we continued to circle the bronze. It may have been minutes or hours. The night was lost to the ritual and I could not tear my gaze from the metal to look skyward for the moon's hour.

'Stop!' commanded Tara. 'Watch!' We all stared as a single bubble slowly birthed itself in the orange liquid, its languid beauty so miraculous that I began to weep as others were weeping. The sun's blood was in our pot.

'Now,' shouted Tara. 'Step back!'

Two women stood in wait with wooden paddles. They wore pads of sheepskin over their arms and chests. For the first time I noticed the earthen mould propped with sticks in a pit beside them. The two women stepped forward and lifted the crucible. A branch near the fire ignited.

'Quickly!' Tara called.

The bowl was brought to the mould. I feared it would spill. I had heard stories of smiths burned to death in this rite before.

The women positioned the crucible above the mould's small entrance. Others prepared smaller paddles to dam the charcoal that had flown into the bowl.

All of us were chanting loudly.

'Pour!' screamed Tara and the bowl was tipped. Molten metal ran from the crucible deep into the mould. The women howled in pain but they held firm to the paddles. The mould filled and the surface sank as the fluid settled into its shape.

'Again!' screamed Tara and the women prepared for a second pour. They had seconds before the bronze was too hard—already it moved more slowly.

'To the water!' cried Tara once the mould was filled. The women rushed it to a trough where the water boiled as the mould was plunged into it.

We were drenched in steam. The mould hissed and spat until the water worked its power and the sword was silent. The women whispered incantations to bless the bronze and hold the sun spirits within its form.

The first streaks of the new day coloured the sky as we gathered around the mould, which had been placed on the ground. With a small axe, Tara carefully broke it open and inside, too hot to touch, was a perfectly formed grey-yellow sword.

'We are blessed,' said Tara.

The sword was laid in a grove of oaks to rest and we went to the huts to sleep. For all the next day I lay between black lambskins in a dreamless oblivion that rested my aching body more deeply than it had been rested for weeks.

At evening time, we gathered around the embers, sipping sheep's milk and honey. I listened as the women chattered, their cheeks rosy and chafed from yesterday's fire. Of the twelve houses in the hutgroup, three were used for sleeping. The others, I was told, were forge-houses, store-houses and places for the design and blessing of weapons. They were simple huts, built in an old style of river stone and daub. There were still some of this type in the oldest streets of Cad.

Tara was not among us. They explained that she sat alone in communion with the sword and would return by tomorrow. One of the women replenished our horns with milk.

'Thank you,' I said as she poured mine. 'I will need the strength to face what awaits me at home.'

'Home?' said the woman who sat beside me, the same woman who had attended my arrival. Her name was Meb. 'Why do you speak now of home?'

'Why should I not speak of it?'

The others stopped talking and turned toward me.

'Do you know nothing of why you have come here?' continued Meb.

'No,' I whispered, my fingers tightening around my cup.

'You are here to learn. Only when you have learned will you be free to go home.'

My pulse quickened. 'And if I leave now?'

'You may try,' said Meb. 'But you will not be able to.'

I looked around at their strong and beautiful faces. I knew Cookmother and Bebin would be frantic by now, and that Fraid would never forgive such an absence, but it was as if I had drunk of the henbane, lulled by an assurance that all would be well. 'What, then, am I to learn?'

─

The next morning I awoke to see Tara beside my bed with the fresh-cast sword in her hand. 'Come,' she whispered.

I dressed and followed her to the forge-hut.

She placed the sword on a bench and began to work the blade with a piece of leather that had been coarsened with resin and river sand. It was a small sword, like the ancient weapons, barely two handspans long. A sword for use, not Ceremony.

She handed me a second piece of leather and showed me how to buff the bronze. The fine frill of metal around the blade edge, where the bronze had seeped into the tiny cracks at the mould-joins, had been chiselled off, along with the pouring cup at the sword's tip. 'Firm strokes, do you see? It will take a day to work it to a half-sheen, then we will form the cutting edge. Two more days buffing after that.'

'And then?' I asked.

'Then you will learn how to use it.'

I looked up, speechless. In Cad swords are made only for Elders and tribekings and only once in their lifetime. Even lesser warriors had to go to battle with arrows, knives and spears, so powerful were the swords. 'Is it to be mine?' I asked, unbelieving.

'Perhaps,' she said.

I rubbed the bronze in silence, lost in the fathoming of these events. It had been two nights since I met with Taliesin in the forest, or was it three? My sense of time was drifting.

'So let us begin,' said Tara, continuing to polish. 'What did you learn from the pouring of the sword?'

I opened my mouth then closed it, mute. It was wondrous and I was changed by it but I could not say what I had learned.

'Then answer me this,' she said. 'The tin that was dug from the ground and put over the fire. Does it now exist?'

I thought for a moment. 'No, it does not.'

'Yes, it does.' Her black eyes burned. 'It was changed by heat: deeply, irrevocably altered. But it still exists.'

I nodded, wanting more.

'This is the lesson of the fire. Form can be changed. Shape can be shifted. But nothing is lost.' She stroked the sword steadily. 'So it is with the human soul. It will pass through many births, many bodies, but the soul, like the cosmos, is indestructible. This is what feeds our courage. This is what is true.'

I set down my leather cloth and stared out the open doorway. The day would be cloudy. Tara's words led my thoughts to Taliesin, and I wondered if he had learned the lesson of fire. If he was nourished by this truth, as I was.

'Why do you cease?' asked Tara. 'Are you troubled?'

'No,' I shook my head. 'I am thinking of a knave I have met near here.'

'A knave?' She sounded surprised.

'Yes—of some height with dark hair.' I looked at her. 'Have you seen him? Do you know of whom I speak?'

Her strong brow furrowed. 'No,' she said. 'He has not come here. And it would not be well for him if he did. This is a women's place. Men are not permitted here. Men will not survive here.'

I was trained by Tara herself. We ate more flesh than I had ever eaten, we worked our bodies for all the hours of the sun. At night I slept, exhausted, by her side, more soundly than I had ever slept.

The sword that I had watched being created was made complete with a bone handle carved with secret messages. Every morning I trained in its use. Less the use of the weapon to render a kill (although this, of course, we learned), than the opening of my spirit to that of the sword, the summoning of the forces that had formed this weapon.

At highsun we ate, then I spent afternoons learning the art of the fight. I was taught to stand firm and draw spirit through my bare feet

144

into my task. I learned how the fury that possessed me when I came upon the slaughtered fawn could be harnessed to my will.

My skills blossomed. I parried with many tribeswomen, each bringing a different pattern to the battle's dance, and I learned to match and better them all. Three full moons passed in this learning. My mind became sharp and precise like the blade I swung, more alive than it had ever been. And Taliesin's presence was bright, as though my learning brought him close.

Yet when I thought of anything beyond him, beyond this gathering of women, my thoughts became veiled, as though I was recalling a dream. I asked the women many times, as we sat by the fire at day's end, where I was and why I had come, but they only chuckled at my confusion and wondered that I had not been better prepared.

What I dared not ask them of was skin. Like outcasts, they did not greet with it, they did not speak of it. I could only imagine that they assumed I was skinned, and I said nothing to correct them. For the first time—by some twist of grace—I was learning, and I would not endanger it for anything.

Eventually I asked nothing at all, because deep in my bones I knew where I was and why I had come. As my learning grew, I let myself think what I had not dared think, and hope what I have never dared hope: that these were neither outcasts, nor even journeywomen. These were the Mothers and I was walking among them. Not fleetingly, not by spirit, but by flesh. I was in the Mothers' realm. I had journeyed without skin.

I should have been frightened. But I was not.

Boundaries

The boundaries between realms are potent,
bound by many taboos.
Realms must align for souls to pass.

SUMMER WANED, REPLACED by a crisp autumn.

I sat polishing the sword beneath flame-leafed trees at the edge of the hutgroup, waiting to begin the morning's training.

Meb approached and I rose to meet her. 'There will be no training today,' she said.

'Why not?'

She paused. 'Today you will fight.'

I nodded and collected my polishing leathers. I had been told this would come. I knew I was to be matched with one of similar strength, perhaps a little stronger, as it should be a good fight, one to test my knowledge of swordcraft, my communion with the metal and, of course, my courage.

Meb was quiet as she prepared me in the sleep hut.

As she readied my washwater, she yielded no word of my foe. Surely they would not have me fight Mandua, who was like a she-wolf in battle, or Sirit, who could summon glamour almost as powerfully as Tara.

Meb bathed me and painted my skin with ground red stone. She was coiling the last of my braids when the horn call sounded.

Outside, the women had formed a circle. They parted so that I could enter, and waiting within—naked, with owl feathers in her hair and swirling patterns on her chest and face—was Tara herself.

I looked back at Meb, who nodded with encouragement.

They were testing me well in this match. So greatly did I honour Tara that I was already weakened. But I had been taught to fight, so I would fight.

I walked in, unsheathing my sword. Already the bone handle I had so lovingly polished felt like part of my body as I grasped it. We stood before each other, swords raised, as the women chanted the invocation to fight.

Mandua sounded a shrieking cry and the spark of combat ignited.

I took an instant to form strategy and Tara exploited it, her weapon whistling as it tore through the air. I lurched back, lifting my sword in a powerful block. The tone had been set: she would not win unchallenged.

She drove me back with three lateral swipes.

I struggled to parry them, sensing their position by the movement of wind as they descended. Then, in the split second she took to shape her next stroke, I lodged an attack: two sharp lunges that forced her retreat. Our audience took breath.

'Ha! The learner is bold,' she hissed.

I knew that at any moment she could enchant me and my terror would be too great. So I whipped the sword furiously before me, the clang of metal ringing in the air.

We locked eyes and I saw hers darken. I swiped into the space between us. In the next instant she loomed, her skin alight, so dazzling that I could not see her edge. Her strikes came one each side in a steady rhythm.

Blinded, I swung my sword wildly back and forth to protect myself, but I was beginning to stumble. 'Mothers, help me,' I called from my heart. The weapon grew warm in my hands. Time slowed. I paused, at great risk, to draw spirit through my feet. First of the earth, then yet deeper, fire.

Tara was upon me. I felt her sword's breath before its cut, painless at first, a clean slice, then a fierce sting as blood pulsed from the wound. It was long and bone-deep in my swordless arm. But I had drawn. Spirit was within me.

When Tara halted at the sight of my blood, I attacked with four driving swipes. She staggered back. All around us, the women shrieked, inciting us to fight without mercy. Tara's face was a grimace of rage as she swore and spat at my strikes.

But I was not angry. I was at peace.

My handle grew slippery with blood, but I drove forward with unwavering force until, with my fiercest blow, Tara lost her footing and was down on the ground. I straddled her with my sword at her chest. Though she was trapped beneath me, I feared her still. 'What am I to do?' I whispered. In training, fights finished with laughter and a shared piece of sheep cheese.

'Kill me,' she whispered. 'That is your task.'

I looked frantically to Meb, then to the women around me but no one disputed her command.

I turned back to Tara's fine face, her chest pounding under the point of my blade. Then I stepped away, casting my sword to the ground. 'If that is my task, then I have failed it. I will not kill without purpose.'

Tara rolled over then jumped to her feet with throaty laughter. 'Oh, you are good! We've not seen one such as you for some time.' She picked up the sword and handed it to me. 'This is yours. You have earned it. Now go to the healing tent and tend your wound. Then we will eat and drink for the last time. Tonight you leave us.'

Evening drew and the women led me to the mouth of the forest track that would carry me away from this place. Excitement danced in my belly as I glanced at the rising moon, as full and golden as the one that had carried me here.

I wore a woollen shawl and leather cloak over my own summer dress. Though my wound ached beneath its flax dressing, my muscles were hard from training and from the animal flesh I had eaten in such abundance. I was ready to face whatever my return to Cad would bring.

I embraced Meb and the other women in turn, until I came to Tara.

She kissed my cheeks, then held my sword out before her on flattened palms. 'This sword is our body. It is your body reborn. Carry with it the knowledge of fire.'

'Thank you,' I said, as I grasped it. It was weighty and warm like a living creature.

Tara met my eye. 'The sword will bend the world to your will, Ailia. But once it takes life, it will have no greater power than that. Do you understand?'

'Yes,' I nodded, although I could not fathom how it would serve me.

'Keep it well hidden until it is needed.'

I nodded again and strapped the sword, sheathed in leather, beneath my skirts. It was short and light enough that I could bind it to my thigh—a little awkward as I walked, but nothing compared with my pride in possessing it.

Tara handed me a torch and stepped away.

Suddenly I was frightened. 'How will I find my way back?'

'By our song.'

I went to query her but she silenced me.

Softly, the Mothers of fire began to sing. It was low at first, in unison, on deep, rolling breaths. Then it built, until song poured like water, filling the dusk. It spoke to me of all their wisdom, the gift of fire, and the birth of my learning. I began to walk. They were singing me out of their place and back into mine.

For several hours I walked, guided by their voices. As they grew fainter, the night air grew hotter. Eventually I stripped off my shawl and cloak, wedging them under my arm. When they became too cumbersome to carry, I left them behind on the path.

Finally I heard the voices no longer. My torchlight spluttered. I was at the forest's edge.

A dog barked. With a surge of joy, I burst free of the trees and there, to my disbelief, was Neha. I buried my face in the folds of her neck, drawing deep breaths of the crushed-grass scent of her fur. 'Were you waiting for me?' I marvelled. Surely she had not kept vigil since I entered the forest? I stroked her flank, but she was no thinner, and bore no sign of having lived wild. It was as though no time has passed.

The creamy moon lit our path back to Cad. By its height, the hour was not long past midnight. As I walked on, I imagined the words that I would tell Llwyd: that the Mothers had called me, that I was worthy of learning despite my skinlessness, and he must teach me at last.

After a short way I was sweating. It was yet warmer here beyond the forest. What strange autumn was this? The air was as hot and noisy with insect hum as it was when I left, a whole season hence. I stared around me. The crops were still thick in the fields and there were berries on the bushes that lined my path. There was something tilted here. I had been gone for several moon turns. At least the turn of the season. But I was returned to the scents and fruits of midsummer.

Had I slept in the forest and dreamed my passage? No, there was a wet bandage around my arm and the dull throb of the cut. And bound, chafing, to my thigh, was the sword I had been gifted. It had been no dream.

The sight of my hilltop town brought a wave of relief. For the first time since I had left, I yearned to see Cookmother and my worksisters. But with each step closer, my excitement gave way to dread. The lulling haze that had wrapped me as I trained with the Mothers was now truly lifted. I had no idea of what furies Cookmother would deliver, what Llwyd would say of my learning without skin. My boldness, my new strength, were ebbing away.

I stole through the gates and into the Tribequeen's compound. In the odorous heat, Cookmother, Bebin, Ianna and Cah were sleeping soundly. Cookmother was alone. It was odd that she had not called one of the others into her bed when I had been gone so long.

Then I noticed what was strangest of all. Spread across the floor was the same upturned basket and spilled barley that I had kicked as I left.

I stood paralysed, my mind reeling. I had returned to the same night that I left. Had they all been captured in some stillness of time? There had been some deep magic here and for the first time, far away from the light of the Mothers' fire, I felt sickened with fear for what I had done. It could not be right to have passed time in one place without time being spent in another.

I pulled off my sandals and lay beside Bebin, who stirred and murmured without waking. Despite my exhaustion, sleep would not come. What had happened was wrong. I had journeyed—this much I knew—but it should not have happened in this way. I had the journeywoman's gift but not the learning to support it.

How could I explain my months with the Mothers when there had been only a passage of one night? I would not be believed. Or I would be punished for walking where I was not permitted.

I could not ask Bebin, who had warned me, nor Cookmother, who had forbidden me. I was alone.

Steadiness

There are years of good harvest and years of bad.
We must not cling to our joy nor despair of our suffering.

I OPENED MY eyes to Bebin's face watching me as I slept.

'Tidings,' she whispered.

The morning was full of birdsong, yet the kitchen was still. 'Why have none risen?' I murmured.

'Do we not always lie late after festival?'

'Festival?' I asked, too drowsy to think.

Bebin frowned. 'Solstice, you goose. Are you still dreaming?'

'Of course,' I nodded, masking the jolt as it all returned to me. Though they had long since cooled in my memory, the solstice embers would still be warm on Sister Hill.

I rose to tend the fire. It was bewildering to be reunited with my worksisters when I had not seen them for many months, and yet to know that, by their reckoning, there had been no absence at all.

Cookmother did not protest it when I brought her goat's milk to sip in her bed, but nor did she thank me, and I knew I was not forgiven.

I joined Bebin at the fire as she prepared the breakfast. 'Tell me of the feast.' I urged. 'I'm sorry I did not help—'

She waved my apology away. 'It was lively,' she said, tipping meal into the cookpot. 'Fibor drank half a barrel and was asleep by highsun. And—' she glanced at me. 'There was news from Gaul.'

'Well or bad?'

'Mixed.' She stirred the porridge. 'The best of it is that there has been mutiny among the Roman forces.'

'The mighty Romans?'

'Yes!' she laughed. 'Plautius commanded the legions to board the ships but they refused, too frightened.'

'Of what?' I scoffed.

Bebin shrugged. 'Of us. Of Albion.' She scooped some water from a bucket beside the fire and poured it into the pot. 'They think this place is the edge of the world.'

I smiled. 'An army of field mice.'

We giggled together over the bubbling porridge. It felt good to laugh.

'What was the worst of the news?' I said, quieting.

'The numbers.' Her face grew still. 'The rider said that forty thousand soldiers, and as many horses, are gathered on the shores of Bononia. Two thousand ships wait in the tides, laden with grain and weapons.' She looked up from the pot.

Such numbers were beyond my imagining.

'If they do find their courage,' she said, 'then how will we defeat them?'

When I walked to the well after breakfast, Cah stood there, laughing with the strangemaid, Heka. The sight of them stopped me in my path. I had rarely ever seen Cah so at ease, so lost in her laughter. At the sound of my footsteps, they turned, and their smiles dropped away.

By late morning the sword had rubbed my thigh skin to an angry rawness. Desperate to ease it, I released the leather binding while the kitchen was empty for a moment, and buried the sword deep in my bedskins, where Neha proceeded to snuffle for it beneath the blankets.

'This will not do,' I murmured, pulling Neha off to fish it back out again. Glancing over my shoulder, I pushed aside Cookmother's rosewood chest, which covered the opening to the storepit below. Little was held there now and it was rare that Cookmother bade us enter it.

I dropped down on the wobbling stepladder into the chill of the dark chamber. It was barely tall enough for me to stand. In the light that seeped through the opening above, I could just make out a few grain pots, some old metal tools, and a mound of straw that would once have been bed to winter's smoked carcasses. I wrapped the sword in my leine and stashed it beneath the straw.

Cah entered the kitchen just as I was pushing the chest back over the opening. 'What are you doing?' She watched me from the doorway, clutching an armful of wood.

'Looking for a pot lid Cookmother has lost,' I murmured.

'Find it?' Her mind was sharp as flint. She walked to the woodpile. 'You are holding secrets—do not think I will protect them. You are favoured enough as it is.'

I crouched beside her as she stacked the logs. 'Why do you offer your friendship to Heka?'

Cah shrugged. 'She helps me with my tasks for nothing more than a cup of ale. And I like her. She has no one—no suck-mother to protect her—and yet she survives. She does not look down on me.'

I nodded, ignoring the jibe. 'Do you know what has brought her here?'

'No,' she said. 'She doesn't speak of it. She is a spirit that wanders. She follows pleasure and takes it heartily.' Cah stacked the last log and got to her feet. 'She did ask of you often when first she came. Though thankfully her interest seems to have waned.'

'She has cruelty in her nature, Cah,' I said, as she walked toward the doorway.

She turned briefly. 'Perhaps that is her strength.'

I sighed. 'Perhaps.'

I had greater concerns at this moment than Heka.

I was grinding wheat with Bebin after highsun when the doorbell sounded. We jumped to our feet as Llwyd entered.

'Be at peace,' he said, waving away our reverence. 'I come to speak to Ailia.'

Cookmother hurried my worksisters out of the roundhouse then busied herself at the cookpot.

'Might I be alone with her, Cookwoman?' Llwyd sat at the fire.

Cookmother eyed him, then ladled a large bowlful of porridge and set it with a clatter on the bench beside him. 'Of course.'

'Thank you, Cookwoman. Your graces are, as ever, enchanting,' he said with a faint smile as she trundled toward the door. He turned to me as I sat beside him. 'How do you fare, Ailia?'

'I...am well,' I faltered. Did he see change in me?

'I would speak of the warning in yesterday's fire.'

The memory, softened by the Mothers, was now knife-sharp here. 'Yes,' I said.

156

'It would seem that the Mothers have marked you,' he said slowly, 'to be woven, somehow, into the fate of this tribe. But I cannot understand the omen because you are without skin. You will never journey or even train.' He shrugged. 'I can make no sense of their intentions.'

He had opened a crack I could not let close. Before I could stop myself, I had reached for his hand and grasped it firm.

It was cold and bony and returned my hold.

My voice trembled. 'Journeyman Llwyd, honoured Elder, will you teach me?'

His grip tightened.

'I think there is knowledge in me.'

He nodded. 'I see it. And the fire saw it too. But without skin, you cannot be taught. You must learn within the fabric of your skin. This is what the Mothers require.'

They themselves have already taught me, I wanted to wail. But I was afraid to confess the warped shape my journey had made. If I wanted to go back to them I had to find a sanctioned way.

'And even more so because of the seer's prediction that blood will run,' he continued, 'we must show the most loving observance of the skin laws.' He frowned. 'Or they will not protect us.'

'From what?' I breathed, daring to ask what I had never been taught. 'What is the danger?'

He winced, as if struggling to resolve what should be spoken. 'It is not just our souls that are wrapped in skin,' he began. 'The hardworld itself is held in its layers. It is spirit skin that separates the realms and holds us intact. And if it is ruptured or torn, then the wound can infect and spread. Knowledge is the blood that sustains this skin, Ailia. Only knowledge holds the hardworld in place. If knowledge is breached, it will bring chaos and damage upon us all.'

My stomach lurched. I had made such a breach with my untrained journey. I knew I must never repeat it, and yet I could not go back to the darkness of life before I began to learn. I had to convince Llwyd to teach me. 'I am without skin, that is so, but Llwyd, there are other truths that mark me for learning.'

He frowned. 'Go on.'

You asked me once if I saw an animal,' I said, my thoughts racing. 'I did—a fish. A salmon attended me.'

He raised his chin. 'What else?'

'A geas,' I spilled, 'that I set and healed. It carried the weight of death.'

His breath caught. 'Is there anything else?'

The sword lay in the chamber beneath us. With a word I could tell him that I had walked with the Mothers and my learning was greater than he knew. But my unlawful journey had already wrinkled the seasons, and I was terrified to confess it. I shook my head.

'Upon these truths alone, you cannot be trained,' he said, 'but if there was more evidence of your knowledge,' he urged, 'then perhaps, Mothers willing, the Isle would take you.'

'The Glass Isle?' I whispered. 'Could it be so?'

'I have never known a skinless woman to be trained, but if the knowledge gift was strong enough, then teachers of the Isle may want to shape it...' He gripped my fingers until they ached. 'Show me more, Ailia, and I will call Sulis.'

I nodded, blood pounding in my head. Llwyd saw knowledge in me. There would be more. I would find a way to show him.

'But please—' his voice wavered, '—you must not go near the sacred places, especially the Oldforest, when you are untrained. You could bring great injury to the tribes.'

I stared at the bone talismans that hung from his belt and hoped he could not see my chest thumping beneath my dress.

He looked at me, reading me. '*Have* you, Ailia? *Have* you breached the forest's edge?'

'Most certainly not,' cried Cookmother, bustling back. She must have heard every word. 'I've not let her slip from my view since—'

'Since what?' said Llwyd.

She stood at the hearth, her arms folded across her chest. I knew she was thinking of my first sighting of the Mothers.

'Since...the early harvest,' she stammered. 'There's nothing in it, Llwyd. She's a kitchen girl, nothing more. She's of no more consequence to the fate of this tribe than the mice in the kitchen.' She picked up her ladle and churned the porridge, flicking scalding droplets onto my forearm.

'Which can be of great consequence, as you know, if they get into the grain pits,' said Llwyd. 'It is not my way to command your honesty, but it is your conscience upon which it will rest if you are wrong.'

'Do you say that I lie, wiseman?' Cookmother snapped.

'No. But we both know that you have cause to.'

A burning silence flared between them and for a moment I was forgotten.

Cookmother stirred the pot as though it was a hide needing beating and Llwyd stared, unmoving, at the fire.

My eyes darted from one to the other, unable to fathom this tension between them.

Finally, Llwyd turned back to me. 'The Oldforest?' he repeated.

I looked up at Cookmother. Her rigid jaw revealed a fear I had never seen before. My thoughts raced. Cookmother knew that I had walked the forest and yet she was determined it should not be revealed. It was difficult to lie to Llwyd, but it was Cookmother in whom I trusted. I shook my head.

Llwyd sighed and the lines scored in his cheeks seemed to deepen. 'I hope it is so,' he said.

I shifted on the bench, my thigh still smarting from where the sword had been bound.

Llwyd stood to leave. 'Do not breach the forest's edge, Ailia. Do not weaken what protects us.'

I nodded, vowing in my heart that I would not defy him. I would not risk harm to the souls of the tribespeople. I prayed that it was not too late.

When Llwyd had left, Cookmother stood before me, her cheeks flushed with anger. 'I repeat what I have told you,' she said. 'If you step once more into the forest you will not sleep in this kitchen again. You will not be my work daughter.'

I nodded, stunned by her threat.

Then with a sob, she lurched forward and took me in her arms. I rested my head on the fat-stained breast of her cooking tunic and, for the first time since I was much smaller, she rocked me and sang my childhood song:

> *Ailia Ay,*
> *Ailia Oh,*
> *Through shadowed lakes we travel,*
> *To land's deep heart we go*

As she stroked my arm she found the bandage around my fight wound. Wordlessly, she unwrapped it. 'Why do you bandage this perfect skin?'

I looked down. My arm was unscarred. Already my knowledge was receding. Without answering, I rested my head back on her chest. Perhaps I would have to accept that this seed was not destined to fruit. I could speak of it with no one in Caer Cad. There was only one to whom I could confess my journey, and I had vowed not to enter the place where he waited. If I wished to meet with Taliesin again, I would have to find a way to call him to me.

Early next morning, I was returning with bread when Neha streaked ahead, darting behind the kitchen. A hare? I wondered. There was a flood of barking before she bounded back, snapping at my skirts and bidding me come.

'I don't want to see your kill,' I chided, shooing her away.

But she kept up her barking until I followed.

When I turned into the narrow pathway behind the kitchen, it was not a hare carcass I found, but Heka, sitting on her haunches with a torn piece of linen and a small pot of beeswax on the ground before her.

She looked up at me, her face triumphant. Across her lap, one hand rubbing its blade and the other grasping its handle, lay my bronze sword.

My fingers tightened around my basket. 'How did you get this?'

'Cah asked me to order the store pit and I found it hidden there. I thought it was so pretty I would clean it. For its lucky owner.'

Neha yapped relentlessly at the weapon.

'Hush!' I hissed, crouching before Heka. 'Has anyone seen it?'

'No,' she said. 'I kept it out of sight as I wanted to attend to it myself.'

'Not even Cah, who bade you?'

'Only me. Why do you ask? It could not be yours.' Her feigned innocence chilled me. 'Swords cannot be held by those without skin.'

'You know that it is.' How did she seek and find what was most precious to me?

Footsteps passed just beyond the curve of the kitchen wall. 'Give it to me, Heka, and speak of it to no one.'

'For what reward?' she said.

'What is your price?' I spluttered. 'Coin? Food?'

She leaned back against the kitchen wall, savouring her moment. 'Coin, for now, enough that I need not find work for a moon turn or two,' she said, 'and some of the honey cakes that Bebin has just put into the oven.'

'Yes, yes,' I gasped, giddy with relief that the sword would not be exposed.

She stood, letting it fall to the ground, and kicked it toward me.

I stared at her, confused by her trust. 'How do you know I will honour my promise?'

'I do not like you,' she said, 'but I know that you are true.'

I snatched up the sword and stowed it beneath my shawl. 'Wait here until I can procure Cookmother's purse,' I said. 'And when you have coin will you be gone from this kitchen?'

'For now,' she said. 'Ugh, you bleed!' Recoiling, she pointed to my arm.

I looked down. Fresh blood streamed down my elbow. The cut had opened again.

'A fight wound!' Her eyes blazed.

'No...' I said. 'A carving wound.' With my hand pressed around it, I hurried away, calling Neha to my heel. I had to be on my guard with Heka. She was cleverer and more poisonous than I had realised.

Virtue

Pain is not evil. Nor suffering. Nor death.
The only evil is moral weakness.
The strongest weapon against it is knowledge.
Learning is the root of all virtue.

THE SUMMER HARVEST came. I did the same work I had always done—the milling and storing of the Tribequeen's grain, the fleecing of sheep—but I was not the same woman. I was feigning contentment, sitting by the fire each evening with my work-sisters, attending their riddles and gossip, when the whole of my being yearned to proclaim what I had learned.

I became practised at wearing the sword, releasing it deftly as I undressed for bathing, disguising it in my skirts and refastening it by touch, so that no one could see. It stayed bound to me always, even as I slept.

My hunger for skin endured, sharpened. With skin, I could be trained to journey to the Mothers with full sanction. With skin I could return Taliesin's skinsong. The sword—which rubbed my thigh to rawness, to weeping sores, then finally thick calluses—was useless without skin.

It was one moon after midsummer. I was sweeping the floor of the grain hut when I heard the bell announcing visitors to the Great House. At the sight of the horses tethered outside, I flew to the kitchen.

'Quick, give me bread and an ale pot,' I commanded Bebin, brushing clean my skirts. 'Uaine and Ruther are returned!'

Bebin loaded my tray with loaves and a jug and bade me send Uaine to her when their business was finished.

The benches in the Great House were draped in gleaming, sky-hued fabrics, fragrant with spice. Boxes spilling with gems were spread over the silks and Fraid sat tall in a white gossamer shawl, clusters of green stones cascading from each ear. 'Ailia,' she called, 'come and help me with these trinkets.'

Sitting by the fire, his hair cut short and face shaved like the merchants of the First City, was Ruther. His eyes turned to me as I entered, yet bluer against his sun-darkened skin.

I set down the tray and walked to Fraid, feeling Ruther's gaze hot upon me. Uaine was beside him, and opposite them both, with no interest in the eastern finery, sat Llwyd. He smiled briefly as I passed.

Fraid held up her mirror as I fastened a snake-shaped clasp around her neck. 'These are beautiful, Ruther.' She turned her cheek. 'How does it stand at the coast?'

'They are ready to sail,' said Ruther. 'This is why we return. We have passed close to the Roman camp, and learned much of their intent.'

Fraid put down her mirror. 'We know they wish to subdue Caradog—but surely they do not look to the peaceful tribes?'

'It would be false comfort to think so,' said Ruther. 'They want the isle of Albion in its entirety. This is Claudius's goal.'

I stood behind Fraid, staring at Ruther. Was it only I who read the trace of excitement beneath the concern in his face?

Fraid motioned me to unfasten her neckpiece. 'We are not his war trophy.'

'But he would have us be,' said Ruther. 'And this, I know, is not all, Tribequeen.'

I sensed the blood quickening under Fraid's skin as I unclasped the metal.

'Speak,' she said.

Ruther's gaze flickered to me before returning to Fraid. 'Durotriga is of particular interest to the General Plautius. Our tribelands are fertile and rich in metal.'

Fraid paused before responding. 'I don't see how any of this can be true,' she said. 'There have been several riders from the east telling us that Plautius commanded them to embark but they were too terrified of our tides and would not board their ships.'

'Such a mutiny occurred, yes,' said Ruther. 'But the Emperor sent Narcissus to stand before them. He is a great speaker. He countered their fears with reason. They are once again ready to sail.'

'When?' asks Fraid.

'Within days.'

She stared into the fire. 'So it is war.'

I stood, motionless behind her, watching Ruther's eyes jump from her to Uaine, then back again.

'Is this the only way, Tribequeen?' said Uaine carefully.

Fraid looked to him. 'Clearly you think not. Speak.'

'If they are seeking to expand their territory, it is to their advantage for local leaders to remain in place,' said Uaine. 'Rome will offer client kingships, generous kingships, to those tribekings who do not oppose them.' He paused. 'Many of the eastern kings are already planning such negotiations.'

Was it the draft from the doorway that made the hairs on my neck rise?

'This is not the way of the Durotriges,' said Fraid.

'Wait,' Llwyd raised his hand. 'What would this mean?'

'Foremost an arrangement of revenue,' said Ruther. 'Taxes paid to the Empire in metal and slaves and an allegiance to Claudius. Beyond this, freedom. To live as we have always done.'

I startled as Llwyd broke into a loud laugh.

'Do I amuse you, wiseman?' said Ruther, frowning.

'I laugh at your knowledge of freedom,' said Llwyd. 'Tell me, by what laws do we live in these client kingships?'

'For the most part, tribal law is upheld.'

'But ultimately?' said Llwyd.

Ruther's lips tightened. 'We would be held within the protection of Rome.'

Llwyd nodded. 'Within the Empire, laws are strictly enforced, are they not?'

'The penalties for disobedience are indeed strict,' said Ruther. 'The law is strong.'

'And upon this law rests the virtue of Roman citizens?'

'Yes. For fear of death,' said Ruther.

I shifted on my feet, sensing the conflict seeding between them.

'And yet the city is strewn with criminals,' said Llwyd. 'I hear they run like rats in a drain. Fouling the water.'

'There is virtue and order in the city of Rome that Britain is yet to know,' said Ruther, bristling. 'Great cities cannot be built upon chaos.'

'I agree,' said Llwyd. 'Chaos will always prevail.'

Ruther frowned, shaking his head. 'I am lost by your Journeyman's reckoning. Speak plainly, wiseman, if you wish to be understood.'

I flinched at his treatment of his journeyman Elder. There had been a hardening in him since I last saw him.

Llwyd rose and stood closer to the hearth. His skin was made smooth, youthful, by the firelight.

'As you know well,' he began, 'in this isle of light we live by the laws of skin.' He fingered the sprig of mistletoe that hung from his belt. 'Those who truly know the laws will love them. The order of Albion is freely consented. Taught. Not enforced. Whoever does not comply by their own judgment is not virtuous, but captive. Teach what is true, then allow each soul its choice. This is freedom. This is virtue.'

And what of those who cannot learn? I ached to ask. Where is their freedom? Where is their virtue?

'Thank you,' Ruther's voice was cold, 'for your illumination. But wise words will not win a war. Tribequeen—' he turned to Fraid, '—despite these compelling discussions of freedom, the Romans will come, and we will fare better if we meet them with some willingness to make terms. If we resist them, they will take their desire by force—and on that count we cannot match them.'

I stared at him. This was not the warrior's way. There was something he sought to gain in this.

Fraid turned to Llwyd. 'I have heard your protest, Journeyman, and understand it. Still, Ruther's advice must be considered, if the legions do indeed reach our borders. Do you agree?'

Llwyd stood at the hearthstones, his voice low. 'If you submit us to their laws, Fraid, you will destroy us.'

'Do you rather we fight a battle we cannot win?' said Ruther without patience.

Llwyd lifted his face, his voice now strong. 'With the Kendra's blessing, we will win.'

Ruther snorted. 'Of what Kendra do you speak?'

'She will come,' said Llwyd.

'You are waiting for the past,' said Ruther.

I gasped and Fraid hushed me.

Llwyd did not respond.

The room rang with the clash of their minds.

'I will summon the council to meet tonight,' said Fraid. 'You will attend, Ruther, and we will discuss the news you have brought.'

'Ailia!' Ruther held out his cup. 'I am empty.'

I took the jug to him. As I poured, he slipped his hand beneath my skirt, trailing his fingertips over my calf. Though I angered at his claim of me, my blood coursed at his touch. 'There is something else you must both consider in relation to the intentions of Rome,' he said to Fraid. In a moment he would know my sword. I pulled away and returned to my place.

'Speak,' said Fraid.

'Romans do not judge their women as we do here,' said Ruther.

'Yes,' Fraid scoffed. 'I have heard they do not head tribes or fight...'

'Nor choose their leaders,' said Llwyd.

'Not publicly, at least.' Uaine laughed.

'The wives exert power enough,' said Ruther. 'But not to command soldiers. I've heard them mocking the tribes that are led by queens: the Brigantes, the Iceni. And us. To their minds, these are weak targets. Easiest to destroy.'

'If women are so poorly esteemed,' said Llwyd, 'then how is their knowledge heard in statecraft?'

'Beyond bedchamber politics, it is not,' said Ruther.

'There are virgins,' countered Uaine, 'the Vestels, who keep the fires. They are always present at state ceremony.'

'Virgins?' Fraid snorted. 'What do virgins know of the power of the Mothers?'

'Little,' Ruther laughed. 'In this matter, the women of Britain are greatly superior. But we are already a target, due to the fortune of our geography,' he continued. 'To be led by a queen makes us yet more vulnerable.'

'So you suggest a change of leadership,' said Llwyd, 'to address this problem?'

'Without doubt a tribeking would present a more daunting opponent to Rome,' said Uaine.

This man loved Bebin, I mused. How could he question the Mothers' strength? Was it Rome that infected him, or Ruther?

'It may favour our hopes, Fraid,' said Ruther, 'if you were to hand the leadership to another.'

Fraid's shoulders stiffened.

'Fraid is our chosen consort to these tribelands,' said Llwyd. 'Deeply loved.'

'I acknowledge it so.' Ruther bowed his head. 'I think only of the tribe.'

'And who should replace me?' asked Fraid. 'I have no sons. We both know my brother's temper is too poorly restrained.'

'Perhaps you suggest that we select from the other high warriors, Ruther?' said Llwyd. 'Or their sons?'

'I make no campaign,' said Ruther to Fraid. 'My loyalty is sworn. I merely bid you think on this and exploit me, if it serves you. I have rank and friends in Rome. I am in a strong position to negotiate when I return to the east.'

None spoke.

My eyes were fixed on the plush hide at my feet. I was rocked by the pride in Ruther's petition and by the dawning reality of this attack.

'Thank you, Ruther,' said Fraid, standing, 'for your information and advice. But I am Tribequeen of Northern Durotriga. Whether we fight them or submit, it will be under my rule.'

My heart swelled with love for her.

I returned to the grain hut after Fraid had dismissed me and it was here that Ruther found me when the day was late. He approached my turned back, winding his arms around my waist without a word of greeting. I knew him by the scent of his sweat and foreign cloth.

'Come walking with me,' he urged.

'I am not finished here.'

'Yes, you are.' He pulled me by my hand toward the door. 'I am sure I could have the Tribequeen's pardon if you need it.'

'And Cookmother's?' I snatched my hand away. 'Gain her permission and I will walk with you.'

He sighed. 'Where is she?'

'The kitchen, I expect.'

'Wait here then.' He strode out the door.

I swept the sheaves that had fallen to the floor. I had not expected Ruther's interest to endure his journey, and I had to find a way to tell him I was no longer free. My hope for Taliesin was fruitless, but the months of separation had not lessened my wanting of him.

Ruther pushed back through the doorway, smiling broadly. 'You have the Cookwoman's blessing to walk with me.'

I set my broom down, surprised. 'She's not let me walk for weeks. How did you gain it?'

'As I always gain what I wish.'

I shoved his thigh with the broom end for his arrogance.

We walked through field lanes to Sister Hill, talking all the way. There was no danger of silence with Ruther. He regaled me with tales of mishaps from his travels. How Uaine's horse, weary with heat, and with full packs upon it, mud-rolled to cool itself in a bog and Uaine had to ride naked for a day while his tunic dried. How, lighting candles in their Roman guesthouse, their man attendant set his beard alight and had to douse it with the pisspot.

I laughed freely and it was easy between us, despite his long absence, despite another's claim of my heart.

As we climbed the slope our conversation quieted and I was

sure he was remembering, as I was, the Beltane night we spent here. Breathless, we sat down at Sister's summit, looking westward toward the dusky township. The days were beginning to shorten and a cool breeze rolled up from the valley. Ruther leaned on one elbow to face me. 'Have you been feeble with the want of me?'

I laughed. 'Not in the slightest way.'

'Good then,' he said, 'nor I for you.'

I glanced at him. 'You have cut your hair like a man of the Empire.'

'Better in the heat,' he said. 'You prefer me with clansman's hair and beard?'

'I prefer you neither way. I only make an observation.'

Now it was he who laughed. 'Ailia, I've missed your tender ways.'

'You seem to have found your comforts in Rome.'

'Jealousy becomes you,' he said, eyes shining.

'I meant the city,' I said quickly. 'It sounds like it has ensnared you further.'

'I am willingly trapped,' he said. His face softened. 'I wish I could show you, Ailia. It is an otherworld—'

I touched my finger to his lips to silence him. 'Enough. You already look half-Roman, now you sound it, too. The tribespeople will begin to doubt your loyalty. Especially when you make claims for the Tribeking's crown.'

He shook his head. 'I am a loyal clansman, Ailia,' he insisted. 'I love this country and I wish to see it prosper as I have seen other lands prosper. The wiseman, Llwyd—' he grunted in frustration.

'Hush,' I chastised. 'He is our Journeyman Elder—'

Ruther exhaled heavily. 'But he cannot see beyond the old ways. He sees the Empire only as a threat, but perhaps it is a gift.' He turned to me. 'The Romans will bring their crafts, their villas, their roads, their waterways, their fightcraft. There is so much that will be gained—for those with the eyes to see it.'

'But will not the gains be paid heavily in losses?' I asked.

'What will be lost?' he said. 'Our mud huts? Our buckets?'

I stared at him in shock. 'Is your tribesman's learning so faded? I am untaught yet even I know what will be lost. The most important thing: they will not cherish the laws of skin.'

He met my gaze. His eyes were like a summer sky. He would have been the finest of men had I not known another finer.

'How are you so loyal to what has abandoned you?' he asked. 'In Rome, there are so many different gods and ways to worship them, that no one even asks of your totem. Skin is what can be touched on your cheek. Nothing less or more. You are your word and your deed and you are judged so. Does such a world not appeal to you, Ailia?'

I did not answer. A world without skin terrified me. Where were its roots? How was it fed?

Ruther shifted in the silence. He seemed to be searching for words. 'You are a servant woman of unknown parentage.'

'Cleverly observed.'

He smiled. 'Do you dream of something more?'

For what was he digging? 'I am not wanting.'

'You are not wanting of your own house, a marriage bed, fine jewellery?' As he spoke he was fishing in his belt pouch and finally pulled out a gold pendant, tear-shaped in the Roman style. He laid its chain over my bent knee like a small, glittering snake. A dark red stone sat like a bead of blood at its centre.

'What is this?'

'A gift.'

'I cannot wear such a gift. What would my worksisters think?'

He rolled back his shoulders and spoke to the horizon. 'They will think you are first consort to Ruther, son of Orgilos, High Warrior of Cad.'

My mouth dropped open in surprise.

Swinging around to kneel before me, he gripped my shoulders. 'This is what I offer you,' he said. 'Leave the Tribequeen's kitchen and come to my house. You will travel with me and share my bed until I marry—and beyond.'

My thoughts spun. He had offered me servitude before, but not to stand, as honoured companion, at his side. I would see the Eastlands of which he spoke. I would draw yet closer to the knowledge of statecraft that he commanded. But I would never see Taliesin again.

'Why do you not answer?' he pushed. 'Surely such a bond to a high warrior is a future greater than you have ever imagined.'

My anger rose. Indeed his offer should delight any woman without skin, but who was he to define the limits of my hopes? 'No greater or lesser than any future lived by the laws of the Mothers.'

He warmed to my anger like it were fire, taking my face in his hands and kissing me greedily. Heat surged through my body at his touch. Like fat in a cookpot, I could not hold my shape.

'You have grown more womanly, more beautiful, in even this short time,' he whispered.

'I am no great beauty,' I scoffed, drinking his kisses like water.

'Yet you bewitch me still.' He grasped at my belt.

I braced my hands on his chest to hold him back. 'Ruther—'

He silenced me with a more determined kiss.

'Ruther!' I insisted, 'please steady this.'

'Why do you parry me?' he asked, frowning. 'Has there been another since I have left?'

I went to answer but the words would not come. I had not yet lain with Taliesin. There had been no bond made. I did not know if there would ever be.

Ruther's hands were upon me and under my robe. My mind protested his free admittance to my breasts and thighs, but my body knew a different logic, filling with blood and warmth where he touched. My hunger for Taliesin gathered and hardened at the chance of release. I would betray both men in this and yet I had promised nothing to either. Taliesin had my heart but he would not lay claim to my flesh. Right now this was Ruther's and I gave it freely.

'Wait,' I whispered. I tugged off my cloak as he untied his belt. Then, with his mouth at my throat, I loosened my sword from my leg and hid it, one-handed, under my cloak. 'It may be the time for seeding me,' I whispered into his hair. 'So spill outside. A babe now will not be well timed.'

'I will spill outside,' he assured me.

My hip grazed raw against the pebbly ground, this time there was little gentleness in it. We coupled frantically, violently, on the hillside, each taking our fill of the other. I looked up to the night's first stars as he moved above me. It was not a joining, but a feeding, and afterwards, as I lay with my head on his chest, my body was sated but my heart was even emptier.

Ruther wrapped his thick arm around my shoulder. 'I take this as your agreement,' he murmured.

'No,' I said before I could stop it. Quickly, I softened my refusal. 'You flatter me too much. I must take some time, to know if I can step up to such an honour.'

The muscles of his chest stiffened. 'I will give you one night. Not a moment longer. By tomorrow, market day, I want your answer.'

Only after darkness fell that night did I recall the pendant, which must have slipped, forgotten, to the grass.

—

We were back just in time for the meeting of council. It was still warm enough to gather outside. The discussion was lively with the new threat to Durotriga.

I heard scattered talk as I went back and forth to the kitchen, replenishing platters of oatcakes and jugs of ale. But as the moon crept high and the voices rose, I stalled in the darkness to listen.

'I cannot see their purpose in pursuing these tribelands,' said Fraid. 'We have been ready partners in trade. They skim the cream of this country without the burden of administering it. What do they truly seek?'

'The Empire is a living beast.' Ruther sat opposite Fraid in the visitor's place. He had dressed in his clan tartan to meet with the councillors and looked like a tribesman again. 'It follows the urge of all life: to grow. Now it would feed on this rich ground. The question is, can we turn its hunger to our advantage?'

'Or should the beast be slain?' Fibor's voice was a growl.

Amid the rumble of agreement, Llwyd rose beside Fraid. 'Today Ruther has suggested that we submit to the rule of Rome.'

I flinched at his naked account.

Llwyd waited for the murmurs to subside, before he continued, bracing himself on his staff. 'Let me answer that suggestion. Ruther speaks of growth,' he began. 'None understand the forces of growth more deeply than the tribes of Albion. In all that we do, every blessing we call, every bowl of milk we cast upon the ground, every time we lie down in the fields at Beltane, we proclaim that the Mothers are fruitful. Their fertile bodies are our country and our knowledge is the seed that ripens them. Without our rituals, their milk will dry, their wombs will wither, and their song will not be heard. We do not ask of the Mothers more than what they are able to renew. Rome's hunger cannot be met. It should not be met. We do not submit to Rome.'

I clutched my jug, quenched by his words.

Most of the councillors were nodding, united in our Journeyman's wisdom. Most but not all.

'Should we not at least consider what Ruther tells us?' said Etaina.

'After all, he has been where we have not.'

'I still say they are too fearful to breach our shores,' said Fibor. 'Let them first come and then we will talk of clientage.'

'I agree,' called Orgilos, Ruther's own father. 'If their fear of this island is so great that it caused four legions to mutiny, it will take more than one man's speech to quell it.'

The council murmured its agreement.

'You are in a world of dreams if you think they will not come, Father,' said Ruther. 'And if you think we can fight them when they do.'

Fibor's mouth twitched. 'Ruther, you believe they are the light of the world.'

Ruther met his gaze. 'If you saw their cities, you would agree with me.'

'Enough!' Fibor jumped to his feet. 'He praises our enemies! He calls for our submission! This will not be tolerated.' He drew his sword.

I took a few steps back. It had to come to this. None sought to stop it.

Both men moved clear of the circle and Ruther drew.

They fought briefly, skilfully, the moonlight catching their flying blades. Fibor was one of our finest swordsmen but it seemed only moments before he was down on his back, Ruther's blade at his throat, while his own lay struck to the ground.

Etaina helped her husband to his feet, praising Ruther for sparing his life.

I gathered the cups as the councillors readied to leave in silence.

None would speak against Ruther now.

I recounted all of the day to Bebin, huddled deep in her bedskins, where no one could hear us. When I had described every detail of

Uaine's costume, his beard and his bearing, I told her of Ruther's desire that I come to his service.

'Show caution,' she counselled. 'The honour of the tribes is slipping from him.'

But she need not have worried. I already knew what I would do.

The Earth

The earth receives all seeds, all ideas.
The earth is our bridge to truth.

STORM CLOUDS GATHERED the next morning and there was talk of heavy rains. Ianna was my companion to market as Bebin was waylaid skinning a goat. I was glad of it, for Bebin would have proved a greater barrier to what I had determined must happen this day.

The stalls were abundant with late summer fruits, and the crowds were anxious to find the best of them before they turned. 'Pears or apples? Which should be sweeter?' mused Ianna, bent over the baskets.

'It could not concern me less,' I snapped.

She looked at me in surprise. 'I would have thought I stood with Cah.'

'Forgive me,' I sighed. I picked out some pears and put them in my basket. The sky darkened. This was my moment. 'Ianna, by the look of the clouds there is not much time until they open. Perhaps you should finish choosing the fruit and I will search for Cookmother's powders?'

'She told us to stay together. She told me to keep you in my sight.'

'But we will be soaked through if we are not quick,' I urged. 'I won't be far. I'll make rose cakes this afternoon,' I added desperately, 'and you can have the first one.'

She nodded hesitantly and before she could change her mind, I took my basket and strode down the tradeway, ducking from sight so she could not follow. I walked through the medicine sellers, where the crowds were thinner, then out of the stalls and down to the Cam, unsettled under the grey sky.

Alone finally, I stood close to the bank, feet firm on the grass, and began to breathe as I was taught by the Mothers of fire, to focus my will, to draw from the veins of spirit that flowed beneath me. It was hard to concentrate with the sound of the sellers in the distance and the knowledge that at any moment I might be discovered. But I stood tall and deepened the call of my breath, and soon the familiar quiver in my hands and legs told me I had awoken the forces that I sought.

'Taliesin,' I whispered into the heavy air, 'come.'

Water lapped at the banks. Nothing else moved.

Taliesin had come to me beyond the forest before. Never this far from its edge, it was true, but perhaps, if my call was strong enough, he would reach me. And if he did not, then I would know he was lost to me and Ruther could have his desire, for I could not breach the Oldforest again.

'Taliesin,' I whispered again with all my strength. A long rumble of thunder rolled over the fields, stirring the air with its charge. I glanced to the horizon and, when I turned back, Neha was bounding upstream, where a figure crouched at the bank.

The pears from my basket fell to the ground as I ran. 'By the Mothers,' I murmured into the folds of his shirt. 'You are here.'

179

We clung to one another, without words, until my heart felt it would break with happiness. 'You are breath to me,' I sighed, now shuddering at the thought of Ruther's offer. Even if I never saw him again, I could love only Taliesin.

He smiled in response but his luminous eyes were ringed with shadows. He was thinner than I remembered. I curled my fingers around his forearm. It was cold, the sinews and muscles almost visible through his delicate skin. 'You are unwell—'

'No, I—' His words caught.

'I have little time.' I glanced back to the stalls.

He gave a despondent laugh. 'Be assured you have longer than I do. It may only be moments until—'

'Until what?' I urged.

He looked to the ground.

'No! Do not turn away from me. Now you must speak, Taliesin. There is no more time for mystery. Tell me how you are caught and why you cannot walk here freely—quickly, before I am called away.'

He shook his head. 'There is nothing to be gained in the telling of it.'

'You are more stubborn than a goat! I will not endure another day of this. I am living an agony without you. And now I am wanted by a man of high birth, who offers me more than any woman without skin may hope for. And I would shun it all for you—who offers me nothing!'

'Take it, Ailia. Take his offer.'

I felt my face crumple. 'Why do you urge me so?'

'Because we cannot help each other. I thought we could but we cannot. We will only cause each other sorrow in the attempting of it, and there has been enough of that. Without skin you can never come.'

'But you are wrong!' I cried. Thunder rolled, louder now, and the market sellers began to call the day's close. I clutched his wrists, damp with a cold sweat. 'Taliesin, I have *been* to your place. I have walked with the Mothers.' I almost sobbed with the relief of speaking it.

He stared at me. 'It is not possible.'

'It is true,' I said. 'They have taught me the fighting arts and given me this.' I pulled up my skirts to reveal the bone handle above the sword's leather sheath.

Taliesin reached out, brushing the skin of my thigh, then the sword with his fingertips. He paled as he stared into my face, then light stirred in his black eyes. 'You have journeyed.'

'Yes,' I said, half laughing, half crying. 'I have the journey-woman's gift.'

Then he was kissing my face and shaking his head in disbelief. 'I knew it was so,' he murmured. 'I knew you would come. Now you will be trained, you will come again...'

'No.' My smile fell away. 'I am not to be trained. I have told no one of this. I cannot. The turn of the seasons fell askew when I returned. Winter was as summer. I have been warned that a skinless journey can cause immense harm to my people.' Now it was I who looked to the ground. 'I have been too afraid to confess it.'

He lifted my face with his hands. 'You have been called by the Mothers. It is greater harm if you deny them.'

'I hear their call, Taliesin. I hear it and feel it, but I do not have enough learning to answer it.'

'Precious girl.' He pressed his cool lips to my temple. 'You must not be frightened. You must tell your Tribequeen and your wisepeople. You must train so that you can journey again. For my sake, you must.'

'Why?' I asked.

The darkening sky flashed with light.

'So that you can bring me home.'

I watched, frozen, as the skin of his brow moistened with a slick sweat and began to blister into a ridged texture before my eyes. 'What ails you?' I gasped.

'I cannot hold myself here any longer.' He was shivering, his very breath struggling to come. 'There are only moments left.'

'How...how will I tell them?' I was frantic.

'Your knowledge will tell them. The Mothers will call you again and when they do, do not deny them—' his eyes began to glaze, '—show yourself.'

'Ailia!' Ianna's voice was shrill in the distance. 'Where are you?'

'Hurry.' I wrapped my arms around his neck. 'Kiss me for luck.'

Rain broke on our faces as I swam in his kiss.

For three days and nights the skies opened. The riverways filled and spilled their banks. Our drain channels flooded and water seeped through the thatch on our roofs. Our bedding was sodden and nothing could dry.

Cookmother took ill with the damp. I tended to her constantly, refusing to see Ruther, who came several times to our door. He left Cad for Rome without an answer from me, bearing news, no doubt, of Fraid's refusal to make terms.

On the morning of the fourth day, we were trying to stuff dung in the roof leaks when one of the stablemen burst through the door. 'Women, quick! There is trouble streamside. We may need herb lore soon enough.'

Dropping our bowls, we followed him out, our skirts dragging over the muddy ground. The rain drove down in sheets as we descended the hill.

A great crowd was gathered at the Cam. The banks were breached and a mother stood too close to the frothing edges. 'My boy!' she screamed, and though she held one babe safe in her arms, it was clear there was another in danger.

I grabbed Mael the baker's arm as he passed. 'What has happened?' I shouted over the drum of water.

'A child, swept off the banks. No one has seen him rise.'

Townspeople were shouting, hysterical, along the banks downstream, casting offerings into the water. I ran toward them.

'Ailia, come back!' It was Cookmother's shout. She had followed from her bed.

I slowed for a moment but I could not heed her. As I ran, I looked into the water, thick as cream with the churning mud. I kept running. Beyond where any other looked. After a few more strides, I stopped. The river was wider now, tangled with reeds. I closed my eyes. I knew the child was here. I knew the child was alive.

I had to be quick. I tugged off my cloak and sandals and stood at the surging edge.

The crowds had reached me, shouting, questioning why I would enter the water here when there was nothing within it.

'Ailia, no—' commanded Cookmother. She halted, gasping for breath, at my side. 'I'll not give the life of you to pull out one already gone.'

'He lives,' I said, readying to jump.

'You cannot swim!' She tried to restrain me, but I wrenched free from her grasp and jumped. The water was ice-cold and angry. I braced myself against the force of it, clutching at reeds, but I could not find the riverbed, nor see anything through the muddied water.

I had lost the knowing of the child. I found footing on a river stone and paused. Again, I knew he was here.

My feet wobbled on the shifting stones. Then my toe touched a soft-skinned form, lodged by the current in a crag between boulders. Dropping beneath the surface, I stretched out my fingers but could not reach the child. I needed to go deeper, but if I moved further into the heart of the current we would both be gone. With one final stretch, my fingertips found a small foot. I grasped it and pulled. The body came easily and I hauled it to the surface and then to the bank.

Tribespeople gathered as I dragged him from the water. 'Shake him!' they cried. 'Give blows to his back!'

The boy's skin had begun to grey. His closed eyelids were thin and veined. There was no heat in him. No breath at his mouth.

As I watched him dying, I saw a vision of him as he was in life: blond and rosy. His blue-eyed gaze met mine before he turned away.

'Suck the river from him,' hissed Cookmother. Though her lips were at my ear, I heard her only faintly: 'Cover his mouth with yours and suck.'

I set my mouth over his and drew a breath as deep and strong as a smith's bellow. His ashen chest did not move. He was walking away, his fair hair glinting under a bright sun.

My dripping braids curtained his face as I sucked again. From the base of my spirit I called him back. A cry so raw that it split the hardworld.

The walking child slowed.

I sucked once more with the last of my strength. This time a rush of water and bile flooded my mouth and he was back, convulsing with life as he retched, vomiting onto the ground.

There were many gathered around us now who had seen me pull this child back from death. Some were falling to their knees in reverence.

Then Llwyd stepped forward, his eyes shining with a wild excitement. 'You saw that boy!'

'Ay, in the water,' I gasped.

'No. Not in the water. You saw him when he couldn't be seen.'

'She merely caught a glimpse of him as she passed,' said Cookmother.

'No, woman.' Llwyd spun to face her. 'Do not close my eyes to what lies before them. This is not your story to tell.'

For the first time in my memory, Cookmother was wordless.

The boy's mother broke through the crowd and fell to her knees beside the child.

Llwyd placed his hand on my shoulder. 'Go back to the kitchen, Ailia. Dry yourself and take food. When you are rested, I will call for you.'

As I walked back along the river, the rain lessened and finally stopped. People murmured as I passed them. All of Cad had witnessed my finding the boy and bringing him back to life. All were asking how it came to be.

———

I waited through the afternoon and into the next morning. The kitchen was a forest of wrung-out robes and blankets draped on poles by the fire, pouring steam as they dried. Gradually Cookmother, Bebin and I sorted through the store pots, burning the herbs and meal that had gone mouldy and upending baskets to dry. By highsun the following day, the kitchen was restored but my nerves were in disarray. When would Llwyd call for me?

For want of busying my hands I took a ground bird, freshly slain by one of the stablemen's sons, and began to pluck its feathers for cooking. The bird was still warm under my fingers as I tugged each plume with a pop from its pore. Blood smeared the table.

The doorskins stirred and Cookmother came through. She had to wait out an attack of coughing before she spoke. 'The Head Journeywoman Sulis has just arrived from the Glass Isle,' she panted. 'Wash your hands, Ailia, and put on your cloak. She is with the Tribequeen and Llwyd in the Great House. They call for you now.'

I swallowed. 'Will you accompany me?'

'No, girl, I am not permitted.'

Lingering moisture weighted the air as I walked to the Great House. For all my grown life I had attended here, polishing the carvings, sweeping out floors and serving food. Never had I entered as guest. I stopped at the threshold, shivering inside my still-damp cloak. I knew that I would not leave this place the same woman who entered it. Suddenly I wanted to run. Then I reached down and squeezed my sword handle through the fabric of my skirt. I straightened my cloak, hooked the loose strands of hair behind my ears and pushed through the doorskins.

Fraid was at the strong place behind the fire, facing the door. Llwyd sat on her left, and on her right was the journeywoman of whom Cookmother had spoken. She was no larger than a child, with silver braids that hung to her waist and a staff upright in her hand.

They turned to me as I entered.

'Come,' said Fraid.

I walked past the hearth and stood before them. The fire was hot on my back.

'Ailia,' said Fraid, 'this is Sulis. She has come from the temple at the Glass Isle.'

I had never met a woman who had trained to the white cloth. Twenty summers. I dropped my head and kissed her outstretched fingers. They were clawed with age, and smelled faintly of limewater and onion. 'Let me look at you,' she said.

I raised my head and met her gaze. The angles of her face were entirely unsoftened by flesh: no lips, hollow cheeks, a large, bony nose and jutting chin. Yet her wide, grey eyes cast her harsh features with a deep soulfulness.

'Do you understand why we have called you?' she said.

'The child in the river...' I faltered.

'Because you have shown strength in the visioning arts and it may indicate you for the Isle,' she said bluntly.

'It must be confirmed,' said Fraid.

'She has shown it,' said Llwyd.

'Still—' Sulis quieted them with a raised hand. 'It must be proven. Sit.'

I lowered myself onto the small stool they had placed before them.

'Tell me, girl, is it true that you have reached beyond the gates of Caer Sidi, and that you brought a child back from death to life?' Sulis asked.

I looked to Llwyd, who gave the smallest hint of a nod. 'Yes,' I whispered.

'By what means did you find the child beneath the dark water?' asked Sulis.

'I saw him.'

'But he was deep in the river, how could you see his form?'

'Not his form.' I frowned, trying to find the shape of what had happened. 'I saw something else...'

Sulis leaned forward. 'And how did you retrieve him?'

'Cookmother told me to suck the water from his chest with my own breath—'

'No,' she said, sharply. 'What made him turn back?'

I paused. 'My call.'

Sulis nodded. The firelight made her grey eyes glitter.

What did she make of me? Would it be enough?

'Journeyman Llwyd tells me that this is not the first time you have bent life to your will?'

'Ay. I know plantcraft by my Cookmother—' again I glanced to Llwyd, who bade me continue with a trace of a smile, '—and I have set a geas that brought a maiden to death's threshold.'

'And she died?' said Sulis.

'No. When I saw that I had done it, I lifted it.'

Sulis rubbed the carved indentations of her staff's handle. 'And the fish?'

'The fish?' I stammered. 'Yes...it appeared to me.'

'And where did it lead you?'

My mouth opened to speak but a stab of trepidation silenced me. Admission to the learning I had so long craved was just within my grasp. I could not risk it now with a confession that I had breached the tribe's most sacred boundaries. 'The fish appeared only briefly and was gone again. It led me nowhere.' I exhaled silently. The lie felt comfortable. There was enough without this truth.

'Good.' Sulis smiled for the first time, revealing small, even teeth, and looked to Llwyd. 'I will have her. I will school her at the Isle.' She turned to me. 'Tell me, Ailia, are you Cad-born? Are you skin to the deer?'

I stared at her in shock.

'Did Llwyd not speak of this before, Sulis?' said Fraid in surprise. 'The girl is unskinned.'

'Unskinned? This I was not told,' said Sulis to Llwyd.

Llwyd's expression did not falter. 'She has been raised since suckling in Summer,' he said. 'She is wedded to this tribeland by time and service to its Tribequeen. And she has shown spirit enough to learn.'

'That is all of no consequence,' said Sulis. 'You surprise me, Llwyd. You know we cannot bless her learning or submit her to the temple if she has no skin. She is half-born. She cannot learn.'

'She has a command of life I have rarely seen, even among those of high training. We cannot let it lie fallow.'

Sulis shook her head. 'I'm sorry,' she said. 'Half-born, I will not train her.' She rose, readying to leave. 'You are poorly considered, Llwyd, calling me here in haste to look at a girl without skin.'

Despite my fears, I could not allow this doorway to close. Once Sulis had gone she would not return to consider me again. I remembered Taliesin's words. It was the Mothers' rains that had revealed me and now I must answer to their call. 'Journeywoman Sulis,' I said as she walked to the doorway.

She turned.

'I honour your judgment.' My voice trembled. 'What would you say if I told you of another woman without skin, without training, who had walked with the Mothers of fire? What would you say if I told you she had learned with them and carried now, as we speak, their knowledge with her? Would you admit this woman to the Isle?'

Sulis frowned. 'I would say that you are a fool and she is a liar. Only from the Isle can women journey by flesh to the Mothers, and only then after many years of training. The only one who could journey beyond the Isle and without training, as you have described, is the Kendra herself.'

My breath stopped. I could not think.

Llwyd stared at me. 'Is this what has happened, Ailia? Are you she who has already walked with the Mothers?'

'Yes,' I whispered.

'She lies,' said Sulis. 'She lies to gain her admittance to the temple.'

'It is no lie. I can prove my claim.'

'Then show us your evidence,' said Sulis.

In one fluid movement, I stood and lifted my skirts, taking hold of my sword and drawing it from its sheath. The dull bronze gleamed as I offered it flat in my palms, firelight flickering over the shapes carved into the handle.

There was a long silence before Llwyd stood, then lowered himself to his knees.

Sulis also bowed her head.

Fraid looked to them, unknowing. 'What is it?' she said. 'Why do you bow?'

'It is the Kendra's sword.' Llwyd began to weep. 'She has been given the sword of the Kendra.'

Trees

A tree is an echo of the cosmos.
All trees are branches of the one great tree
that spans all consciousness.
Its branches sprawl infinitely above,
its roots infinitely beneath.

THE ROOM SWAM as I stared at their stunned faces. There was terror in this. It was too great a leap. I could not bridge it. I sat down, legs shaking beneath my skirt, and laid the sword across my lap.

'She cannot be Kendra,' said Fraid. 'Not without skin.'

Sulis returned to her place at the fire. 'Indeed she cannot,' she said. 'And yet she is marked.'

Llwyd rose and kissed my face, his beard scratching my cheek. 'Bless you, Ailia.' He turned to Sulis. 'What say you now on the matter of bringing her to the Isle?'

'I do not know,' said Sulis. 'Never have I known an unskinned woman to be called—'

'And yet there has not been a call for many summers.' Llwyd stood beside me, his hand on my shoulder. 'We all know there is great need.'

I glanced up at him, astonished. He believed I was called. He saw no error.

'Do you know anything of your people?' Sulis asked me. 'What hope is there of learning your skin?'

'I...I was left newly born at the time of the Gathering. I know nothing of my people.'

'Still,' said Sulis, 'if anyone knows your story, then this news may call them forth...'

'Will you train her?' pressed Llwyd.

I was taut with hope, as Sulis sat, deep in thought, before me.

'If the Mothers so mark her, I have no choice.' She gripped her staff with both hands. 'I will take her to the Isle,' she said, 'though I am unsure of it.'

Llwyd squeezed my shoulder.

I said nothing, but my heart was exploding like a rising sun.

Llwyd looked to Fraid. I was under her queendom. The final decision would always be hers. 'This is greatly unexpected,' she said, 'and yet somehow I am not surprised.' She smiled at me. 'Perhaps we should drink some ale...'

I went to serve from the heavy flagons on the shelves near the door, but Fraid rose first and motioned that I remain seated. She poured four cups of the dark syrup and handed one to each of us. When she came to me, she paused, then held the cup forward for me to take. Of all that had occurred today, this was the strangest.

I sipped the fragrant ale and it rolled, heavy and sweet, down my knotted throat. We drank in quietness. Outside, a pig squealed and I heard the laughter of young men, for whom today was like any other. Slowly, the joy began to seep into my body. I would be further trained. I would gain the learning to journey to Taliesin.

'When will you take her, Sulis?' asked Llwyd.

'Tomorrow. While the skies still favour travel.'

'Tomorrow?' I yelped before I could halt it. 'I cannot leave Cookmother so soon.'

Sulis frowned. 'This call is an honour above honours, especially for one without skin.' Her voice was hard. 'Your kitchen tasks are of no consequence now.'

I nodded, beginning to falter. In all my yearning to be taught, this was a truth I had not thought of. 'When will I return to Caer Cad?'

'You will not leave the temple until your training is complete,' said Sulis. 'Three summers at the fewest, almost certainly more.'

'Cookmother cannot work the kitchen without me for such a time.'

Fraid smiled as she sipped her ale. 'It would seem that your days in the kitchen are finished, Ailia.'

'And when you return, you will be sought on matters of Ceremony and judgment,' said Llwyd. 'Your Cookmother would find you a most unreliable kitchen girl.'

I looked around at the three faces staring at me, the most powerful tribespeople of Summer. It was almost unbearable to be so revealed. I had been given a gift beyond imagining, and yet I had to face a future bereft of all I had known.

'Are you doubting the call of the Mothers, Ailia?' said Sulis. She looked to Llwyd. 'She is weak enough without skin. If she is not firm in her conviction, I cannot take her.'

Llwyd crouched before me. 'Ailia.' His voice was kind yet unwavering. 'If this sword speaks truly, then you are the woman who has been chosen to hear the first songs of our tribelands. To bring them back. We face an invasion of people who threaten to sever our ties with the Mothers. You alone can keep them close.'

'What is your response, girl?' said Sulis. 'Will you answer this call?'

I was held in Llwyd's gaze. Its brown depths stirred up drifts of courage in the riverbed of my ambition. 'Yes.'

'It is decided then.' Sulis pounded her staff. 'But hear this, girl—' Her eyes hardened and there was no more gentleness in them. 'You are marked to be our highest wisewoman and I will see that you are trained to this purpose. But with or without the sword, until you find skin, you will never be Kendra.'

—

I walked back to the kitchen as if in a dream. Manacca and the stable-hands who passed me glanced at my sword that hung, now exposed, from my belt. Never before had I felt myself to be of such consequence. I had craved the chance to be taught but now it had come, I saw what safety there was in unknowing. What peace. How could I be the Kendra? I anchored my fears with thoughts of Taliesin. I would see him soon.

Cookmother sat alone in the kitchen, spinning flax by a dying fire. She turned to me as I entered, her eyes dropping to my sword.

'It is the Kendra's sword,' I stammered.

'I know.'

I wondered how she could know it, when even Fraid had not.

'Are you to go to the Isle?' she asked.

'Yes.'

She did not respond.

'Why do you let the fire burn so low?' I chastised, striding across the floor to refuel it.

'When will Sulis take you?'

'Tomorrow.'

She whimpered as if physically struck. 'Beloved girl.'

I stared at her. How could I leave her? 'Would you have me stay?'

'It is not for me to speak against the call of the Mothers.' She turned the spindle slowly and would not meet my eye.

'But I cannot go without your blessing.'

Then I saw her stiffen. 'Do not be stupid, girl. You are going. My blessing has little to do with it.'

Before I could argue, Bebin, Ianna and Cah burst through the doorskins and the kitchen was filled with shrieks and tears at my news. There was talk enough about my Isle training, but questions of my sword were left unasked. A Kendra had been chosen yet could not rise without skin. None could fathom the Mothers' intentions.

When the hour for sleep fell, we were all kept awake by Cookmother's cough.

I rose and boiled herbs to soothe her.

Ianna tried to assist me but Cookmother would not permit it.

'Only you, Ailia,' she whispered as I held the cup to her mouth. 'Only you.'

When she finally slept, I lay down next to Bebin.

'Will you care for Cookmother?' I whispered into her ear. 'Cah is too unfeeling and Ianna too daft. It is only you I can trust.'

'No harm will come to her until you return.'

My eyes drifted closed. 'Have you seen Uaine?'

'Yes.' I heard the smile in her voice. 'Ruther bade him return to the east, but he has decided to stay.'

'But are they not the firmest of companions?'

'Something has come between them. Uaine would not say what it was.'

—

Early the next morning, Sulis sent word that we were to leave the following dawn. I began my last day in Caer Cad sowing parsnip seeds in the kitchen garden, the topsoil warm and crumbly between my fingers. Cookmother worked wordlessly by my side until the chime of our doorbell pulled her, grumbling, back to the kitchen.

Footsteps approached, but my gaze stayed fixed on the ground, lulled by the scooping and sprinkling of seeds. 'Who breaks our peace at this early hour?' I asked, expecting Cookmother.

'A thoughtless journeyman,' said an old man's voice.

'Journeyman Llwyd!' I scrambled to my feet to bow. 'Why did you not announce yourself?'

'No need. Continue—' He motioned to the garden. 'I'll work with you a moment.' He knelt beside me and began to dig. His hands reminded me of Taliesin's, fine-boned and long-fingered, weaving through the soil like needles through cloth. 'How are you bearing this Kendra's cloak that falls to your shoulders?'

'I will wear no Kendra's cloak without skin. This is what Sulis has said—'

'The Mothers are mischievous. They toy with us in choosing you. But they have called you. They will give you your skin.'

'But the Mothers of fire said nothing of my skin.' I said.

A frown crossed his face, then he shrugged. 'The others will help you.'

'The others?'

He smiled. 'I forget how little you know. There are twelve circles of Mothers. Each keeps its own knowledge.'

My eyes widened. 'Will I meet with them all?'

'You will be called only by the Mothers whose knowledge you do not already possess.'

'Then that will certainly be all of them.'

'We shall see.'

I nodded, unsure. It was all still barely true, a poet's tale I was hearing at feast.

Llwyd sensed my hesitance. 'When I was first called to the Island of Mona to train, I was scared to my under-robes.'

I looked up. 'You?'

'And why not? I was just a son of a silversmith before I became this towering greatness you see before you.'

I laughed. Here, stooped in the garden, Llwyd mocked himself, but I had seen him summon forces that came from the most disciplined learning. He was indeed towering. Indeed great. In confessing his fear, he began to dispel mine. 'There is still one thing that holds me...' I faltered.

'What is it? You must be free of any doubt—'

'Cookmother.' I glanced back nervously for her return. 'She does not offer her blessing, and I cannot embark without it.'

Llwyd sighed. 'There is a reason your Cookmother withholds her blessing and it is time you knew it.'

I stared at him. 'Will you now tell it?'

'I cannot. You must ask her—'

The thunder of a galloping horse shattered the question between us.

I helped Llwyd to his feet and we hurried out to the courtyard.

'Message from the east!' cried the rider. 'I ride from Mai Cad. Where is the Tribequeen?'

'I am here.' Fraid emerged from her sleephouse, unadorned. 'What do you bring?'

'News of great consequence.' The rider dismounted and bowed.

'I will leave,' I whispered to Llwyd, turning away. It was not for the servants to hear news as it was given.

'No.' Llwyd grabbed my wrist. 'Listen.'

'There has been an attack on the coast of Cantia,' said the rider, 'and a two-day river battle with the legions led by Aulus Plautius. The tribes of Albion are defeated. King Togodumnus, brother of Caradog, is dead.'

There were gasps and murmurs among the townspeople who had followed him in.

'And what now of the legions?' said Fraid. 'Is this the extent of their claim? This defeat in the east?'

'They make camp outside Camulodunon and replenish supplies,' said the rider. 'They wait for the Emperor Claudius himself to arrive, then they will march on the capital.'

The gathering crowd fell silent, marvelling, as I was, that Camulodunon, the capital of the most powerful tribe in Britain, could fall to Rome.

'The great Catevellauni are subdued,' said Fraid. 'What says Cun?'

'The King of Mai Cad asks that you travel south with your wiseman. He calls all the Durotrigan heads to discuss an alliance in the face of this attack.'

'I wish him luck,' said Fraid. 'If he can unite the tribes to one strategy, then he has statecraft even the Mothers lack, but I myself will certainly come.'

The messenger nodded, relieved. 'Cun calls you to return with me today, that you may meet tomorrow.'

'Well then,' said Fraid, 'I must ready myself to travel. Llwyd, you will ride with me.'

Llwyd nodded and Fraid turned back to the sleephouse door.

'I must prepare her,' I said, moving to follow her.

Llwyd halted my path with his arm. 'Rather prepare yourself,' he said. 'You will also accompany us to Mai Cad.'

'For what purpose?' I asked in surprise.

'You are journeywoman initiate, you must learn the workings of the tribes.'

'But I will understand nothing—' I gasped.

Llwyd lifted his hand to silence me. 'Do not argue with your Journeyman Elder. You will attend the talks. You will understand.'

'But what of my travel to the Isle?' I asked. 'Sulis has told me we leave at dawn.'

'Sulis will wait.'

‏⸗

We left for Mai Cad, casting jewels and weapons into the Cam to bless our journey; then we rode south, through pastures and fields of wheat and barley. The sun drew high as we reached the woodlands that marked the southern border of Summer. These were not forbidden forests and I could enter them unskinned.

Fraid and her stableman rode ahead. I rode beside Llwyd, soothed by the steady thud of my grey mare's footfall and her warm strength beneath me. Along the path Llwyd pointed out fragments of forest life, the track of a fox with an injured front foot, the call of a thrush fallen too soon from the nest. As the forest turned from beech to ash, then to oak, he explained the different qualities of the trees. How one was used in binding work and one in dispelling. How a wiseman would come to one part of the forest to vision the future and another to remember the past. I gleaned that there was meaning in every stone and leaf and trickle of water.

We had been riding gradually uphill. When we emerged from the woodland in the late afternoon, we were at the crest of a ridge that looked to the west. Fields, grasslands and settlements spread before us in shades of yellow and green, with silver streams threaded among them and boulders scattered like crumbs. It was stonier, wilder than Summer. Beside us was a spring that bubbled from within the hill, ringed with stones and carvings left by others who had worshipped here.

'We will rest the horses before we descend,' said Fraid.

We dismounted. By the spring Llwyd began murmuring a chant to the Mothers.

While the stableman tethered the horses, I pulled strips of dried fish from my riding pouches and sat overlooking the flatlands to eat them. Llwyd settled beside me. The late-day sun was sinking before us, soaking the country in rose-gold light.

'What is it that we stare upon?' he asked.

I looked at him. Did he trick me? 'It is Central Durotriga...?'

'But what do you see in it?' He bit into his fish.

I frowned. 'Fields, rivers, many stones...'

'When you train you will see it in a different way.' The sun turned his brown eyes to amber. 'You will see the stories.'

I knew he could not tell me the stories until I had skin, but he wanted me to know they were there.

'We alter the land,' he said. 'We speak with it. We take from it in our farms and give to it in our rituals. But we don't change it too much, or the story is changed. Think on this as we meet with Cun.'

'I will try.' I drew my cloak against a needling wind. There was so little I knew.

'Prepare to mount,' called Fraid.

'Llwyd—' I touched his cloak as he went to stand. 'I go to these discussions without even the most basic learning.'

He crouched back beside me. 'Then let me give you what I can now.' He leaned close and I smelled the woodsmoke caught in his hair. Years of reckoning were held in his face. Like the tribelands he loved, it was more story than flesh. 'Two things above all others guide the journeymen and -women of Albion,' he said. 'The first is knowledge so that we may deeply understand what is true and what is false. The second is freedom to choose between them. With knowledge and freedom, a soul may be enlightened. Without them, it will never be.'

Fraid called us to depart.

Llwyd caught my wrist. His grip was strong. 'All the power of the tribes rests in knowledge and freedom. The Kendra must protect them.'

'But I will not be Kendra, Journeyman!' I whispered, suddenly frightened by the gravity of his charge. Was there wrongness in this? I was unskinned. Was I falsely chosen?'

'You will be Kendra.'

'How can you know it?'

'You have the Kendra's heart.'

Strong People

Our wisepeople are spiders, weaving order
from the chaos that would otherwise consume us.

WE APPROACHED MAI CAD as the sun turned crimson. The hill reared from the lowlands, its walls wrapping around the slopes, like the Mothers' fingers. This was said to be Albion's largest, most splendid hillfort. Only when we were climbing the paths of the eastern entrance did we see the dizzying depths of the ditches and the sheer-faced height of the walls.

When our horses were stabled and we had washed in the guest-house, we were led to the Tribeking's Great House. His servant told us that the other tribal heads were not expected until tomorrow morning. Tonight, we three alone would meet with Cun.

The Great House was lined with torches and well-shined weapons. Durotrigan banners of war hung from the walls and a full cauldron of fragrant stew simmered over the fire. At the strong place sat a dark, well-muscled man, wearing the thick torque of a king. Cun. But where were his wisemen? His warriors?

There was one other with him, whom I had not expected to see: Ruther. My instincts sharpened. Why was he here?

His eyes widened when he saw me. It seemed he, too, was unaware that we were to meet, although he did not betray this surprise when he bowed to kiss my fingers and to greet me as a high guest. Our eyes met for a moment and I wondered if the others in the room could feel the ribbons of energy that spun between us.

'This is a great surprise, Ruther.' Fraid's voice was guarded. 'How is it that you have come?'

'I bring knowledge of the campaign and—' he glanced at Cun. 'I have met with men of the legions.'

'The Romans themselves?' said Fraid. 'You are at the heart of things.'

Cun shifted in his seat as we all took ours. It was clear that Ruther did not have his trust.

I was introduced to Cun as the servant poured us cups of strong ale. 'And who are you to be brought here so young?' Cun asked me. 'Do they train statecraft at the tit nowadays?'

'She is as yet untrained,' said Fraid slowly. 'We think she may be knowledge-gifted to the Kendra.'

'The Kendra?' Cun raised his eyebrows. 'I have not known one since my boytime. This will hearten the warriors.'

Ruther's stare bore into the side of my face as Cun described the attack to Fraid. 'The landing at Cantia was unopposed,' he said, a tendon twitching in his throat.

'Where was Caradog?' asked Fraid, shocked.

'He withdrew his men after the mutiny,' said Ruther. 'The legions took him by surprise.'

'But he rallied to meet them at the Medway,' said Cun. 'The

Romans were greater in number—thousandfold—but Caradog held them for two days in the wetlands. The tribesmen knew the riverways, but Plautius brought warriors from Gaul, trained in water crossings. In the end, Plautius scraped together a feeble victory.' Cun spat on the floor. 'Though the Romans call it glorious, as Togodumnus is dead.'

'And Caradog?' asks Fraid.

'In retreat,' said Ruther. 'Though he gathers forces among those who have not submitted. The Romans now send two forces. One northward—' he paused, '—the other westward. Flavius Vespasian heads the legion that is moving west—at least ten thousand men.'

Fraid inhaled. 'It could take years for a campaign of that size to reach the western tribes.'

'We should send fighters to Caradog now,' said Cun, 'to halt the advance before it comes too far.'

Fraid shook her head. 'The strength of Durotriga has always been our independence. I will not invite attack by joining against them unprovoked.'

'And when they arrive,' pressed Cun, 'will you defend?'

Fraid lowered her cup, her knuckles white. 'What is the thinking of the tribes, Ruther?' she asked. 'The Regni? The Belgae?'

'Eleven kings have pledged their loyalty. Now they strengthen Plautius's forces through their knowledge of rivers and trackways,' said Ruther.

'Others have fought,' said Cun.

'And?' said Fraid.

'None have succeeded in it,' said Ruther.

Fraid leaned back, colourless even in the fire's warm light. It was the first time I understood the weight she must bear.

'Ruther, you have seen it,' she said. 'In truth, how strong is this army?'

'Their strength cannot be overstated,' said Ruther. 'They fight in a manner most unlike our own. It is not simply courage they call on, but strategy. They work as one force. A greater force than brute strength.' He paused.

'Speak on.' Cun frowned.

'The mind of their fighting men is quite other than ours. They do not fight to display their own courage. There is no battleglory for one man alone. Each is committed, above all else, to the glory of their commander.'

'What kind of fighters are these?' smirked Cun. 'Driven by mindless obedience. That does not sound like a strong army, but one fuelled by fear.'

'Exactly so,' said Ruther. 'They are trained to fear their commander more than their enemy.'

'I do not fear Vespasian,' said Cun. 'The warriors of Durotriga are the fiercest in Britain.'

'And man against man we will always beat them,' said Ruther. 'It is not courage in question. They fight in perfect unity of style and dress, with short swords behind large shields. One beast instead of many. Our weapons are useless against a wall of their shields. And they are well armoured. They make jokes of our robeless warriors and call them children—'

Llwyd raised his hand to silence him. 'Our warriors fight naked to draw of the forces in the earth beneath them. Their courage is sacred. These Roman ways are without spirit.'

'There are spirits enough when they drink to their victories,' said Ruther.

I flinched at his disrespect.

'Enough, Ruther,' said Fraid.

Ruther sipped his ale.

My thoughts sped.

As he set down his cup, Cun's forearm clenched thick and hard as a taproot. 'We will gather an army that will make them soak their skirts—'

'Or?' said Fraid, interrupting gently. 'What do *you* advise, Ruther?'

Ruther paused. 'I have spoken of it before, and it was not well heard. Plautius pursues a peaceful presence and offers an alliance. A friendship that preserves the tribes, that strengthens them. Many are taking the offer. It would bring us benefits.'

Without warning there were words on my tongue. 'Though far fewer benefits than it brings to Rome.'

All eyes turned to me. Ruther looked bemused.

My heart pounded. I glanced to Fraid and she nodded me to continue. 'Is the knowledge of the journeypeople upheld under Roman *friendship*?'

Llwyd smiled at my weight on the word.

Ruther paused before answering, holding my gaze. 'The journeymen are not well loved by the Romans.'

'But if Durotriga submits, as you are suggesting—' my voice quavered. 'Do we uphold the journeypeople's learning?'

Ruther's lip twitched. 'It would not be to our benefit to do so.'

'So we lose both our freedom and our knowledge.'

A flash of anger crossed Ruther's face. Then it was gone and he softened, speaking as if only he and I were in the room. 'Do not fear change, Ailia,' he said, 'not one so alive as you. The invasion comes. If we cannot hold it back then let us shape it to our gain.'

'And what of the Kendra, should she become known,' I continued. 'Will she be honoured under Roman law?'

Ruther met my eye. 'She would not.'

'There are warriors waiting beyond this door who would knife you for these words, tribesman,' said Cun.

Ruther turned to him. 'Then tell them to think of the solstice wheel,' he said.

'What?' scoffed Cun. 'I am in no mood for riddles.'

Ruther leaned forward, wiping ale from his thick blond moustache. 'It is forward motion that keeps the wheel upright as it rolls burning down the hill. When it stops, it falls, and its flames are extinguished. We are as the wheel. And this invasion is the ground before us. If we do not roll forward, our fire ceases and we will fall.'

'A pretty image,' said Llwyd. 'But what if you told them of the oak. Life in its most sacred form. The seasons turn around it, the winds shake its branches, but it remains still, its roots fixed in the ground.' He looked at me. 'Which is stronger, Ailia, the wheel or the oak?'

I had no answer, compelled equally by each image.

'We are neither trees nor wheels,' said Cun, shaking his head. 'And we have never been under anybody's rule. Even when the Great Bear took the tribes on three sides of us, we remained untouched.'

Ruther gave a resigned snort. 'Do not worry. Our dissent is well known to the Romans,' he said. 'It is the very thing that will incite them to subdue us.'

'Then let them come.' Cun stood. 'You make your choice, Fraid. Every man of Mai Cad will die fighting before I kiss the feet of the pigs.'

'And so they shall,' said Ruther.

—

Talk of Rome was put aside until the meeting of heads on the morrow. Tempers were soothed by Cun's rich beef and turnip stew, dark ale and vulgar jokes. The meal lasted late into the night.

I sat between Fraid and Llwyd, saying little and growing exhausted.

Ruther's eyes had barely left me, and when I stepped outside the Great House to cool my face in the autumn night, he was swiftly at my side. 'Ailia, I would speak with you.'

'Then walk with me for a while,' I said, 'I need air.'

We turned down one of the wide and unfamiliar streets.

'Why did you not see me in Cad?' he demanded. 'I asked of you.'

'There has been too much afoot,' I answered in truth. 'I am to go to the Isle.'

'Impressive. And without skin.' He shook his head in disbelief. 'Did I not pick you for the temple when first we met? And I was your fire-lover!'

'Hush.' I smiled.

The house beside us was noisy with babe-cry and the dog at its threshold growled as we passed. In truth, it was a relief to be with someone who treated me as he always had. 'I cannot believe that I will go to the temple,' I whispered, taking his arm.

'And then?'

'And then...' I hesitated. 'I will serve Summer as journeywoman.' The words felt foreign. 'And if, somehow, I learn of my skin—' I paused; it still felt unutterable, '—I will train to be Kendra.'

'A very ancient wisdom,' said Ruther. 'It has served a long time.' He glanced at me. 'Is it the best pathway now to take?'

I stopped and turned to him. 'Do you speak against your history?'

'I love my history as deeply as any tribesman. It is the future of which I now speak.' He stepped forward so that our faces were close. 'I have known since we lay at Beltane that you had a great strength. When you train, it will be even greater. Then you must decide how to use it.'

I looked at him in shock. 'It is foretold how I shall use it.'

He pulled me by the hand and led me through a narrow passage between two houses. Before us was the township's wall. We hoisted ourselves up and sat, our feet overhanging the plummeting ditch, looking out at the grain fields before us. The moon glowed at half strength behind drifting rags of clouds and I shivered in the wind.

Ruther unpinned his cloak and wrapped it around me. It was thicker and heavier than mine, scented with leather, sweat and smoke. He shifted closer until our shoulders were touching. 'What if I were to offer you marriage?'

I almost laughed. 'Do you forget I am unskinned?'

'That is no obstacle to me,' he said. 'I will have you unskinned.'

'But no such marriage could be rightly made,' I said, incredulous, 'without the blessing of my totem.' While Taliesin breathed, I would not marry Ruther, yet still his boldness intrigued me.

'It will have to survive on my blessing alone.' The moon shone on his pale hair.

'You honour me,' I said, 'but it is no longer my question to answer. I am to be given to the temple and then to service...' Still I did not confess that there was another.

'Is this your choice then?' His voice was sharp.

'It is not my choice to make.'

'But it *is* your choice, Ailia. Do not be commanded by others. If you do not desire the journeywoman's life then speak it so and take a different way.'

'There is no other way.' His words were unsteadying me.

'You could have a place beside me, Ailia. My family is powerful in Cad. The Romans will talk to me...they *have* talked to me.' He paused. 'They offer great reward to those who receive them well. With our strengths united, there is no barrier to what we may build together—'

I stared at him in horror. 'Are you saying you are in league with the Empire?'

'I am in league with what is inevitable. Cad cannot hold back the Empire, nor can Cun. No one can. For the well-eyed among us, it need not be feared. I will need a woman beside me, a woman to whom the people will listen. I already have the trust of Rome and you will keep the trust of the tribes.'

I shook off his hands. 'As if they would listen to me in this—'

'Do you not understand? You have a gift. The journeymen think you are called to be Kendra—but it is something far less shrouded in mystery. It is the gift of leadership. An allure, a natural wisdom that others will follow. The men of Rome who possess it rise to Consul or Emperor.'

I was spun beyond speaking. The Kendra's call was no mere gift. It was a cry from the Mothers. Undeniable. 'This is desecration,' I said.

'By some, yes, but true nonetheless. Ailia, I love you and I am choosing you. I can offer you a great deal. Consider your decision.'

I reeled from his words, from his love. 'You ask me to deny what has always been.'

'Nothing remains the same. Is that not the first lesson of the journeypeople? Change will happen. The great among us will ride it like a chariot.'

'Stop. You are speaking against the truth of our wisepeople. The truth of the Mothers.'

'The Mothers are revered by those who have not seen what men can do. It is not the hidden forces, Ailia, that strengthen us—it is our own forces.'

But were they not the same force? That which was hidden in the rivers and trees, and that which moved through us as breath and blood? How could they be separated? How could one be greater than the other?

The stars above us began to sway and the wall itself seemed to lurch beneath me. I braced my hands on the stone for balance.

Ruther sat solid as iron beside me. How tempting it was to yield to the assuredness he offered. To be part of his certainty.

The other way I was alone. The strength I needed would have to be mine.

That night I dreamed of Taliesin.

He was calling to me across a river of stones, his face in bright sun. My feet were bare and the stones were jagged. As I ran to him, I slipped on my own blood.

My heart bashed me awake and I lay in the strange bed at Mai Cad, unable to find sleep for the brightness of his face in my memory.

I thought of the two men who had entered my cosmos.

Ruther was a cloak I could wrap around me.

Taliesin was an arrow that had pierced my soul.

Ritual

Our tribelands are nourished by ritual.
Flood, disease and weak crops occur where bonds
with the Mothers have not been renewed.

THE TRIBAL LEADERS of Durotriga could not agree.
 The same independence of spirit that had kept them free of
the Great Bear—and free of each other—now meant that whatever
the Roman forces brought each region would face on its own.

Ruther left in disgust for the east, on bad terms with Cun and
several others.

I was the only one he sought out to farewell.

Our party left late in the afternoon and arrived at Caer Cad by
highsun the next day. By the time of our return, all of the tribespeople
had heard that I was to go to temple. Many rushed out to offer greetings as we rode in through the gates, casting petals that caught in my
hair. Others hissed and spat as I passed. There was great joy that the

Mothers had finally marked a Kendra, but it was utterly bewildering that it fell on a skinless woman. They knew that without skin, my Kendrahood, so deeply craved, would never be realised.

I stared down at the upturned faces, full of questions and hope, and I felt, for the first time, the kindling awareness that my knowledge was not only for me, nor even for Taliesin. It was for them.

Ianna and Bebin ran out to meet me at the stables. As I dismounted and kissed them, the greatest excitement was Bebin's. Uaine had sung her the song of skin while I was gone and she would marry him this moon.

'Be prepared for Cookmother,' Bebin warned as we walked to the kitchen. 'Her chest is worsened and it spoils her temper.' She glanced at me. 'That and the loss of her favourite workdaughter.'

Cookmother was resting in her bed. Her face was pale and her forehead, when I crouched to kiss it, was damp with sweat.

I propped her more comfortably and brewed her a tea of yarrow leaves for fever. Despite my care, she was determined to deepen the chasm between us. She watched me as I unpacked my bundle. 'What is that?' she said as I lifted out a fine bone brooch.

'A gift from Cun.' I held it forth. 'Look—the sweetest carving of a thrush.'

She turned her face away.

I tried again. 'Have you survived well enough the attendance of Cah while I was gone?'

'Most perfectly well,' she grunted over her shoulder.

Sulis had left word that tomorrow's mid-morning was favourable for departure. These were my last hours in the kitchen. I could not bear that they would be spoiled in this wordlessness. The ill temper Cookmother had always shown to others, but never to me, was now to be my farewell gift.

We had but one day to make and dye the wedding cloth, for Bebin wanted my blessing in it.

Ianna was using the warp loom to speed the fabric, with Bebin at her side. Together they walked the length of the loom and back again, passing the shuffles smoothly between them. Cah was weaving ribbon on a small tape loom and I was crushing blackberries and scraping the pulp into a steaming pot of dark blue liquid. Cookmother slept, snoring noisily.

We had placed juniper outside the doorway to warn our men not to enter. Dying was strictly women's work and the presence of a man would curse the cloth. Especially near wedding time.

Only those skilled in plantcraft could work the dye pots. Cookmother usually left it to me, as the pots were too heavy for her now. I was dying berry for good fortune and kelp for protection. Both pots had to be mixed and dipped by the end of the day. Tomorrow the moon would turn and it would be a poor time to fix the colour and craft into the cloth.

The air was pungent with the aroma of bubbling fruits and the large pot of stale urine in which we would soak the cloth so it would better take the dye. Often we would sing stories into the flax as it was woven, but today there was too much to discuss.

'Sisters,' I said, 'with two of us to be gone from the kitchen, I am worried for Cookmother. The sound in her chest is not good and she needs to be tended.'

'Then we need another girl,' snapped Cah. 'My days are too laden as it is, and I would take marriage if it were offered.'

'She will have my loyalty,' said Ianna. 'I am not sure I will ever marry.'

'Oh, Ianna.' I smiled but I was far from comforted. 'Are you quite certain,' I asked Bebin, half in jest, 'that you prefer Uaine to the kitchen?'

'Oh, I'd prefer him,' burst Ianna, 'he is handsome as a king.'

'There are many you'd prefer,' said Cah. 'But none who'd take you.'
Ianna made a face.

'Bebin?' I pressed.

'I am pleased to marry Uaine, as you know, Ailia,' she answered gently. 'I will come to Cookmother every day and tend her well. But I suspect that it is not *my* certainty you are questioning.'

I stirred the boiling liquid. She was right. My heart was not resolved to leave the kitchen and I did not know how to make it so.

'Cease,' called Ianna. There was a clack as the last length of twine sent the warp weights knocking against the loom frame. 'Look!' She reached up to unhook the cloth from the upper pole, 'I have tied off my final loop. Now we have a wedding cloth to dye.'

I stood by the well trough at sunfall, scrubbing the last stains of blue dye from my hands. Dogs drifted around the quiet street. Blackbirds keened. My last day in Cad.

I did not notice Heka approaching until she was right beside me. I nodded a greeting. I had not seen her since before the rains. She had gained a small amount of weight, braided her hair, and washed the dirt from her moss-coloured dress. But although the corners of her face were softened, the pall of anger around her was not.

'It is said you are to leave Cad. And Bebin to marry.' She appeared sober and clear-minded, and for this she made me more nervous.

'How have you heard it?'

'Cah,' she answered. 'She is not afraid to companion me.'

Cah is not well supplied in companions, I thought to say, but did not. Heka was like green wood in a fire. 'She has told you true,' I said, 'I leave tomorrow.'

'My friend Cah,' she continued, shifting on her feet, 'thinks it well that I come into the Tribequeen's kitchen when you and Bebin are gone.'

'It is not for Cah to determine.' I dried my hands on my skirt. 'You know it is impossible.'

'Why?' Her eyes darkened. 'Do I not deserve for a few seasons what you have enjoyed for all the summers of your life? Or do you prefer to see me cast to the fringes over winter?'

'I do not. But Fraid would never bring you into her service,' I said.

'Why not?'

'Because you are...' I paused, struggling myself to name the nature of her breach.

'What?' Her lip curled into a snarl. 'Too impure?'

'Perhaps.' I sighed, suddenly sorry for her. She had not chosen whatever had befallen her. 'We have spoken on this before, Heka. I told you then I had no power to help you.'

'But you are marked to be the Kendra now.' She savoured the observation. 'Fraid will heed your influence if you speak well of me.'

In truth, I wished Heka no further ill, but the thought of her lying in my bed was horrifying. I shook my head as I gathered up my brushes and soap. 'I cannot recommend you to Fraid. There are others who await the places before you.'

She trailed one hand over the surface of the trough water. We both watched the ripples that rolled out from her black nails. 'Your mother would not have thought well of such coldness in a daughter.'

The early night air became solid in my chest. 'What do you know of my mother?'

Heka stood very still. 'It was her way to look after those in need.'

A crow's cry halved the sky.

I could scarcely speak for the violence of my heart. 'Heka, if you have true knowledge of my mother, you must tell me now.'

'Hah!' She leaned closer, her breath sour. 'Knowledge is a heat that makes the metal more pliant.'

I took hold of her sinewy forearm, steadying myself against the wild hope that surged within me. 'I beg you, tell me.'

'Secure me a place—your place—in the Tribequeen's kitchen and I will consider telling you my knowledge.'

I clutched her arm tighter. My voice was thin. 'Tell me now.'

She peered at me. Unglazed by ale, her eyes were green and sharp. 'When it suits me to tell you, you shall know.' She pulled free from my grasp and turned away.

'Heka—'

She spun around.

'Why did you not speak of this before?'

'You did not have the teeth to help me before. And besides,' she said, her face hardening, ugly again, 'I liked to watch you flounder in your skinlessness. To be without hope of finding it.'

Gradually the floating truths began to make a whole. 'You know my skin,' I whispered.

'Yes,' she breathed.

I was as abject before her as a hatchling fallen. 'Will you give it to me?'

'Speak to Cookmother,' she said, 'and speak of this to no one, or you shall learn nothing more.'

I walked back to the kitchen formless, as if my body had dissolved into the night air around me.

The Mothers had answered me.

I would learn of my skin.

—

My sisters were gathering and feeding the yardstock when I returned. Cookmother was alone, sitting by the fire.

I placed my hands on her rounded shoulders. 'Will you take some elder water if I warm it?'

216

'With thanks, I will not.' She did not look up, but the tendons of her neck softened beneath my touch.

I could not tell her what I had just heard or why my fingers were trembling on her shoulders. But, by the Mothers, I would not leave Cad without healing what was torn between us. 'May I speak?' I asked without lifting my hands.

She said nothing but did not protest it.

'You know, more than any other, how much I have wanted to learn,' I began. 'You have been my teacher when I could not be taught. I have wondered lifelong of the Isle. And now, even beyond the laws of skin, I am called to it.'

Her shoulders stiffened beneath my fingers. Still she did not speak.

'Durotriga is under threat, Cookmother. I have heard it clearly spoken at Mai Cad. By some mystery it is thought I could be part of its protection. I want to do what is right by the tribes, by Llwyd and Fraid. But more than anything, I want to do what is right by you.' I stepped closer that my belly felt the warmth of her back. 'You have birthed me with your teaching, with your care.' I closed my eyes. 'You are my mother.'

She remained silent but reached up for my hand.

My questions spilled over. 'Why have you pushed me from this path?' I asked. 'You have warned me from the forest so harshly. Are you so fearful for me? Do you not believe that I have the journey-woman's strength?'

She turned to face me, crushing both of my hands so firmly in hers that I winced. 'I know you have the strength, Lamb. I have always known it. Oh, I am a stupid old woman and only now do I see it. Fetch some elder water, after all. You will need drink for what I must tell you.'

I poured us both tea and sat beside her at the fire.

She took a long draw, holding her cup in both hands. The hot steam unsettled her chest and for several moments she was bent in a spasm of coughing. When she straightened, her breath was rasping. 'I fear for you, Ailia, because I, myself, have walked with the Mothers.'

I stared at her face, unable to speak. She was my constant, the one thing that had been unchanging. 'You are a journeywoman?' I finally breathed.

'I was,' she said. 'I trained at the temple. I walked once with the Mothers.' Her face darkened. 'But they cast me from their place against my will.'

I shifted closer and pressed my temple to hers, marvelling at the unlived greatness of her. She was a kitchen servant but had possessed the power for so much more. She must have wondered of it every day. I drew back my head. 'Why did you cease to be journeywoman when you returned?'

'I was too angry. I lost something to the Mothers that they would not give back.'

'Could you not retrieve it? Could you not journey again?'

'I tried with all my strength, but I could not pass back.' She looked to me. 'Then I found you, laid down on the step like a flower—I am selfish.' Her face twitched. She was unpractised with tenderness. 'I wanted to keep you safe—'

All I was sure of began to unravel. 'What was it, Cookma?' I asked. 'What did you lose?'

But her face reddened with tears and her breath started to heave. She shook her head, nose streaming, too grief-stricken to speak any further.

As I tightened my arms around her, it struck me that I had never seen her cry.

As her sobs subsided, I asked her a final time. 'What should I do, Cookmother, with my call to the Glass Isle?'

'Go,' she whispered, crushing my hand. 'Go.'

That night I told Cookmother and my worksisters that I had asked Heka into the kitchen. There were protests and questions and I parried them all, arguing and appealing, until Cookmother agreed to suggest her to Fraid, and I knew it would be so. It was a physical pain not to tell them I had learned of one who knew my skin. But Heka's way was as vengeful as an angered wasp. If I breached her terms, she would give me nothing.

Dawn came late on the morning of my departure. But it mattered little, for I had lain awake for hours. Never had I been so aware of the sounds of my kitchen home: the whispering embers, scuttling mice, and the murmurs and grunts of bodies asleep. I could think of nothing but Heka's words and the promises they ignited. With knowledge of my skin, I could journey to Taliesin. I could become what the sword foretold. I could, in truth, become Kendra.

When the light finally seeped under our doorway, I was glad for the distraction of the morning. The first hours of the day were the busiest in the kitchen and my leaving day would be no exception.

I visited Mael, who gave me currant cakes for my journey, then dressed Fraid, finished hemming ribbon for Bebin's dress, and helped salt a late-season calf for drying. But as the hour of my departure neared, I ceased my work and hurried to the fringes in search of she who knew my skin.

It was the time of day when men and women of able body were all at work, but Heka was lying on her side by a peat fire with others of her fringe kin, gnawing on bread torn from a loaf on the ground.

At the sight of me, she staggered to her feet, ale-addled once more, and pulled me a few paces away. Her companions whistled at the tidy robes of a Tribequeen's attendant.

'It is done,' I told her directly. 'Cookmother awaits you when I am gone.'

'Well done.' Her face creased into a smile. Her gums were crimson with infection. I could easily soothe them with comfrey, I found myself thinking, but her comfort was not my concern.

'Cah will instruct you,' I explained. 'You know her already. Ianna is gifted at weaving but little else—though don't tell her I said so. And Cookmother—' I paused. 'Cookmother is not well.'

'Have no fear,' Heka said. 'I will care for her.'

Instinctively, I shivered. How could this woman care for another when she cared so little for herself? All of my being lamented this decision, but I could not protest it.

She knew my skin.

I met her gaze. 'I have kept my part in our bargain. Now you must keep yours.'

She stared at me, her expression bemused. 'Ah yes. Your skin. Are you so certain you want it? You are temple-bound. You already have all you could wish for.'

'No...' I whispered, my heart thundering. 'Do not play with me, Heka.'

'Why not?' she challenged. 'I am fond of games.'

'Tell me, you stupid woman!' I spluttered, almost crying. 'Do you not know what is at risk in my not knowing?'

She laughed. 'Risk? I will comfort you with this: you are born of those who are lucky in risk.' She turned back toward the fire, still laughing.

'Stop!'

Slowly she turned.

'Is that all I shall know?' I gasped, incredulous at her deceit.

'I shall tell you more when I have reason to do so.'

'You are lying. You do not know my skin!' I wailed. 'You invent stories for your gain.'

'Perhaps.'

Please, Mothers, I prayed, let her not be lying. 'I will withdraw your place in the kitchen—'

'Do so if you will.' She nodded to the misery around us. 'I will be no worse off. And you will never know anything more.'

I brimmed with fury at the weapon she made of her knowledge. 'You inflict an unspeakable cruelty with this,' I whispered.

Her eyes blackened with contempt. 'It is nothing to what has been inflicted on me.'

My temper erupted. 'That was not my doing!' I shouted. My legs were trembling with the injustice, the indignity of anger.

Her fire companions turned at the noise. One sprang to his feet, hungry for trouble.

Then Heka screamed, her teeth bared like an animal, 'Yes, it was!'

I heard it ringing in the marrow of my bones.

I ran, shaking, through the streets of Cad. I could not fight this battle now. Heka knew my skin. She was telling the truth. I could feel it within her. To protect this knowledge, I had to protect her. When I returned I would find a way to make her tell me. But now I had to steady myself. Now I had to leave.

I had time left only to pack my few belongings: my shawl, a water-skin, a bone comb and the golden fish pin. They fitted easily into a pouch I tied across my back.

Ianna had made rye porridge but I could not eat. Bebin brushed and re-braided my hair and, too quickly, I was ready.

Neha was not permitted to accompany me. She had been tethered to a pole at the stable, out of sight, so she would not see me leave. I went to her one last time and crouched to farewell her, rubbing her muscled shoulders and soft belly. She stared up at me, her odd eyes questioning, and I fought back the wave of sorrow that told me not to leave without her.

I walked to the Tribequeen's gateway, where Fraid and my house kin waited to bid me leave. Llwyd was already leading the horses through. He would accompany Sulis and me on the day-long ride to the lakes.

I stood first before Fraid. She straightened my cloak. 'I am proud of you,' she whispered as we embraced. 'Continue to make me so.'

I kissed the cheeks of each of my worksisters, murmuring blessings for Bebin's marriage into her ear.

Then there was only Cookmother. Her hold threatened to crack my ribs. I pressed my face into her hair and drank the thick, smoked smell of her: burnt milk, sour bread, nettle, sage and a thousand other herbs. The smell of my girlhood. I filled my lungs till they took no more.

'Go well, daughter,' she muttered hoarsely, 'go bravely.'

I nodded vigorously, unable to speak.

The next moment, she had released me and pushed me away.

I walked through the gateway without looking back. Llwyd waited with my mare just beyond the queen's wall. Only he saw my face collapse.

At the final rampart of Cad Hill, a messenger stopped to tell us his news before he took it to Fraid.

The stammering, limping leader of Rome, the Emperor Claudius, had landed on British soil and led the legions into Camulodunon. On his ships, he had brought more men, jewelled chariots and beasts from foreign lands to make up his procession. The animals that bore him into Camulodunon were as moving stones: hairless, grey and as big as farmhouses, with curved, white swords that grew from their faces. They were said to be the mightiest and greatest beasts that walked the land, all under the Emperor's command. He appointed General Plautius as Governor of Britain.

I looked to Llwyd, white-haired and stooped, on his brindle pony. What hope did we have?

Reaching the Mothers

People of Albion do not seek to invade other lands.
We seek to invade the lands of our souls.

WE RODE WEST along the Nain, turning north into the vast wetlands that bordered the great lakes. Already I felt the pull of the water as we travelled the wooden causeways that spanned the marshes. Already it seemed as a spirit world, where land and water slipped into each other without boundary.

Llwyd and Sulis said little as we rode. Where the pools deepened, or the willow trees were grouped in a certain way, they dismounted and stood by the water, chanting and casting in pieces of silver.

By late afternoon we had reached the lakes. Never had I seen such breadth of water. I squinted into the distance as we approached, trying to find the shape of the Isle.

'It would not be called Glass,' smiled Llwyd when he saw me craning, 'if it were easily seen.'

'Do not tease, Journeyman,' called Sulis, who rode ahead. 'You will see the Isle clear enough, girl. But it is still a night's boat journey away.'

'Further than the Mothers' world,' I joked to cloak my sudden nerves.

'Indeed,' said Sulis, unsmiling. 'The Isle is hard, but the realm of the Mothers is reached easily from its shores. This is why initiates train there. And why you, especially, must be careful.'

When we had reached the place where the lake became deep, Sulis stopped. A wooden canoe knocked against one of the causeway's pylons. As we dismounted and Sulis untethered the boat, a thick mist poured in across the lake's surface.

'Come, girl.' Sulis was lowering herself into the canoe.

'Do not betray my faith in you,' whispered Llwyd, as we embraced farewell.

'I will not,' I murmured into the folds of his collar. I stepped into the wobbling boat and sat opposite Sulis. 'Journeyman—' I knew the answer but I could not help asking. 'Can you not come with us?'

'It is not the Island of Mona,' he chuckled. 'You'll find no men on Glass.' He unhooked the rope and cast it into the boat. 'Or none that hope to return.'

I shuddered as he pushed the boat away with his foot. Taliesin was such a man: caught in the wrinkles of a place where he did not belong. Not the Isle, but somewhere more deeply hidden: the Mothers' place. I prayed that the Isle would admit me to him.

As Llwyd faded from view, the mist wrapped around us, and soon I could not see land in any direction. Sulis rowed without speaking. At times we passed a gliding nightfowl or a quiver of reeds, but otherwise the lake was as lifeless as a tomb, and only the splash and drag of the oars broke the silence.

Though we faced one another, Sulis kept her eyes averted. She was among those who did not trust the Mothers in choosing me. Soon my eyes grew heavy and I dozed, while Sulis rowed through the night.

A dull dawn met us as we pulled onto the beach. I glimpsed grassy banks, startlingly green. But what stilled me, as I stepped into the shallows and stood on the Glass Isle for the first time, was a mighty, steep-banked hill rising out of the mists, like a cry from deep in the earth, a crag of stone at its peak. 'What is it?' I asked.

'The Glass Tor, our most scared place.' Sulis glanced at me as she dragged the canoe up the pebbly shore. 'You are forbidden to climb it. And you are forbidden to walk on the west side of the Isle. It is our burial place.'

I nodded, following her up a woodland track until we reached a small group of huts dotted amid beautifully tended gardens and fruit trees at the foot of the Tor. A round, stone temple welcomed the sun, surrounded by a labyrinth of narrow streams and springs.

Sulis waited as I walked, delighted, among them. The rocks lining the streams were stained deep rust. Even the water itself appeared rose-tinted. 'What is this redness?' I asked, peering into the deepest pool.

'It is the blood of the Mothers,' said Sulis. She took a cup that nestled in a low rock wall and handed it to me. 'Drink.'

I crouched at the pool and filled the cup. The water was cold and tasted of metal. No one could have missed the magic in it and I was glad I had come.

We entered the temple house where the journeywomen were preparing to take their morning meal. Sulis had told me that I would not eat, and that none would acknowledge me, until I had been ritually admitted. I sat at the outer edge of the curved room, watching, listening. There were women from all tribes of Albion, many in the green robes of the initiate, others in the blue that marked the ovate's learning. The teachers wore undyed cloth and sat closest to the fire.

Sulis stood in the strong place to dedicate the food, her staff in both hands, her head lowered. For the first time, I heard her speak the three laws that would become the shape of all my learning: 'Remember the Mothers,' she began. 'Seek their world. And know your own.'

That night, an older initiate led me wordlessly to the sleephouse where I was finally permitted to rest. The day of admittance had been long. I had been bathed in the red pools—not once, nor twice, but five times—scrubbed, soaked and skin-roughed in between with salt and herbs, fresh leaves and blossom. I had been naked in the groves, surrounded by women bearing fire sticks held at the outer points of me, and had smoke washed through my skin and hair. The chanting was ceaseless, its breath warming my bare thighs and shoulders in the autumn chill. I had not eaten or drunk all day and, even as the sun had fallen, my growling belly was not given a crumb to relieve it.

The sleephouse was sparse, its floor swept and without skins. Six tidy beds lined the walls and sage smoke rose from the scent pots beside them. For the first time since I had arrived, I missed Cookmother so sharply that I would have gladly gone another day without food for one embrace against her grubby breast. But I was to have neither. 'Where are the others?' I asked my companion, suddenly terrified that I was to sleep alone.

'They will come.'

In a moment the hut was full of giggling voices, busied hands and discarded robes: the music that is many girls.

Sulis threw open the doorskins. 'Silence, initiates! To sleep without delay. The new one needs rest.'

The room fell quiet but I lay awake, sleepless in this strange place. 'Friend,' I finally whispered to the girl beside me, the one who had led me in. 'Might I sleep in your bed? I am not accustomed to sleeping alone.'

'Come then.' She held open her bedskins.

I curled against her bony back. It was not as comforting as Cookmother's, but still drowsiness descended at the touch of another.

'Enjoy it now,' she whispered as I began to drift. 'There will be no such relief when you go to the forest for the long night.'

'What is this?' I asked, fully awakened.

'We all fear it,' she said. 'At the end of the first lustre you must sleep alone in the wild places of the Isle. With only forest food and water.'

'I cannot do that,' I said, horrified. 'I cannot sleep alone.'

'We all must endure it,' she said. 'But do not worry. It is many moonturns away.'

The very next day I commenced the first lustre: the degree of learning. It would last one year, or several, depending on my speed and strength.

Each day was without variation. We awoke two hours before dawn to sit on long benches under the open sky. Even as the autumn rains came, running in icy rivulets down the necks of our cloaks, we had to sit unmoving, bearing witness to the Mothers' birthing light, training our breath to align with its rhythm.

After sunrise came our day's first meal of sheep's curd and bread, taken in the temple house. We huddled and chattered, thawing our damp robes against a fragrant birch fire, initiating friendships despite the many tongues that were spoken between us. These were young women selected for the deep seams of their thoughts, and it was easy to feel at peace among them.

The hours of the sun's ascent were given to lessons. We sat in the gardens learning the poems by tireless repetition. Writing had come to Albion, but the poems were too sacred to be given to letters. Their power lay in the months it took to seed them in memory.

We walked with the teachers through the forests and grasslands of the Isle, learning survival arts of fire, water-gathering, wild food and shelter—arts that would be tested in the long night.

I pushed my terror of this night from my thoughts. We were told little of it, only that it would come without warning, and that it would separate the weakest from the strongest of the initiates.

In the afternoons, we tended the hutgroup: weaving, thatching and herding the sheep that fattened on the lush pastures surrounding the Tor.

We ate our only other meal at sunfall: an unvarying stew of mutton and roots. There were no rose cakes, no honey glaze on our bread, no fruit wine or other Roman delicacies. Rome had not touched this place.

Over many weeks, I learned the stories that formed the Isle, the stories of which Llwyd had spoken. The magnificent Tor was the longest poem, a well of sacred lore, and I wept, sitting in the grass beneath it, on the drizzling morning when Sulis nodded that I had spoken its final verse without error.

We learned the laws of fair treatment of one person by another, the moral truths, the correct attitudes to pain and death. Slowly (for it would take twenty lustres to say I had truly learned) I began to see the patterns that lay over all things: the veins of a leaf, the cast of the stars, the bones of a robin. I saw the shapes mirrored between these and everything beyond, and I also saw the pricked holes of difference that threw the Mothers' light in its infinite directions. I saw that it was neither Llwyd's oak nor Ruther's burning wheel alone that was truest, but the two set in perfect balance, one at the heart of the other, the stillness created by ceaseless spin.

Every day I was more fully awakened. But the truth remained. I was still without skin. At first it had caused sharp words among the teachers, and some had refused to give me lessons. But gradually, as my strengths were seen and the story of my sword was repeated, I was taken by them all, until there was only one lesson I had not yet commenced.

—

I had been two moon turns at temple. Sulis called us to the red springs before dawn, and we gathered drowsily, stamping against the cold. 'Sit,' she commanded and began passing out cups of dark liquid that she ladled from a bucket. 'Not you,' she warned, as I reached for a cup. 'You will watch only. You will not journey.'

'No, Sulis—' I protested before I could stop it. Surely she would not withhold me from this.

'Silence,' she said. 'Without skin, you are unguided. We cannot sing the spells to prepare you. We cannot protect you. It is for your own sake as well as ours.'

I watched wretchedly as my sister initiates drank the herbs and raised the chants that would prepare the passage. Over many hours I bore witness as they fell into trance, their bodies emptied, quivering, as they made their first spirit flights toward the Mothers.

Sulis wandered attentively among them, guarding their passage.

'Let me journey, Sulis,' I cried as she passed. The lure of the Mothers was an ache in my chest.

She crouched before me, her grey eyes alive to this rite. 'The danger is too great.'

'But I am not scared.'

'I know it. But there is more at risk than you alone. Skin holds us all. It must not be breached—'

'*Why not?*' I whispered. 'What is the risk?'

'Infection,' she hissed. 'Disease of the hardworld. In shape and form we cannot imagine.'

'Then when?' I lamented.

She scowled, searching my face with her journeywoman's sight. 'I can see that they want you. But you must go on our terms, held fast by your skin.'

From that day onward, I sat beside my sister initiates through all their journeys. I watched them commence each morning, eager and rosy, then emerge hours later, pale and exhausted, their eyes black and glazed. Sulis asked if I would not rather spin or harvest late-autumn herbs while they practised, but I chose to stay with them, wanting to be close to the rite that my soul craved.

Sometimes the call was so strong that even without the medicine, without the chants, I began to slip into trance, plunging toward the Mothers in a wash of elation.

Sulis stayed near me always, watching for the loll of my head, the whimper of my breath, so that she could rouse me and bring me shuddering back to the wet ground of the temple garden.

I was marked to be the Kendra, yet forbidden the journey that would birth me.

On nights when the moon phase bestowed sufficient protection, Sulis kept me in the temple house after all others had retired to sleep, to teach me what she could of Kendra law. Enough to protect me, but not enough to endow me: it was not permitted for any to touch the Kendra's head; only the Kendra could ascend to the summit of the Tor; her purpose was to bring the Mothers close to the tribes and to nourish the hardworld with their song.

Sulis spoke with expressionless eyes and a voice as cool as night.

My questions bubbled over, yet few were answered. Still I did not have her trust.

'How is she made Kendra?' I asked. Winter was approaching and we sat under heavy blankets beside the fire.

'She must endure a long night more terrifying than those of all other journeywomen.' Sulis paused. 'For her long night is in the Mothers' realm.'

'My pulse hastened. 'And if she survives it,' I asked, 'what marks her transition?'

'The Singing,' said Sulis. 'She is Kendra when she has sung.' She laid down her blanket and rose to stand. 'That is enough. Let us return to the sleephouses—'

'But might not any of the initiates say they have sung in their journey?' I asked. 'And claim the Kendra's title?'

She stared at me. 'None would be so devious.'

'Yet if they were?' I persisted.

Sulis hesitated, displeased at the question. She breathed heavily and sat back down. 'I had not intended to speak of it, but I will tell you only this: she who has sung is given a scar. The Mothers cut her.'

My gasp was audible in the quiet night. 'What if the scar is falsely made?'

She laughed. 'Have no doubt, girl. It cannot be falsely made. Now ask nothing more. For until your skin is claimed by a totem, the Mothers will never scar it.'

We returned to our beds with no further word. Sulis could tell me of the Kendra's duties and her taboos. But the rest of it, the thrumming heart of it, I had to learn with the Mothers. As I drifted to sleep, I consoled myself that I would learn of my skin.

That I would journey again.

That Taliesin would wait.

Flight

She who understands has wings.

I HAD BEEN four full moons at the Isle. It was a wane day, a day of rest. They were granted to us once in each moonturn.

I was scouring the Isle's forest for late peppermint, vervain and pansy leaf for Sulis's lessons. None of the girls had wanted to walk in the rain, preferring to sit by the temple fire, telling stories from their villages and sewing charms for the young smiths or warriors who waited for them there.

The rain padded down on my back as I stooped to tug out plant stems. Black soil clumped at the roots, oily between my fingers, like bloodcake. With my eyes locked to the ground, I did not expect it when I found myself at the other edge of the forest. We had been told it was a full day's walk, at least. This was the western side of the Isle, the burial place. Sulis had said that herbs grew well here, but that I must not come here to harvest. Those of later lustres may come here for trancework, she had said, but never initiates.

I peered out from between the trees. Despite Sulis's warning, the country looked inviting. The hills were lushly grassed, thin streams of mist settling in their shallow gullies. I saw no burial mounds or marking stones. A heavy bank of vervain, with lingering purple blossom, lay just beyond the forest's edge. I darted out to pluck one quick stem. The vervain was beautiful, mature and strong—perfect for a tincture for Sulis's lesson. I walked a little further to gather more.

A movement in the distance caught my eye. Squinting against the drizzling rain, I saw a figure with dark hair and a fineness of stature that I could mistake for no other. 'Taliesin!' I shouted, running toward him, without a thought for Sulis's warning.

He was too far away and could not hear me.

'Taliesin!' I shouted again and this time he looked toward the call. I was directly in his sight but he continued walking.

'Wait!' I screamed with all my breath.

He glanced back once more but did not stop.

Why did he not see me? I paused, panting. To follow him I would have to run deep into these lands of the dead. But I could not let this chance pass. I let go my basket as I launched down the slope. A gully of mist lay between us and I prayed, as my feet pounded toward it, that he would not be gone before I could reach him.

As I headed into the first drifts of mist in the crevice of the hills, there was an odd thickening of the air that slowed my pace. I pushed on but it grew yet more dense, repelling me, until finally I could press no further into the whiteness without it holding firm, like flesh, against my weight. Was this some contrivance of wind and water that I had not yet known? Why could I not pass?

Every moment took Taliesin further away.

With all my strength I pushed against this vaporous skin. It was impenetrable. With a wail of despair, I wrenched my sword from my belt and stabbed furiously at the barrier before me. Through my wild strikes, I saw the mist shiver and bend with the force of my sword, and a small fissure break open around its tip.

I worked my arm through the tear and felt the cold, strange air on the other side. Again I slashed into the veil and a strong, living smell, like blood or milk, rose to meet me as I cut. Soon I could wriggle my body right into the hole. With tendrils of torn membrane brushing my face and arms, I stepped through.

The valley seemed darker, disturbed. Had I angered the Mothers with these steps? I could not think of it. I started to run.

Taliesin was no longer at the rise of the hill where I had seen him. I screamed his name and ran westward, as he had headed. As I rounded the hillside, I stopped in surprise, gasping with joy and relief. A hutgroup stood before me. I had found him.

The houses were like none I had seen before: small stone domes wedged deep into the slope, their roofs covered in grass, hidden in the hillside. Smoke snaked from the roof peaks. I hesitated as I approached. We had not been told of any settlements on the Isle, other than the temple hutgroup. Perhaps it was a lesser village of the temple or a place for retreat. But why was Taliesin here?

I saw the signs of a ritual slaughter. Hoofs, ribs and knuckles of spine, stripped clean by birds, lay scattered along the path. 'Taliesin?' My voice snagged in the silence. Doorways were closed and no one answered my calls. Beyond the last house was a stream that ran from the hilltop, and beside it on a fallen branch sat a small, trance-stilled woman with moon-blonde hair. Her skin was translucent, the flutter of blood visible in her upturned wrists. With the crunch of my footsteps, her eyes flickered open.

I startled at their lightness. A blue so pale it was almost white. 'Tidings,' I ventured, stepping toward her. 'Forgive my disturbance but I can find no other. There is a man I seek—his name is Taliesin. Is he here?'

She frowned and her eyes drifted shut.

Had I roused her from a spirit journey? 'Please,' I urged. 'Have you seen the knave? Are you a sister of the temple?'

Her eyes sprang open. 'I am not,' she said in a high, clipped voice. 'I am sister of no temple.'

My belly stirred with a rising unease. 'Then who are you?'

'Do you not know to whom you have come, Ailia?'

At the sound of my name I sickened. Had it happened again, as it had when I fell through the waters? Had I slipped, once again, to the place of the Mothers?

My thoughts were churning. I could not stay. I had to leave straightaway and tell Sulis the entire truth. Of Taliesin. Of Heka. 'Lady?' I said, unsure how to address her. 'There has been some mishap in this. I have not been sent here under the blessing of my teachers. I have stumbled through in pursuit of my own desire and now I must be restored to the proper place.'

'Do not worry,' she said. 'This is the proper place.' She had the voice of a child but the command of a tribequeen.

'Please, I am a temple initiate of less than one lustre. Tell me how I can get back to the temple.'

'You cannot leave until it is done.'

My innards clenched. 'Until what is done?'

'Until you secure our wisdom. This is why you have been called.'

'But I beg that you hear me—I received no call!'

'Something led you here. Otherwise you would not have come.'

Now I was certain that I had transgressed the sacred boundary and entered the Mothers' realm. Already I felt the numbing wash of stasis, of acceptance, begin to descend and disperse my doubts, just as it did when I walked with the Mothers of fire. I had to convince this woman, while my mind was still hard. 'Steise,' I said, for already I knew her name, *I do not have skin.*'

She stared at me. 'Skin is not needed here.'

I frowned. Did she mistake my words? I mean that I have no totem kin...' I stammered. 'I am half-born...I cannot be in this place.'

Steise looked at me as if I spoke in a foreign tongue. 'You are here because we wish it,' she said. 'It is not your totem, that determines it.'

My blood halted in my veins. There was no sense in this. She did not observe the demands of skin. Yet the Mothers were the very origins of skin. Was this a demeanour of the Mothers I had not yet learned of?

I floated, dazed, toward the stream and sank to a flat stone at its bank. I sought learning so desperately, yet I became more and more trapped in my own ignorance. Sulis had been right to doubt me. I should not have come to the Isle without skin. I was too unformed. I looked out over the darkening valley to the forest. Might I not simply walk back the way I had come? But I knew already that the Mothers would hold the mist firm.

The grey sky began to spit. I looked back at the hutgroup, unearthly in its stillness. There was still one hope. It was Taliesin who had led me and I was certain he was here.

I cupped my palms in the rushing stream and quenched my sudden thirst before walking back to Steise. 'What am I to learn?' I asked. 'What is the knowledge that you keep?'

She nodded at the question. 'We keep the wisdom of change. And of death.'

'Whose?' I gasped. 'Taliesin's? My own?'

'Neither of these,' she said. 'But you will touch death here, Ailia.' She looked to me. 'And it will alter your form.'

My thoughts raced. I had heard of such learning. Forbidden in the hardworld to those without skin. 'And the knave?' I asked. 'Is he here?'

'Yes.'

I could not stifle a joyous laugh that became a sob.

The sky deepened. The day was waning. I tightened my cloak around my shoulders. Death was present here. I felt it in the cold ground, I saw it in the dark stones that studded the hillside, and in the clutch of bare yew trees that circled the hutgroup. But I did not fear it. I was calm. Like the Mothers of fire, this woman, this place, was unbound by skin. I could make no sense of it. And yet if the Mothers themselves did not demand my skin, then who was I to question it?

'As you wish,' I said. 'I am ready to proceed.'

When I had been bathed and tended by Steise's own hand, she led me to the Great Hut, where the Mothers were gathered to mark my arrival. Noisy chatter and aromas of meat seeped from the doorway as we approached.

The room within was warm and crowded. The women were captivating to look upon: each small in stature, like Steise, yet each possessing, in varying hue, the most disarming gaze.

As I searched for a place, my breath stilled. Pressed close between two of the Mothers, and laughing as he sipped his ale, was Taliesin. I startled afresh at his beauty, the blade of his jaw, the song of his eyes.

Steise gripped my arm as I surged forward. 'No,' she hissed. 'You will sit here.' She motioned to the furthermost place from where Taliesin sat. 'When you have learned, you will speak with him.'

I silenced my cry of disbelief. There was only one path with the Mothers and that was by their ways, their wishes.

Taliesin's gaze flickered toward me. A twitching smile betrayed his joy. But he had clearly been given the same instruction, for he did not approach.

Steise went to the strong place, spoke my welcome, and dedicated the meal. Although I was hungry, I could not eat. Taliesin was too vivid before me. I spoke to no one, nervous of these strange and powerful women with eyes like spears. My bowl untouched in my lap, I leaned against the wall and watched. I was a stranger here but Taliesin was not. This was his place. Never before had I witnessed him in the presence of others.

He sat sprawled on the bench, devouring his stew, his face animated in the firelight. The women grouped around him, smiling, attentive to his every word.

For the first time, I saw that his magic did not exist for me alone. He drew all who met him. Who was I to deserve such a prize? I shrank further against the wall.

Then he looked up, our eyes met, and there was nobody else. I swore to myself that I would learn hard and swiftly. I would learn the lesson of change from this group of Mothers. I would cross this last barrier between us.

Finally I ate and the women around me began to speak, asking me of my township, my learning, my strengths and skills. But never of my skin. It was sweet relief to be free of the question, but I was disturbed by its absence. I had learned too well that skin should be asked of.

I grew tired and asked Steise's permission to sleep. She took me back to her hut and stoked the low fire. I undressed and lay down, my thoughts still drumming as I listened to the muffled sounds of the feast and Taliesin's laughter.

The next morning my work began.

What I learned that day and for the months that followed was everything that Sulis had denied me at temple. The trancework of breath and voice cycles that plummeted me deep into the journey-state; the changework that allowed me to glimpse outside the circles of place and time; the learning that was so dangerous without skin. I was taught to seek and cook the plants that would tear open the layers of sight. I was taught to bend my senses to see the shapes that lay beneath the first form. I was taught the long, knotted poems that mapped the journey paths and ensured I would find my way back.

On the first morning of winter, I was taught to vision in the seeing hut, in a basin of water drawn from the spring. The earthen bowl was painted with dogs and birds—the seeing animals—and I had drunk distillations of watercress and thyme to sharpen my eye.

Steise sat beside me, leading the chant. For half the day we sat and nothing appeared. 'Take a little more,' she urged, passing the vial of juice.

I drank. I breathed. And then it came. Hard as a blow to my back. The water was full of sight and I lurched above it, nauseous with the strain of making it clear. I saw Heka, yet stronger, and Fraid, looking drawn. In the days that followed I saw tribes of an earlier time, walking among stones, then other tribespeople in Roman dress.

Each time I visioned I was exhausted beyond speech and had to sleep for several hours. Each time, when I had finished, I suffered a deep sense of loss, of grief. Is this the death, I wondered, of which Steise spoke?

That I was without skin was never questioned again by me, nor by the women. It troubled me as would a distant scream, faintly heard, signalling a danger from which I was too far to prevent.

Winter fell. Snows blanketed the hills and only the hardiest, most determined herbs survived beneath it. I harvested daily, curiously peaceful in this bleak country, missing only Taliesin and Neha, who loved the snow.

Through all this time I did not meet with Taliesin. Some evenings, as I walked through the hutgroup, bringing water or an armful of stems, I saw the edge of a dark figure as it turned into shadows. I did not see his face. I did not hear his voice. But I felt him waiting.

I was fully with the Mothers now. They would not release me until I had changed my form.

—

The Mothers were gathered in the Great Hut, drinking a broth of river eel at day's end. We were in the darkest moon, one turn before the deepfall of winter.

The cook ladled out bowlfuls, but Steise lifted her hand when it came to my turn. 'Take no food, Ailia,' she said without gravity. 'It is time.'

'Surely it is too soon?' asked Ebrill, a quiet, watchful woman, who had been quicker than most to offer a second strip of meat at breakfast, an extra sheepskin by night.

'No, she is ready.' Steise sipped her broth. What say you, Ailia? Will you enter the cave of heat?'

Ebrill was frowning.

'She has been quick to see difference in form around her,' Steise said to her. 'Now we must know if she can alter herself.'

Her light tone belied her words. Though I had never seen one, for they were deeply forest-hidden in Summer, I had heard whispered stories of the heat caves from Bebin and Cah. They were the crown of changework, the sweltering cauldron wherein human bones took animal form. Those journeypeople trained in change could inhabit many animal shapes. Not the skin totems—they were too close—but other shapes, other forms, that opened the eye of the soul.

It would be the greatest freedom I had ever known, yet I knew, from Sulis's teaching, that it was utterly forbidden to those without the protection of skin.

'Ailia?' said Steise. There was grit within her babe-like voice.

The Mothers ignored my skinlessness, but could I? Lodged within me, disguised by my learning, hid the kernel of fear that this was not right. I buried it deeper. I had given myself to this learning so I would find Taliesin. And I had to proceed if I was to see him. But it was more than that now. I, too, wanted to know if I could change. I wanted to know if I could open the eye of my soul. I wanted to know how far I could go without skin.

'Yes,' I said. 'I will go.'

Throughout the following day I was given nothing to eat or drink, and was told to speak to no one as I went about the harvesting and extracting of the plants that would carry me that night.

Before sunfall, Steise called me to the Great Hut. She tipped a fine brown powder into a cup of broth and handed it to me. Immediately I recognised the pungent smell of fly agaric, a fungal herb forbidden in Caer Cad for the violent displays of strength it would incite among the warriors. I retched against its bitterness. 'What is it for?' I gasped when it was swallowed.

'To change form takes courage,' Steise said. 'The powder dispels the fear.'

It did not stop my heart thundering as we walked to the cave, a small stone dome at the edge of the hutgroup. Ebrill and the other Mothers waited near its entrance, tending the fire that was heating the stones. Steise commanded one of the lesser Mothers to take the stones into the cave and pile peat over the smoke hole to trap the magic.

At Steise's word, I stripped to nakedness and handed her my dress and cloak with trembling hands. The women began a low chant, whipping branches of birch against my bare arms and back.

I had learned of the risks in this journey. The body could be torn apart as the bones transformed, or the animal form that claimed the soul may refuse to release it. Sometimes the magnitude of the deformation could cost a life. I picked up the basket of bottles and powders

I had prepared.

Steise held open the doorskins.

I crawled into the dark cavern, feeling my way over the thick straw that covered the floor, struggling to breathe in the steam. Only by heat did I know where the scorching stones lay. 'Steise!' I called. 'Are you still there?'

I could hear the women wedging rolled skins around the doorway to make a seal. 'We will wait you through the night.' Steise's voice was muffled through the leather door.

I closed my eyes and tried to lessen my heartpound. If I was steady with my breath, there was just enough air to allow my chest its rise and fall. Wet herbs hissed and steamed in the stone pit, and in moments my skin was soaked in sweat. A slow, sweet calmness washed through me. The fly agaric was working. In the blackness, I traced my fingers over the bottles beside me, and drank three drops of artemesia, followed by six of selago. Softly, I began chanting the first poem.

For many hours I sat, sipping, chanting, calling the change. Every so often the door was undone and Ebrill brought fresh-heated stones into the pit, briefly breaking the darkness with their soft red glow. The cave became hotter, the fragrant steam thicker. But still I was woman. Still I was here.

It had not been done correctly. I had not learned enough of the herbs, the quantities, the poems. I chewed some mugwort but it only muddied my memory for the poem. What would bring the change?

I leaned forward to tip water from a jug over the stones, my skin searing in the rush of steam. I began a chant I did not know well. A raven chant. The words would not come. But then they did and I cycled them over until the poem became fluid. Shaping.

There was someone in the cave with me. It was not Ebrill, it was Heka. And she was not angry, nor ugly. She was beautiful. She knelt before me and handed me two vials from my basket. Wolfsbane and mistletoe. A dangerous blend. But I trusted her. I drank them both and she was gone.

Now the spirit could dislodge from the bones. The heat bore down as the plants pushed from within. Rivers of sweat poured down my back, but my mind began to lift beyond the cave, beyond my curdling body. I felt an intense prickling beneath my skin. My eyes sprang open but there was only blackness. I tried to steady myself, but could not lift my arms. They spasmed mercilessly as their shape was shifted and bent. There was an agony of bursting as a thousand tiny arrows broke through my skin. My head dropped forward and I vomited with the pain. I was being wrung by the laws that make one thing this and another that.

Knowledge and Love

Some say they are the same.
What you truly know, you will also love.

BRIGHT LIGHT. A wide sky above me. I had never known such sharpness of vision, every pebble, every crawling beast, clear under my gaze.

I staggered on clawed feet, lifting my arms to steady myself, but they extended endlessly to each side, black and glistening, their weight almost toppling me. Others of my kind reeled through the sky.

I was near a deep pit. Something within smelled good. I tried to lift myself in flight, but my command of my wings was weak and I fell to the ground, plummeting back into the darkness and heat of the cave, before I stood as raven again.

Once more, I attempted flight, but could only hop awkwardly on the stony ground. I lurched to the pit's edge and peered in. There was a carcass, a human form. I was hungry. I launched down onto its leg and jabbed and pulled. The meat was tough but sweet. It was newly dead and did not tear as easily as an older kill. The eyes would yield more readily for a quicker meal. I hopped to the shoulder, then the forehead, cocking my head.

The sight of the face, rictal in death, hurled me back to the cave, naked and human, wailing at the doorskins. 'Let me out!' I screamed. 'Let me out! She is dead!'

The door released and I threw myself out onto the icy ground where Steise gripped my shoulders. 'Tell me what you saw, girl? How did you travel?'

'I took raven form,' I sobbed. 'I saw Cookmother, my suckling mother, in the burial pit.'

The Mothers dressed me and comforted me, murmuring about the raven, the most powerful messenger of death.

'Come,' Steise, said, frowning. 'Let us go to the seeing hut. We will observe what has befallen her.'

Steise filled the basin with water, tipping in a small jug of hare's blood that poured in thick clots. Swirling the water, she began to chant.

I waited beside her, stricken with fear.

'Breathe,' she commanded. 'Open your spirit eye that you may also see.' We chanted in a shared rhythm until she gasped at a sight. 'There is pattern in the water,' she said, moving aside. 'You make the final clarity. The image in the bowl resides in our knowledge. The water is only its mirror.'

I leaned forward. Despite the dawn's cold stealing in through the doorcrack, I began to sweat again with the exertion of summoning vision. Another blink and it was there. 'Cookmother!' She was alive. The raven had taken me to what had not yet occurred. Could I prevent it? She lay on a healing table with Cah and Ianna beside her. When did she become so weak?

I reached out to touch her through the veil of water.

Steise grabbed my hand. 'You will disturb the sight,' she hissed. 'Just look.'

I saw Ianna wiping Cookmother's face and Heka mixing a tonic at the table. I could not see the herbs but I knew she did not have the plantcraft to heal Cookmother or aid her passage into Caer Sidi. 'I have to go back,' I murmured.

The image began to disperse. Frantically, I splashed my hand through the water to make it return, but it did not. 'I have to treat her,' I said. 'This is why the raven took me to her—to call me back.' I was fastening my cloak, ready to run back to the gully or forest or wherever I could pass.

'You cannot go back now,' said Steise. 'The bend of the flesh into animal shape can cause infection. If illness comes, you must be within our protection.'

'No!' I shouted. 'She has only a short time.' I was filled with a panic so blinding, I scarcely noticed Steise's form, suddenly tall before me. I had never seen her draw, or take on a glamour.

'You must hear this truth.' Her eyes were white flames. 'Or you will never find the path. If we do not bless your passage, there is no way back.'

'It is different for me,' I cried, refusing to shy from her. 'I have journeyed before, unblessed, unprotected.' I pushed past her. Only the love of Cookmother gave me the courage to do it.

Outside, the winter sun had risen and the valley was pale with a milk light. I fetched my sandals from the sleep hut and bound my sword-sheath to my belt, my heart thudding in my defiance of Steise. Then I ran from the huts, into the gully that trapped the mist, and up onto the hill beyond.

But it was as Steise had said. There was no mist. No border to cut. The trees and stones around me looked suddenly familiar. I was back at the huts of the Mothers of change. Steise waited in the doorway of the seeing hut. Unspeaking.

I tried again from a different direction. This time I ran straight toward the forest. I ran until the trees became thick, until I broke into a clearing, breathless and panting, right back near the huts from where I had come. I fell exhausted to the ground. I was trapped. I could not escape here without the blessing of the Mothers. My bones were aching and my skin was damp, despite the cold.

Ebrill helped me to my feet and led me back to the sleep hut where I fell into a feverish sleep.

—

I slept for several days and nights, drifting in and out of dreams. Whenever I roused, Steise was beside me. Each time I asked her when it would end.

'Soon,' she promised, though her pale eyes were full of uncertainty.

Finally my fever lifted. Dull evening light crept under the door-skins and a fierce wind wailed outside. Steise sat, waiting, by the fire.

'Is she dead?' I asked.

'Not yet.' She handed me water and a bowl of porridge, my first food since I had fallen ill. 'You have taken raven form and survived it,' she said. 'You may leave. If that is still your desire.'

'Yes!' I sat up, the room spinning. 'I will leave as soon as I have eaten.'

'Is there not one you would like to see before you leave?'

I looked up. Her half-smile confirmed it. I had earned the right to see Taliesin just as I was determined to leave. I did not want to leave Cookmother in her illness for a moment longer. And yet, she had survived the past few days. Surely the shortest delay would cause no harm. 'Does he know I am still here?'

'Yes,' Steise said. 'Shall I tell him that you will come?'

I looked down at my sweat-soaked under-robe and arms still streaked with soot. 'Might I wash first?'

I wiped my body with sage water and re-knotted my braids. It was almost sunfall. I would speak with him for the fewest of moments, and then I would leave for Caer Cad.

With wind whipping our skirts, Steise led me to a solitary dwelling hidden among a clump of trees just north of the hutgroup. I had noticed it as I gathered plants, but never had I seen smoke from its roof peak. Steise stopped a few paces from the door. 'He is there,' she called over the roar of the wind, and turned back.

My heart jumped furiously in my chest. Since we had last spoken, I had been marked as my country's Kendra. I had journeyed and known animal form. Would I appear the same to him? Would he to me?

I rang the bronze bell and blotted my palms on my skirt.

The skins were pulled aside and he filled the doorway, his tunic falling open around the hollow of his throat. For a moment I was frozen, unsure, and then a frown flickered over his face, and I saw how deeply he had yearned for me. Without breaking his gaze, I reached for his hand.

He pulled me to his mouth. We had kissed before but never with such fierce intent. Never with such freedom. 'I knew you would come,' he murmured.

'I have only moments to speak with you—' I said, as he pulled me inside.

The doorskins flapped behind us in a burst of wind. As Taliesin retied them, I waited by the fire. The hut was sparse and well kept. I picked up a woven basket from the floor, its pattern and style oddly familiar.

'My mother made it,' he said, standing beside me.

I put the basket down and we both sat on the floorskins, close to the fire. 'Tell me the truth of you,' I said. 'Is this your home?'

He took a deep breath. He was more assured here but somehow even sadder. 'Often I am in the forest,' he said, 'hunting and fishing for the Mothers. I sleep there sometimes. Otherwise this is my home.'

'But this is a women's place. And a place of death. Why have you come?'

'I didn't come.' He stared at the ground. 'I was always here. I was born here.' I heard his breath hasten with agitation.

'Please,' I urged. 'There is so little time. Tell me how.'

'All right!' he said. 'But do not forget, when you have heard it, that you desired to know it.'

I nodded. 'There is nothing that could turn me from you.'

He faced the fire and did not meet my eye. 'My mother was born of the hardworld. A gifted journeywoman. She was carrying me when she walked with these Mothers and I was brought to flesh here, where I should not be.'

'Why did she not take you back?'

'She could not. The boundary yielded for her alone but with me she could not pass. Because I was born here, the Mothers had claim of me. Knowledge has its own will.'

'Yes,' I nodded. 'I know it.'

'She stayed for my first four summers, although the Mothers had finished with her. She promised that she would never leave without me. But one morning she went harvesting and did not come back.' He paused. 'In the end, she broke her promise.'

'She must bear a heavy loss for that choice,' I whispered.

'If she does, I do not know of it.'

'So you have lived all your life in this place?' I said, struggling to imagine it.

'Yes,' he said, without emotion.

I reached for his hand, warm and fine-boned, like a small creature, in mine. 'With no one to teach you the ways of men?'

He frowned. 'I have been raised by teachers. It is not knowledge I have lacked.'

I was quiet in the thinking of it. He was trapped, with no kin, in country that was not his own.

'Do not pity me,' he said, reading my silence. 'My kin ties were torn, but I have walked and slept all my summers on Mothers' land. I have made kin of sacred places, sacred waters. My mother left me with skin-law, and I have kept it strong.'

Indeed I had not met one whose skin was stronger. 'Yet the Mothers themselves do not honour skin?'

'No, they do not. I have been alone in it.'

There was too little time to ask of the Mothers, when there was so much else I needed to learn of. 'How then did I met you in Summer?' I asked.

'It was as I swam in the river last spring. There was a red hazel berry of such brightness floating at the water's surface. I was compelled to bite it and, the moment I did, I was pierced through the mouth with a hook and dragged deep beneath the water. My arms were as fins and I could not loose myself from the hook—'

I nodded, urging him to continue.

'My bones and skin were all turned to fish,' he said. 'There was pain in the transition.'

'You are the fish...' I murmured, my mind twisting in the figuring of it.

'When I finally found the light of the surface, I was in a different place. The hardworld. You were there and I was man again.'

'That was the first time? When I found you with the hook?'

'Yes.'

I stared, incredulous, into his dark eyes. He took fish form, unaided, without intent. He was the most gifted of journeymen. 'Am I the first you have known then, other than these women with whom you live?'

'Not the first. There have been other visitors here, other journey-women. But none as strong as you. You are the first who has lured me out of this place. If only for a short while.'

I leaned forward and pressed my lips against the ridge of his cheek, flooded with tenderness toward him. He was at once so needing of care, yet so firmly held within his own skin, as if my love would roll off him like water.

The wind squalled outside the hut and I heard distant shouts from the Mothers as they secured their doors.

There was little light beneath the doorskins now. I burned to be gone, but I could not leave now, not without hearing the whole of it. 'Why did you not tell me this as we met?'

'Because I did not understand. I no longer knew myself.' He glanced at me. 'All I knew was that I was under some kind of spell and I could not venture more than a few paces beyond the edges of water before I was bound by the way of the fish.'

I nodded, speechless at the workings of the realms.

'With every passage, I saw more clearly what had happened. But my love for you had grown also. I thought you would not wish to meet me if you knew the truth.'

I squeezed his knuckles, still held in mine.

'How could I tell you that I had only a few hours or less to walk on your country before I would feel the ache of the fish in my flesh? And that I must enter the water or I would change right there on the ground and die with your disgust as my last memory?'

'Disgust? It could never be.' I stared at his profile, choking with love. There was such intimacy in this truth, and yet the facts of it brought us no closer. 'But how did you know when to come?'

'I could feel through the water when you were near. At first I could reach you outside the forest. But then I could no longer take form as man unless I was within the forest's bounds.'

'If only I had known this—'

'I sang you my song! You did not return it. There was no purpose in telling you. But when you showed me the sword—' His face buckled then hardened. 'I don't belong here, Ailia, I belong in the place where my mother was from, where you are from—'

I stared at him. I had no words, no answers. All I could offer were my arms, my mouth. And these he accepted. He swung around to face me, loosening my robe with one hand while the other pulled me close.

'I have to leave,' I whispered.

His lips brushed my bare shoulder.

Our fingers trailed, trembling, over each other's arms and necks, then beneath our robes, the secret places that made us both shiver and gasp, before we shed our clothes and fell naked on the furs that lined the floor.

Now he did not pull away. Now he was here, above me, around me, grasping me to him as though life itself depended on our union.

We rocked together as one: of bone, skin and muscle, faces buried in each other's shoulders. Yet still we were not fully joined. Would he betray the force between us again? 'Now,' I whispered.

He raised himself above me and, with eyes locked to mine, entered my flesh and, with it, my spirit. Our movement hastened, our bellies slipped with sweat until we were clinging to each other as our world broke open.

We lay speechless, keeling.

His seed coursed within me. My flesh hummed as though made of light.

As the world re-formed, it was something other.

When my breath was quiet I sat up. 'I have stayed too long, my love.' I said, reaching for my dress.

He rolled over and did not respond.

'What is it?' I asked, leaning on his shoulder.

'I have given you all and now you will leave—'

'It is not my will to leave,' I said, anguished that he would think it so. 'Were it not for my Cookmother...I will return as soon as I can.'

'And I must wait.'

'Can you come with me?' I asked.

'How?' he said, as he turned back to me. 'I will die beyond the waters of the forest. Have you not heard me? It is only as fish that I breach the veil between the realms. I cannot come through as man.'

As I listened, a truth began to form in my thoughts. 'Taliesin, if you were made kin to the hardworld—by marriage—could you come through as you are?'

He gave a despondent laugh. 'I should not be surprised that you have reckoned it. This is as the Mothers have always told me. They will release me by my marriage, but that it must be true kinship, a marriage of souls. That means only you, and you do not have skin. You cannot marry.'

'Yet the Mothers do not call for skin!' I said.

'They do not,' he said. 'But I belong to where it is hard. I belong to where skin is needed.'

Again, there was no time now to unravel what he might tell me of the Mothers' freedom from skin. There was only time to forge our future. I paused before I spoke it. 'I *do* have skin. I have met one who knows it.'

Something shifted with the utterance.

'Has this person told it to you?' he breathed.

254

'No,' I said. 'But she will.'

I reached for the soft, dirty fabric of my under-robe and tore a long strip away from the hem. 'We cannot marry yet...' I pulled him to standing. 'But this I promise you: I will learn of my skin and I will return for you.' Hurriedly I laid my left arm over his and bound the strip tightly around both our wrists as a handfasting, a rough betrothal. 'Taliesin of the Salmon, do you bind yourself to me?'

'Yes,' he nodded, laughing.

'Now you...' I urged, when he did nothing more than grin.

'Oh.' He took a deep breath and lifted his chest. 'Ailia of skin unknown, but who hails from Caer Cad, do you bind yourself to me?'

For an instant, I saw far into the depths of him, and stood, teetering, at this precipice. 'For all time.'

His kiss earthed me.

'But now I must go. It is already dark and I must travel by torch-light.' I unwound the rag from our wrists.

'Ailia—' He frowned as he caught my spinning hand. 'Stay this night.'

I shook my head. 'My suckling mother ails—'

'Give me this night and go back at dawn tomorrow to tend her. You do not know when you will return to me. Give me a night to hold as a talisman.'

I hung poised, trapped by his gaze. He loomed before me, his eyes pleading and yet challenging.

My breath caught with a sudden sense of danger but I clung to him, as if he were all that was safe. I pressed my cheek to his bare chest, inhaling his soursweet skin.

'Why have they kept you?' I murmured. But even as I uttered it, I knew the answer.

They wanted him because his bruised light knew all the world's shadows, because anyone who encountered him would want to be close, as I did, to the tattered wholeness of the universe that turned within him.

I stared at him, so grateful, so disbelieving that he was mine. If I had nothing else, this was enough. 'One night,' I said.

25

The Guarding of the Dead

*After a burial, the closest kinswoman must pass
the first night in the bed of the dead.
This will prevent the spirit stealing back from the Otherworld.*

I SLIPPED INTO Steise's doorway just before dawn, poorly slept, churning with worry for Cookmother. I washed and dressed, then Steise walked with me to the edge of the hutgroup.

'You have done well,' she said. 'You can hold strong change.'

I nodded miserably. I had not done well. I had delayed my return to the one who had given me all. 'How shall I get back?'

'This way.' She pointed toward the western horizon. The hills and valley were bleak in the struggling light. 'There is a track.'

'But that is the opposite direction from which I came,' I said. 'I must return to the temple and travel by boat...'

'Go.' She waved me on.

I strode down the hillside and followed the track into forest, staying faithful to Steise's direction, though this was no Isle country that I recognised and I drew no closer to the temple. As I neared the forest edge, I sensed the same thickening of the air that I had met in the gully. I laboured to gain enough breath, but, despite the discomfort, I did not need my sword to cut my passage. The realms were aligned and I could move through.

The trees receded and I was in open grassland. It took a few deep gulps of this new air before I realised I was staring at the fields of Summer. The Mothers had sent me directly home. I wanted to weep with gratitude, but I began to run. As each foot hit the ground, I prayed. Let it not be too late. Frost crunched on the mud as I ran up the entranceway of Caer Cad. It was deep winter, as it was with the Mothers. I could be thankful, at least, that the seasons had not been turned by my journey.

The cold had driven people indoors and the streets of Cad were empty. I knew I should go directly to the Great House to announce my return but I stopped, breathless, at the kitchen door. The willow wreath had not been placed. She lived. I rang the bell then pushed straight through.

The kitchen was greatly altered. I scarcely recognised it. The clutter of cook tools and piles of baskets were neatened. Heka and Cah sat at the fire.

'Where is she?' I cried. 'Where are her things?' Then I saw Cookmother lying in darkness, Ianna crouched beside her.

'Ailia!' Ianna looked up, her face wretched.

'Are you returned from the Isle already?' asked Cah without greeting.

'Not yet.' I tugged off my cloak. 'I've come to tend Cookmother.'

'You are too late,' said Heka. 'She died not yet an hour ago. We have not even placed the willow.'

An hour! I ran toward her. Perhaps she had fallen into a half-death. Perhaps her spirit was still within reach.

I knelt down beside her, stroking strands of hair away from her forehead. The folds of her skin fell smooth as she lay and her face looked as gentle as a babe's. I put my arms around her. She was nothing but bones. Her bedsores leaked a wicked smell and I winced as I held her. She had been poorly tended.

The girls murmured behind me.

'Go away!' I shouted. 'Let me be alone with her.'

As they shuffled outside, I turned back to my suckling mother. 'Tidings, Cookmother,' I whispered. I watched her closed eyes, her chest, for a shadow of movement. 'I am here.'

Did her cold fingers clutch back as I squeezed them? Quickly, I built a drying fire with spruce and birch brush, washed and dressed her sores in flax, and laid her on fresh straw. I warmed stones in the fire and placed them on her chest to draw out the wetness, then I boiled ivy and coltsfoot and dribbled drops down her throat from a bronze pipette. This I did for many hours, while Ianna, Heka and Cah kept their distance. Finally I sat still beside her.

A rough tongue greeted my hands as I rested them in my lap.

'Neha.' I rubbed her thick winter coat and kissed her head.

I waited a long time for Cookmother to awaken. But when Neha barked at the silence, I knew she had seen what I could not: the spirit's flight.

I walked out into the cold night and looked up at the clouds that emptied the sky of stars. A horn call sounded from the shrine. It was midwinter. The very night that she had found me.

How could I not have come?

Ianna emerged behind me. 'Ailia,' she said. 'Oh, Ailia.' She leaned against me and I held her, dry-eyed, while she wept.

I deserved no comfort.

We took elder tea by the fire before hanging the willow to announce the death. There would be little sleep that night.

'How soon did she worsen after I left?' I asked, cradling my tea.

'She grew well after you left,' said Ianna. 'It was not until the following summer that she caught damp sickness again. Then it worsened with the cold.'

I stared at her. 'But I left only last autumn—how long, by your reckoning, have I been gone?'

'I thought *you* had the knowledge gifts,' scoffed Heka.

'You left the autumn before last,' said Ianna. 'Grief has confused you.'

I nodded and sipped my tea. I was wrong. There had been a distortion. But this time, seasons had been lost, not gained. A second solstice horn call tore my thoughts from the figuring of it. By turns of the hardworld I was sixteen summers.

'Are there not solstice fires this night?' I asked.

'The legion is too close now,' said Cah. 'Since last Beltane, Fraid has ceased the fires.'

Ianna helped me weave the wreath while Heka and Cah took the news to the Tribequeen.

'Did she know much pain?' I asked. 'Who made her medicines?'

'I did,' said Ianna. 'Mostly hogroot and verbane.'

I withheld a frown. These were poor treatments for fever.

'She was maddened with heat by the end,' Ianna continued. 'But there was one thing she said, over and over, when death was close.'

I looked up. 'What was it?'

Ianna faltered, suddenly hesitant.

'Tell me,' I urged.

'*My boy*,' she answered. 'Over and over. *My boy*.'

All through the night, tribespeople came and went, offering their blessings to Cookmother on her journey to Caer Sidi.

Fraid arrived first with Llwyd by her side. Bebin was called from her marriage house, swollen with child. Too stricken to speak much beyond greetings, I embraced them all and told them only brief news of my time on the Isle.

Heka and Cah served thick stew and warm honey beer. Amid the crying and keening for Cookmother's death in this world was laughter and celebration for her birth in another. All who came left a small trinket—a silver statue, a carving or a small bone comb—for her to take to Caer Sidi. By the end of the night there was a pile of gifts two hands high beside her.

When the visitors were gone and the girls had fallen to sleep, Fraid and Llwyd sat with me, taking a last drink. At Fraid's temples were thin streaks of silver that were not there when I left Cad. 'Who will wake her?' she asked.

'I will,' I said. 'I will wake her for seven days.'

'A long wake,' said Fraid. Seven days was the wake of a high warrior or a low king, not of a cookwoman.

'She is deserving of it.' I had not been here to prolong her life. I was determined to care for her in death.

Fraid looked to Llwyd, who nodded his head. 'Seven days,' she said.

Draining their cups, they rose to leave.

'Journeyman—' I touched his cloak. 'Can you stay?'

Fraid departed and he sat back beside me. He waited, but I could not find my words.

'She was well loved,' he said at last. 'But by none more than you.'

'And yet I did not come.'

'You were her greatest comfort,' said Llwyd. 'You were her renewal.'

I shook my head then looked to him. 'Ianna said she spoke of something as she died.' I paused. 'She asked of "her boy".'

261

Llwyd flinched.

'Was it just the fever?' I whispered. 'Do you know of what she spoke?'

He ladled some more warm ale into our cups. 'She has told you, I expect, that once she was a journeywoman? That she walked with the Mothers?'

'Yes,' I nodded. 'And that they kept something she treasured. She said nothing more.'

Llwyd sipped his ale and stared at the flames. 'It was a child,' he said. 'A boy. This is what was lost to the Mothers. This is whom she called.'

For a long time we did not speak, only the fire's crackle breaking the silence.

'How long ago?' I asked.

'She was not long returned when you were found,' he said.

'So the...boy—?'

'The boy—the man, if he lives—would be nineteen summers. Twenty, perhaps.'

A shiver ran through me. 'I see.'

When Llwyd had gone, I walked to Cookmother, lifted her coverings and climbed in beside her. She was cool and unyielding, but I curled up around her familiar shape. 'I have found him,' I whispered, my lips at her cheek. 'And he is beautiful. He is the most beautiful soul I will ever know.'

The night was icy and I pulled a heavy skin over us both.

'I will bring him back,' I promised, cradling her. 'I will give him the love that you could not.'

For the last time, I slept beside her.

After a few short hours, Bebin returned, and she, Ianna and I washed the body with rosewater. I mixed a resin paste with salt, honey and sawdust, infusing it with herbs to help her safe passage. For several hours I pressed the mixture over her skin, into her creases, her mouth and nose and all the entranceways of her body. We wrapped her first in an inner shroud, then a woollen outer shroud, filling the folds of the cloth with resins and powders so she would be sealed from rot while she was waked.

The girls prepared me food and water.

Then I sat for seven sets of the sun. I sat at her head, giving thanks for her. I honoured her strength and her suffering. I thought of the times I had been vexed by her and how I would have given my fingers to be vexed so again. I thought of how I did not come. How I had chosen to spend her final hours with my lover. How my lover was her son.

When I became tired, I lay on the floor beside her and slept. I was clinging to her spirit. I had not released her.

She started to bloat and her frothing insides soaked into the shroud. I stomached the smell gladly in her honour. But by the last day, none other than I could be in the house without retching. She had to be buried.

It took several men to lift her out of the kitchen and onto the bier. We covered her with birch brushes and began the long walk through the northern gate, down the hillpath and through empty fields, to the part of the river Nain that protected our dead. The whole township followed. Llwyd was waiting at the head of a freshly dug shallow pit.

Her gifts and provisions were laid in first. I placed a comb, a nail file, a joint of pork, a bladder of mead, a drinking horn, a summer cloak and her favourite games and brooches. I had left her plant oils in the kitchen for my own gift. Tribespeople clapped their hands vigorously up and down the length of her, banishing bad spirits and summoning good, before her body was lowered into the grave.

Llwyd dedicated her soul to the Mothers and sang her Amra, the lamentation that spoke of her greatness in this life. He sang her true name, Ceridwen. The crowd sang back when they concurred with his praise, then branches and sticks were cast down upon her. She would be left uncovered by earth, so that air spirits and ravens might relieve her of flesh, and her soul could journey, weightless, to the Otherworld.

Many wailed and howled as the branches were dropped in. I remained silent. My cheeks dry.

I could not cry for her until I had brought back her son.

'Can I sleep by your hearth this night?' I asked as I walked back with Bebin. 'I do not know if I can abide the kitchen without her.'

'It would not be a peaceful night,' Bebin said. 'I am roused twenty times in the night to the piss pot with this—' She motioned to her giant belly. 'And besides—,' she looked to me, '—you know you must pass this night in her bed.'

I nodded and we walked on in silence.

'But come for food at least,' she said, taking hold of my arm.

It was still early evening when I returned to the kitchen from Bebin's fire, having eaten little. Ianna was visiting her family and had taken Cah. Heka was nowhere to be seen. Bebin had told me she was often out, back with those of the fringe fires, making kin of drink. I sat down at the fire. Its light on the walls made the red spirals dance. They at least still spoke of Cookmother. For the thousandth time, I pored over the shape of her illness. How could I lament her death when I chose, by absence, not to prevent it?

A dark weight descended as I sat slumped at the table. It seemed that I was knowledge-gifted without sense or instinct to use it well.

264

The purpose of journeying was the pursuit of light. Yet by my journeys, light was lost. It was all for the lack of skin that I failed. Skin would have held things firm. If Heka would not grant it to me before I left Cad, then I would be destined for this darkness.

I stood up and walked to Cookmother's bed. The bedding was worn and old, still soaked with the smell of her nightsweats. I lay down and rolled myself in its familiar comfort. Here, at last, I let myself cry. I cried from my bones, for the mother she was and the mother I missed, for Taliesin, who would never see her, and for the flaw in me that kept us apart.

Through my sobs I heard a shuffling in the dark. 'Who is there?' I called, sitting up.

Heka walked, bleary-eyed, into the firelight. 'I was asleep,' she said, 'until your noise woke me.'

'I did not see you.' I straightened my dress and wiped my face. 'Why do you sleep so early? Why did you not announce yourself?'

'Announce that I am sleeping?' She walked to the breadpot, pulled out a loaf and sat by the fire.

So quiet was the kitchen that I was almost glad to see her.

She tore the loaf and passed me half as I joined her. The oat bread was fresh and I realised how hungry I was. We sat, chewing in silence.

'Your loss is deep and I am sorry for it,' she said.

I looked at her in surprise.

She wore a winter shawl dyed a deep blue. She was fattened by her time in the kitchen, her body strengthened by the work. There was something close to beauty in her face in the firelight.

'Thank you,' I said, 'for what part you played in her care.'

'She called for you,' Heka said, staring into the flames. 'Ianna will not confess it. But I thought you would like to know. Especially on her last day.'

My stomach constricted. 'I could not hear her.'

'She was in much pain.' Heka looked up from the fire, her beauty gone. 'She asked many times why you did not come. I tried to reassure her. But she died with your name at her lips.'

I stared back at her. I saw her savagery, how she stabbed at my softest parts. I was suddenly desperate to be gone from her. But this pitiless woman held the secret of my skin and if I was to learn it, I had to stay. I was coming to know now that Heka could not be matched by force. Only by cleverness would I gain what I sought.

I drew my shawl around my shoulders. 'You have done well here in my absence,' I said. 'I will speak to the Tribequeen about keeping your place in the kitchen.'

'Ay, I was going to ask you to ensure it.'

'And I will.' I placed two large logs into the fire and we watched the flames rise. 'Are you content here, Heka?'

'Ay.' She looked at me warily.

'It has been fortunate for you that our paths crossed.'

Her chin lifted. 'My contentment is deserved.'

'I have given you all you have asked of me. Do I not deserve some repayment?'

She smiled, as though expecting the question. 'Not yet.'

'Why not?' My battle plan fell away. 'I have helped you. I help you still!'

'And yet look.' She stretched out her arms, each weighted with metal armrings of Fraid's favour. 'You are losing your power to help me now.'

She was right. Ianna had told me that she had worked hard in the kitchen and Fraid was pleased with her. My ability to shape her life was weakening.

Yet Taliesin's future hung on my skin. Albion's Kendra hung on my skin. I drew the one tool I had not yet used: the truth. I told Heka what I had told no other. 'There is a knave—a man—I have met in my learning time. His name is Taliesin. He is of the hardworld, but he is trapped, by birth mischief, with the Mothers.'

Heka watched me with a faint scowl.

'He is skin to the salmon and by salmon flesh he travels here for just a day's journey or less. With knowledge of my skin I could aid his return—' I paused, '—through marriage.'

Heka's eyes widened and I saw she was caught in the tale. 'You love this man.'

'With all my being.'

She nodded, slowly. 'A pretty problem.'

'Will you help me?' I whispered. 'Will you give me my skin?'

Her face twitched. 'No. I shall not. You have been truthful with me and I will return it.' She wiped her nose with her hand, her manners still of the fringes. 'Your skinlessness has bought my comfort. And your skinlessness preserves it. While I have your skin, I have your protection. I am not stupid. If I gave it to you, you would cast me away.'

'I will protect you!' I cried. 'You are safe, I can promise you this.'

'Your promise is strong but my knowledge is stronger.'

My balled fist slammed down on the bench beside me. 'I will speak to Fraid. I will tell her to exile you from Cad. She will heed my command. I am the Kendra in training.'

'Do so if you will,' she said, unflinching. 'But you know, as I do, that if I am cast from Caer Cad you will never have the knowledge you seek.'

My shoulders fell. 'When will you tell me?'

'Perhaps I will never tell you,' she sneered. 'That is the chance you take.'

A vast depth opened beneath me. I had not imagined that Heka might never tell me.

The doorbell clattered.

'Who comes?' Heka and I both called at the same time.

'It is Llwyd's manservant.'

I straightened.

'The Tribequeen and Llwyd require Ailia in the Great House as soon as she is ready.'

Self-knowledge

We are each responsible for our own enlightenment.
Praise and honour go to those who possess sovereignty of self.

DESPITE A WELL-BUILT fire, the cold seeped into the cavernous room. Fraid and Llwyd huddled under heavy blankets and I drew a deerskin over my legs. They told me how Roman rule was now well established in the eastern tribelands and how the campaigns to the west and north had moved forward. I was tired to the marrow with no hunger for talk of Rome.

'Strong tribes have submitted,' said Fraid. 'Even Cartimandua has made a treaty.'

My eyes widened. I knew Fraid looked to this powerful tribequeen of the north in matters of queenship. 'And what of Caradog?' I asked. 'Does he submit?'

'Not him,' said Llwyd. 'He runs free and attacks the Roman camps by stealth.' He gave a small chuckle. 'The Romans hunt him like a pack of wolves. Plautius has set thousands of men to the task. But none can draw him from the forests.'

'He gathers his own army,' said Fraid. 'He incites breakaway forces among those tribes whose leaders favour Rome.' She worked a gold-knotted ring over her middle knuckle. 'This war is turning tribesman against tribesman.'

'He must be well spined,' I mused, 'and steadfast in his bonds to Albion.' I warmed to the image.

Llwyd nodded. 'He is a true leader.'

'Or a leader of trouble,' said Fraid. 'He is not far from Cad, at this moment.'

'Will he come here?' I asked, curious to meet such a man.

'No. He heads west for the mountain tribes, who offer him their fighters,' said Fraid. 'He has asked if the warriors of Summer will join him.'

'And what have you answered?' I said.

'I will supply him with weapons if he needs them,' said Fraid. 'But I cannot grant him our fighting men. I will give Rome no good reason to enter our tribelands.'

'But is it not certain that they will enter?' I asked. 'Ruther has said that they seek Durotriga.'

'My hope is that they will desist,' said Fraid. 'The Empire now has full control of the eastern tribelands, the gateway for all the wealth of Albion. We do not threaten their position. We are peaceful. There has been little fighting in the past few months...'

Her frantic tone made me fearful. Fraid had always been clear-eyed about danger. It had been one of her greatest strengths. Her denial now made me realise how afraid she was.

'We have both heard the messages, Tribequeen,' said Llwyd gently. 'Vespasian's Second Legion camps at the southeast border, building supplies—'

'Perhaps if I offer more generous terms for our tin—' Fraid rubbed her eyes.

'They do not want better terms,' I said, turning to her. 'They want the country.'

'But already they take our metals—' said Fraid.

'Not our metals...' As I spoke, an understanding was finding shape in my thoughts, faint, yet alive as an image in the visioning pool. I closed my eyes, willing it to come clear. 'They want our waters.'

'Speak, Ailia,' said Llwyd, seeing my knowledge form.

'We are the most richly veined country in Albion,' I said. 'Rivers run from the south to the north of us. With control of our waterways, they would not have to sail the cliffs of Dumnonia to supply their armies in the north and west, would they?' I asked. 'And are those tides not the death of ships?'

'You are right,' said Fraid. 'They need our rivers to take the furthermost parts of Albion.'

'But the waters are sacred,' said Llwyd. 'They cannot fall to such a purpose. If you are right, Ailia, then we must protect them.'

I nodded. 'When is it thought that the legion mounts the next drive, Tribequeen?'

'Preparations are slow because their supplies come south by the Avon—'

'And the current works against them,' I finished.

'Yes,' said Fraid, her brows raised at my statecraft. 'Cun believes Vespasian will make his attack this spring.' She met my eye. 'We still have the choice to resist or submit.'

'This is no question,' said Llwyd calmly. 'We do not submit our knowledge. We do not betray our Mothers.'

'An heroic stance,' cried Fraid, 'but look at the two paths before us!' She steadied herself with a breath. 'This is an invasion like none we have ever seen. Their numbers, their battle plan, their weaponry—'

She grimaced. 'We are told of attacks where arrows rain down from over one thousand paces.'

'No man can strike an arrow that far,' I said.

'It is not the work of their bowmen,' she said. 'It is machines that do their bidding.'

'Machines?' I asked, disbelieving.

'And the arrows carry flame.' Fraid looked to Llwyd. 'How can we defeat such an attack on Caer Cad? Would you have me lead our tribespeople to their death?'

'Would they not be glad to die for their freedom?' Llwyd's voice was calm but the hand that clasped his staff was shaking. 'These are the Mothers' tribelands. They will not fall to Rome under the Mothers' protection.'

'Why did they not protect the eastern tribes?' cried Fraid.

'Where they are not honoured, they cannot be strong.' His fingers whitened on his staff. 'We are among the strongest tribes in Albion. The Mothers will protect us if we give them the chance. Why do you doubt them?'

Fraid lowered her head. She deferred to Llwyd but I felt the doubt in her silence. This faultline between them was not good.

Llwyd rested his staff against the bench and leaned forward. 'The Romans are skilled soldiers, it is true,' he said, 'but their sharpest weapon is not their blade. It is their scorn of our knowledge. Warriors of Albion have always lived and died by the truth of their tribelands. Now the Roman leaders tell them a different truth.' He looked to Fraid, to me. His faded eyes blazed. 'This is a greater death than any death by arrow. It is the death of our Mothers, our skin.'

'You are right,' whispered Fraid, her shoulders slumping.

I watched her thin wrists below her heavy cloak. She looked like an old woman now and I had never thought her so. 'You are frightened,' I said. I meant no insult to her Tribequeen's courage; it was our kinship to these ancient tribelands that suddenly seemed as fragile as a first green shoot.

'Yes,' she said. 'I am frightened.' She glanced at Llwyd. 'About the problem, we are both in agreement. It is the solution that divides us.'

Llwyd sat unspeaking for some time, then turned and looked to me. 'It is the Kendra's knowledge that must decide whether we fight or submit.'

'Yes,' said Fraid. 'You are right.'

It took a moment for me to understand what they were asking. 'But I am not the Kendra...' I faltered.

'But you are chosen by the Mothers,' he answered. 'If you did not possess knowledge, you would not have been chosen.'

'It is true I have learned with them...' I grew more panicked. 'But I have not asked them such questions.'

He met my gaze. 'It does not need to be asked. It is within you because you have walked with them. You must claim this knowledge, Ailia, and tell us your counsel.'

My thoughts began to fragment. The clarity, the knowledge, I held only moments before was entirely lost. I thought of the Mothers who had taught me. Of Tara. Of Steise. What would they tell me now? Nothing came. 'What said Ruther?' I spluttered. 'Does he still advise we form bondage with Rome?'

Llwyd sighed and looked away.

'Ask not of Ruther,' said Fraid. 'He has not been often among us and when he is, he speaks highly of the Roman commanders. I meet with him because he holds knowledge of the invasion but—' her eyes darted from Llwyd to me, '—do not trust him, Ailia. He has great allure but he is not clear in his alliances.'

I braced my palms on the boarskin beneath me, my fingers finding the hard, wrinkled tip of the snout. My heart started to race.

'Ailia?' said Llwyd, imploring. 'Do not give us another's answer.

It must be *your* knowledge. The Roman forces prepare to attack and we must decide which is worth more: our freedom or our lives. What does the Kendra's knowledge say?'

I looked to his face and then the Tribequeen's and I was sickened to realise that this was no longer a test, but a true question. That Fraid looked to me, that Llwyd himself required my guidance, set me reeling. I was not ready. It was beyond my learning. My need for Taliesin was blinding now. 'I...I do not know.'

I pushed myself to standing on unsteady legs, gasping for air. 'I must be gone,' I stammered. 'This is a mistake. I am without skin. I cannot yet give what you seek. Perhaps I cannot ever give it.'

'No, Ailia—' Llwyd stood. 'Wait!'

But I stumbled backward, bowing quickly before I rushed out of the room into the dim winter moonlight.

The icy air rushed into my lungs as I ran through the township. Soon my chest ached but I pushed myself faster down the hill and into the fields. I wanted my heart to feel nothing else. This was my truth: moving in secret, untethered, unknowing. I should not have sought to know my skin. I was born not to know it. The unknowing shaped me. Knowing now would have broken me apart.

I ran the river path toward Taliesin. If I could not bring him here then I would go to his place. If I could not help him then I would be lost with him. What Llwyd was asking I could not give.

A heavy snow began to fall, iceflakes prickling my face as I ran. Ahead was the Oldforest, black under the swirling sky.

'Ailia!' A figure loomed before me, tall and strong-shouldered, his face shadowed in the grey light. I gasped. It was Llwyd. He was young and beautiful, his long hair dark. He could not have pursued me here by flesh. He had travelled by spirit drawn from the time of his young man's strength.

I stood in the tumbling snow, awed in the face of the skill he had used to shape this change. But I would not be swayed. 'I am going to the Mothers!'

'You cannot,' he commanded, his voice resonant. 'You are still without skin.'

How could I tell him that the Mothers cared nothing for skin? For it would desecrate his knowledge, and he would never believe me. 'You ask too much of me!' I cried. 'I am mourning my milkmother. I have lost all that binds me to Cad. Now you ask me to give wisdom that determines the life or death of the tribe. Wisdom that I do not have. Do not keep me here.' I went to push past him, but he blocked my way.

'Then think of others,' he said. 'Think of the tribespeople. If you force through now, you will tear open the skin that holds us all.'

I stopped, wondering fleetingly if he spoke the truth. But then my thoughts filled with Taliesin. It was he alone who drew me on, nothing else. What harm could arise from our union? 'Do not burden me with what I cannot carry, Llwyd. I do not have the power you think I have.'

He stood firm in my path, snow mounding on his cloak. 'Do you not think that I, too, have felt unworthy of knowledge?' he said. 'There is no one born who does not doubt themselves before it. I, too, struggled to hold what was handed to me...' He paused.

I stared at him as glinting iceflakes caught in his beard. For Llwyd not to have learned would have been a terrible loss. But I was not like him. The knowledge had been poorly matched to me. 'I will never be Kendra!' I shouted. 'I will never have skin.'

'You *will* be Kendra,' he said. 'You will hear the Singing and you will return to us with its truth.'

'No!' Tears fell from my cheeks.

Gradually his glamour was subsiding and he contracted to his old man's shape. 'You must—' His voice was aged and rasping again.

'Or else we are all lost in a world that only you have the power to understand.'

I could not hear any more. He was wrong. I pushed past him.

'Ailia!'

I did not look back. I had my own knowledge of the Mothers. I had walked with them and knew they did not ask of my skin. And had I not cut through the realms once before with my sword? I was outside the laws of skin. I would set my own path.

Llwyd's shouts grew fainter behind me.

I ran straight through the Oldforest until I reached the hazel pool. Its black water churned. 'Taliesin!' I screamed. 'Taliesin, come!'

My words condensed in the cold air.

There was a strangeness to the water when I crouched to quench my thirst. It was as thick as syrup in my cupped palms and no sooner had I sipped it than I spat it back. It was foul with the taste of rot. Was this the Mothers repelling me? But I thought only of Taliesin and how it would feel when he held me. I cared not for the warning of the river, nor for the doings of the Romans, nor for the harm of which Llwyd spoke. I did not want to be Kendra. I wanted only to join with Taliesin and stay with him in his place. I was fit for no other.

I tore off my cloak, dress and sandals, shrinking against the furious cold, and refastened my sword belt over my under-robe. At the river's edge, with the shallows shooting ice currents up my legs, I was caught by a moment of fear. I had journeyed through this pool only once before and that was by the guidance and seduction of my fish. Alone, I had no recollection of how far or how deep I needed to swim. I could only jump and trust that Taliesin would take me through.

I braced to jump, my feet numb in the water. I would not survive long submerged in this coldness. This passage would be death or a return to Taliesin and I would take either.

I closed my eyes and launched into the deep centre of the pool, then turned and swam down, face-first into the drop.

Soon the breath drained from my chest and I was dizzied with cold and pain. Pressure squeezed my ribs as I kicked downward, my lungs screaming for air. Finally, I opened my mouth and sucked in a mouthful of cold, silty water. It filled my chest to breaking then, somehow, I found the air in it. The pressure lessened and the pain subsided. The water flowed in and out of my lungs. I was breathing it.

I could see nothing in the blackness, but as I swam my fingers brushed against walls of stone beside and above me. I was under-ground. I swam effortlessly, water coursing through my body like blood. There was bliss in it, sustenance, and I was not afraid.

Soon there was a glow ahead. I eddied forward, drawn to the light, then I was free of the underwater chambers and rising toward a bright moon. My face broke the surface and I gasped air, a human breath.

I was within a wide lake, a shoreline not far in the distance. It was still dark but the air was warm; the seasons were askew again. I had journeyed. Joyously, I took another breath and began to swim. Yet as I drew closer to shore, I recognised a shape rising out of the water, lit by the three-quarter moon. It was Glass Isle's mighty Tor. I remained in the hardworld. Yet had I not travelled by trance to come here? By journey?

Night mist clung to the shore of the Isle. I crawled onto the pebbly bank and collapsed on my side. It was the same bank that met the canoe when I first arrived with Sulis. I was sure of it.

I stood up, wringing the lake from my under-robe. I could not find the shape of what had happened. If I had not journeyed to the Mothers—if I was still in the hardworld—then how had the season been turned? How did I swim such a distance?

I checked the strapping that held my sword to my waist. I would rest in my temple bed this night and leave at first light. If I walked the same forest path that led me to Taliesin, the same mist-filled gully, I would surely be able to cut through once more to the place of the Mothers who held him.

I walked the treeline in the darkness, searching for the opening that led to the temple. But when the shore began to curve to the north and I had been walking almost half an hour, I knew I must have passed it.

I walked back, scouring the forest edge as I went, but still the path was not revealed. At last there was a small gap in the trees, marked with a clump of buckthorn heavy with berries. Had the path been so narrow and unformed? I did not recall it so. I took a few steps but the spongey ground and overhung branches soon turned me back onto the shore, my skin prickling with fear. I walked back and forth with a quickening pace, but the line of trees was as dense as a wall. This was maddening. There was nothing for it but to return to the buckthorn path. It had to be the path to the temple. There was no other.

I would be through in moments, I told myself as I stood poised at the mouth of the track. I had walked the Oldforest by night before, so why did this path set my heart thumping?

The moon scarcely penetrated the forest canopy. There was a bank of sheared earth to my right and I trailed my fingertips tentatively along it. Soon all light was banished. Whether my eyes were closed or open made no difference. I pawed forward over the uneven ground, my arms outstretched, groping into the space before me.

I tried to calm myself, to argue with my pounding heart, but my muscles were strung taut, alert to every sound that echoed in the blackness. Was that the rustle of a wolf? An animal smell rose through the odour of wet leaves, but I was so addled by loss of sight that my mind was surely bending my senses. I had to be nearing the temple clearing. Or was I wandering deeper into the Isle's forests? I stopped. I had lost all sense of direction. Moments as long as hours passed while I stood, unmoving.

The darkness began to attack, full of spirits, circling and readying. I spun toward the sound of footsteps behind me, then others in front. There was a wailing cry and I did not know if it was my voice or another's.

With a jolt, I realised what was happening. This was my long night. My trial. And I was failing it. The making of fire or finding of food was beyond me now. The test of the long night was to banish fear. But with every shaking breath, I summoned what waited in the darkness. The rot beneath my feet was not leaves, but bodies, infected, predatory, clamouring for me.

Even in my terror, I recognised this darkness. There was something monstrous in me that called it forth. What I had feared my whole life was upon me. I was utterly alone. It was my punishment. Deserved. For placing my lover before my milkmother, for shunning the wisdom of my Elders, for thinking I could live outside skin. If fear could be withstood during the long night it would not return again. But fear had slaughtered me.

I sank to the ground and curled into a ball, my body aching with the need for sleep. But there would be no escape from the full passage of this terror.

I lay for many hours, rigid.

I learned the true shape of my fear.

I learned what it was to be only myself.

—

Dawn came like a kiss, its flesh light filling the forest. Never had I been happier to see the day. The scene of last night's torment was now so tranquil, the path clear when I turned to find it. I had survived.

I moved slowly, fractured by the night that had torn through me. But when I finally stepped free of the trees, there were no temple huts. No initiates. There was nothing here at all. 'Sulis?' I called feebly. 'Taliesin?'

Had I wrought this change by my tearing of skin? Was I to remain alone here as punishment? Last night's horror began to stir and I knew I could not endure it again. I wondered if I should leave the Isle while I had light. But there was no boat to travel back to Caer Cad over the water and I would never find the passageway that brought me here under the vast lake. Still I was not even sure if I stood in the hardworld or on Mothers' ground.

Perhaps I had died this night. Perhaps I had come to Caer Sidi. Part of me wished it so. But my hunger, my exhaustion, my grazed skin, my loneliness all felt very much of the living.

It was only the thought of Taliesin that bade me walk on. But there was no forest track, nothing I recognised here except the Tor, looming before me. Was that a thread of smoke winding from its summit? A fire?

I blundered forward, ignoring the teachings that forbade me from ascending the mountain. It was steeper than it appeared from below. Panting, I clambered up a winding path through dense wildflowers and mountain shrubs. Near the summit the path became stony, banks of low cloud drifting past. I kept my eyes on the ground, the smell of the smoke urging me on.

When at last I reached the peak I was in a clearing ringed with rough-cut branches, buckthorn and stones. A woodfire burned in the centre but no one tended it. No one was here. I collapsed on a log, my legs shaking, and closed my eyes. I had been truly cast from all I knew.

Then on the howl of the wind, I heard a human breath. When I looked up there was an old woman sitting cross-legged behind the fire. Had she been so still that I did not see her? With a cry of relief, I ran forward and crouched to greet her.

She was older than Cookmother, older than Llwyd. But beneath the droop of her brow, her eyes were the colour of the greenest water. She stared at me then spread her arms. Without pause, without thought, I climbed into her embrace. She wrapped her arms around me and kissed my forehead with the love of a mother. I burrowed into the warmth of her lap, sinking deeper as she yielded to my weight.

For a teetering moment, I could have pulled myself back from her embrace and returned to the solid ground of the mountain. Even as I fell into it, I knew there was risk in this pleasure that I may not return. But her hold was so blissfully tender after my night alone that I no longer cared for anything else.

I closed my eyes and let her skin and muscles grow around me until I was entirely buried, submerged in the current of her blood. Soon there was no more flesh and I was falling, surrendered, into emptiness. My journey was over.

Language

To know the earth, we must learn to hear it
in a way that reveals its language.

PAIN SEARED THROUGH my centre.

Something had caught my fall.

When I clutched my belly I felt a cord, warm and sinewy, coursing with blood. This was what held me. In agony, I grasped it and hauled myself up to lessen the strain.

I did not want to be caught.

Bearing my weight with one hand, I reached for my sword with the other. This was its promise: to do my will. It would slice through the cord that halted my fall. Even a flash of Taliesin's face, vivid as flame, could not bid me stay.

My fingers tightened around the cord as I readied to cut. Then, through the membrane of skin, I felt a vibration. A hum. Faint, as though from a great distance. I raised the sword. But the humming strengthened. It was a voice, a song. An illusion, I told myself, a trick of the mind. One last barrier to pass before I could enter the freedom of the fall. Again I lifted my sword. A wave of song poured into me like breath, pure and spinning with light.

I hung, suspended by the cord, by the song. Beneath me was an infinite dark. Above me was the light. And the song. I looked up and I pushed the sword back into its sheath. I could not defy this sound.

Slowly I placed both hands around the cord and began to shunt myself up. It took many hours to make the ascent. Soon my shoulders ached and I was dripping with sweat. It was only the song, ever louder, that urged me on. Just as I could not heave myself up one more length, the cord thickened, becoming fleshy, muscular. Then it was a hand and an arm and I was being pulled back into the lap of the old woman.

But when I opened my eyes, it was not her, but the flat ground that cradled me, and the fire that warmed me. I lifted my under-robe and rubbed the place where the cord had attached. Now there was only smooth skin and some tenderness where it had pulled.

Still the air was full of song. I looked up to see a river of women in ceremonial furs surging past me, down the mountain. Straightaway I recognised their bearing, though I had not seen their faces before. I was indeed with the Mothers. It was their singing that had called me back from the fall. With a gasp, I recalled what Sulis had told me and I reeled with the question: had my long night been of the Mothers' realm? Were they preparing me to be Kendra? It could not be so. I was not ready.

Hesitantly I rose to follow them, my hair whipping in the wind, then I paused and turned back. I wanted to see the view from this height. At the summit's edge, I drew breath in wonder. I had never seen so much of the world. Woodlands, meadows, mist-crowned rises, irides-cent rivers and, beyond these, the endless lake, all spread in a vast living cloth. In the distance I saw the hill that marked the salmon's nose, the river of its spine and the jutting stones of its tail tips. The totems of dog, crow and many others were clear also, marked in the earth as they were in the night sky. I saw the land's stories of which Llwyd had spoken.

Through the howling wind, the Mothers' chant drifted up the hill. I walked to the other side of the summit and peered down. Hundreds of women, all singing, were pouring into the flatlands beneath the Tor. This was not just one group of Mothers, nor two, nor three. All the Mothers were assembling.

I scrabbled down the path, behind the women who descended, their sound unceasing. I alone did not sing.

At the base of the mountain I stood against a sheared stone bank and watched the Mothers gather in their circles, in turn making one great circle around a central fire. For what purpose did they gather? I shrank further back against the crumbling earth.

The greater circle was nearly complete. As the last women trailed in from the forest paths, my heart jumped.

'Tara!' I rushed forward to greet her.

She did not break her song, but her eyes told me she was pleased to see me and I took refuge beside her. 'Is this all of the Mothers?' I whispered.

Tara nodded, still singing.

'Tell me of them,' I said.

She halted her song and looked to the circle beside us. 'They are the Mothers of grain.' She turned to the next. 'They keep the language, and they the children...' One by one, she named each of the knowledges: nine I had not yet been called to learn, and one that I had. Steise and the Mothers of change stood across the great circle. I craned, searching for Taliesin, but he was not among them.

Tara nodded to the women who had sung me back from the fall. 'They are the Mothers who keep the renewal of laws. And she—' she pointed to an old woman who stood at the heart of the circle, raised high on a platform of interwoven branches, '—she alone keeps the twelfth lesson.'

It was the woman who had cradled me as I fell.

'She is the Mother who makes us all one.' Tara glanced at me. 'Once you have met with her, you will not return to the Mothers.'

I stared at Tara in shock. I had met with the old woman. But surely this could not be my last time with the Mothers? For if it was, I could not yet bring back Taliesin.

Tara took up her tone again and motioned that I leave. Distressed, I walked back, beyond the circles, to listen and watch.

The old woman stood with her arms raised, her gaze flickering around the circles. Then slowly, when every eye was upon her, she lowered her arms and the Mothers were silent.

She held one hand out to Tara's circle, the Mothers of fire, summoning their song. When the sound was strong, she used her other hand to call for another group and then a third. The exquisite blend of the three tones coiled through the air, soothing my fears and winding around my spirit.

With this, the old woman began an intricate dance of gestures, silencing one circle, summoning another, calling five, six, even ten at once. I listened spellbound as, with threads of song, she wove the fabric of the world around me.

I looked up at the great Tor and the trees covering it. They were made of song as much as of wood and earth and I could not tell if I was hearing or seeing them. The ground hummed beneath my feet and I looked up to a sky full of sound.

This was the Singing, the birthing of our country.

Slowly, I understood why skin was not part of the Mothers' world. They were before skin, beyond it. Skin was what held the hardworld in place. Skin was our name for what they created.

Slowly, I understood that our world could not exist unless the song was heard that made it so. And I was the woman who heard it for my people.

There was an abrupt silence as the old woman quieted the Mothers and raised her left hand high above her head. I watched her, without breathing, as she lowered her arm toward the place where I stood, until finally it came to stillness pointing directly at me.

I froze.

She wanted me to sing. She wanted me to answer. But what would I sing? I had no skin. I had no song. I looked at the old woman and then around at the Mothers, all silent, all staring. I met Tara's eye, then Steise's.

I opened my mouth and drew a lungful of air. My breath reached where it had never been, into the deepest core of my being, where I sensed something dislodge and take form. It rose from my core, then broke from my throat on trembling air. A note, as sweet and thin as a shoot of grass. And as it was uttered, it took root, strengthening, until it was as dense and textured as the ground beneath me.

I knew it. It was my song. My part of all creation.

I did not have skin, but I was the Kendra.

Bridging the Worlds

The hardworld and the Mothers' world
are bridged by our Kendra.
Only she can witness the making of time.

THE SUN ROSE and set three times as we sang. Sometimes the women lay down to sleep. They left to drink water, to piss, or fuel the fire, but the song remained unbroken.

During these days I learned the songs that made the mountain, the wind, the trees and the seasons. I heard the words that made the human and animal shapes, and I echoed them until I knew I would never forget them. Each circle of Mothers had a song for their part of the country. I remembered them all.

By the Singing, I knew that I would never see the hardworld in the same way now. I would always hear the songs that gave it form. By the Singing, I knew the counsel that I would offer Llwyd and Fraid when I returned: we would fight the Roman forces. We would defend the songs with our lives. For without it, there would be no life.

It was the dawn of the fourth day. My legs ached from standing, my vision was blurred from tiredness but still I sang.

The old woman summoned Tara and two others of the Fire Mothers to my side.

Tara drew her knife.

I knew what they were about to do. I trembled as the two Mothers braced my arms and Tara released the fastening of my robe. She placed a wad of tightly rolled linen into my mouth and raised her blade. The old woman summoned volume in the song. Every Mother was singing me into being. The sound was deafening.

I buckled, biting hard on the linen as Tara cut a spiralling shape into my chest with her knife. The hot pain brought a deep release as blood dripped in the dirt at my feet. This was the wound that would hold the song. The scar that would mark me in the hardworld.

Tara left my cut untended and returned with her women to their circle.

I tried to resume my song but, in my exhaustion, my voice began to fail, and with it, my vision. The temple house emerged before me, its stones not solid but sheer as a veil, the circles of Mothers still visible behind it.

I squeezed my eyes closed, but when they opened, the temple was yet clearer and I saw Sulis push through the door and walk toward me, a jug in her hand. 'Sulis!' I cried. I stood directly before her but she neither saw nor heard me. She did not witness that I stood with the Mothers as they sang.

The Mothers' song shifted, strengthened, and Sulis faded from sight.

I stared hard at the circles of Mothers, watching and listening, before once again the temple huts and gardens took shape before me.

My sister initiates were tending the temple grounds, chattering as they filled buckets from the pools. They were not firm-fleshed, but wrought of some mist that thickened then waned with the rise and fall of the song.

This was no trick of the eye. This was my return to the hardworld.

For most of the day I was cast backward and forward between these two visions. The Mothers' song poured forth unbroken while the temple initiates carried out their tasks in the same place, the same moment. I saw both truths at once. One a little clearer, then the other.

As the sky deepened, the temple at last grew solid and the circles of women ebbed away. As I watched them fade I felt a wash of grief, then I recalled Tara's words and they hit me like a slingshot: I would not be called to the Mothers again.

'Taliesin! Tara!' I shouted, calling them back, swaying with the effort and the pain of my wound.

The shape of the Mothers strengthened once more. I ran among them, searching and calling.

Shrouded by trees, beyond the edge of the circle, he stood alone. At the sound of my voice he turned. I had never seen him look so fragile or so beautiful. He wore a summer tunic, dyed with bark, as dark as the shadows that ringed his eyes. The bones of his shoulders hunched forward as though caging his heart.

'My light,' he whispered into my hair when I reached him. 'Can you free me? Have you learned of your skin?'

I shook my head against his chest. 'The woman who knows it will not yield.' His heart quickened beneath my cheek and I tightened my hold. 'There will be a way.'

He pulled back to stare at me. 'There is no other way.'

Through the translucence of his throat and arms, I saw the faint forms of the temple huts. 'No,' I cried. I could not let him fade from me. By the force of my intent I hardened the realm and he was once again solid. But there was little strength in me to hold him much longer.

Think, I commanded myself, over the crash of my heartpound. I searched my memory for the ways I had journeyed forth and back from the Mothers: by the drop in the pool, by the Mothers' song, by cutting the mist in the gully. The mist! I gripped Taliesin's forearms. Why had I not seen it before? 'My love,' I gasped, 'when you come to the hardworld, is it always through water?'

'Yes. As fish. I have told you—'

'There has been no threshold, other than this?'

The bones of his wrist started to soften as I grasped them. He was slipping. 'There is another threshold.' He frowned. 'But one I cannot breach.'

'Describe it,' I urged.

'It is a thickness, a barrier that rises near the river when you call to me. I have tried to push through it as man. Sometimes I see you beyond it. Once you even heard me call through it. But only as fish, beneath the water, can I pass.'

I was shaking in my excitement. 'Is it a mist? A watery barrier?'

He nodded. 'It is that.'

Then I was laughing and sobbing. 'Mothers be praised, Taliesin. If you can stand at that veil, then I have means to cut it. I can bring you through as man.'

'How?' he asked, unbelieving.

'This!' I cry, lifting the weapon still bound to my waist. 'My sword has cut such a mist before. My sword will cut your passage.'

'No.' His face knotted with doubt. 'No sword can cut the realms.'

'But it has! It has cut through when skin could not.'

His smile was unsure.

My hold of him was weakening. In moments he would be gone. 'You must go to that place,' I told him. 'You must stand at that mist.'

'When?' he breathed. 'Now?' His flesh grew yet sheerer.

'Not now,' I cried, desperate. 'If I cut from here, I do not know where we will emerge. I must cut from Summer and bring you there.' I looked to his face. 'Beloved Taliesin, can you wait a little longer to come home?'

He answered me with a kiss that turned my flesh to water.

'Wait for my call,' I instructed when he pulled away. 'I will go to the forest and call for you. I beg that you hear it. But do not sink beneath the water. Do not come as fish. Find the mist and stand before it as man. That is my only chance to make you free.'

He stared at me, his dark eyes ebbing. 'Are you true?'

I staggered. His wounds were deep to question a heart as sure as mine. He was dissolving quickly now.

'Listen for my call!' I commanded as he faded.

He nodded, and met my gaze for one last moment. For the first time, I saw an echo of Cookmother's eyes in his. It was too late to tell him now. I would tell him when he was free.

He turned as he disappeared.

It must be true, I assured myself. My sword would cut what lay between us. The Mothers had promised me this: if it took no life, it would do my will. And this, above all else, was my will. At last my legs, which had stood for four days, could carry me no longer and I sank to the ground.

—

'Ailia?' The sharp voice was familiar.

I opened my eyes to see darkness had fallen.

'Rise, girl.' Sulis crouched beside me and aided me to sit.

The temple garden was quiet now. The Mothers were gone.

'Am I returned?' I murmured, dizzy from change.

'Yes,' she said, scowling, 'and I do not need to ask whether you have been with the Mothers. I see how you are drunk with journey.' She offered me her water pouch and I drank thirstily. 'How did you reach them?' she asked. 'By medicine? By chant?'

By my love of Taliesin, I wanted to answer, recalling the pool, the swim. 'By their ways,' I said.

'By skin?' she persisted.

My face fell. 'No.'

Her eyes closed then opened, her brow furrowed. 'You will not disturb the initiates with any account of this. You will sleep this night in my hut and resume training at sunrise.'

I stared at her, terrified that she would not release me. 'But—I cannot go back to my training,' I stammered. 'I must return to Cad—'

'You have been almost three summers gone from temple. There is much you have missed.'

Breath caught in my throat. Yet another year passed in a matter of days. I wanted, with all my being, to free Taliesin, but even more than this, I wanted to give my people their Kendra. Was it too late? 'There is counsel I must give Fraid and Llwyd—'

Sulis shook her head. Her voice could not contain her displeasure. 'You have journeyed again to the Mothers without skin, without sanction. You are in breach of our most sacred laws.' Her hands trembled as she interlocked them. 'You will stay and resume your learning. And try to make right what you have wronged by these journeys.'

'I have been given knowledge, Journeywoman! I must bring it to Cad—'

She crouched unmoving. 'What knowledge have you received?'

I paused, suddenly frightened to utter it. But there could be only truth now. 'The song,' I answered. 'I have heard the song.'

Her eyes widened. 'Whose song?'

'The Mothers' song. The creation song.'

'And you, girl…did *you* sing?'

'Yes,' I said, my heart soaring at the memory. 'I sang.'

'You lie,' she hissed.

We both looked up as an initiate passed, holding a blazing torch. Suddenly there was light enough for Sulis to see the dark stains that soaked my tunic. 'Mothers of earth, what is this wound?' she cried.

Before I could tell her she tore open my robe and bade the light be held nearer to my bleeding cuts.

The initiate gasped.

'As the moon is my witness.' Sulis was trembling. 'It is the cut of the Kendra.'

'Yes,' I murmured.

Sulis stiffened. 'Was it you?' she whispered. 'Have you wrought these cuts to claim the Kendra's title?'

'No. They are true.' My voice was a whimper.

Slowly Sulis placed her fingers to the edge of my wound and her eyes closed.

I watched her. These cuts were my only evidence. Why did she touch them?

A frown twitched across her brow as if she battled another expression. Her eyes sprang open. 'I hear it.' Her voice was unsteady. 'I hear the song.'

I slumped, weakened, as though her touch had drained me of blood. But even in my frailty, my whole being was lit by the revelation: this was how the Mothers claimed me as their own. Their song was in my wound. This was what I would carry back. And no one could deny me.

Initiation

Knowledge is shared only between the initiated.
Only the initiated have the power to prevent death, recapture
souls, and understand the depth of the human mind.

AD 46

W E REACHED CAER CAD in the bright light of the next
afternoon. Sulis had brought me by boat across the lake
and we had walked the day's journey back to my hillfort home at a
tireless pace. Save for the brief words of wayfinding and the sharing
of dried fish, our travel had passed wordlessly. I was unsure of how
I stood in her eyes. She had recognised my mark, she had heard its
song, but she had not yet called me Kendra.

Spring blossoms dotted the hedges along the laneways. Three
seasons. By hard time, I was seventeen summers. How close would
Rome be now?

'Speak nothing of your marks until I meet with Fraid and Llwyd,'
said Sulis, as we reached Cad Hill. 'We must determine what shall be
done.'

'But they must learn that I have been made Kendra straightaway,' I said. 'There may be little time to wait.'

'Hush,' she spat, panting with the ascent. 'I know not what skewed spell-craft you have used to purchase the marks at your chest, but you will stay silent now.'

I pushed down my protest. Sulis did not recognise me. Would anyone? The Mothers had made me Kendra, because they were not beholden to skin. If the tribes were to accept me as Kendra, I would have to convince them of this new truth. But would they hear it?

The gates were unattended as we entered Cad. My heart swelled at the sight of the familiar houses and roadways, yet something was altered here. The township was too quiet. I glanced to the daylight moon. It was no wane day. Where were the craftsmen and the sellers? 'Perhaps there has been a death?' I wondered aloud. 'Are they all at burial?'

There were no deer antlers adorning the doorways of the central street and many houses were emptied of their shrines. 'The totems are abandoned,' said Sulis. 'This is not well.'

Both wary of what we might find, our pace slowed as we approached the Tribequeen's compound. We passed through the gateway, and what we saw brought us to stillness.

Clustered around the entrance to the Great House was a large gathering of my townspeople, some sitting, others sprawled on the ground. At the sound of our footsteps, they turned to us with an inhuman slowness. Their eyes were dark and staring, their faces gaunt.

'What is this, Journeywoman?' I whispered, filling with dread.

'This is Troscad,' said Sulis with shock in her voice. 'The ritual fast. They are hungering against the Tribequeen's injustice.'

'But why? How does Fraid betray them?'

'We cannot ask them. Troscad prohibits both word and food. Go to your kitchen house,' she commanded under her breath. 'Wait there for me. Speak to no one. Not a word. I will go to Fraid and learn what has happened.'

Cah was alone in the kitchen, at the quern stone, grinding wheat. 'You are back,' she said, standing.

'What has happened?' I asked. 'Why do the townspeople make Troscad?'

She knelt back down at the quern. 'Your bedfellow has taken Caer Cad.'

It took me a moment to realise she spoke of Ruther.

'Ay,' she said, working the stone. 'He appealed for clientage with Rome but Fraid would not agree. Then he worked secretly last winter to gather support from the warriors. He challenged for the kingship and won it by one vote in the council.'

I gasped in astonishment. 'Where is Fraid?'

'One of the farmhouses gives her refuge. I know not which.'

'And Llwyd? Surely he has not sanctioned Ruther as Tribeking?'

'Of course not. But Ruther does not care for the ways of the journeymen now. Amusing,' she snorted, 'that his great love is a journeywoman in training.'

'I am no love of his.'

She poured a fresh cupful of grain into the quern hole. 'Do not say so too loudly. It is rumoured that he is still angered by your marriage refusal, despite that it is three seasons past. If you were clever, you would keep far from his sight.' She chuckled and looked up at me. 'Not the welcome home you were expecting, eh?'

'I must find Llwyd,' I murmured, too distracted to respond.

'Be careful,' she warned. 'Ruther has cast Llwyd from the walls of Cad. He forbids the townspeople to see him and he is not a forgiving Tribeking. Many townspeople are fasting against his kingship and he'll see them die for their effort, I'm sure of it.'

'And you? Do you not fast against this wrongdoing?'

'I'm busy enough cooking here with only Ianna to help me. Whether I make bread for Fraid or Ruther, it is all the same to me.'

I flinched at her heartlessness, then realised that she had mentioned only Ianna. 'Where is Heka? Does she not help you?'

Cah raised her eyebrows. 'She serves in Ruther's house. He looked favourably, as I did, upon her spine and grit and likes her to attend his person.' She looked at me. 'I miss her being here,' she said. 'She was good company.'

Ignoring her, I turned and walked to the door. 'Cah,' I said, turning back. 'Where is Neha?'

'Heka took her. She preferred Heka to all others when you were gone.'

I took a sharp breath then turned and left.

I stood at the southern gate, looking over the fields of Summer in the afternoon light. Any one of the farmers could have been hiding Llwyd and would not have said so. But if my sense of him was true, he would be ritualling in response to this crime and there was a place I might find him.

The shadows were long when I reached the Oldforest. If Llwyd had been challenged—if he could not ritual freely by the river—he would come here.

I held to the river track, peering among the trees. At last I saw the shape of his pallid robes, stark against the dark trunks that ringed my journey pool. He had marked out a circle of branches close to the river and had placed within it small carvings and statues that honoured the deer. I stopped at the boundary, still wary to enter a journeyman's circle without my skin. 'Journeyman?'

He startled at my voice. 'Who is there?' His vision had weakened. 'It is Ailia. Returned.'

'Ailia!' His steps were laboured as he came forward to embrace me. Through his woollen cloak, I felt the bones surfaced by his fast. 'Have you learned of Ruther?' he asked.

'Ay. But little else. I know nothing of the invasion—'

'We are to fall, Ailia.' His voice was empty. 'The Romans have claimed Stour Valley, Brae Cad and Caer Hod. We are clear in their sights.'

I stared at his face, ashen with hunger. 'How does Ruther propose to meet this attack?'

'With full submission. This is his purpose. We are to be slaves of Rome.'

I shook my head. 'He cannot be Tribeking without your sanction.'

'He does not observe our laws now. And he has the support of the warriors who betrayed Fraid.'

'But the township hungers against him.'

'Yes. They still love Fraid. There is great division.'

Evening had began to dim the forest. Llwyd motioned to a fallen log, covered with moss, and we sat. 'We will go to him together,' I said. 'He is a tribesman of Durotriga. He must listen to his Journeyman Elder.'

'He will not. He is of the Roman mind. He listens to his own counsel and that of other warriors.'

Llwyd shivered in the cooling air and I moved closer to him, placing my hand at his back. 'Stay steady, Journeyman,' I whispered. 'We will survive this.'

He turned to me. 'Will we? It is the journeymen and -women who are first slaughtered. Most violently. Most publicly. There is no better way to subdue a tribe than by destroying those who hold its knowledge. The Romans know this. Whole towns are made subject by the slaughter of wisepeople.'

My heart quickened.

'If we are killed,' he continued, 'who will ensure the laws of skin

298

are not broken? Who will listen when the Mothers speak?' His voice, so resonant at festival time, was hoarse and feeble. 'I did not think this could happen, Ailia. I thought our knowledge was beyond destruction.'

I looked to the coursing river, to the oaks rising like warriors around us. I remembered the Singing and it filled me with strength. 'It *is* beyond destruction.' My voice was steady. 'This land is our knowledge. They are one and the same. Come.' I reached for his hand, bidding him rise.

Llwyd did not move. 'It is too late. They are too strong.'

'We will be the first to fight and win against them,' I urged. 'The first of Albion to keep the laws of our choosing. They will not have us. Others will see our triumph and be strengthened by it.'

Llwyd stared at me. 'How will we succeed where Albion's greatest fighting tribes have failed?'

'Because...' My answer crumbled. Sulis's doubt had seeped into my sureness. I could find no words to tell him. Yet I was the being he had yearned for, the soul that would protect the knowledge he loved.

With shaking fingers, I unfastened the neck of my robe and pulled away the soaked wad of dressing. Then I took his hand and pressed it to my chest. 'Because we will fight with the blessing of the Kendra.'

I flinched in pain as his gnarled fingers traced over the raw crusts of my cut. A deep ache arose as he touched.

Slowly his face lit as he read the round, spiralling shape of the mark. Then his breath caught. 'There is song in the wound,' he gasped. 'You are made Kendra—?'

'Yes,' I said.

'But what of your skin?' he whispered, hope thinning his voice.

I re-pinned my robe, terrified to answer. How would I hold the title if Llwyd would not acknowledge it? 'The Mothers have marked me without skin.'

His face blackened. 'No,' he muttered. 'They have not. They cannot mark a Kendra without skin.'

'But yet they have,' I said, praying that he would hear me. 'And there is sense to it...there is a reason—'

'Stop!' He rose to his feet. 'There can be no reason. You are in grave breach of law with this. I can hear no more—'

'Wait!' I cried as he walked away. 'I told them I was skinless! I asked them to return me, and yet...' I paused.

Llwyd stopped.

I took a long breath. I could be shunned anew, or worse, for the words I was about to say. 'The Mothers have no need of skin.'

Slowly, he turned to face me. Never, even in the peaks of ritual, had I seen him so inflamed. He sank to the ground, where he knelt, calling on the Mothers, bidding me to silence my violation.

I crouched before him, clutching his arms, which shook me away with unexpected force. 'You speak against skin!' he cried. 'Against the very source of skin!'

'I do not, Llwyd! Hear me!' I pleaded. 'It is ours! *Our* truth! It belongs to the hardworld. Skin is *our* understanding of what *they* create.'

He stilled for an instant and looked at me.

'Their creation is beautiful beyond measure,' I said, 'and skin is how we know it, and how we protect it, but they themselves do not need skin. *We* are bound by it. But the Mothers are not.'

A deep confusion darkened his gaze.

'For us, skin is life itself,' I continued, 'and by the Mothers, I would give my own eyes and tongue to have it. But I do not. And yet the Mothers want me as Kendra. And if you want my knowledge, Journeyman, you must accept me.'

Llwyd's stare was cold and bewildered. 'I have loved you and protected you and trusted in your gift. But you are asking me to speak against the truth upon which my life is built...'

My heart clenched. Could I ask this of him? I had no other choice. If he did not hear me, there would be no Kendra, no future. 'It is a greater truth that I bring,' I said. 'A new understanding of the Mothers' greatness. How powerful are they who are more powerful than skin?'

I watched his face closely as this new truth—that our spirit beings, our Mothers, did not need skin—moved through him, shifting, turning, then embedding.

'Perhaps,' I continued, 'the Mothers have chosen me precisely because I am unskinned, because they want us to know that skin is *not* theirs. It is ours.'

He sat motionless.

We both turned at the rustle of an animal close behind us. A honey-coloured doe lifted her head from the forest floor, tasting our scent on the breeze. It took two delicate steps toward us, then paused before taking flight into the evening. 'My totem appears...' murmured Llwyd, staring after it.

He turned to me then dipped his head to kiss my fingers. 'Kendra,' he whispered, his breath warm against my knuckles.

—

Llwyd knew where Fraid was hidden. As he led me north through the laneways in the last drifts of dusk, we shaped a strategy.

'I will speak with Ruther,' I said. 'There is still a chance I can turn his view and gather the allegiance of his fighting men.'

'Speak with him,' agreed Llwyd. 'You alone could sway him. But do not speak in anger. He will always match it. Use the power you hold over him—it will be even greater now. Use his love for you.'

'It should be the Mothers he loves,' I said.

'He loves them no longer, but he loves them in you. Let him see them that way.'

I glanced at him. 'You are the cleverest of us all.'

'Remember, he does not look well upon me now,' he said, waving away my praise. 'Do not tell him that you have met with me.'

We arrived at a farmhouse, nestled among apple trees on the banks of the Nain in outer Cad. It was well kept and not long built, one of many belonging to Fibor, and leased to farmers for a share of the grain. Here, at least, antlers hung from the lintel and pots of burdock smoked in the shrine. We bowed before them and sounded the bell.

A gap appeared in the doorskins and Manacca, now as tall as my shoulder, peered out. She threw her arms around my neck when she saw me. Behind her was the housewoman, whom I had aided several times in birth and sickness. She beckoned us through, her two young sons at her skirts, clamouring to see the visitors. 'Greetings, Ailia,' she said. 'You have beaten the Romans by only days.'

The southern wall of the room was thick with Fraid's shields and weapons. Fibor, Etaina and Fraid were at the fire. Between them, in the strong place, sitting so still that at first I did not see her, was Sulis, her face pale.

Fraid rose to greet us. She was unmetalled, plainly robed and her hair fell unbraided over her shoulders, but her presence filled the room. 'How do you fare, Ailia?' She embraced me firmly. 'Will you offer your guidance now?'

'Yes,' I said, taking a place at the fire.

Llwyd sat at my right, closer to Sulis, who had not yet looked at me.

'Mead!' exclaimed the housewoman, striding to the hearth. She ladled steaming cups of honey beer from the firepot and passed them to each of us.

Manacca clucked at a woodfowl chick that roamed on the floor and Fraid hushed her. The room fell quiet, choked with questions, awaiting my word. Had Sulis told them yet of my marks?

'How far away are the legions?' I asked, stalling the news of my ascent. 'How long do we have?'

'They are camped at Hod Hill, throwing up new defences,' said Fraid. 'We do not know how long they will remain there or where they will next strike.' Her cheeks hollowed as she sipped her ale.

'But Hod is a foot journey of two days at most—' I said.

'Ay, they are close,' said Fibor. 'But some think they have Mai Cad in their sights before us. The riders bring different messages...'

'Have you spoken with Cun?' I asked.

'Ruther controls all contact,' said Fraid. 'The petty tribes are ignorant of one another and Ruther would keep it so. It is too late to join together now.'

My anger flared. Who was Ruther to keep his people in such darkness? 'Tribequeen, do you still hold the faith of the warriors?'

'I believe so,' said Fraid. 'There are only five, maybe six, who side with Ruther. At least ten are still aligned to me but quieted by fear.'

'And if I could convince Ruther to fight with us,' I continued, 'would your men join him?'

Fraid nodded. 'The tribe would follow a leader into war. But above all else—' her brown eyes glittered in the firelight as she lifted them toward me, '—they would fight for the Kendra if she commanded it.'

Now it had been spoken.

In the sudden silence, Sulis's breath was a faint hiss. The housewoman pretended to busy herself at her spindle.

'I...have sung with the Mothers,' I faltered. 'I return as Kendra.'

Fraid gasped. 'This is welcome news indeed,' she said. 'But how have you come to skin?'

Fibor and Etaina turned to me, their faces bright with hope.

My cheeks burned hot. 'I remain unskinned.'

303

Fraid's smile dropped away. 'Then how do you name yourself Kendra?'

I turned to Llwyd. We both knew it must come from him. 'The Mothers name her,' he said, unflinching. 'They have marked her with the scar.'

He nodded to me. With a galloping heart, I unpinned my tunic and pulled it part open to expose the cuts.

Etaina snorted in disbelief. 'Llwyd, this is madness! She makes these cuts by her own hand.'

'She does not.' Sulis spoke for the first time, her gaze locked to the flames. 'I witnessed her as she hardened from journey. The cuts were fresh. They were Mother-made—' she paused, '—they carry song.'

'Impossible.' Etaina shook her head.

'I have heard it by my own touch,' said Llwyd.

'And I,' said Sulis, her voice tight. 'I heard it, yet I did not hear the skin in it. Her mark is true. But it is falsely got. She is no Kendra.'

My heart plunged. 'Please, Sulis.' I could not let her rob me of this. 'When I tell you of my learning—'

'I acknowledge your learning, Ailia,' Sulis said. 'I am humble before it. But the skin totem is the truest shaping of us. The tribes will not follow a woman whose soul is still without form.'

I closed my eyes against the truth of it.

'It is so,' agreed Etaina. 'The tribe accepted Ailia as journeywoman initiate. But how can she wear the Kendra's robe without skin? Surely the Mothers would forbid it.'

I turned to Llwyd. Would they heed their highest Journeyman? His eyes were lowered. Did he begin to doubt? He looked at them. 'We can receive this Kendra,' he said. 'It does not breach the Mothers' law.'

'But *skin* is the Mothers' law.' Sulis's voice trembled.

'No,' Llwyd replied. 'Skin is *our* law. The Mothers are greater than skin.'

'Llwyd?' questioned Fraid, her face fraught with confusion. 'Do you speak against skin?'

'I love skin more deeply than ever,' he answered. 'But I have seen a shift in its meaning. We need skin, but the Mothers do not. And Ailia does not.'

I could not stifle my gasp. He had spoken too brazenly.

Sulis rose and walked from the fire, murmuring a low chant.

'This is greater than me,' said Fibor, also rising. 'I am a man of sword law. I will wait outside until it is decided.'

'Stay,' commanded Fraid. 'I want your ear on this.'

Llwyd took up his staff and looked to his tribespeople, his voice barely a whisper. 'I am also deeply confused,' he began. 'But this woman—this woman without skin—has felt the Mothers' knife at her chest. She has felt their song in her breath.' He glanced at me, his staff trembling. 'She told the Mothers of her lack of skin, but they did not protest it.' He paused again. 'They saw no lack.'

'We will be punished for this,' murmured Sulis from the darkness of the room's periphery.

Fraid leaned forward, searching Llwyd's face intently. I knew she had the fire of mind to hold this truth, but only if she was convinced. 'Are you saying,' she began, 'that of all the generations of our journey-women who have walked with the Mothers, none has ever discovered that the Mothers do not acknowledge skin?'

'I have wondered of this,' I interrupted. 'I have no answer. Perhaps I was the first to test it, for I was the first to journey without skin.'

'No,' said Llwyd. 'It is not this. Skin is a powerful light for the journeypeople. Perhaps those who are led by it have never been able to see beyond it. Perhaps it has taken one without skin to see the Mothers' freedom from it.' He looked directly at Fraid. 'The Mothers have chosen this time to reveal their truth, and have sent Ailia as its messenger.'

Fraid looked shocked as she grappled with these words from her most trusted advisor. 'So...do you suggest that we are to discard our belief in skin at will, then?' she stammered. 'Do we send any fringe-child to the Mothers now?'

'Of course not!' said Llwyd. 'Skin is the thread that leads us back to the Mothers. It will always be this. But Ailia holds a knowledge I have not seen before. A knowledge so strong that it carried her to the Mothers when skin would not.' He laughed in amazement. 'Ailia alone has transcended skin.'

'Mothers spare you, Llwyd,' muttered Sulis, stepping back into the fireglow. 'Even if she is truly chosen, she cannot transcend skin here, where the world is hard, where skin lives. It will tear our world open.'

'But it will not,' I said. Llwyd's defence had strengthened me. I had to make them see. 'We have never known an invasion like that which stands now at our doorstep. I bring a new knowledge from the Mothers, so that you may receive the Kendra they have chosen. It is I who will protect you, if you will let me. It is I who will teach you.'

'What do you teach?' Sulis scowled. 'That skin is nothing? That it is weak?'

'That it is beautiful!' I cried, gripping the edge of the bench. 'That it pours from the belly of the Mothers in infinite rivers to us, who name it and sing it back. That it is not rigid. It can bend and move. It can be cut and healed. It can hold more than we ever knew. Because it can hold unknowing.' I paused. Every eye was upon me. 'Llwyd spoke once that laws are true only when they are honoured in freedom. How can we truly honour skin if we are not also free of it? The Romans come. They will rob us of our skin and we must choose to fight for it. Only then is it true. This is what I teach of skin.'

Llwyd stared at me in wonder. 'You are the flaw in skin that proves its strength.'

The only sound was the fire's soft crackle and the clack of the spindle as the housewoman turned it nervously. I looked around at their troubled faces, wrestling with my words. I had given them almost enough. Almost, but not quite. There was one more truth to be shared and if this did not convince them, then I had nothing that would.

I rose to my feet and wrenched open my tunic, fully baring my marks. 'Touch!' I commanded. 'Then you will know if I am your Kendra.'

'You will grow too weak,' Llwyd protested.

'But they must hear,' I answered. 'They must hear what is within me.' With the force of my words the wounds had split and were beginning to run.

Manacca whimpered at the sight of the blood.

'Touch me, Fraid,' I urged. 'Tell me what you hear.'

Fraid stood hesitantly and walked to me, then laid her palm on my chest. I winced at the pressure. Again, there was a stirring, an ache, in the wound. The fire had burned down and the air was suddenly cold, but the housewoman did not tend it. All eyes were on Fraid.

Slowly her face broke into a smile. 'It is creation,' she whispered. 'It is beautiful.' She closed her eyes, pressing more firmly against my flesh. I fought a wave of dizziness as she drank of the sound that poured from my wound. 'I cannot deny it,' she said, withdrawing her hand, 'you are right, Llwyd.' She met my eye. 'Kendra,' she said and lowered her head.

Sulis moaned and sank to her seat.

The housewoman comforted Manacca.

One by one I commanded them all to touch.

Once Etaina had pulled her hand away, wet with blood, eyes shining with wonder, I slumped to the bench, gulping a long draught of mead. When I looked up, all heads but Sulis's were lowered around me. Her blank stare held an unnamable dread.

Many moments passed in silence.

'We will name you in the water tonight,' said Llwyd.

'What do you mean?' I asked. River initiation had not been spoken of.

'The Mothers have scarred you, but you must also be initiated in the hardworld as Kendra,' said Llwyd.

Fraid drained her cup, enlivened by the hope that was gathering around this plan. 'She will be recognised above even yourself as a knowledge-keeper, Journeyman. The warriors will find great strength in it.'

'It will mark the end,' said Sulis to herself.

Llwyd turned to me. 'Will you permit me to initiate you, Ailia?'

My fingers tightened around my cup as I battled a surge of doubt. With his initiation I would be wholly born to the hardworld. But without the skin to know my place in it. I thought of the Mothers. This was their will. But would it tear yet greater holes in what they had created?

'Ailia?' Llwyd urged.

I carried the song. There was something sacred within me. Something powerful. My Tribequeen and her councillors could not deny it now, nor could I. There was no other way that my knowledge would be seen. 'Of course,' I whispered.

⸺

The night was cold and the moon well hidden.

It should have been done at the Cam, near Cad Hill, but it would have been too great a risk for us to go so close to the township. Instead

Fibor, Etaina and I marked out a hasty circle in branches next to the Nain behind the farmhouse, while Fraid held a torch close by. Working quickly by its weak light, we buried meat and bread at the easternmost point of the circle and threw the last of Fraid's gold finger-rings into the river.

Sulis stood at a distance, watching.

Llwyd began the chant. He took a long time to walk the many circles moonwise that would bind our ritual to the rhythm of the sky. But at last it was done and there, within that small, cramped circle of ground, he sang me the poems that revealed what he knew of the Mothers. Sloughed of any encasement in skin, the stories were still as beautiful and transforming as dawn.

They stripped my clothing and laid me on the ground where Llwyd cast handfuls of cold dirt over my skin. 'This is the body of the Mothers, which is now your body,' he said as I shivered. He handed me a horn of ale, gritty with antler scraped from the shrine.

As I leaned up to drink, the bitter liquid spilled from my mouth.

'This is the spirit of the Mothers, which is now your spirit.'

Thick deer and cattle pelts were laid over me. I could not breathe beneath their smoky weight.

Llwyd's voice trembled as he peeled them back. 'From this moment you are born to the world and all knowledge is entrusted to you.'

I lay naked on the ground between them, the force of their gaze like a flame to my skin.

Llwyd led me to the river's edge and bade me enter the shallow water. Sharp stones pierced my back as I was pushed down, my face held to one side so I was fully submerged in the icy flow. His voice was distorted through the water and I could scarcely hear the last of his calls, but when I climbed back onto the bank, shaking with cold, it was done. I was sister of the Mothers. Daughter of the Mothers. Kendra of Albion.

Llwyd stood beside me, weeping openly.

Fibor cheered and Fraid stepped forward, arms outstretched.

Fighting my own tears, I returned her embrace. Immediately I could feel a new edge, a new surface. But beneath it, something was not right. Something remained unaltered.

Over Fraid's shoulder, I saw that Sulis had drawn closer.

As I had no skin talismans, Llwyd loosened the deerhide pouch at his belt and pulled out an amulet of adderstone. He kissed my forehead with cold lips as he handed it to me. 'Daughter,' he whispered. 'You are born.'

Aided by Etaina, I dressed quickly, strapping my sword and the amulet to my belt. Was I born? Llwyd had called it so and it would be true for my people. But wisdom should know itself and I did not feel this knowing.

Sulis stepped forward to offer her grim acknowledgement of the rite. The moon broke from behind the cloud, lighting her face, and I could see in her stare that she saw: she saw my doubt.

We walked back to the farmhouse in silence. With each step my hesitation grew. I knew I was chosen; I knew I had sung. So why did I now feel the Kendra's soul ebbing away?

Yet even as I wondered, I knew. The Mothers' place was free of skin, but here in the hardworld I was bound by its laws. This birth was a layer, a cloak that would be seen by the tribespeople. It gave shape to my surface, but not to my bones. It was not true.

It was not skin.

We pushed through the doorskins and I gathered my cloak in readiness to leave. It was too late now. I had to ignore my doubts. I had to be strong. I had to be the Kendra.

Poems

We recognise a speaker of truth
by the words that flow from her lips.
Words are the power that brings all into unity.

ALONE, I WALKED the laneways to Cad Hill.

Only Heka could give me what Llwyd could not. Heka, who was lost to the light. Who had vowed to give me nothing. I forced thoughts of her aside as I strode up the ramparts and through the entranceway. However it had come, this new birth had strengthened me. I hoped that I had enough to protect the township, enough to cut free my love.

As I turned into the Tribequeen's compound, music and laughter spilled from the Great House. Ruther was at feast, the townspeople hungering at his threshold in even greater numbers.

I darted behind the kitchen, stealing toward the sleephouse, unseen. It was not yet late. I had time to hide myself before he returned. Waiting silently for Cah to pass with a platter of cakes, I crept to the doorway and slipped inside. Praise the Mothers, no one was there.

I looked around the room in which I had attended Fraid for all my grown summers. It was different now. Weapons were stacked along the western side—the resting place—and the bed had been moved to the east, the place of light. Lavish new pelts and weavings lined the walls, and cups and jugs of Roman design filled the shelves. It was no longer a tribequeen's house. It was full of the sharp smells of a man.

I hid myself behind the falls of cloth that lined the walls in the darkest part of the room and soon I heard Ruther's ale-soaked voice approaching the door. As he entered, I heard a woman's laughter. He was not alone. Had I to wait out his coupling?

'The hungerers are stubborn, I'll give them that,' said Ruther to his companion.

'Then disrobe!' The woman laughed. 'And let me feast if they will not.'

I startled, peering out from the cloth's edge to confirm what my ears could not believe. The voice was Heka's.

They were untying their belts and pulling off garments amid drunken shrieks.

With a pounding heart, I flattened against the wall, trying to close my ears to the rut and grunt that followed. Mercifully, it did not take too long until I heard the familiar pant and rising moan that told me Ruther was close to the end. But the name he cried, when his pleasure reached its peak, was not Heka's but mine.

'What said you?' Heka's voice was sharp with fury.

'I said nothing,' Ruther muttered into his bedskins.

'I heard you call Ailia,' she spat. 'Does that serpent poison all? Crawling even between me and the man I am fucking?'

'Leave then,' he commanded wearily. 'You are not even a drop to her river.'

Despite her venom against me, I was angered by his dishonour of her.

When she had left, taking her hateful murmurs into the night, Ruther walked to the night pot. As he steadily filled it, I stepped out of my cover. 'Donkey,' I said softly when he had finished.

'Ailia!' he gasped, turning. 'What are you doing?'

'Waiting for you.'

He came to me, taking my face in his hands. Even in the dim firelight, the blue of his eyes was startling. 'You are strengthened,' he said, seeing the change in me.

'And you also have risen since I have been gone—Tribeking.' I pulled free of his hold.

He gathered his trousers from the floor and tugged them on. His chest and arms had thickened, hardened. His warrior stature stole my breath. He was worthy of a king's title. But not this way.

With a loud sigh he sat down on the bed. 'I have simply done what needed to be done. We are fools if we fight them and Fraid could not see it.'

'Am I then to be counted in your band of fools?'

'If you cling to a chariot that is speeding toward a cliff edge, then yes—you are a fool.'

'Foolish is one who insults the Kendra of Albion.'

He looked up in surprise. 'Is that who I see before me?'

For a moment I wondered if, here with him, I could hold myself to the title. His respect meant more than I had realised. I drew up, feeling my skin prickle with light.

'Do not try and summon your glamour against me,' he warned. 'I will not be swayed by spirit-craft. But talk to me and I will hear you.'

I sat beside him on the bed. It was still warm and smelled faintly of his spill. 'Why do you force your tribespeople to surrender to the invasion?' I asked calmly.

'You would sooner they were forced by blade?'

'Then at least they die in the light.'

'But what are they dying for? Why do you not listen to one who has seen? I have left the shores of Albion. I have seen beyond. If we fight, we are fighting to remain in the darkness. If light is your love, Ailia, you will find it in Rome. There, you may live like a god.'

I watched how his beliefs enlivened him. They were truly held, if poorly formed. 'There is something I love more than light,' I said.

'Is it me?'

I had to laugh. 'No, you fool, it is freedom. Their god's life is bought by our freedom if we allow it. It is not for any man or woman to live as a god.'

'But there is a new freedom in what Rome wil bring,' he insisted. 'In the cities, I see the vision of men set free—'

'And what of the Mothers?' I filled with anger. 'Where are they to exist in these cities of men? Do you put your own creation above that of the Mothers?'

He turned to me, grimacing in his conviction. 'Our creation honours the gods. Our greatness is theirs. If you could only see—'

'Let me tell you what *I* have seen, Ruther. I have seen the Mothers at work. I have heard the songs that are the making of the very air we breathe and the ground we tread. If these songs are not honoured, there will be no cities. There will be no ground. There will be darkness. It may be falsely lit by men. But in time that will fail. Only the Mothers' light will endure.'

He snorted. 'The knowledge of the new world is no false light, Ailia. It is reshaping our world. Even the paths of rivers can be redrawn by this knowledge. The leaders of Rome are craftsmen, Ailia, and the world itself is their clay. Are you so wedded to our simple ways?'

I stared at him. He was as assured as the sun, ignoring all shadows. His certainty cast its own light and for a moment it blinded me. He was untouched by doubt, unwounded. I thought of Taliesin and the bruises that coloured him, his knowledge wrought by his wounds. I felt a rush of yearning.

'Nothing is more sacred than the waters,' I said steadily. 'A fool's risk is taken in reshaping them.'

He recoiled from my insult.

'You call the ways of Albion simple,' I continued, 'but, forgive me, Ruther, it is your own wilful ignorance that sees it so. You know there is wisdom embedded in every stone and river. It is intricate beyond measure, beyond comprehension.'

He looked away. In the flickering light I saw traces of the boy he once was. 'Why have you betrayed the old ways?' I asked gently.

'Because they do not serve me.' He avoided my gaze. 'Plautius has promised me leadership of Summer, Hod and even Ham Hill. All of central Durotriga, with his soldiers at my flank, if I stand beside him.'

I stared at him in disbelief. 'You hunger for power, yet there is already power in you, equal or greater than any man.'

He whipped to face me, ignited by my praise. Our eyes locked and then, before I could halt it, we were embracing, drawn by an animal bond I could not sever.

'You weaken me, Ailia,' he said, pulling away. 'Listen—' he gripped my arms, '—the legion will be here in two, perhaps three days. They will arrive peacefully. I will ensure it. But even so, they will seek you out. They do not trust the journeypeople. You and Llwyd will be killed.'

I stiffened. 'I am not afraid.'

'You should be.' He swung to the floor before me. 'I asked you once and you refused me but there is still a chance for us. The townspeople will follow you. Will you join with me to rule these tribelands under the law that will be strongest?'

The fire made a soft silhouette around his head.

'You are the bravest fighter of Summer,' I said. 'The Mothers have

315

gifted you courage and skill but you will not repay them for it. I will join with you, Ruther, but only for one purpose. I ask *you* now for the last time: will you stand strong with me against the Romans?'

'As husband?' His voice was unwavering. 'Do you offer yourself to me as wife if I turn on Rome as you request?'

My thoughts swam. Was this what I must do? Marry him to turn his mind? The sacrifice was too great. 'I cannot,' I said. 'I cannot offer myself as wife.'

'Then damn you, Ailia,' he said in a low whisper. 'You will die when they come and I will not seek to stop it.'

I stared, stunned, then rose to my feet and walked to the doorway.

'Wait,' he cried, following me and grabbing my wrist. 'I did not mean it. I am sorry.'

'Do you want a wife who lives against the very core of her conscience?' I spluttered. 'Is that what you seek in a woman?'

He shook his head, his expression anguished. 'I want you.'

We fell against each other, exhausted.

'Stay,' he murmured into my neck.

'You have just been spent, and with Heka of all people,' I said, pulling away.

'I took her because she is sharp-witted like you, and well practised in the coupling arts,' he said, holding me firm. 'But she is not even your shadow.' He kissed my throat.

Despite the heat that flared in my centre, I pushed him away. 'I cannot lie with you.'

'Am I not good enough for a journeywoman now?' he jeered. 'In Rome a man may take his woman as he wishes without penalty.' He reached for me again but I strode to the door.

'I spit on your Roman ways.'

I walked back through the silent township and mourned for the waste of him.

'How did you fare, Journeywoman?' Fraid greeted me at the farm-house door.

'He is resolved,' I said. 'He will not fight the legion. He has already met with envoys to plan his succession.'

When I walked inside there were twelve or fourteen tribespeople gathered around the fire with Fibor, Etaina and Llwyd. They were councillors and warriors of Cad, weak from Troscad, but now hungrily eating bowls of a rich-smelling stew. Among them was Orgilos, Ruther's father. They dipped their heads as I stood before them. 'Why do you eat?' I asked in astonishment. 'Have you broken Troscad?'

'We no longer oppose the decision of our leader,' said Orgilos, gnawing a knuckle of bone.

'But Ruther's position is not changed,' I said.

'We are loyal to another now.' Orgilos's eyes met mine. 'If the Kendra will bless the battle, then we will fight.'

'I have sent word to many townspeople, many warriors,' said Fraid, making room for me on the log at the strong place. 'Although they will not admit it to Ruther, I still have their loyalty. When I told them of your initiation, they pledged to support you. See here—' She lifted a basket filled with tokens: arrowheads, spearheads, knives. 'They are ready to fight for Summer. They need only the Kendra's word on the battle outcome.'

My chest burst with pride at their courage. 'Ruther said the legions are two or three days from approach.'

'Or closer,' said Fibor. 'Some scouts report they have already left Hod Hill.'

'They could take one of two paths,' said Fraid. 'I suspect that they will move on Mai Cad first. They will know it is a threat.'

'Our only choice now is to move the farmers into the hillfort and defend the ramparts,' said Fibor.

'Ruther must not learn of it,' I murmured.

'How are our weapons stores?' asked Fraid of the warriors.

'I have spoken to the makers,' said Orgilos. 'They are ready to work hidden by night to ready us for battle.'

'We will need to position our weapons and stock the ballista,' said Fibor. 'This, too, must be done at night. By the time the Romans are upon us, Ruther will have no chance to intervene. There will be war and he will have to fight, either with us or against us.'

'Ailia.' Fraid turned to me. 'We need you to sight the battle and secure it with your blessing.'

The blood quickened in my neck. 'Perhaps it should be Llwyd—' I stammered. 'He has blessed many battles.'

'No,' Llwyd said. 'You are the Kendra. I will assist you, but you alone can foresee this battle's outcome.'

'There are few hours left until dawn,' said Fraid. 'Let us all take sleep. Ailia, you will have but one day to see and sanctify this battle.'

When the warriors had departed and we were preparing our beds, I asked Fraid where Sulis was.

'She left for the Isle,' Fraid answered.

'By night?'

'She would not stay.' Fraid smiled as if to reassure me. 'She holds her knowledge too firmly,' she said. 'Do not heed her.'

I had not heeded her. And I hoped I was not mistaken.

⸺

At daybreak, Llwyd and I walked to the Oldforest, where we could work unseen. An ovate followed, carrying the pots and herbs, and leading the calf whose blood would summon my sight.

Llwyd led us to the pool where I had twice met Taliesin.

'Here,' said Llwyd.

As we positioned our tools, the familiar mist rose up from the water, obscuring my view to the other side. I knew Taliesin waited beyond it. But I could not call him now. I had to wait until I was alone. I had to wait until the battle was fought and won.

While Llwyd sat in silence, watching for portents of birds or hares, the ovate prepared for my seeing. Deftly he slayed and skinned the calf and set about making a broth of its blood over a fire of oak.

I sat on the forest floor, facing the sunrise, the river gurgling before me. The ovate laid the calfskin, fleshside out, over my head. Beneath this heavy tent, I smelled the dung warmth of the animal's pelt and the tang of its blood. I was handed a cup of broth and I sipped, closing my eyes.

It could take many hours to bring me to sight. With the ovate and Llwyd keeping vigil beside me, I began the deep, rhythmic breaths, and the chants I had learned from Steise, to coax open my eye.

Soon there were moments of sight: Ruther's face, Taliesin's. I saw fragments of Cookmother, Heka, then at last there were soldiers in red tunics at camp. *See!* I commanded myself, but I pushed too hard and the image slipped like vapour. I needed the raven eye to make clear sight. I needed to change form. 'Heat me!' I cried to the ovate.

They fuelled the fire, setting steaming bowls beneath my calfskin, and passing me medicines. I dizzied with heat and dripped with sweat, but the raven form would not come. *I changed with the Mothers*, I anguished. *Why not here?*

And yet I knew why. My doubts had been founded. I was free with the Mothers, but here I could not take form without skin. *Then why?* I agonised. Why had they chosen me? Here I could not take form without skin.

I laboured to see what I could, grasping at the wisps of sight at the edges of my vision. I saw Ruther gathered with two men of the legion, talking with purpose, but I heard no sound. 'I cannot hear what is said!' I lamented aloud.

Llwyd's voice came as if from a great distance. 'Call to the Mothers, Ailia. Make sight of the battle. Make sight of our success—'

Images of our fighting men painted for battle, eyes alight, flashed before me then faded. 'It is a blur!' I cried. 'It does not come.' I weakened, near fainting beneath the heavy cloak.

'It will come, Kendra, do not desist.'

But it did not.

Though Llwyd asked and coaxed, I said nothing more as I sat and waited. It could not be known that my eye would not open.

Finally it neared day's end. Exhausted, I pulled the skin tent away from my shoulders.

'Do you have an answer for the warriors?' asked Llwyd.

I had heard the song. I knew it must be defended, whether or not I had sighted the battle. For why else had I been chosen? 'Yes,' I said.

—

We walked back to the farmhouse in dusk. All the way, I silently crafted the words that would give the warriors strength.

'Have you seen us victorious?' Fraid asked as we arrived.

There were several more warriors gathered around the fire, including some with tartans from townships in greater Summer. Among them was Uaine, Bebin beside him, a plump boy child squirming in her arms.

I looked around at the faces staring at me. They had asked me to guide them. Their future hung on my answer. What I could not find with my sight I would create with my words. No one would know that the sight had not come.

I bade them be seated and stood before them in the strong place. Then I began. 'Our fighters are fewer in number than Rome's but we hold one incontestable weapon.' I paused to quell the shake in my voice. 'That weapon is truth.'

A long silence greeted my statement. But they were listening.

'If you strengthen truth, it will strengthen you.' I took a deep breath, drawing on the words of the Mothers, of Taliesin, of my own heart. 'If you guard truth, it will guard you.'

As I looked around at the warriors, I saw a kindling in their spirits.

I stepped onto the bench so that I could see, unobstructed, all to whom I spoke. 'If you honour truth,' I continued, 'it will honour you. If you defend truth, it will defend you.'

My heart quieted. I was clear in what I must tell them and the words rose up from my learning like water. 'For it is through truth that great tribes are governed.

'Through truth every law is beautiful and every cup is full.

'Through truth, mighty armies of invaders are drawn back into enemy territory.'

Their eyes were ablaze.

'For so long as you fight for truth, it will not fail you and you will not perish.' I paused to take breath, the will of the warriors pliant in the fire of my words. 'As Kendra, I tell you that we will fight, men and women of Summer. And truth will make us indestructible.'

The warriors broke into smiles and cheers.

I stepped off the bench with trembling legs. I knew I had done the right thing. They had to believe in their strength. This would be enough.

In the hum of chatter and strategy that followed, I gathered with Fibor and Llwyd.

'We will prepare this night,' said Fibor. 'There will be little time to dress and paint—'

'Ruther must be distracted,' said Llwyd. 'He still commands several warriors—'

'And we cannot risk him sending scouts to the Roman camps,' said Fraid, who joined us.

Fibor exhaled with a grunt. 'He must be detained and his men told not to disturb him. Otherwise the risk of discovery is too great.'

'I will distract Ruther.' My steady voice belied my knotting stomach.

'No, Ailia,' said Llwyd, 'we need you with us.'

'But she is the only one,' said Fraid, 'who can weaken him.'

'Commence the preparations,' I said, fastening my cloak. 'I will make sure Ruther is mine until dawn.'

'Go now,' said Llwyd, kissing my cheek. 'We need every minute.'

As I stepped out of the warm farmhouse into the dark spring night, I was met with an overwhelming dread. Of all the fears I had known in my lifeturn, this moment felt the most ominous. A brutal force lay in wait, seeking to tear us from our roots. The people of Albion were no strangers to battle. It was the way of the tribes to fight for their boundaries, to display their bravery. But this was not battle sport. This was an attack on our very existence. We must defeat it or we would not survive it.

I quickened my step. I had to keep my wits sharp now.

One of Ruther's men stood at the sleephouse door and I bade him tell Ruther I was there. I drew up, taking on a small glamour, while I waited to be admitted, not too much, lest Ruther be suspicious. I was called through.

He looked weary as he drank by the fire, but straightened at the sight of me. 'What brings you back?' he asked.

'Does the girl Heka share your bed this night?'

'No. She is cast from my favour.'

'Good.' I dropped my cloak and moved toward him.

Disturbance

To deny our kin is to disturb our soul.

I AWAKENED JUST after first light. The cries of the smiths drifted up from the craft huts and I wondered if their night had been fruitful, if I had bought them enough time.

Ruther murmured and I watched him sleep, the same fine face that woke me from my first Beltane. His eyes flickered behind closed lids, dreaming perhaps of his beloved city. I opposed him but I could not hate him. In his own way, he acted in truth.

I placed my lips on the ridge of his cheek, then sat up, reaching for my under-robe.

In a flash he had roused and pulled me back down. 'Do you think I will let you go now you have come to me?'

'I cannot stay,' I protested, wriggling from under him.

'So you have not changed your mind?' He propped on one elbow as I dressed. 'You did not come to stay?'

I shook my head. 'Last night was my farewell gift.'

'Ailia—' His tone became grave. 'In truth, it is best if you do not go. Let me hide you until the danger is passed.'

'Never,' I said as I stood. 'I will not be hidden away.'

'You must trust me. You will not be spared.'

'For how long would you have me hidden?' I scoffed, strapping my sword to my belt.

'Until I have gained their trust. There are scouts from the legion in the township already, surveying the land, seeing who is dangerous. Please let me protect you.'

'Impossible.' I pulled on my cloak, eager to be gone from him. He was too insistent now.

'If you will not see sense, then I will see it for you.' In the blink of an eye he had sprung up from the bed and was pulling me across the room. Gripping me around the waist, he kicked away the basket that covered the opening to the storepit beneath.

'Stop—' I struggled against him but he was as strong as a bullock, determined to force me into the narrow opening. I fought, raking his skin with my fingers, but he held my arms like a vice.

With his final shove, I tumbled down the ladder. I sat, shocked, on the dirt floor, scratches bleeding on my hands and legs.

'You will have food and drink—you will be safe!' called Ruther from above.

'And when will I be released from this cage?' I shouted up at him.

'When it is done and I have their trust. Then I will release you.'

'No!'

But he was drawing the bolt of the trapdoor and my scream was deadened by the damp earth around me.

The storepit was cold, airless and entirely black until Ruther opened the door and descended the ladder with a torch that he fixed into a wall bracket. In the weak light of the flame, I saw there were blankets on the floor, a pot and a jug of water. He had prepared for this. He had intended to trap me and I had walked straight to him.

'You snake,' I whispered in disgust.

'You will be grateful.' He turned to the ladder, then back to me. 'Give me your sword.'

'No.' I panicked. He could not take it. 'I will cause no further trouble if you leave it with me. This is my promise.'

He stared for a moment then snorted with indifference. 'There is little harm that can come of it here. Tidings, Ailia.' He climbed the ladder and shut the trapdoor beneath him.

I heard the iron latch slide shut and I sank to the floor. The warriors would think I had abandoned them. They would doubt their strength. 'Fight,' I urged them with my mind's voice as I sat for hours in the dank silence.

Later, one of Ruther's attendants brought food, but would tell me nothing of what was happening in the township. I begged and cajoled him but he handed me the bread and stew without a word and latched the door again.

What torture it was to be powerless in wait, while the tribespeople were working to face the darkest enemy we had yet known. What kind of Kendra was I who allowed herself to be hidden and protected while her people put their lives at risk? Who could not even give them the seeing that was needed?

I could not eat the food. It was as though my body was making Troscad of its own will, protesting the confinement that I was neither strong nor clever enough to protest myself.

Again there was scuffling above me and the sound of the latch being drawn. Strange, it was only moments since the attendant had left. Was he back for my bowl so soon? I stood, ready to pass it to him, untouched.

A woman descended the ladder. The fine hairs on my neck bristled. It was Heka. 'What are you doing here?' I whispered. 'Does Ruther know you have come?'

She pulled the door shut above her. Her business would have to be swift or the servant would find it unlocked when he returned. When her feet touched the floor she turned to me, her eyes glittering in the torchlight. There was mud on her skirts and her hair was strewn with straw. 'He does not know,' she said.

She looked to the bowl by my feet.

'Take it.'

She crouched on her haunches, devouring the meal. 'You have come to greatness, Ailia,' she said, chewing a large mouthful of stew. 'Or must I call you Kendra?'

'The news has spread quickly,' I said.

'This is not all I know.' She scraped the bowl with her fingers. 'You have been with Fraid and the Journeyman. I know you have sanctified a plan to fight.'

I was astonished. 'How can you know this?'

'We are not so far from one another as you would wish,' she said. 'I followed you to the farmhouse. I have heard your talk.'

Once again, I was shocked by how brazen, how sly, she was. If she used this against me, Ruther would not spare Fraid or Llwyd, or any of those who had pledged to fight. 'Heka—' My voice was low. 'For the final time, I ask you: what do you want of me? Why do you pursue me?'

She set down the empty bowl. 'The Roman army comes. They are hours away and I do not want to be among the dead. I need a horse and cloak and coin to escape. Give this to me or I will go to Ruther.'

I stifled my laugh. 'Coin? And where, please tell, will I get your coin?' I motioned around at the chamber. 'Do you see a horse here between us?'

'Ask Ruther, when he comes, to arrange it and I will wait for it—'

326

We both looked up as the door creaked and was tugged open. The servant had come to take my bowl.

Heka caught my glance and her eyes flared with panic.

'Quick,' I whispered. 'Lie still under the blanket. Stay there!' I called to the servant. 'I will pass up my bowl.'

'Why was the door unlocked?' he growled as he reached for the bowl. 'Has Ruther been?'

'No,' I answered quickly. 'You must have forgotten to draw the latch.'

The servant grumbled as he hauled himself up from the opening. 'I will not forget it now.' The door thudded shut and I heard the bolt slide.

Heka threw off the blanket. 'Now I am caught here, curse you!'

'Good then.' I sat beside her. 'This may serve us both.'

Like any journeywoman, I did not have much by way of metals, but I had the favour of those with wealth and could easily have her provided for. My only treasure was Taliesin's love. As long as I had this, I could promise her anything. 'I will give you coin, Heka. I will give you horses. I will give you all that I have to give. But first you must tell me the truth. You must tell me my skin. You must tell me everything you know of my family. Not just one question answered, but all. Without this—tell Ruther what you will—you will have nothing.'

She looked at me and I saw she was startled by my boldness. 'What promise do you make me,' she said slowly, 'if I tell you all?'

I took deep breath. My words, when they came, were raw and meant. 'You will have what is mine, Heka, or you shall own my freedom.' It was a form of geas that I offered. Under it, I would be cursed if I acted outside her will: a debt of obligation that surpassed all others.

'You would put yourself under my geas?' She was stunned.

'Yes. Even my freedom is useless without skin,' I said. 'I am nothing without skin.'

She nodded.

'Who are you, Heka?' I murmured.

'Ay then, I will tell you.' She turned from me and spoke into the darkness, her voice softly rasping. 'I first came to Caer Cad when I was seven summers old. It was the time of the Gathering. I came with my father and mother. She was huge with a babe. They offered me for the gift. Perhaps it was the shock of the ritual or the relief that I was not chosen, but Mam's pains started early, and soon it was plain that she was going to have the babe that night. There was a birth hut in the town, but Mam wanted to be near the river. She insisted on it. So we all went down: the midwife, me, others as well. I was scared,' said Heka.

'Two girls came from Mam that night.' She paused. 'The first was Kerensa. Mam was still strong after her, lying on the riverbank and smiling at her sweet face. But when the second child set to follow, Mam started twisting and crying to get into the water. She kept screaming, "Let me under", and trying to crawl in. The river was icy. But maybe she thought the cold would ease the pain, so we helped her in, me on one side, a woman on the other, and the midwife in front to catch the child.

'She tore right open with the coming of it. The night water ran black with her blood and when the babe was lifted out of the water, she was so slippery that the midwife lost the grip of her ankles and she was washed downstream where she lodged on a log. Nearly drowned in her own mother's blood, before I got to her.' Heka turned to me to see if I understood.

'It was me,' I whispered. 'I am the child in the river.'

Heka nodded.

I could not breathe. Heka was my sister.

'It was I who hauled you out and laid you on the grass next to Kerensa, while our mother bled to death in the river. You came hard and stole her life to buy your own. If it were only Kerensa, Mam would still be alive. She was whole after Kerensa.' Heka closed her eyes for a few moments before she spoke again.

'You were not sameling twins; you were odd. When we got back to the camp, my father said we could keep only one and the other had to be left somewhere to be safe and fed.

'I begged him to let me keep you both: the two bits of life left from Mam, but he knew—and he was right—that with only seven summers, I could carry one babe and still be helpful with the cattle, but not two. It was no difficulty to choose whom to keep. Kerra was the most likened to Mam and the one whom had left Mam well. The other—you—I took to the Tribequeen's kitchen door on the night you were born.

'I cried when I farewelled you, despite all. There was a newling's loveliness to you in your own way, though, even then, you had the look of one who would fight for herself.' Heka paused once more.

The scowl scored in her face began to make sense.

'I did not forget you. Not for one day. Every sun turn I thought of the sister who was growing in Fraid's town. And I worried, too, that you might *not* be growing. If you had died or gone to fosterage I would never have known of it. And I did not forget either, that you did not know your skinsong and you would be suffering the lack of it.

'When I saw you again it was seven summers past, at the next Gathering. I had dreaded and craved that day all at once. The moment we arrived I wanted to find you and tell you that you had kin and let you meet your womb sister. Our father was dead by then—but I was kept on by the farm that he had worked, and we cared for each other greatly, Kerra and I. We wanted you to come home.'

'What happened then?' I asked. 'Why did you not find me?'

Her face twisted. 'Because it was Kerensa who was given, torn apart that day.'

I reeled back as if struck in the chest. 'That was my sister,' I gasped, remembering the child who had been chosen as the gift, 'and you were the one with her.'

Heka's eyes closed against the memory. When they opened again they were burning. 'It was *you* the Journeyman chose for the gift that winter. You were the most pleasing, the special one, but because you were with the Tribequeen's woman—ay, I saw her speak for you—they took my Kerra instead. The most precious thing I would ever know. You bought your life a second time by taking one of mine.'

I was silent. Reliving that unspeakable day. Was it as Heka charged? Had my life been wrought by others' deaths?

'I had some sister's love for you when I came that year, but it was nothing next to my love for Kerra. If I had been given the choice between you and her—there would have been no question in it—I would have kept my Kerra.' Her eyes bore into me and I saw her face begin to twitch and change with the anger that shaped it from the inside. 'What did you whisper to the wiseman to buy your life?' she growled. 'What words bought the death of my sister?' Her face crumpled as she slumped against the wall.

I said nothing more.

She was my kin. I felt the earth shift to make room for the knowing of it. 'Why did you not tell me? Or Cookmother?' I asked.

Heka stared at me in disgust. 'Because both of you killed my sister. I felt nothing but hate. Cookmother must have seen it in me because she drew you close and turned away as I passed her after the giving.'

The torch flame flickered. It would not bring us light for much longer.

'But *you* didn't turn away,' continued Heka. 'You looked straight at me with those round eyes, full of innocence. The same strange colour of sun in muddy water. You have none of the heart of her but your eyes are all Mam's.'

And with those words a ribbon of wind drifted into the core of me, gently awakening the knowledge that I had come from a mother—my mother. Now I knew that I was born to a woman who had gifted me the colour of her eyes and may have gifted me the world's love if she had lived to do it. I was bound to other souls, dead and alive, and now sitting here before me.

'So there it is,' said Heka. 'You had all of it. I had nothing.'

'Nothing!' I cried. 'You knew your skin. This is something I have never known.'

'Do you not think I would have gladly traded my skin knowledge for just one moment of the care you have known by your cursed Cookmother? From seven summers I was motherless with none to replace her.'

I frowned, seeing the truth of it.

'I have found friends enough to drink with but I have never known a moment's kinwarmth since that day. Do you know what love has been to me, sister? It has been a man's prick and the money he'll give to use me freely for its pleasure. This is what I have known of love.'

'And now?' I asked, suddenly exhausted. 'Why did you come back?'

'Justice,' she said. 'After seven years of grieving Kerra, I woke up. The wrong needed to be righted. I knew you should help me or suffer for it if you would not. That is what brought me back.'

'And what of me? Did you care nothing for me as your sister?'

'Ay. I cared. I did not know—right up until the very moment I saw your face at the door—whether you would be kin or enemy to me when I found you. But when I saw you so rosy and tended and then not letting me have even a crumb of it, like I was less than shit on your sole, well, I knew then you were no kin to me.'

'But I *am* kin!' I cried. 'I did not know—how could I have known?'

'You, the knowing one! Did not even know her own sister. Not then, nor months after. Never until this moment. What kin does not know itself? No, sister. I say you knew. You knew you owed me some life somehow, but it was sweeter for you not to grant it.'

I spun from her words, fathoming what truth they held, and stared into her face, now seeing its echoes of my own. 'And now?' I asked. 'Am I your sister now?'

She would not meet my gaze.

I watched her profile. Now I saw more than the worn skin at her jaw, the lines gouged in her brow, her sunken temple. Now I saw our story.

'This has shaped me, Ailia. I cannot change what I am.'

I wanted to comfort her. I needed comfort from her. But the wrongs she had done me had shaped me also and I was scarred from the knowing of her. Like hers, my cuts could not be washed away.

We sat beside each other, locked in the chamber, listening to the rise and fall of each other's breath.

Then, in the silence, Heka began to sing. A sweet, lilting song, in a voice made husky from ale, that called to the wisdom, the loyalty, the kinship of the dog. She sang it once. Twice. Three times.

On the fourth cycle I began to whisper, joining with her as she sang. My voice strengthened as I learned the song, making it more precise, more true, each time I sang it through. After many cycles, we were singing together in perfect unison.

The song soaked into my bones, finally giving shape to what had been formless. Naming what had had no name.

This was our skinsong.

I was skin to the dog.

32

Destruction

Our world is a braid, made up of three strands:
our land, our laws and our rituals.
Take away any one of these, and our world
will be altered beyond survival.

hours passed and Heka drifted into sleep. Her body slumped sideways and her head fell on my shoulder. I breathed her hair, musty, like the nest of a kitchen mouse, and a wave of exhaustion rolled over me.

In the lull of half-sleep, something was stirring. The new parts of my story were intermingling and fusing with those I already knew. Layers were shifting with the birthing of skin. The change that had pressed so close but could not break through in the forest, now entered me.

With skin, my sight came. My knowledge awakened. With skin, the Kendra was fully born.

In my dream it was almost dawn. I was a raven, black and strong, soaring over the fields and forests of my country. I was flying southeast toward the vast water, nearing Mai Cad. I passed over a tall ridge and there was the hilltown spread before me. Straightaway with my raven's eye I saw something was wrong. The pink sky was stained black with smoke.

I dropped forward to gain a closer view. Smoke stung my nostrils and eyes. A foreign banner, bearing an eagle, flew at the eastern entranceway. I circled over it and saw men with the close-cropped hair and red skirts of the Roman legions. There were only a few, gathered around fires, laughing together as they ate from steaming bowls, jovial with their success. Were the rest hidden in the tents, tired from their night's work?

I dipped my left wingtip to turn and sail over the town.

Where were the huts? I dived in closer. Where were the tribespeople?

I flew toward the western gate and there the full breadth of this attack was laid before me. The sight turned my avian bowels to liquid.

I came to perch on one of the tall posts that stood each side of the gate. The few who remained alive were digging furiously, deepening the grave to hold the mountain of dead beside them. They were digging with stones, branches, their hands, so urgent was it that they laid their kin to rest before the daylight alerted the Romans to their task.

I cawed in despair and a young boy looked up to see the day's first bird.

With a chest full of stone, I lifted off the post into the sky and began to fly back to my home, where Rome would come next.

When I reached Caer Cad, no matter how loud I cried that the resistance must be ceased, that we had to surrender to this force if we were to protect anything of ourselves, no one could understand the bird. No one could hear me.

I awakened with a jolt, Heka still heavy against me.

Skin had given me sight in the hardworld and I had seen what would happen if the tribe fought. I had ordered a battle we could not win, that would injure our people beyond healing. I had to get word to Llwyd and Fraid. I had to tell Ruther that I would marry him and concede to the Empire. I would do anything to halt the massacre I had seen and that moved toward our township. To live by Roman law would wound the Mothers, but the blood of whole tribes soaked into their ground would destroy them.

I wriggled out from under Heka and climbed the ladder to pound at the door. 'Ruther! Come!' I shouted. 'I must speak with you!' There was no response. I shouted again, pummelling the door with my fists till they ached.

Heka roused with the noise. 'What are you doing?' She yawned.

'I have made sight, Heka—I have seen the Roman attack on Mai Cad. I have to call back our warriors.' I started hammering on the door again.

'For Mothers' sake, shut up!' cried Heka.

I dropped down from the ladder and stood before her. 'Listen,' I commanded. 'I have seen an attack more terrible than your worst imagining.' I paused, trying to gather my thoughts. 'If my vision is in true time, then we still have some hours, even days,' I muttered. 'Their soldiers must replenish and rest, then make footjourney from Mai Cad. But if I was looking into old time, then...' I looked up and met Heka's gaze.

'They may be upon us,' she finished, understanding me.

'Help me,' I said. 'Help me scream so that one of the servants may hear as they pass.'

'Strange that no one has come with food or fresh water,' said Heka, getting to her feet. 'We have been here some long time.'

I glanced at the torch, burned almost to its base. She was right. Why had no one come?

We locked eyes again and neither of us spoke.

Slowly I climbed the ladder once more, but this time I did not bash against the door or cry out. This time I drew the underbolt closed so that it could not be opened from above.

I did not know how long we waited, huddled together in the chamber. Without sun or stars to guide us, there was no way of knowing if the moments were hours or even days. We sipped what remained of our water and waited.

A sudden thump startled us both from a half-sleep.

Immediately my senses were sharp. There was anger in the force of the strike. The thump was followed by a second that sent us cowering against the wall.

'*Patefacite*!' The Latin command to open was shouted through the wooden door.

We clutched each other, my heart crashing, as showers of grit rained down from the edges of the opening. Then, for a moment, all was quiet.

'Have they gone?' whispered Heka.

'Perhaps,' I breathed.

Another splintering strike sent us shrinking into a huddle. Now they were using a tool.

Heka began to whimper, grey with fear.

'It will be all right,' I heard myself tell her.

The axe was almost through. I saw the door bend and shudder under the blows and I heard the sound of wood beginning to split. Two more strikes and I saw the glint of the axe edge.

336

I stood and inhaled to draw up power from the earth, but it did not come. I remained a mere girl. Against this enemy, my strength would not come.

They had made a hole in the door.

I was chanting, calling on the Mothers, drawing up from their deepest spirit. Why would they not come?

Sandalled feet slid through the hole. Then the rest of the Roman: young, stocky, dressed in the short tunic and leather skirt of the foot soldier. His face was partly obscured by his metal helmet but his eyes shone, dark and aroused.

A second soldier dropped down behind him. They both guffawed at the discovery of us, loosening their sword belts. From the words they exchanged I recognised only 'lupa', a she-wolf, and also a woman who lay with men for payment.

I stood before them while Heka crouched against the wall behind me.

Suddenly their swords were drawn.

'What do you want?' I screamed.

They shouted back and the first soldier moved forward, pushing me away, bidding Heka to rise, his sword at her throat.

She shook as she stood.

There was a shout from above. The second soldier bounded up the ladder in response to it, but the first remained. He bellowed at Heka.

She stared back, uncomprehending.

Then he was upon her. He twisted her around, shoving her hard against the wall.

She lifted her head to scream but the soldier pushed it back down with a sickening thud. He rummaged within his tunic, readying to take her.

I stared, frozen in horror. It was so fast. I saw the pale flesh of her flank as he wrenched up her skirts and forced her thighs apart with his knee.

Just as he was about to breach her, it finally came. A white blaze of rage. I drew as I have never drawn. The full power of the Mothers exploded within me. I pulled my sword from my belt and lunged forward.

The soldier leaned over my sister.

With all my strength, I drove the sword deep into his back. First high, to puncture his lungs, then lower, into the orbs and pockets, twisting the blade to ensure he would not survive it. To ensure I took his life.

He slipped to the floor.

Heka sank down beside him. 'Thank you,' she wept as I crouched to embrace her.

I held her tightly with one arm, my sword in the other, as the soldier's blood pooled at our feet.

33

The Kendra

She alone has been touched by the Singing.
She has a light that belongs to no other.

ᕼEKA GREW WHITE and silent with shock.

I wrapped her in blankets. 'Stay here and make no sound,' I whispered. 'I will come back for you.'

My legs trembled as I climbed the ladder.

First the smell. Of smoke and blood.

Then the quiet. The inhuman quiet.

But it was the sight that met me when I stepped out of the sleep-house that finally told me we were lost.

The smoke wrought a sinister false darkness. Caer Cad was an underworld. Every hut was burned to the ground. Smoke drifted from blackened stumps, from charred remains of children and livestock scattered through the smouldering ash. Strewn across the ground before me were the bodies of the stablemen and Ruther's servants.

I began to walk.

Ianna and Cah lay near the scorched ruins of the kitchen. Their chests and bellies opened, skirts torn away, their bodies defiled before they fell.

I walked through the Tribequeen's gate into the central street of Cad. Here were the men, women and children of Cad, hacked and slain.

I found Fraid. She was stabbed in the face beyond recognition. I knew her only by the arms and feet I had washed and tended for many years. Near her lay Fibor, Etaina and the other warriors who had fought close at her side. And Manacca, slain at her mother's skirts.

I viewed it as though in a dream. As though it were not true.

Farmers, smiths, builders, musicians, weavers I had known since sucklinghood lay scattered, staining the streets black. Their hands were shredded from lifting their arms to shield themselves without weapons. Others lay face down, the wounds struck to the backs of their legs as they had tried to run.

This Roman army had not come to fight. It had come to wipe us away.

I drifted, like a spirit, through the bodies, toward the shrine.

There were a few yet alive. Crouched on the ground, they rocked back and forth, singing their low songs of mourning. They called to the Kendra as I passed. Would she help them? Would she sing their dead to Caer Sidi?

I could not go to them. I did not even look at them.

I walked down the spine of Caer Cad. All around me was the smell of burnt flesh and bowels opened in terror, the sound of wailing, and the fallen bodies like autumn leaves on the ground.

If there were any dead among the Roman soldiers, they had been carried away.

This was no honourable battle. These Roman soldiers had slain people who could never have equalled them in strength or numbers. Babes. Old women. Even animal kin. This was a massacre, as Ruther had forewarned it. What was their purpose in this? How did they earn glory by this inhuman fight?

And yet I saw my hand in it. Because they had expected compliance, and found resistance, the Roman soldiers had fought angrily, impatiently. The killing was worse because I had told the tribe to fight.

Near to the bread house—the oven still standing—I found Uaine almost, but not completely, beheaded. Bebin lay a few steps on, terror frozen in her face, the gash in her throat bearing strings of white tendon.

Her injured boy child kneaded her breast, still seeking milk, his plump cheeks sprayed with her blood.

I lifted him and saw the wound at his side. Too deep to treat, yet shallow enough that he may have lived another hour or two. I pulled Bebin's knife from her hand, stilled him quickly and walked on.

From the peak of Cad Hill, I saw the camp in the west, the soldiers gathering around fires next to the Nain. Their work was complete.

At the door of the shrine was a pile of old man with pale robes and silver hair. The sight of him ignited me and I ran the last few steps to his side. He was sliced neatly beneath his left ribs, his face drained to the colour of chalk. He would not have fought. He would have stood before them with the names of his beloved Mothers on his lips. But what was this? Blood still seeped from the wound in a weak pulse. He lived.

I dropped to my knees. 'Journeyman?'

At the sound of my voice his eyes drifted open. In them, I saw the courage and faith that had never wavered, and it broke me in half. 'I was wrong, Llwyd.' My voice was hollow. 'I needed skin to protect you.' I paused, scarcely able to breathe. 'I did not transcend it...no one can—'

He frowned, his lips parting as blood welled at the corners. 'And now?' he uttered, searching my eyes. 'Do you have skin now?'

'Yes,' I whimpered, wincing at its uselessness. 'But it came too late. I am sister to the dog, Journeyman! The Mothers did not need it, but I needed it. Forgive me, beloved Llwyd. I am no Kendra. I have betrayed you all.'

'No,' he rasped. His face was greying, yet his gaze sharpened. 'The failure is ours. You have shown us the truth. Skin is the law of all life—' he paused, his chest rattling as he laboured for breath, '—but it is something other than what we have known.' His eyes closed. Then slowly he looked upon me once more. 'You always had skin.'

I stared into his eyes. Even moments from death, his strength held me.

'You were always the Kendra,' he whispered.

Then I heard his final breath and watched his life end.

I rose to my feet. With his death I was at last awakened to this slaughter. 'Do you know this man you have killed?' I screamed into the smoke-filled sky. 'Do you know his greatness? Do you know what you have destroyed?'

I ran to the outer wall of the township and looked down. Our most sacred part of the river Nain was where they washed their knives and rinsed their dirty bowls. They camped in the Mothers' place, the northwestern place, where my womb sister had been slain. That death was a gift, offered with love and great reverence. That was how we killed. Not like this.

Standing high above their smoking fires, I held my arms to the sky. With every part of my being I drew spirit to set a geas against them. A sudden cold wind curled up from the valley. The smoke clouds shifted and swirled. My Kendra's power was summoning weather. I reached my fingers into the furious sky. 'I curse you soldiers of Rome,' I screamed down to them. 'For this devastation that you have inflicted, may you be crippled by anguish and shame. May you be overcome with the weakness and suffering of a woman raped. May this remain on you for every night and day of your lives.'

My curse echoed like thunder and the soldiers below looked up at its sound.

If I were caught I would be killed. I strode back to Llwyd and quickly whispered the chants that would carry him to Caer Sidi, tucking his adder stone talisman into the front of his robe. I pulled the knife from his belt so the Romans could not take it, and ran back to the sleephouse, murmuring what blessings I could, as I passed, to honour the dead.

Heka waited in the storepit just as I had left her.

'Come,' I urged, pulling her gently to her feet. 'Do as I say and we may be safe.'

She was weak and compliant as I fastened her robe.

I led her from the chamber and through the township to the northern gateway, steadying her as she took in the sight of the slaughter.

We kept ourselves hidden by the hedges that lined the field lanes, but there was a short distance where we would need to pass close to the legion's camp, if we were to reach the river track.

I stood at the end of the hedge, Heka behind me, and peered around at the camp. The men were so strange, so different from us, yet all dressed alike: one beast made of many, like a swarm of wasps. I picked up only fragments of their Latin tongue, but their laughter, the irreverence with which they sat on our sacred place, was unmistakable. They were the mighty and all others must fall.

Some of the tribesmen of Cad sat at the camp's periphery, unwounded, but bound by rings about their necks or ankles. One of them stood and, with what little movement the chain at his leg afforded, took a few steps to the edge of the camp. He stared southward toward the hill. It was Ruther. He had been spared.

Despite my stillness, his eyes fell upon me.

With Heka's hand gripped in mine, I took a step forward.

His lips parted. Would he call my name? He glanced around at the camp, the soldiers lulled and drowsy with their morning's kill, then looked back, nodding me on.

We moved lightly, with the rhythm of the wind.

The Mothers protected us. Ruther alone saw us pass.

The farmhouse was empty, but two grey horses still grazed the house paddock. We ate bread and milk that we found inside, then I roped the stronger of the two horses and helped Heka mount.

'Ride to the north,' I told her, pushing the last of the bread into her belt pouch. 'Head for Siluria, where Caradog hides. It may take some days, but his people will give you refuge. Tell what has happened. Tell to all the nature of this enemy.'

'And what of you?' she said. 'There is another horse. Will you not come?'

'No.' I handed her the head rope. 'I am still needed here.' I untied Llwyd's knife from my belt and gave it to her. 'This will gain you much coin.'

She hooked her tangled hair behind her shoulders and gathered the reins. 'Thank you,' she said.

I looked up, my hand resting on the mare's smooth flank. 'Thank you also,' I said. 'Thank you for giving me my skin.'

'It came too late,' she stated.

'It came by its own course.'

'Farewell, Ailia.' She stooped down to kiss my mouth. The first and only kiss I had been given from kin.

'Farewell, sister,' I whispered as she rode away.

Only when Heka was disappeared from view did I allow my legs to weaken, my breath to shudder in grief. I sank to the ground and lay on the grass. As much as I tried to still it, the shaking would not cease. Too many had died. How did I deserve to survive? Llwyd was wrong. I was no Kendra. There was nothing I could bring to my people now.

As I curled in a ball, something rustled behind me. The soldiers had found me. I buried my face in my arms. Let them come. Something nudged the back of my neck. But it was not a sword or a soldier's foot. It was a whiskery snout and a cold, wet nose. I lifted my face, disbelieving, then reached out and pulled her to my chest. Her rough tongue scraped my cheeks.

'Neha.' I breathed her warm fur. My sister dog.

We lay unmoving together, her heart whirring under my grasp, until I had the strength to rise again. 'Come.' I brushed the grass off my skirts. 'It is time for us to get Taliesin.'

She trotted beside me as I walked to the Oldforest. At least I would be safe there from the soldiers. With every step I forced myself to silence the warning of the Fire Mothers. I forced myself to hope that my sword would still cut.

At the mouth of the Oldforest, Neha stopped.

I turned back to face her. 'Do not abandon me,' I whispered.

For the first time, she came.

Already the forest was lively with the dead, howling and unsettled, as they moved among the trees. I sensed their panic in the shadows and in the bleats of the owls. They were calling on me to give them their rites so they could passage in peace to Caer Sidi.

I staggered among them, cycling the chants and poems that would free their souls. There were so many. The light deepened. At last my voice was hoarse and my legs were buckling, but the forest was quiet.

I returned to the path. There was one left still to save. My sword had killed. It would need every shred of my strength, my knowledge, to bring Taliesin through.

As I walked onward, I thought on what we would do once he had been freed. We could not return to Cad. We would have to stay forest-hidden for some time. Taliesin was skilled in hunting arts and I could help us find our way northward until we reached safer tribelands. There would be no hardship with him at my side.

We came to the pool. A fine mist rose off the water, coiling around the hazel branches, staking, with its watery tendrils, the boundary between our place and the realm of the Mothers.

Neha stood beside me at the water's edge.

Through the thickening veil, I sensed the presence of Tara, Steise, and all the women who kept the knowledge in their magical other-world. Their voices echoed over the distance, mingling with calls and rustles of the forest.

The mist started to close in, heavy and wet.

'Taliesin!' I cried. *Let him come. Let him come.* 'Taliesin!' My voice was ugly with fear. I stared hard into the whiteness, unsure if he would appear.

And then, just as it had rolled in, the mist began to thin before me, and he was standing on the other side of the river. Thinner, weaker, beneath his rough shirt and trousers, he seemed altered. But still it was *his* form that waited, hopeful, before me. His beautiful spirit. 'Ailia?' he called, his expression uncertain.

'I am here!' I cried, laughing with relief. I could scarcely hold the sight of him as the mist ebbed and surged with its own living force.

A smile broke over his face. 'I can hear you!' he called. 'But I cannot see you. Can you cut the mist?'

Frantically, I tugged free my sword and plunged it into the space between us. The air shuddered and rippled from where my strike had disturbed it, but no hole was cut.

'Ailia?'

'Yes! I am here.' I slashed into the vapour, 'Stay near!'

Neha stood beside me, her head thrust forward, hackles raised. She growled warily at the eddying vision.

I stumbled into the shallows, stabbing at the veil. But the membrane did not yield. Again and again I struck it, willing the skin to tear with all my being. It bent and moved, yet held intact.

Although he stood only paces away, Taliesin was frowning into the distance, unable to see me. 'I can hear you, my love. Why do you not cut?'

'I cannot,' I said, beginning to weep. 'The sword will not cut.'

'Try again!' His voice rose in panic. 'Ailia, do not fail me. You are my only chance.'

Over and over, I drove my weapon into the mist. Surely the force of my love would pierce it? Each time it merely quivered and settled back to quietness. 'No...' I gasped. It could not be so. I threw the sword behind me onto the bank and pushed forward with my bare hands, waist deep in the water. Perhaps, if I could touch him, I could pull him through. 'Taliesin,' I wept, clawing blindly into the vapour, 'can you still hear me?' But I knew, even as I pushed against it with all my strength, that the skin between us would not be breached. The Mothers would not permit it.

Finally, my arms fell to my sides. I crawled from the water, where Neha waited for me, and collapsed on the bank.

'Ailia?' Taliesin called, fainter now. 'Are you still there?'

I turned to face him. 'I cannot cut you free.'

We both stared across the chasm, him unseeing, and me watching his face turn to stone. The air clouded and he was gone.

My scream cleaved the sky. I grabbed my sword, hacking wildly at trunks, hewing leaves from branches, stabbing the blade into the earth itself. 'Damn you, Tara!' I screamed at the forest, 'Damn you, Steise! Damn you, Mothers! You have stolen my love.'

With Neha close at my heel, I walked back to the place where the river emerged from the forest. The place where I first met him. Perhaps he would be able to walk one last time as man. Before I had the Mothers' knowledge, he had come to me several times in this way. Could it not happen again?

But even as I hoped for it, I knew in my Kendra's wisdom that he would not find form here again as a man. The Mothers would not allow it. He had been the lure, the seed that conceived me as Kendra. Now I was born, they had no need to release him, even for an hour. The Mothers cared for my learning. They did not care for the longing of my heart.

As we approached the place in the river where I first found him, I saw something twitching in the grass on the bank. The moon was not long risen and I could not make it out. But when I reached it, its form was clear. It was Taliesin caught in the fish's shape. His scaled flank shimmered as he whipped back and forth in the hard air. He had journeyed as fish and had leaped to the bank in search of me.

I dropped to my knees, touching his side, slick with its jelly coating that yearned for the river. The vents in his flesh were fluttering as he struggled to draw air. He needed the water.

'Taliesin,' I murmured, 'I am here.'

I slid my palms under him and lifted him up. For a moment, he lay still in my hands and I felt his heart humming beneath his fragile skin.

I brought him to the water's edge, then lowered my face, pressing my lips to his skin. 'I am sorry,' I whispered. Then I crouched down and let him slide from my hands back into the water.

I watched long after he had swum away.

Neha had been keeping her distance, sitting a few paces away, wary of the strange smells of the water animal.

I called her to my side, took off my sandals, and sat down on the riverbank, letting my feet trail in the flow.

Nearby a wolf howled. Ready to hunt.

By my command, hundreds had died.

How I longed to slip into the water, like Taliesin, and let it close slowly over me.

I could not return to Caer Cad. Even if they allowed me to live I would not survive among men who did not love the Mothers.

My sister was gone. She would endure. Her alone, I had protected.

Taliesin was held. I could not free him. But he lived.

There were no others living who were kin to me by blood, nor by love.

I was kin only to knowledge. That was all I possessed. All that I was.

Everything changes. Yet nothing is lost.

How I longed to return to the water.

There was a whimper beside me. Neha was guarding the gateway of the realms. Her ears were petal-soft as I caressed them.

'Do not worry,' I murmured. 'I am not yet leaving.'

I chose to seek Taliesin where the forest forbade.

I chose to learn, though I had no skin.

I chose to slay he who violated my sister.

I was born by these acts.

And through them all I now understood, with deep-water clarity, the meaning of skin.

That skin was an act of love. Love of the earth. Love of kin. And love of the truth.

No one would hold us to this love but ourselves. Not the Romans. Nor the Mothers. For truth answered only to itself. And bestowed its light and protection on those who chose to seek it.

What Heka had given me was only part of the truth. My soul had been shaped long before by what I had loved: Cookmother, Neha, my tribelands. And Taliesin.

All these were my skin.

This was why the Mothers had chosen me. This was the new truth I revealed: that skin was far greater than something simply given. It was something that must be grown, understood, chosen and loved. Something that must be taught.

I did not know what shape this new truth would take in Albion's future. I knew skin was needed for the hardworld to endure. And I knew that if I, as Kendra, was to teach anything, it would be that no one could be denied learning.

No one could be denied skin.

It was Taliesin who had led me to knowledge. This was his gift to Albion. And he was still imprisoned in the giving of it. I would live my life in honour of that gift.

I was Ailia of Durotriga. Skin to the dog. Seventeen summers. Tall for my tribe and strong. I had been a kitchen girl. A privileged servant. Now I was something other.

I pulled my feet from the water and strapped my sandals.

I would go to Caradog. I would offer him my knowledge. I would find a way to fight for skin.

For Albion had needed a Kendra. It needed her yet.

I called Neha to my side and began to walk.

Author's Note

AILIA'S STORY IS fictional, but her world is not. Caer Cad is Cadbury Castle, an ancient hillfort in South Cadbury, Somerset, the site of which remains today. One can still see the remnants of undulating banks and ditches, now covered in grass, which would once have protected this mighty tribal centre.

The characters and events relating to the Roman invasion are drawn from history; the events preceding it, however, have been compressed to serve the purposes of fiction. There were in fact two or three years between the death of tribal chieftain, Cunobelinus and the Romans' landing in AD 43, although this is a period of only a few months in *Skin*.

My 'journeypeople' are, of course, the druids. Archaeology reveals almost nothing of these mysterious philosophical and religious leaders, but many Roman historians bear testament to Britain's deep reverence for their people of knowledge.

Acknowledgments

MY DEEPEST THANKS and appreciation must go to Penny Hueston at Text Publishing who has guided me through this endeavour with extraordinary grace and skill. Thank you also to Michael Heyward, Alice Cottrell, Kirsty Wilson and Léa Antigny for their work in promoting the book, and to Imogen Stubbs for her beautiful design.

The manuscript has benefited greatly from the expertise of archaeologist and author, Francis Pryor, who generously read the whole thing and spent a very pleasant morning with me touring Flag Fen in Peterborough, UK. His books, *Britain BC*, *Britain AD* and *Seahenge* were key sources of historical detail. All errors of fact are mine.

In understanding the elusive teacher/priests of ancient Britain I have drawn heavily on the work of Peter Beresford Ellis, particularly *The Druids*, which led me to several ancient texts. The riddles that Taliesin asks Ailia are taken from the 'Wooing of Ailbe', a medieval Irish manuscript. Instructions of Morann Mac Cairbre, recorded in the *Book of Leinster*, inspired the speech Ailia uses to the rally the warriors. Ailia's curse on the Romans at the end of the book is a reworking of Macha's curse in the Irish saga 'The Debility of the Ulstermen'.

The writings of James Cowan informed my knowledge of Australian totemic spirituality. In particular his *Mysteries of the Dream-time* and *Aboriginal Dreaming* offered much inspiration for several of the 'lessons' that precede each chapter.

I am grateful to Writers Victoria for awarding me a Glenfern Fellowship in 2012, and to the Australian Society of Authors and the Copyright Agency for Sue Gough's fortifying mentorship in 2010.

The Australia Council's ArtStart grant provided funds for a much-needed space to work. I have been housed by Mary Delahunty's delightful 'Rosebank' property near Lancefield and by 'Duneira' at Mount Macedon. Thanks to the S.R.Stoneman Foundation for allowing me to be Duneira's first writer in residence.

Heartfelt thanks to my teachers at RMIT: Sally Rippin, Clare Renner, Olga Lorenzo and Toni Jordan. Your encouragement and knowledge were transformative.

To my fellow writers who have read my work patiently for many years, I owe a huge debt of gratitude: Brooke Maggs, Michelle Deans, Richard Holt, Carla Fedi, Melinda Dundas, Jo Horsburgh, Simon Mitchell, Melissa Keil, Jacinda Woodhead, Benjamin Laird, Nean McKenzie, Lucy Stewart, Vivienne Ulman, Anthony Holden, Jason Cotter, Damean Posener, Suzanne Donisthorpe and Danielle Binks. And especially to Suzy Zail, who has walked beside me unwaveringly.

I am indebted to Sarah Butler, who first took me to Glastonbury over twenty years ago. We climbed the misty Tor at midwinter and the seed of *Skin* was sown.

Thank you to Lyn and Tim Nitschke, for caring for my children during the years of writing and to Jane Mills for the same, as well as her reassurance and love.

And to Adam, Toby and Amaya: my earth, sun and moon.

Ilka Tampke
MOUNT MACEDON, NOVEMBER 2014